BULLETPROOF DAMSEL

AMELIA HUTCHINS

Copyright ©October2020 Amelia Hutchins

This book is a work of fiction. Names, characters, places and incidents are either the product of the author's imagination or are used fictitiously. Any resemblance to actual persons, living or dead, or to actual events or locales is entirely coincidental.

This book in its entirety and in portions is the sole property of Amelia Hutchins.

Bulletproof Damsel Copyright©2020 by Amelia Hutchins. All rights reserved, including the right to reproduce this book, or portions thereof, in any form. No part of this text may be reproduced, transmitted, downloaded, decompiled, reverse engineered, or stored in or introduced into any information storage and retrieval system, in any form or by any means, whether electronic, paperback or mechanical without the express written permission of the author. The scanning, uploading and distribution of this book via the internet or via any other means without the permission of the publisher is illegal and punishable by law. Please purchase only authorized electronic editions and do not participate in or encourage electronic piracy of copyrighted materials.

This eBook/Paperback is licensed for your personal enjoyment only. This book may not be re-sold or given away to other people. If you would like to share this book with another person, please purchase an additional copy for each recipient. If you're reading this book and did not purchase it, or it was not purchased for your use only, then please return to place of purchase and buy your own copy. Thank you for respecting the hard work of this author.

The unauthorized reproduction or distribution of

this copyrighted work is illegal. Criminal copyright infringement, including infringement without monetary gain, is investigated by the FBI and is punishable by up to 5 years in federal prison and a fine of $250,000.

Authored By: Amelia Hutchins

Cover Art Design: Eerily Designs

Copy edited by: Melissa Burg

Edited by: Melissa Burg

Published by: Amelia Hutchins

Published in (United States of America)

10 9 8 7 6 5 4 3 2 1

Dedication

For my first pet Tyler, the best dog ever. Thank you for being my first real friend and walking me home from school every day, even if you did growl at my teacher. You were the best dog, my first friend, and the model in which I aim for every dog to be. Now, if you could give Gunner (Sir Barks-A-lot) and Milo (Satan) some lessons, that would be amazing.

BULLETPROOF DAMSEL

AMELIA HUTCHINS

Chapter One

The headlights of an oncoming truck blinded me on the two-lane highway. Traveling at a steady pace, I was making great time over the passes, and through the backroads of Washington State, heading to the last place on earth I wanted to go: Home. I hadn't been home in over five years, and while I'd missed it, I hadn't missed fighting with my overprotective mother. I also didn't miss the ugly argument we'd had on the day I'd left to join E.V.I.E. to fight on the right side of the war against immortal beings that preyed on the weak.

I could still hear her screaming at me, even though my memories were blank in places, something those at the E.V.I.E. compound had noted upon my entry. It was as if someone or something had messed with them, but there was no proof, so there was no reason to go digging into my head for more information since that was both dangerous and time-consuming.

Studying the mountain range ahead, I frowned,

remembering how I found this place and thinking how perfect it was. I'd spent years moving around with my mom until we'd finally settled in the Inland Northwest, nestled high in the mountains.

It should have been safe enough, but she was fearful of being discovered, and it had driven me bat-shit-bonkers. My mother's endless talk of the Van Helsings finding us and removing the threat we posed had driven me insane. She'd homeschooled me, forcing me into a life where I had no outside contact with anyone. Not until I'd finally run away and discovered an entire network of creatures that hunted down bad guys.

At seventeen years of age, I'd done what any other teenage girl would have done. I joined an army-type hunter's guild that secretly kept humans safe from the otherworld creatures. I had gone through years of rigorous training, learning how to hunt and bring down immortal beings.

By the age of eighteen, I'd mastered weaponry classes and graduated as a hunter. By twenty, I'd become the head weapons master of the Pacific Northwest, and created tools used to hunt our enemies without the body count of agents being a factor. I had done things most adults hadn't accomplished in their entire lifetime. Of course, my mother hadn't seen it that way.

She was the reason I was coming home today. She'd failed to answer mine or my sibling's calls for the last two weeks, which was unlike her. I turned off the highway and headed up the old gravel road that led deep into the woods. I cursed, hitting deep ruts in the road with the expensive Audi I'd loaned from E.V.I.E. to return home.

Living in Seattle inside the bunker, I didn't need an expensive car, let alone own one. Driving in Seattle was crazy enough, so thankfully, we had drivers who took us where we needed to go, and everything else we ordered online. It reduced our chances of being caught outside the company, but they also liked us to stay close in case the need to relocate occurred. Luckily, that was something that had only happened once since I'd joined.

Pulling up in front of the cabin, I narrowed my gaze, inspecting my surroundings. The rocking chair on the porch lay on its side. The windows had shattered, apparently from the inside since the light from the headlights revealed glass outside.

Swallowing, I frowned, chewing my bottom lip as I reached for the glove box to pull out the handgun stashed inside. Slipping it into the holster on my hip, I retrieved the flashlight from the middle console before grabbing my phone as I slid out of the car.

At nine o'clock at night in the woods, it might as well have been a blackout. The sliver of light from the moon offered nothing to help me see the footpath to the cabin. At the door, I pushed my phone into my pocket and clicked on the flashlight, noting the salt line in front of the door was disturbed.

"Mom?" I called, praying she answered, and it had just been a spell that had gone awry.

Silence met my call. I shook off the sensation of unease as I slowly stepped into the house, turning on the light switch. Nothing happened, which caused my frown to deepen. My feet crunched over broken glass as I moved deeper into the house, withdrawing my gun, and pointing the business end to where the flashlight shined.

The cabin wasn't huge, but then my mom bought it because it sat on the ley lines that made our magic more potent when casting. It boasted of a large, open front room, kitchen, and small dining area with two bedrooms and a full basement converted into an armory. Shining the flashlight toward the kitchen, I found the table smashed into two wooden pieces, the scent of rotting food and magic assaulting me.

Ignoring the signs of struggle, I walked on shaky legs into the bedroom, opening the door with my foot. I took in the disheveled bed and broken picture frames that covered the surrounding floor. Tears pricked my eyes as I turned, moving toward the one other room in the house, clearing my old bedroom, and the bathroom.

Whispering a prayer to the witches of old, I heard the sound of salt scraping over wood as it recreated the barrier around the house. Slipping my gun into the holster, I dialed my oldest sister. The call went straight to voicemail, and I muttered my message before hanging up.

"What the hell did you do, Momma?" I aimed the light around the floor, before lifting it toward the wall, finding silver bullets pebbling the plaster along with blood spatter. "That can't be good."

I ran my fingers over the bullets in the wall, brushing them over the dried blood. My phone chirped, scaring the life out of me, and I frowned at my response, rolling my eyes as I answered in a singsong tone.

"Remington, what?" Winchester Silversmith demanded coldly.

"I do hate it when you use my full name, Winnie," I groaned, hearing the all too familiar grunt of her response.

"And I hate it when you shorten mine. To what do I owe the displeasure of this phone call? I intend to murder my phone after we've finished the call."

"Have you heard from mom lately by chance?" I asked, still smiling at the displeasure I imagined was on her too-perfect face.

Winchester Silversmith was blessed with the Silversmith looks. Unlike my red hair, she was born with the stylish silver-blonde strands known for the Silversmiths. My eyes were electric-blue, giving away pretty much every emotion that went off inside of my head, while hers were ice-blue and as cold as her insides. I loved her, but she made the arctic look warm and fuzzy on her best day.

"No, I have not. I don't make it a habit of knowing our mother's every move as you do, Remington. She's probably sitting at home trying to figure out how to answer your call."

"Nope, because I'm standing in her house, and it's a mess."

The call went silent, and I held it away from my face to make sure she hadn't hung up on me.

"What?" she demanded carefully. I took a moment

to enjoy the fact that I'd made her speechless. "Why are you there, Remington Silversmith?" I frowned at her sharp tone.

"I'm in her house, Winnie. Someone cut the table into two large, upturned pieces, and scattered potions all across the floor. Either silver bullets have become all the style as wall décor, or she used them to attack someone. There's only a little bit of blood, which is good. Her bed is a mess, and you and I both know she wouldn't leave the house without making it first. Tidiness is how a lady starts her day, after all," I repeated the mantra my mother had sang to me every freaking morning as she loomed over me, ensuring I had made my bed before stepping foot outside my bedroom.

"What else do you see?" she asked softly, her voice finally holding the panic I felt standing in the shattered mess of my mother's home.

"Someone or something breached the salt line, and the windows are all broken, blown *out* of the house instead of inward. Rotten food was on the counter, along with a half pot of coffee that smells like shit." I walked to the pot, tilting it as my nose turned up, and the sludge within it made a sickening noise as it moved. "I can't smell anything else over the potions shattered on the floor." I moved toward the bedroom, pushing the door open to survey the room. "The power is off, and the pictures on the walls are broken, missing the frames' photos." I stopped in front of my mother's desk and balled my hand into a fist at the spot where I should have seen the family bible. "The bible is gone, and all the desk drawers ransacked. Someone was in here looking for something unless all they wanted was our bible." Some asshole had taken our family bible, which didn't actually contain our real names.

"You need to leave, now, Remi. You need to get into your car and go home to Seattle."

"I'm not leaving until we find mom," I groaned at her tone. "I'm not a child anymore, Winnie. I'm the weapons master at E.V.I.E., and I have assisted on countless missions."

"You're twenty-one years old, Remington Alaina Silversmith!"

"And you're two-hundred and seventy-five. Yes, I get it. I'm a child in your world, but I am not a little girl anymore. I hunt bad guys, and they're some pretty big bad guys, sis!" My tone was childish, but she was being an asshole.

"You hunt unclaimed vampires without houses to back them. If someone came for Elizabeth, they did so under the backing of a house or houses. You need to go back to E.V.I.E. where you're safe and out of their reach. Now! That's an order."

"I don't follow your orders anymore, Winnie. You're in Paris, Colt is in Ireland, Sig is in Russia, and the others, well, honestly, I don't even remember where they escaped. I'm here, and you're not is my point, in case you missed it." I bristled, uncertain why she thought she could boss me around from her current location.

"Remi, you need to get somewhere safe. For once in your life, listen to me, please. If they took our mother, it means something big is happening. There are things we hadn't told you. Things that you weren't ready to learn when you ran away," she muttered.

"I'm ready now, Winnie." I placed my hand on my hip, waiting for the line to go dead as it normally did when I asked her questions. When it didn't, my jaw almost dislocated.

"Do you remember mother telling you about the Van Helsings?" she asked guardedly, her voice lowering as if she feared they'd appear like *Bloody Mary* if she said it too loudly. At my affirmative reply, she continued. "They promised to eradicate all Silversmiths, which is why we don't stay together. We keep ahead of them, or we did until you ran away. Mother refused to leave because you were in Seattle. A newborn Silversmith in the hands of a Van Helsing would be a catastrophe. Now go home!"

"You're saying this is my fault?" I snapped harshly, running my fingers over the bullets in the wall, feeling the call of silver that hummed as I touched them.

"No, but if the Van Helsings have our mother, they won't let her go easily. If one house has a Silversmith on their side, they're damn near invincible to the other houses. The Van Helsings lost their footing when we cursed them, but also because we no longer had the alliance to create their weapons. Once upon a time, Silversmiths were bonded to them and only them. Silversmith marriages were arranged with the Van Helsings because they fought to protect us from the other beings, and we created their weapons. There's a lot more to it than that, but it isn't something to discuss over an open-line. Just trust me—you need to run and let us handle this."

I frowned, considering doing as she asked while I moved into the kitchen. Shining the light onto the counter, I scanned a piece of paper lying across it. I lifted a flyer from the stack of mail and studied the logo on it carefully.

"Did you know there's a bar in this town called Hunter's Sanctuary?"

"You're not leaving, are you?" Winnie exhaled, and I didn't need to see her to know she was pinching her nose with exasperation straining her face.

"Nope, but I'll call in a team for protection if that will make you stop demanding that I do."

"Your little hunter's club can't protect you from this one, Remington. You're out of your league here. If there's a sanctuary there, that means there's also a Van Helsing."

"If mom feared these alpha houses so much, why stay here?"

"Because leaving Washington State would mean leaving her youngest daughter behind, and until your twenty-fifth birthday, you're mortal. Add in the fact that should you fall into the wrong hands, you could do something very stupid," she sighed heavily. "Where are you staying tonight?"

"I booked a hotel in town," I admitted.

"Under what name?"

"Remi Cordova, duh," I chuckled.

"Get there. I'll call in some people to come protect you."

The line went dead before I could argue. I pushed the phone into my pocket as suddenly the lights came on and music started playing from my mother's room. Now that that I could see inside the cabin clearly, the entire scene became real. Things were smashed and destroyed, indicating there was a struggle. My heart clenched while I took in the blood spatters, and then I exhaled slowly.

My heart thundered in my chest when I noticed the corpse hidden by the broken table. More blood spattered the kitchen walls, and I noted the black sulfur that ran from the bedroom to the front door. Silently, I moved toward the corpse, using my foot to open his bottom lip to reveal fangs.

Vampire corpse.

Black sulfur.

Broken salt line.

Missing mother!

Vampires, demons, and witches, oh my.

Chapter Two

Once I'd checked into the hotel, I made the call to E.V.I.E., listening as they explained politics in this region of Washington. Help wasn't coming, which figured since they played by a rule of conduct and the local police hadn't invited them. No bodies were piling up, and one missing witch didn't scream foul play on a supernatural level. Not even the vampire corpse had gotten their attention.

My phone rang, and I slid my finger over the screen, listening.

"You do know I can hear your creepy breathing over the phone, right, Remi?" Nyx snorted, chuckling as if she'd amused herself.

"Not a good time, Nyx," I admitted, thumbing through the phone book for the club's address.

"Considering that you called the elders before calling me, I should be offended. However, as your official best friend, I'm going to let it slide this once. I'm currently getting on a plane and coming to you. You're welcome." The boarding announcement for Spokane echoed through the phone, and my lips jerked into a smile. "No, that's mine, it does not go below! What if I need to get off while on the plane? I can't just grab a male and take him to the bathroom with me. That isn't sanitary!" she whined to the man, arguing that she needed to check her bags.

Nyx was a nymph. She fed on men, and she enjoyed it to no ends. Her snappy comments and flippant attitude had made me laugh and feel accepted the moment I'd met her snarky ass.

"Ma'am, your bag will not fit in the overhead compartment, we will need to check it," the flight attendant was arguing.

"Fine, but you may need to service me mid-flight. I get famished on long flights," Nyx murmured huskily.

"It's an hour-long flight, and refreshments are provided, ma'am. Please take your seat."

"Stop moving your hips, Nyx," I grunted, knowing she'd be doing that to make sure the flight attendant got her meaning on the word *service*.

"He's hot," she said, making purring noises at the poor man. "Anywho, your mom's missing, foul play is afoot, and you're standing in a hotel without any protection, where there could be Van Helsings close enough to sniff out your unused vagina. Does that about sum up what I am walking into?"

"My vagina is not unused." I pulled an arrow from my bag, and ran my finger over the tip, placing the call on speakerphone while loading my quiver with Silversmith arrows. "I had sex five months ago, and unlike you, my life doesn't depend on me getting laid."

"Scientists have proven that orgasms reduce stress and are actually good for you." The line went silent for a moment before she spoke again. "I'm sorry about your mom, Remi," she said softly, causing my heart to clench and my stomach to churn.

"Thanks, but let's not bury her just yet." I carefully pushed the arrow into the quiver and then grimaced as it made a soft noise while joining the others.

"What are you doing?" she countered, and I scrunched my face up. "Tell me you're not going hunting without backup. Remington Silversmith, don't you even think about it!"

"I'm just going to take a peek at the bar," I snorted. "There's a sanctuary here, which means there's a Van Helsing. I'd rather find him before he finds me. You and I both know that it's better I learn my enemy rather than give him time to learn me. There's also the fact that it's been two hundred and ninety years since the bloodlines went to war. How long can a feud last? Besides, maybe if I find him, he can tell me what my family has kept from me. Lord knows your version of the truth wasn't accurate. I'm pretty sure your version was more porn than facts, and well, I don't think they started fighting over pussy."

"My version wasn't wrong. It started because the Van Helsings and Silversmiths were born to mate, and trust me; you don't want to find him before he finds you. Not without backup, Remi. The Van Helsings are cursed incubi and therein lays the huge difference between them and normal incubi. You were literally two peas in a gun-slinging pod, once upon a time. You are the silver to their bullets, the wings to their planes. If he senses you near him, he will either hump the hell out of you or try to murder you."

"It's been almost three-hundred years, Nyx. How long can a curse stay that prominent? Besides, he could have my mother. What if the curse is in play, and he's humping my mother?"

"Then… go, momma, go! Not you, though. I need you."

"It's my mother, Nyx. I am not close to my brothers and sisters, but my mom? She knows me, and she gets me. She's my person."

"I thought I was your person."

"You are my person, but so is she. She spent thirteen hours bringing me into this world. Can you say the same?" I slipped my quiver over my back and grabbed the crossbow from the bed.

"Do you want to be in my vagina?" she asked curiously.

"No! What? No, Nyx. Not the point! I'm going. If I'm not back by the time you get here, send out the big guns. We all know that E.V.I.E. only breaks the rules if one of our own goes missing. I'm heading to Hunter's Sanctuary for recon, and yes, I'll be careful."

"My flight is taking off, and you better be. I'll be there in an hour. I've already hacked your email and figured out where you're staying."

"Why would you hack my email? You could have

just asked me where I was staying."

"What is the fun in just asking?" she snorted. "Yeah, I know. I'm hanging up," she promised a man. "The flight attendants are obtuse. I'll call you when I get feet on the ground. You better not die."

"See you soon." I ended the call before muting my phone and slipping it into my pocket.

I glanced in the mirror, staring at my reflection with a slight wince. I looked exhausted and in need of a good six hours of sleep. Pulling up the dark hood, I slipped from the room and started toward the sanctuary that was a mere few miles from the hotel. It took me almost two hours of searching, and moving around the city outskirts to become familiar with the area. Once I had scouted five escape routes out, I'd finally started toward the bar.

I hadn't been aware that there was even a sanctuary bar within twenty minutes from the hotel. I'd booked it for five days, intending to have a place to escape my mother's endless whining about my life choices. All of which were great disappointments to her. Or, my favorite, her threats about coming to bring me home, which was why I'd waited a while before ever telling her where I was.

Winnie was a millionaire, selling silver jewelry she weaved with her metal skills and magic. The others all had some ability to create beautiful things with silver. I made bullets and weapons. I didn't create beautiful trinkets or hold the ability to use magic to peddle my potions or salves as mom did. My other siblings had backup plans to make a lucrative living. Me? I made weapons that were frowned upon when hiding the fact that we were witches born with the ability to craft silver.

Slipping through the edge of town, I listened as a scream ripped through the night. My heart stopped, restarting with a thundering beat. I gave up hiding, rushing toward the sound. At the edge of a large, dark parking lot, men had gathered and were physically fighting. They were blurs, moving faster than I could follow, forcing me to calm my rapidly beating heart rate.

The moment it slowed, I took in the carnage from the immortals fighting against one another. My eyes followed the tallest male, watching his moves. He swung dual-edged blades around swiftly, effortlessly wielding them. He moved like it was a dance he knew by heart. He was skilled with blades, highly trained in weapons, judging by the swift swings that removed heads, sending them rolling across the pavement with ease.

I observed them for a while, and it wasn't until Silversmith blood called to me that my head turned, watching a lone female move onto the scene. I swallowed down the urge to go to her. It was a struggle to ignore the heady siren's call of blood beckoning me toward where she stood. She pushed her hood away from her head, and I paused. Cocking my head to the side, I gazed at her with no recognition of who she was other than we shared magical blood ties. It wasn't my mother, as I'd hoped.

The woman's hand lifted, and I watched her beckoning silver to her, smiling coldly as she pulled more power into her missiles. Silently, I nocked a single arrow, before aiming it at her. Vampires lay bleeding or dying on the ground as a cold-looking male appeared beside her, grinning at the other men's worried expressions. Smoothing his hand down the woman's back, I noted the glimmer of the ring he wore, recognizing the Van Helsing insignia.

Realizing that a Silversmith witch was helping a Van Helsing, I pushed off my hood and redirected my aim. Exhaling, I released the arrow the moment she let loose her bullets for a direct kill shot. The arrow sailed through the air, slamming into the line of ammunition, moving faster than immortals could see. She gasped, and I smirked, noting her wide-eyed look of horror at missing.

Slowly, I reached behind for another arrow, nocking it before moving to stand beside the opposing men, all of whom watched me through narrow-eyed stares.

"Cease, and stand down," I ordered, staring at the silver-haired woman. "On the order of those who hold authority over you, stand down now."

She had fake silver hair, I realized, dyed to fit her role.

She wasn't full-blooded, which meant silver hair wouldn't come naturally for her until she was old enough to have it from aging. All but one of our direct bloodline had silver hair, and that was my awkward ass.

"You don't order me around, sweetheart," she hissed vehemently.

"I won't ask you twice," I warned.

"Only a Silversmith can give me orders. I have orders to assist the Van Helsing in taking the houses of this region!"

"On whose orders?" I countered.

"I don't answer to you!"

"Nor I to you," I smiled cruelly. "I asked you to stand down. If you insist, I will end your life." Her hands lifted in the air, and I observed as silver magic slithered through her.

Narrowing my gaze, I watched the silver lines etching against her flesh as her power erupted in the parking lot. The man next to her was ancient, that much I could feel from the power he radiated. He had dark hair and tattoos covering his arms from wrist to shoulder, with an upside-down cross beneath his left eye.

"She's a Silversmith," the man beside me growled, and I turned, my jaw hitting the ground as he came into sight.

He was wearing a suit and held blades in his hands. Dark, inky hair stuck to his face, covered in sweat from fighting. Azure eyes narrowed on me while my gaze slowly lowered to his chest, which his suit hugged tightly, exposing a long, lean, muscular frame.

Magic exploded toward us, and I turned, lifting my bow that I hadn't realized I'd lowered while I eye-raped the male beside me. My magic erupted without thought, turning my eyes silver as my veins filled with it, pulling the bullets toward me, absorbing them into my body. The woman's mouth opened and closed, realizing her mistake too late. My fingers released the string, watching as the arrow shot through her open mouth, shattering her silver until it looked like glass raining down on the ground as she crumbled.

"What the fuck is happening?" someone asked, and I turned toward the Van Helsing that stood across from us, smiling as my silver magic reflected in his eyes.

"Pretty," he said huskily.

"Did a Silversmith just kill another Silversmith? How are there two in the same town, when a week ago we couldn't even find one?" the voice asked again.

I ignored the men behind me, watching the Van Helsing as he calculated his chances of reaching me before I could react. I lifted my hands, and he stepped back, feeling the undead closing in around him.

The silent monsters hidden within the shadows preparing to attack finally lunged, and I slipped away from the men next to me, offering them a coy smile. I stepped into the opening of the parking lot to fight. Not that I needed much room, but my silver was faster than normal Silversmith silver. I called the silver bullets that the fallen woman had wielded, using them to create a moving shield around me, smiling cruelly while they pelted into the undead that lunged toward me, unable to see the movement of the bullets with the speed in which they moved.

I stared at the Van Helsing, who watched me, lowering his head with a sinfully wicked smirk on his lips as he continued backing away, turning to vanish into the woods. He'd left his undead warriors to die, and that pissed me off since he'd brought them here to fight on his behalf, abandoning them to my bullets.

Exhaustion hit me without warning, and the bullets dropped to the ground, clinking on the pavement. I yelped out in surprise as a vampire lunged, and my hands lifted. I caught him by the shoulders and held his snapping fangs away from me until something sliced through his neck, severing his head from his shoulders. Turning, I found the men standing in the same place as before, as a singsong voice entered my mind.

Chapter Three

"So, just going to look around, hmm?" Nyx snorted, wiping her blade on a vampire's clothes, which had turned into a pile of ashes. "Did you find him?" she continued, staring up at me, narrowing her eyes. Her dark head turned, and she moved her attention to the men in front of us.

Warning bells were playing in my head as I took in the tallest male. Sinfully blue eyes smiled as if he sensed how weak I was in my current state. He took a step closer, and my heart thundered against my chest.

"We need to go," I whispered, turning to run away only to trip over my own feet, landing on my face on the concrete.

"That is an actual blood-heir Silversmith," he chuckled.

Nyx gripped my arms, pulling me up as we started forward. "You were supposed to be the rescue squad!" I groaned, hating that the curse had come on so fast.

We tripped at the beginning of the woods, and male laughter sounded behind us. At least we weren't being chased by the Van Helsing. It was a small blessing, but I'd take it as a win.

Nyx pulled me back up to my feet, and we continued through the woods. But it was futile, considering my curse was pretty much a giant 'fuck you' from the Van Helsings. Every time a Silversmith wielded their power against anyone, it backfired and made us weak and extremely accident-prone for hours afterward.

I slipped on the top of a hill, catching a branch as I went over an edge. Someone plucked Nyx from the air before she could fall over the ledge with me. I peered up at the male holding my wrist, noting his bedroom eyes smiling down at me like he'd just captured a rare prize. My eyes left his to look down at the jagged rocks below as he pulled me up, bringing my body flush against his, then pinching my chin, angling my face toward him, studying me.

"Silversmith, it seems your curse was activated," he murmured, turning my face from one side to the other as he examined me. "You don't look like a Silversmith." His fingers ran through my hair, pulling a strand against his nose as I frowned.

"You planning to eat me?" I questioned pointedly while he sniffed me.

"Mommy wants some. Shit, I'll take them all on right now," Nyx murmured dreamily, causing my head to turn in her direction. I groaned at the look of utter devotion stamped on her face.

"You were supposed to be the rescue squad, bitch," I grunted, and the male smiled down at me as another took my weapons.

"Hey, I came here right from the airport. I was all for playing Captain Save-A-Hoe! I told you to stay away from the Van Helsing, but no, badass Remi has to go check shit out and find him first. I hope you learned everything about him, down to his penis size!"

"Why would I want to know that?" I muttered, dragging my hand down my face. I turned my attention back to the male hanging on our every word. "Who the hell are you?"

"Rhys. Rhys Van Helsing."

"Hot damn! Now you can see if the penis and vagina lore is true!" Nyx hooted with excitement.

The blood left my face as he watched me with a cold smile lifting his lips. "And you would be?"

"Toast when Winchester figures this shit out. I'm in so much trouble," I whined, struggling in his arms as he noted the lack of strength I used to get away.

"Save your fight, pretty girl. You won't win. Not even at your fullest. You're young, aren't you?"

"Why does everyone assume I'm young? What is it? Is there like a stamp on my forehead that says *born yesterday*," I snapped and then squeaked when his hand landed on my ass, and my body went flush against his hard, muscular frame.

"Because you still smell of mortality, and that means you're fragile. Aren't you?" Rhys chuckled darkly. I swallowed hard, watching his gaze narrow as he leaned closer. "Where are the others?"

"What others?" I snapped.

"You're a newborn Silversmith. There's no way you're out here alone, woman." He studied my eyes as they narrowed to mirror his while a frown creased my brow. "Bloody hell, you're on your own. That was stupid and so careless with something so bloody precious and untrained."

"She's not on her own! I'm here with her," Nyx argued, and we both turned, staring at the nymph currently stroking the male closest to her, pretending to dance on his leg, or at least I hoped that was what she was doing. "So, are you going to see if the lore is true?" Her brows wagged up and down before returning her attention to dancing, which hadn't been dancing at all. "Ride that Van Helsing! Get that kitty cat some action!"

My eyes locked with Rhys's once more as I turned to glare at him, and failed horribly. He wasn't just beautiful; he was gorgeous in an old-world way. There was sheer masculinity to him that most men in this day and age lacked. His hair was messed up from the fight and chase afterward. His scent drew me in with a subtle hint of aftershave that was so faint it almost smelled natural. I leaned closer, inhaling him as a wicked smile curved his lips.

"Damn, Remi, you eye-fuck him any harder, and *I'm* going to come."

I pulled back, tossing a glare at her as I shook my head. Rhys lifted me, and I grasped onto him, holding on for dear life. His mouth was close to mine, and I did my best to hold my face away from him like he was contagious with rabies or something.

"Put me down," I whispered, my panic increasing the moment he started moving. "Put me down, or you'll break my neck!"

He laughed darkly, as if he found me cute and endearing. He wouldn't think it was so funny when he ended up with my curse affecting him.

"Do you know how to stop your curse, Remi?" he asked softly, his fingers tightening on my behind, sending a shiver racing up my spine. He smelled like sex on legs, and my body was taking notes, writing things down even as fear hitched up my spine to wrap around my throat.

"Death?" I took a shot in the dark.

"A Van Helsing's touch," he informed coolly, the smile curving his lips, sinfully hot. "I counteract the curse when I touch you. After all, we placed it there. It only seems fitting that we'd also be the cure."

"Death it is, then," I groaned, trying my best to hold my body away from his, failing miserably.

"That's not an option for you now. You walked into my world, little girl. You're in it now."

"You do know we're enemies, and I'm not a freaking damsel who needs carrying around like a worthless sack of potatoes, right? I'm a badass hunter from E.V.I.E. who, by the way, will come to save me."

"Let them come, and if they're strong enough, they can even take you from me."

He sounded confident that it wouldn't happen,

which sent a shiver of unease rushing down my spine. Rhys Van Helsing was carrying me in his arms, and my curse wasn't hindering him at all. My heart was pounding deafeningly in my ears, which I was sure he could feel, judging by the smirk that lifted the corners of his full mouth. He sounded British, or as if he tried to hide the British accent ingrained into him.

"You could let me go," I offered.

"If I let you go, Cole would have you within the hour, and I promise you, I'm much easier to deal with than my brother. Your entire world is about to change, Remi. Don't worry. I don't bite hard."

"I do," I replied, watching his eyes sparkle with laughter. "I totally bite hard."

"Do you know what you are?" he asked.

"I know what I am, and I also know who you are to me. You're my enemy, and once upon a time, our families were united by something greater than either could understand. Then it all changed because your family betrayed mine."

"Do you know why we betrayed you?" he asked softly, without anger.

"I was supposed to get the talk when I turned twenty-five on my rising. I'm not there yet."

"So you're a mortal Silversmith who hasn't been told of the past?" he clarified, frowning as he studied my reaction to his question.

"Does it really matter? I got the whole enemies for life gist of the theme. That was pretty much idiot-proof. There's also the curse, hence the fact that I can barely walk after using my powers, which is your fault."

"You could show her other things that would make her unable to walk afterward. I mean, she's a Silversmith, and you're a Van Helsing. It's like a match made in lore heaven! Oh, and if you can, please elaborate on the porn part of your family histories in vivid detail for the rest of us. She doesn't believe the stories I've told her! I'm totally game to wait for you to remove the cobwebs from between her knees first!"

"Oh, my Lord," I groaned, burying my face in his neck, before realizing what I'd done and yanking away from him. I ignored the curve of his mouth, trying to fight a smile caused by Nyx's outburst, no doubt. "She has no filter. It's like she opens her mouth and words vomit out. It's not the time or place to be talking about *my* vagina, Nyx!"

"Now is the only time! He's a freaking Van Helsing. They're like legends with their swords."

"Weapons. Swords are weapons!" I argued.

"So are penises when wielded correctly. Which you would know if you ever let an actual man near that thing, woman," she scoffed. "You two are literally cursed to fuck each other, so just let that shit happen."

"She's wrong. Right? Tell her she's wrong," I muttered, watching dark eyes shifting to hold mine. "Tell her she's wrong, because…" Rhys's mouth lowered, stilling the air in my lungs as my words hung poised. His mouth brushed against my cheek as he inhaled deeply. "Are you fucking *sniffing* me?"

"You don't smell like magic, why is that?" he pulled back, studying my face. "Your hair isn't dyed, either. It's naturally that color."

"So sorry that I don't fit the perfect Silversmith mold, jerk."

"No, you're actually perfect. No one will realize what I have on my side."

"I'm not on your side."

"You'd rather be on Cole's or another immortal that wouldn't care if you suffered? Because I promise you this, Cole is all incubus, and very little Van Helsing, woman."

"And what is the difference?" I asked carefully.

"I won't keep you fucked stupid. At least, I wouldn't unless you ask me to, of course. I'll respect your boundaries and allow you free rein of my house if you serve me. He'd just chain you up and use you whenever he wanted."

"I pick Cole!" Nyx announced excitedly, like we'd won a prize on a game show. Rhys's words caused me to swallow past the lump in my throat. Winnie was going to roast me over an open flame and then serve my stupid ass up for supper.

"Make me a deal," I offered, watching his eyes narrow before they slid to mine.

"What deal would that be?"

"I am missing something, help me find it, and I will work for you. There's a time limit, though, and once it is up, you'll release me. If you don't, I will rain down hell on more than just your house, bringing it down, unlike anything you've ever witnessed before."

"Wow, who knew the little weapons master could be an evil bitch? Plot twist!"

"Nyx, chuck it in the fuck-it bucket now! This is serious business!"

"Cian, clear the backroom," Rhys said, ignoring us both. "Have some Irish whiskey brought in. After you've finished that, clear out the bar. Cole will be watching for a weakness now, but he'll be cautious about attacking us since he didn't see her go down with the curse. Let's get our little Silversmith to the house as soon as possible. I want a full assault team of knights to escort Remi to her new home."

"Wow, you skipped all the bases and went straight for home base. I don't know if I should be afraid or impressed," I murmured, unable to look away from the stars sparkling in his pretty eyes.

His mouth lifted on one side as he peered down at me. "Careful. That curse is an actual thing, and if you keep looking at me like that, you'll ruin my reputation as a gentleman."

"Wouldn't want that," I muttered.

Chapter Four

The room they gave us was lavish in décor. A crystal chandelier was the focal point, with high-backed chairs surrounding an opulent glass-top table. Beneath the glass, old Victorian-style pictures depicted ageless, beautiful women in risqué poses. It was like we'd stepped back in time.

I reached for the whiskey on the table and watched the glass shatter the moment I touched it. Some days the curse was seriously disheartening, like when facing off against an actual Van Helsing who continued to look at me as if I were something to devour or strangle but couldn't decide which he wanted more.

"Give her a plastic cup," Rhys grunted, watching the server lurch forward to clean the spilled mess of whiskey from the table. I started to stand, only to have the chair legs break, sending me careening to the floor.

I remained on the floor, groaning. I peered at the artwork on the ceiling that I hadn't noticed before ending up flat on my back. Five royal houses, each one with a royal crest that bespoke of their symbol. Van Helsing had swords and a coat of armor. Mine had a potion with silver smoke rising from the vial.

The others had a wolf head, the symbol of infinity, and then one that had the symbol of change for the breeds who continued to grow through the world's evolution and changes. I knew them well, taught to see them on houses to avoid like the plague since before I could even remember.

A dark shadow moved into view, and my gaze slid to the dark blue eyes peering down at me as a sinful smile tipped the corners of Rhys's lips. He was apparently finding great amusement at my curse.

"Bad luck, woman," he said thickly, watching me as I struggled to get off the floor. I placed my hand on his masterpiece of a table which cracked and spider-webbed under my touch. "Stop touching things."

"Like you said, bad luck. Sorry," I returned icily, glaring daggers at him, which only made his lips twitch, still amused. Reaching up to my neck, I touched the straps of my shirt and then winced as it broke, catching the top before he ended up with a full inventory of my goods.

He'd confiscated my cloak and deposed me of all my silver. That included the necklaces and charms that helped to counteract the curse somewhat. Now I was using said curse against him, and judging by the twinkle in his eye, he was fully aware of what I was doing. I smirked, wrinkling my nose, holding my shirt together, surprised when he lifted me off the ground without warning.

"You really like to touch people, don't you?"

"Indeed."

I placed my hands around his neck to steady myself, causing my shirt to drop down the front, leaving my breasts revealed. I slammed against him with wide, horrified eyes as he peered between us, finding way too much cleavage on display for polite conversation.

"That's unfortunate," he chuckled darkly, lifting his pretty hypnotic eyes to hold mine. He sat on the chair beside the heap of ruins where I'd been sitting, allowing me to continue pressing against him awkwardly. "Jamyn, can you please fetch our guest a new shirt? There should be some behind the bar," he mused.

"Do you often have women losing their shirts in your bar?" I asked pointedly, a little ire etching my tone.

"You'd be surprised at how many women throw caution to the wind in my bar. Sometimes people need a place to let loose and not worry about being judged for doing so. I provide them a safe place to do that with the promise of sanctuary throughout that time."

"And if I asked for sanctuary?" I whispered huskily, unable to ignore the heat rushing through me as his fingers slowly stroked my naked shoulder.

"Silversmiths are not given sanctuary inside Van Helsing safe houses, Remi. We're enemies and have been for a very long time. The only way you'd be eligible for sanctuary, was if you worked for me."

"How about other creatures?" I asked, leaning

closer to inhale his scent that tingled in my nose, dancing like a drug through my senses.

"They'd be freely given sanctuary."

"Nyx, ask for sanctuary," I murmured before my mouth opened, and my tongue traced over the pulse in his neck.

"Don't mind me. I'm just here watching the show. If it ends with sanctuary, I'd rather chance death," she chirped from somewhere in the room. But everything within me focused on the male touching me.

"What are you doing?" Rhys asked, and I yanked away from him with wide, horror-filled eyes. I leaned up without warning, noting that he dropped his stare to my breasts. "I'm going to need those barbells, woman."

I gazed down at my nipples, slowly lifting my eyes back to his before bringing my hands up to cover my naked breasts. I had been licking him! I didn't lick people I just met. Nyx licked people! Frowning, I shook my head.

"It's surgical steel," I admitted breathlessly. "What are you doing to me?"

"Nothing," he grinned, bringing his hand up to the curve of my breast. His touch caused the air to still in my lungs. Leaning over, he moved toward my ear, turning at the last moment to kiss my racing pulse at the hollow column of my throat, while his finger touched the metal piercing, brushing against my nipple before dropping to my waist. "They're silver, little liar."

"You could tell just by touching them?" I squeaked, shifting uncomfortably in his lap. The door to the room opened, and a man handed Rhys a shirt, and I flicked my eyes to Nyx, who watched in silent amusement.

"I'm a Van Helsing. Of course, I know what type of metal it is by touch," he answered aloofly, holding the shirt up as he slipped it over my head. "Put your arms through it."

I narrowed my eyes on him, and he smirked, closing his eyes briefly. I uncovered my naked breasts, pushing my arms through the sleeves, quickly pulling the shirt on, discovering heated blue eyes studying me. My hands adjusted, holding on to his shoulders as he searched my face absently.

"How do you have red hair? And your eyes, they're vividly blue instead of the normal ice color that your bloodline is known for."

I twisted my lips into a thoughtful pout as I considered how much to tell him. "We don't know why I came out different, only that I am."

"What else is different?" he asked.

"What is this? Fifty questions with the hostage? You think I'm just going to answer you because I'm sitting on your lap looking cute?"

"You do look surprisingly cute on my lap."

"Why am I in your lap?" I turned as a server approached us, handing me a plastic cup of whiskey, my lips twisting as I fought the smile. I tipped back the cup, downing the contents in a single gulp before handing it back. "You didn't answer my question."

"You didn't answer mine," he smiled mischievously.

The whiskey warmed my cheeks, and I cocked my head to the side, turning to look at the bottle left on the table in the now very empty room. My stare swung back to Van Helsing, who slowly ran his eyes over my face.

"Silversmiths are never born with different coloring. Your hair isn't dyed, and you're not wearing contacts. Your power was intensely strong, yet lacked control. The only time you smelled of magic was when you used it, and for a few moments afterward. Now you smell human and of a meadow filled with wildflowers after a spring rain. Yet when casting, your eyes were indeed silver, as was your hair and aura. I find it highly improbable that you walked right into my path. I've spent months searching for a Silversmith with enough magic within her to counter the Silversmith my little brother stumbled upon weeks ago. I was beginning to think it was hopeless. Yet here you are, literally in my lap. Who sent you?" he asked softly, his keen gaze studying mine.

"No one sent me." I swallowed as his fingers brushed lightly over my exposed midsection.

His touch consumed my mind, creating a red haze that rushed through me violently. A lazy smile played over his mouth before his tongue snaked out, licking his bottom lip, pulling my eyes to it. He sat up, forcing me to hold tighter to him until I realized he was removing his suit jacket. I leaned back slowly, watching as he shook out of it, reaching for the buttons of his white dress shirt that was damp still.

"You don't mind, do you?" he asked, slowly revealing a muscular chest covered in colorful tattoos.

"No," I replied huskily, uncertain why I didn't look away from the washboard abs begging for me to kiss and stroke them slowly. "No accidents are happening as long as I'm touching you. So what you said was true? You're a cure to the curse?"

"I am, as you're the cure to mine. Every curse includes a way to neutralize it," he explained, pulling one arm out of the dress shirt to reveal both nipples pierced, his name covering his forearm and his family crest on his abdomen.

He adjusted in his chair, smiling as he watched me feasting on his ink from beneath my lashes. I pretended that I was anywhere other than his lap. Rhys moved again, and the motion forced me forward, causing my hands to rest on his chest. My fingers brushed against his piercings, and I shivered against the call of Silversmith silver that he wore brazenly. Heat banked in his pretty stare as he hissed under my touch.

"What are you doing to me?" I asked, knowing something was happening.

"Getting answers," he admitted, moving his hands around my narrow waist, pulling me closer. "I'm an incubus demon, after all. You should know that, Silversmith, since your family is the one who cursed me to be this monster."

"I don't know much about that yet," I admitted, turning to look at the whiskey, which would calm the raging inferno within me. "If you plan to interrogate me, you should pour me another drink, Van Helsing."

Chapter Five

He didn't get up to pour more whiskey, choosing to wrap his arms around me as he did the task instead. It was the most awkward and most uncomfortable thing in my entire life to pretend that I wasn't affected by his half-naked body, while literally holding on to it so that I didn't end up on my ass on the floor again.

"How long are you affected by the curse?" Rhys asked casually.

"Shouldn't you know that answer?"

"The more powerful the Silversmith witch, the more powerful the curse."

"So what you're really asking me, Van Helsing, is how powerful am I?" I watched his lips twitch before he stopped them by biting his bottom lip, which was sexy. "Very powerful is the answer to the question you are asking." My hand lifted the plastic cup, downing the whiskey like a frat boy trying to impress the brotherhood of idiots he wanted to join. I smiled at the look of disapproval Rhys offered in rebuke.

"Fifty-year-old Irish whiskey that cost forty-thousand dollars a bottle should be savored, Silversmith," he grumbled, bringing his to his nose to sniff while staring at me over the rim of the crystal glass.

"Why the hell would anyone pay forty-thousand dollars for whiskey?" I asked crossly.

"Because I can?" he countered, sipping the drink slowly. A smile curved his generous mouth as I watched him drinking it slowly. "Who is your mother?"

"Superwoman," I supplied, giving him a half-hearted smile before wiggling my brows.

He tipped back his cup, reaching past me to place it on the damaged table. Wrapping his arm around my back, he pulled me closer to him. His eyes slowly surveyed my face before he dipped his mouth to mine, softly claiming my lips. I brought my hands flat against his chest, trying to remember why this was a bad idea.

The moment his mouth touched mine, all coherent thought left my mind, replaced with need. A groan escaped his lips as my mouth captured it, swallowing it like the whiskey. My fingers ran through his inky dark hair as my tongue pushed past his lips, dueling against his in an ageless dance. My hips rolled, inviting him to do more, which he didn't seem to understand.

One moment led my utter ruin in a charge of sexual tension, and the next, he took control, exerting dominance. His fingers trailed through my hair, controlling my head as he turned it to allow better access to devour me. My hands lowered to his shoulders, unable to touch his flesh enough as I continually rocked against him, moaning unsexy noises like a bitch in heat as he claimed my mouth in a toe-curling kiss.

He pulled away, and my mouth chased his, needing him to continue what he'd started. Or maybe I had started it? Who cared? I felt his mouth twisting into a smile as his hand tightened in my hair, wrenching my head back, exposing my throat.

"Who is your mother?" he asked, and my nose wrinkled up.

"Who cares?" I whispered, listening to his husky laughter.

The music of his deep, rich laughter filled the room, slithering up my flesh as his other hand slipped under the shirt I wore. Pleasure swept over me, and I moaned unabashedly as my body tightened with desire fueled by my need for him.

Rhys brought my mouth back to his, hovering against it with what I needed and desired most just out of my reach. "Who is your mother?"

"Elizabeth Rhianna Cordova Silversmith," I uttered, chasing the pleasure his lips promised. He stiffened, and my mind began to buzz with voices, voices whispering spells that worked on my flesh but did little to ease the pressure between my thighs.

"Elizabeth is dead, Remi. I know. I watched her die," he growled, studying my face.

"She escaped, along with a few others. Beneath the

stairs inside the library was a secret passageway that led deep into the woods where no one was looking. Into the shadows, the Silversmith goes, for the Van Helsing wants to consume our souls. From witch's light, and faraway fright, the Van Helsing comes with all his might, but Silversmith knows how deep to go. Hide from them now. Hide from them all, for we remain the strongest house of all." I sang it for him, my off-tune hum in synchronized movements with my hips as he studied me.

His mouth brushed against mine, holding me in whatever thrall he had over me. My skin glowed, and his eyes lowered, studying the runes before he shook his head, dropping his hands to my hips.

"What are you, Remi Silversmith?" he growled, rocking my body against his. "Tell me to stop. Tell me you don't want me. Tell me to stop this, and it ends now."

I swallowed as my mind slowly took in what was happening around me. My body was strung tightly, pulsing with the need to release the tension he'd created. I could see the tick hammering in his jaw, his pupils dilating with lust as I leaned over, claiming his mouth to stop my brain from stuttering over the reality of what was happening.

He moved swiftly, lifting my body against his before placing me on the table, wrapping my legs around his hips. My hands pushed against his chest as he continued kissing me like I was the air he needed to breathe. His fingers captured the bottom of my shirt, lifting it over my head easily as he broke the kiss, slowly lowering me to the table. His hands trailed from my hips to my belly as he peered into my soul's depths, devouring it with the look burning in his eyes.

My stomach coiled with tension as a wild fluttering began within me, as if butterflies had taken flight and searched for a way to escape. His mouth lowered, clicking his teeth against the piercing in my nipple, pulling against it. I hissed at the pain mixing with pleasure, lifting my hips to roll them as my eyes closed. Absolute pleasure rushed through me from his heated kisses and nibbles.

A knock sounded at the door, and I opened my eyes as he reached between our bodies, stroking against my pleasure zone until I trembled from the pressure. His fingers pinched my clit through my pants as sinfully dark blue eyes slid up to hold mine. I exploded as his other hand lifted, covering my mouth, and he groaned like he was in pain during my sudden release.

"Van Helsing. Cole just walked into the bar!" someone shouted from the other side of the door.

Rhys yanked me up, and my head spun as he grabbed the shirt he'd tossed on the floor, pulling it over my head. He picked up one hand, pushing it through the sleeve before doing the same to my other. His hand lifted, pushing his fingers through his hair as he smiled victoriously at me.

"Don't cuss at me too much, Love. That bloody bastard will see it as foreplay."

"What the hell just happened?" I asked through swollen lips.

"That curse your friend mentioned? It's not real, but the one about our lines being connected most definitely is. If you stay with me, I'll tell you more about it. If Elizabeth is your mother, you shouldn't be trying to find her. She will find you. That woman is relentless when she puts her mind to it."

The door opened, and the tattooed male from earlier in the night entered, his heady stare falling on me as he invited himself inside. His lips curled into a dark smile while he slid his attention down my body to where Rhys held my hips.

"Sanctuary, brother," Cole smirked. "Unless, of course, you intend to break Van Helsing law by denying me entrance?" Cole asked, his eyes sparkled while he studied the way I watched him.

"Granted," Rhys growled as a tick slowly pulsed in his cheek. His dark blue eyes never left mine, not even when his mouth curved into a dark smile. "Cole, meet Elizabeth's daughter, Remi Silversmith."

"Elizabeth's dead, we buried her corpse after we burned them in their home," Cole said coldly, sending a chill racing down my spine as unease entered my mind. "She can't be a Silversmith. The coloring is all wrong. Move, asshole," he ordered, grabbing me and yanking me toward him.

I lifted my hand and shoved Cole back, watching as his mouth curved in a smile that caused my knees to grow weak. He grabbed my wrist, and I moaned, whimpering as the room changed, and both brothers boxed me in, kissing me while hands caressed me. It felt like I'd stepped on a livewire sending waves of need rushing through me.

Their lips caressed my skin, and I moaned,

grinding my body against them. Rhys cupped my breasts from behind as Cole suckled one into his mouth, his hand sliding down my naked flesh. My clothes vanished, leaving me with two very virile, very naked men who were kissing and stroking me until my entire body literally ached with pleasure.

"Tell me your secrets, and I'll bring you to heaven with so much pleasure you'll never wish to leave my cock, little girl," Cole growled hungrily.

"Enough, Cole," Rhys warned harshly, yanking me toward him and out of the illusion Cole had woven. "You're here under sanctuary, brother. Tread very carefully from this point forward."

"She hasn't chosen a side yet, has she? That makes her fair game, and she did just murder the little half-breed witch I owned."

"A witch who held a lot less power than Remi does. She is a Silversmith by blood. That much you can't argue. You saw it as clearly as I did tonight. She had every right to give orders, and those orders weren't followed. So Remi took her life."

"If she were a fucking alpha, brother, then that would be true," Cole snorted, stepping closer, lifting his hand to cradle my cheek. He studied my face carefully through narrowing eyes, running his thumb over my full bottom lip. "She's a little too wild for your uptight ass to handle, anyway. She's got a dark side, and I want to play with it. Care to join me, brother?"

"Remi remains here until she decides which side she wants. She is an alpha, and you know it. Regardless of house status, that stands. Your half-breed should have listened to her, and she wouldn't be dead right now."

I was getting whiplash from their conversation, yet I hadn't looked away from Cole, who was smiling. He screamed King of Wickedness, right down to the tattoos that sat on his face. His power wasn't muted, it continued to pulse like a steady beat through the room, even though it wasn't directed at me since he'd let me go.

"You like what you see, pretty one?"

"Undecided," I admitted.

Who the hell looked like sex incarnate while rocking face tattoos? They weren't supposed to be sexy, but on Cole, they were. His head canted to the side, and the smile that played on his mouth promised pleasure. Shit, everything about both men screamed sex god in pretty packages. Nyx would be in heaven!

"You need help deciding?" Cole asked, slowly stepping closer until I was between the brothers. His hands lifted to my shoulders, while Rhys continued to hold my waist. "You remember the last Silversmith we took together, Rhys?" Cole continued, lowering his lips to my throat while slowly nipping against the racing pulse.

"I'm not interested in sharing anything with you, Cole. I don't think she is interested in being shared, either. Are you, Love?" Rhys asked, his nose slowly rubbing against my ear as their bodies' heat pushed against mine.

My heart pounded relentlessly against my chest. Cole leaned closer, brushing his lips against mine as he smiled. The hands on my hips held me tightly, brushing thumbs over my flesh to reassure me, while Cole claimed my mouth softly, slowly seducing my senses. I moaned as images flashed through my mind. Cole had me seated on his lap, while Rhys sat between my legs, devouring me. Cole held my thighs open, allowing Rhys to stroke his tongue hungrily through my apex's arousal. I watched with a hooded gaze as Cole's fingers began running in a circular pattern against my clit. Rhys's fingers entered my body, filling me until I was bucking against them, coming undone around their sensual assault. I shivered violently, pushing the images away as I tried to determine reality from fantasy.

Freaking incubus demons! Even worse, *brother* incubus demons.

"Enough," I moaned as my head dropped back against Rhys's chest. Cole stepped back, smiling, but the look in his eyes floored me like he hadn't been unaffected by that vision either.

"She's a very dirty girl, with a sinfully delicious imagination. She was imaging you eating her naked pussy, and it is *very* naked, indeed, brother. You're in over your head with this one, Rhys. When she becomes too much to handle, send her my way, and I'll turn her naughty little thoughts into a reality she'd enjoy."

"You finished yet, asshole?" Rhys growled, and yet he didn't release me.

"Nah, I'm just getting started," Cole laughed darkly, letting his eyes drop to where Rhys continued running his fingers over my hips. "I'll see you soon, Sunshine."

"My name is Remington, not Sunshine."

"Remington, what a beautiful name for a little Silversmith," he chuckled, leaning closer to inhale my scent. "Fuck me! You're a newborn. No wonder my asshole brother is trying to claim you. I'm guessing Eliza didn't get to the part where we're the bad guys, did she? Since you're not immortal, I'm going to guess that you know nothing of our world or history. Fuck me, if we didn't hit pay dirt with you."

"You didn't hit shit. I may be young, but I'm not stupid. I'm aware I am in the hands of my bloodline's mortal enemies. I'm very aware of who and what you are. I'm also aware that I'm on neither of your sides, so stop with your demon mind tricks, or I'll make your blood boil with mine. I do promise to enjoy the pretty screams you'll give me. Now get your fucking hands off of me, both of you."

"You sure you want me to do that?" Rhys chuckled against the side of my neck, kissing it softly. "I'm not sure how much more this room can take of your curse. You broke a two-hundred-year-old table that was an heirloom."

"Who is to blame for that?" I countered crossly.

"Touché, but if I release you from my touch, you'll either face plant on the floor or land on Cole, which he is hoping happens. If he's touching you without me grounding you, I can't get you out of his thrall. Decide. It's your choice what happens to you."

"Come on, pretty girl. Come play in my world. I promise you'll like it there," Cole smirked, crossing his arms over his chest, watching me carefully as frustration played out on my face. "I'm much more fun than Rhys's stuffy, prim, and proper ass is."

I didn't trust either of them.

Not one iota.

However, I really didn't trust a man who could sacrifice his men just to make a point. Cole planned to murder his brother. If I hadn't intervened, he very well might have accomplished it.

"I think I'll stay with Rhys for now, Cole. It was a pleasure to meet you, though, and should I need a gorgeous evil villain, you'll be my first choice."

"Who says I'm the evil one, Sunshine?" Cole asked, lifting a brow as Rhys snorted behind me. "Oh, don't let his suit and ties fool you. He's as evil as they come. He just hides it much better than I do. Enjoy your evening. Do try to pull that stick out of my brother's ass, yeah? He's a bloody fucking thorn in my side. It was my pleasure meeting you, Remington. Such beauty and grace have long been forgotten in this day and age. Though, maybe pick your clothes better, and stop letting this wanker dress you. I can send something more… appropriate for you to wear if you'd like. If not, I took it upon myself to pick up your belongings from your hotel. They're being held at the bar since weapons are frowned upon here, especially Silversmith weapons. You have an eye for fine detail, and I must say, I am impressed by your craftsmanship to your personal weapons. I did, however, take one as my price for delivering your things. Goodnight, my lady," he said, bowing at the waist before his eyes lifted. A cold smile played on his lips as he stared over my shoulder. "I'll be back soon, promise."

He left the room, and I spun around, lifting my hand to slap Rhys before he could deflect it. "Do not ever use your magic on me again, or I'll return the favor tenfold, and I only know the nasty spells of my bloodline. If I kiss you, it will be because I *want* to kiss you. If I tell you things, it will be because I want you to know them. Use your demon mojo on me, and I will get evil on you, and you know it, so don't push me. You have things I want to learn about my history, but more than that, you know my mother. Which means you may know who took her or who would want to take her. If you help me, I will help you. That is my offer. Take it or leave it, Van Helsing."

"I only used my influence when I kissed you, and only a sliver of it. I can't make you want me. You're a Silversmith. You're immune to that part of what I am because you cursed me. You're my cure for the incubus magic within me. Yes, I can enhance your libido, and you can enhance mine. That is because we were united, and our bloodlines are the fuel on the fire that ignites when we touch. What Cole did, that is more incubi driven. We're uncertain of why he can wield it against Silversmiths. It has only ever worked on halflings until you. You saw me between your pretty thighs, didn't you?" Rhys dropped his gaze to the pulse on my throat that gave away my lie before I even whispered it. He smiled devilishly, lifting his hand to touch my cheek. "Cole wasn't lying entirely. I'm not a good guy. I don't play by anyone else's rules. When I give my word, I keep it. And the list of who wouldn't want your mother captured or dead is much shorter than those who do."

"Was there a yes in there somewhere?" I asked, exhausted from driving from Seattle to Spokane, across the entire state of Washington. Then to show up to a mess at my mother's house, ending up a prisoner because I hadn't listened to Winchester, who would never let me live this down *if* I survived it.

Chapter Six

Rhys held my hand as we vacated the sanctuary and made a beeline to the waiting sleek, black Suburban. He had an entire caravan of knights outside the vehicles dressed in dark clothing and tactical gear. It appeared as if Rhys expected an assault or was escorting royalty instead of one exhausted Silversmith and a nymph who was currently touching his knights in inappropriate ways.

"Nyx, stop groping them!" I complained, trying to yank my hand back to point my finger toward her, yet Rhys refused to allow me to use of my hand. "It's inappropriate."

"And fun, you should try it," Nyx giggled

"I've done all the groping I want to do tonight. Thank you very much!" I groaned tiredly, noting Rhys's lips that twitched with my words.

"You groped him?" Nyx smiled, wiggling her

eyebrows meaningfully.

I watched as my bag was brought out to the back of a Suburban and tossed inside. My gaze slid to Nyx, who waited for my reply. My teeth worried my lip while I decided what to tell her. I'd been more than groped and had done more than that to the male currently holding my hand.

"I made out with him."

"Is that what we're going with?" he asked, tracing his thumb over the pulse on my wrist. "I'm pretty sure you got a little more than that tonight, Silversmith."

"Indeed, it is. That's all the information anyone needs to know about what happened in that room tonight." My eyes dared him to argue it, his sparkling with amusement before dragging his tongue over his very rideable lips.

"I need more details than that! Did you make her pretty kitty purr? It needs to purr. She's growing cobwebs, and it's such a waste. And considering who Remi is, and what she is, she needs to use those pelvic muscles. Did the curse happen? We're you inexplicably drawn to one another with the need to bend that ass over and spread those—"

"And that's enough from you!" I squeaked abruptly, pausing at the sound of Rhys's rumbling dark laughter. Leveling him with a chilling glare just made him smile wickedly, and his damn thumb found my pulse on my wrist again, stroking it slowly.

"The curse is true. And yes, it has ignited between us, Nyx. Unfortunately, we were disturbed, and our liaison was interrupted. Considering how much magic

Remi wielded earlier tonight, I'm sure we will have time tonight to pursue the end of what we started."

"Nope," I chirped. My heart stopped at his words, starting up again with a thundering beat, pounding in my ears. That cursed thumb paused, pushing against my pulse, and I swallowed as his body got closer to mine. "That is not happening."

"In you go, woman," he announced.

I tried to pull my wrist away from his grip, but he prevailed, holding on to it. I climbed into the backseat of one of the cars, and Rhys followed, pressing his thigh against mine, and finally releasing my hand. I rubbed the skin where he'd held it, feeling the loss of the heat the moment he'd let go.

Nyx crawled in over the top of us, chuckling as we cursed at her unexpected entrance. She climbed over the seat, even though the second row was accessible through the seats' center. It wasn't bad enough that I was sharing a seat with Van Helsing. I also had to deal with my very horny, very inappropriate best friend speaking over my shoulder.

"So, are you going to fuck him, Remi?" she chirped happily. I coughed, covering my mouth with my hand to smother the groan that her words drew from within me.

"That's inappropriate, and no, I have no intention of sleeping with him."

"You'll be sharing my bed unless, of course, your run of bad luck is over," he stated, turning his face toward mine, which was entirely too close.

"Normally, it takes at least a few hours," I admitted, pursing my lips before scrunching up my face. "That doesn't mean I am *sleeping* with you. It means I might be sleeping *beside* you. There's a big difference between the two."

"Remi likes her neck kissed, and her arms held above her head. She's totally into being dominated but hasn't met a man who is alpha enough to accommodate her freakishly kinky needs. I like to be manhandled, you know, in case you were wondering." Nyx offered from the backseat.

I closed my eyes, dropping my head back against the seat, praying for the strength not to throttle my best friend. The hint of a blush burned my ears and cheeks as I felt Rhys's heated stare studying me. Swallowing loudly, I opened my eyes to glare at him.

"What else does Remi like, Nyx?" he asked, watching me through a hooded stare that caused my already rapid heartbeat to hitch to a dangerous rate.

"She likes men who take control and challenge her mind. Pretty boring on the latter part, if you ask me," she announced, inhaling to say more. "Remi has a dark side, one she keeps hidden from the world, but I know because I am her person. She reads romance novels by the truckful, devouring them in one sitting. Candlelight makes her into a hopeless romantic, and she loves music. I've caught her dancing around in her panties more than a few times." I turned, leveling her with a look of betrayal. "She would probably tell me more about what she likes, but she knows I have no filter. Remington's never had anyone go down on her, so there's that too! I'm also unable to keep secrets."

I brought my hands up to cover my flaming face. A redhead blushing wasn't pretty. Not when my hair and face matched, or so my mother had often reminded me. I wanted the seat to open up and swallow me.

"You've never had your pussy eaten?" Rhys asked huskily. His hand moved to grip my thigh, causing my hand to cover his. My angry glare locked with his hooded stare. His touch made everything within me tighten and pulse with a brutal need that eviscerated me.

"It wasn't an invitation," I snapped crossly. "There are a lot of things I have yet to do in my life. That doesn't mean I intend to do them tonight, or with you. If I wanted you to eat my pussy, I'd ask you to lick my pussy. I have not asked you to eat my pussy. Therefore, you should not assume there is an invitation."

The driver sputtered, coughing on the drink of water he'd just taken as his eyes met mine in the rearview mirror. I pulled my eyes from the driver's wide stare to give Rhys a withering glare, but his smile caught me off-guard and gave me pause.

"It wasn't a challenge," I whispered, and then gasped as his hand pushed against my already throbbing core. His nostrils flared, and his head cocked to the side, dropping the smile as something more sinister played out in his eyes.

"Drive, my newest conquest is tired and in need of her rest," Rhys chuckled, releasing my core to pull a phone from his pocket. "Have the room next to mine set up, and have a nightcap ready, along with something… pretty for a female to sleep in." His stare slid to my frame, sliding up and down it before he continued his conversation. "Size four, and make sure to draw a bath for her, ready for when we get there. Not too hot of water, as she is mortal. Have a light meal prepared for her as well, since she missed her dinner. Her traveling companion will need a male to feed from, but have her room down the hall from mine. Get it done. We're less than twenty minutes from the compound." He clicked off the phone and turned his attention back to me.

"You enjoy giving commands?" I asked, chewing my bottom lip, and his eyes lowered to my mouth briefly before lifting back to mine.

"Indeed, I do. I am a born alpha of House of Van Helsing and have been in control of the sub-houses since I became immortal before your mother was ever born. I am always in control and ten steps ahead of my enemies. I also enjoy being in command in the bedroom and controlling pleasure. As you discovered earlier, I am very dominant. When I want something, I go for it." His gaze narrowed, sparkling while he watched my reaction to his words.

"Does he have a brother, by chance?" Nyx asked, reminding us she was there.

"Actually, he does. He promised to show me what heaven was like," I smirked, watching the tick in Rhys's jaw pulse at the mention of his brother, Cole. "I'm considering my options. Both are dominant and deliciously wicked. One seemed a little more... wild, I guess you could say?"

"While you're considering your options, know this, Cole doesn't care about anyone but Cole. He's fought me for my seat as head alpha for one hundred years now. During that time, he's sacrificed thousands of creatures to reach for it. He doesn't even want the seat because he doesn't want the responsibility, he just doesn't like that I have it. Cole is selfish and enjoys sharing his toys to remind them that they are merely there for his entertainment. Tell me, Remi. Do you think you'd want two men destroying you? Because I assure you, I do not intend to let you leave my side, and if you chose him, I'd more than willingly accept his invitation to have you with him."

"No, that isn't something I would want," I admitted, watching his lips curling into a dangerous smile that unnerved me. "Why would he fight for a position that he doesn't want?" I slowly dropped my gaze to his mouth, remembering the feel of his lips against mine. A blush blossomed in my cheeks, and his smile turned wolfish, promising to draw blood.

"Because we both loved the same woman once, and she chose me over him. She was a game to us at first, and then we both fell in love with her. She's been dead a very long time, and yet he cannot let it go. She wasn't the first woman we shared, and I doubt she will be the last," he stated meaningfully, watching my frown deepening.

"She was a Silversmith, wasn't she?"

"Indeed, she was your aunt Roslyn," he admitted, finally looking away from me. "Van Helsings are notorious for fighting over pretty Silversmith women. Even my oldest brother pined for one. Then your family betrayed ours and started a war between the lines."

"And what did we do to betray you?" I snorted, fighting a frown as his eyes slid back to mine.

"Your mother's father raped and murdered my

mother. Donte Silversmith hung my mother from our castle's battlements and left her bones for the carrion birds. He took my family's castle by force, betraying us and murdering hundreds of innocent people who served our family and were under our protection. Your grandfather lost my mother to my father and took issue with it since she was not given to a Silversmith male. He found it to be a slight against him, and the lines that were to be claimed by one of the houses. So, he murdered my mother to send my father a message."

"Ouch," I flinched at the look of loathing burning in Rhys stare as he spoke.

"That isn't the only reason, though. Your mother found us too low in status to marry and turned her Van Helsing match down because she wanted to marry up, and not beneath her. Your family was beneath ours, and yet a single fluke of magic created your line. That magic gave it the ability to control and create weapons that brought down immortal alphas easily."

"And so we became the strongest house of alphas, and the world bowed beneath our feet," I injected, and Rhys bristled with anger while he shook his head. "We rose and chose those in which we wanted to unite. That contract became endangered when your mother, one of the few Van Helsing women, married a demon prince, forbidden to her. Though he was mundane and not dark enough, we fixed that with a curse. You broke the contract first, and in doing so, your mother broke Donte's heart and struck at his pride."

"Donte was a cold prick who enjoyed inflicting pain on women. He was sadistic and raped his bride in front of their entire wedding party while staring at my mother. The issue with it was, he was too strong to fight against."

"And yet you killed him," I swallowed, watching the malice burning in his depths as he recalled the past.

"We did, little Silversmith. We tied his limbs to warhorses, and then we sent them in four directions. Afterward, we set fire to the House of Silversmith and watched them burn. Donte felt the pain because he was immortal. When the smoke cleared, we poured him a solid tomb of iron, forcing him to die repeatedly, until the end of eternity in iron, since silver is too soft to reach him."

"That's horrible."

"Roslyn, who would have been your aunt, enjoyed the power her beauty and line brought her. She used us to gain footing into our world and turned against every lover she took between her thighs. She used Cole and me to lure our mother to your father, and in return, I set her on fire and watched the whore burn. Since that day, we have lured your people in one by one, allowing them to think we love them before we destroy them. You see, we don't allow your kind to reach immortality anymore. Not unless you do so with a vow to be owned by another Alpha House. So if you choose to be free of us, you die, Remington Silversmith. You're either mine or Cole's, but you don't get to walk away without a vow of ownership. Silversmiths become power-hungry creatures, and then they unleash hell upon those stupid enough to fall in love with them."

"I'm no longer calling your family's legend a fairytale. It's more horror than romance, Remi. No wonder you've hidden for your entire life," Nyx admitted.

"Oh, but she's no longer hidden," Rhys chuckled coldly, lifting his hand to push the hair away from my face. "And she already has two Van Helsings vying for her attention. She may not look like a Silversmith, but she is, right down to her silver soul."

"I am not something you can own," I snapped, pushing Rhys's hand away while studying the intensity burning in his stare. "I'm a person, and this isn't medieval England where you can own someone."

"You're mortal, and very young and naïve if you think that the year matters. You walked into my world, and I intend to own you one way or another. If I were you, I'd choose the way that allows you pleasure instead of pain. Unless you're willing to let me give you both," he whispered while leaning over, running his nose against my jaw. "There's also the fact that Silversmiths and Van Helsings are cursed to be together no matter if they wish otherwise. I want you already, and you want me. How long do you think we can hold out against a curse our bloodlines willingly took within them to create a stronger line?"

"There has never been a Van Helsing and Silversmith coupling that created life together, Rhys."

"No, there has not," he agreed, but there was something cold and wicked in his eyes as he watched me. "You have no idea how fucked you are, little one."

I swallowed hard before closing my eyes against the fact that I knew just how screwed I was at the moment. If Winchester and the others figured out that Rhys held me captive, they'd bring down the rafters on the House of Van Helsing. And then they would hang me outside of it as a warning to others.

Chapter Seven

House Van Helsing was a large mansion that stood behind high-security gates. It seemed to go on forever, with small houses spread out through the valley in which it was nestled. The house itself was larger than the building E.V.I.E. had over the underground bunker, and considering the power I felt moving beneath my feet, I was willing to bet Rhys had an underground network of tunnels beneath his house as well.

My things were taken through a side door, while we proceeded through the front of the mansion. I took in the sheer beauty of the entranceway lined in ancient paintings of what I assumed were other homes over their lifetimes. One was of a beautiful palace that had bubbling fountains covering a colorful courtyard.

"Cole called, demanding access to the guest wing. Any idea why he'd want to move home now?" a tall male asked, moving down the staircase that opened onto the upper level in the middle of the entranceway.

Silverish-blue eyes landed on me with curiosity. "I thought we agreed not to bring whores home anymore?"

"She isn't a whore. She's also the reason Cole wants to move home," Rhys stated in an exhausted tone. "Acyn Van Helsing, meet Remington Silversmith."

"Fuck off," Acyn chuckled, slowly coming down the stairs to stand in front of me. "If she's a Silversmith, I'm the head alpha."

"No, you're not, and yes, she is. I'll prove it," Rhys stated, releasing my hand he'd held.

Swallowing hard, I stared around, wondering what would go horridly wrong, and then leaped back. The crystal chandelier above us crashed toward the floor, mere inches from where I'd jumped to keep from it crushing me. Glass shattered across the pristine tile, crunching beneath my feet the moment I moved. I lost my footing, sliding to the floor, and Nyx caught me seconds before Rhys reached over, grabbed my hand, yanking me toward him.

"Well, I'll be damned," Acyn said, pushing his tattooed-fingers through his thick hair. "How did you manage that one?"

"She intervened against Cole and his watered-down Silversmith witch. I guess you could say she saved me, and now her curse is activated for the next few hours."

"And now Cole wants to come home? Bloody brilliant," Acyn snorted and then peered down at Nyx, touching his chest, examining him like she had a doctorate in male anatomy. Considering how many men she'd known and taken to bed, that was probably accurate.

A female, no older than twenty, swept into the room with a beaming smile on her cherry-red lips. "The room you requested is ready and the bath for your lady, Van Helsing. Food and a nightcap were left in the suite too. If you need me for anything, just ring."

"Thank you, Corinne. That will be all, though. Your services aren't needed tonight," Rhys said softly, and she pouted. "The entrance will need sweeping, and a new light fixture ordered, immediately."

My eyebrow hiked up to my hairline, slowly pulling my eyes back to where Acyn was now in a make-out session with Nyx. He grunted as he picked her up, starting up the stairs, leaving me standing with Rhys alone.

Traitor.

"They look entertained. Shall we retire?" Rhys asked, his lips curling into a mischievous smile. "Unless you wanted to tour the house and ensure your mother isn't hiding in my dungeon?"

"You have an actual dungeon?" I countered curiously.

"I do. Some habits are hard to break."

"A dungeon is a habit?"

"Building houses every few centuries to hide the fact that we are immortals, well, it becomes a habit, and each one has a state-of-the-art dungeon built within it."

"I don't know if that's sad or cool," I admitted.

"Indeed," he replied, which I was learning was his canned response when he didn't want to talk about something or needed to end a discussion. "Come, we will withdraw to your room for the night."

Butterflies chose that exact moment to flurry in my belly. I swallowed past the sudden dryness of my mouth, letting Rhys lead me to the stairs, where he paused, turning to look at me as he hesitated. His dark head tilted to the side as his lips curled into a devastating smile.

"Do you prefer to be carried like your friend?"

"I can walk, but thanks?" I answered lamely, inwardly grimacing at my reply. Rhys shook his head, narrowing his eyes as he peered up the staircase where the loud moaning was now coming.

"You may see more of my brother than you wish."

"I'm good with naked guys." I blinked. I replayed what I had just said before snorting as his eyebrows shot to his hairline. "That came out really wrong."

Why was I an idiot around him? I was usually cold and in control. Instead, I'd made out with Rhys, and got my first orgasm in an entire year from the one creature my mother expressively had forbidden I encounter. It was as if his eyes met mine, and all coherent thought stopped, then my body took over.

"Indeed, Silversmith." His free hand rubbed the back of his neck as we started moving up the staircase again.

"How many brothers do you have?" I asked, trying to save face from inserting my foot into my mouth.

"How many siblings do you have?" he countered, turning to look over his shoulder at me with a knowing smile.

"Touché," I muttered. "How often do you have to move?"

"Let's stick with impersonal questions. Preferably ones that don't give away our secrets, shall we?"

"How do you feed?" I asked, shrugging.

"I feed from sex, Remi. Are you offering to feed me? You'd be delicious."

"No, I would not," I rushed out the words, shaking my head as a smile curved his mouth. "You ask something. I'm all out of ideas."

"How old are you?"

"Twenty-one," I replied, knowing he'd already asked me this.

"How many men have you fucked, Remi?"

I swallowed, biting my lip while I decided if I should answer him or not. I hated awkward silence, and the moaning within the hallway was making the walk to his room strange enough. "Three, but one pretty much never got it in before he'd made a mess all over my dress. So I normally don't count him."

"Indeed, poor child," he laughed soundlessly.

"He was twenty-six and not a child," I ground out with irritation.

"Are you defending him?" he asked, and my gaze zeroed in on the way his shoulders shook.

"Not at all," I argued before snorting. "I was just pointing out he wasn't a child, which should have indicated a better adventure into womanhood. The second one was okay, but he wasn't anything to write home about, either. The third, well, he had some kinks that were a little too strange for me, so we parted ways after the first time together."

"How many times have you had sex?"

"Twice," I answered, turning toward the screaming that erupted behind us, but Rhys grabbed me, pulling me forward before I could see the couple going at it hard at the end of the hallway.

"You don't want to see them feeding each other, trust me. Did you say twice?"

"Need me to write it down for you? I don't make it a habit of screwing random people. I work long hours in the armory at E.V.I.E., which leaves little time for me to have much of a personal life, which suits me fine. I'm immortal, so there will be plenty of time to do that stuff."

"You do realize you're mortal until you become immortal, right? And that most potential immortals never make it to the age to become immortalized."

"What?" I asked, pulling on his arm to stop him.

"Did Eliza teach you nothing?" he countered. When I blinked at him, he peered over my shoulder, tugging me with him down the hall. He moved to a door, opening it before pulling me through. "Did she leave you to die?"

"My mother? No. I ran away at seventeen, and

this is my first time home since leaving. She refused to move again because I'd left home and was unprotected. In her words, I was too damn stubborn to not run headfirst into a Van Helsing, and trip, getting pinned on his dick without even knowing it," I said, narrowing my eyes on him as he smirked. "I came looking for you to know my enemy and figure out who to avoid."

"How did that work out for you?"

"Not so well. But this particular Van Helsing doesn't seem so bad yet. Plus, he doesn't seem to want me dead. If that changes, I'll cross that bridge when we get there." I dismissed him as much as I could while holding his hand. Normally when the curse struck, I was in bed, which was on the floor because every frame we'd tried had snapped or given out beneath the curse.

"Strip," he ordered, and I turned, glaring at him. "Do you plan on sleeping in your clothes, then? Might make bathing an issue as well," he said, shrugging broad shoulders as his lips tugged into a frown, studying the horror marring my face.

"I'm not bathing in front of you!"

"I'm about to climb into a bathtub. Unless you plan on standing there holding my hand while I wash myself, you're joining me. I promise to be a gentleman and not fuck you, Remi. I have a routine, and normally I would shower before bed. Considering the day you just had, and your soft nature, I figured a bubble bath with a nightcap would be warranted before you curled into bed beside me. We can discuss whatever you'd like in it, or finish what we started at the bar. But that choice is yours to make."

"You're expecting me to strip naked and bathe with you? Just like that?" I stammered, staring at him as he smirked, lifting my hand to his waist as he released it.

In stunned silence, I watched his fingers slowly unbuttoning his shirt to reveal rippling waves of muscles that covered his chest. Tattoos and muscle with pierced nipples were exposed to my greedy stare as he shook his thick arms out of his shirt. Standing before me in nothing but his slacks, I swallowed a groan. Every time the man moved, his muscles tensed and bunched with the slight movement while I stood silently drinking in the sight of him.

I'd seen men naked before, a lot of men. Not in a sexual manner, but wounded soldiers treated from wounds obtained while on hunts. None of them had shit on Rhys Van Helsing. He appeared to be sculpted by the gods, created to make a girl go stupid from mere sight. His coiled muscles contracted and moved as his hands lowered to the button on his slacks, using his thumbs to unfasten them before letting them drop to his feet. My mouth opened and went dry as his thick cock fell free, bouncing forth before my wide eyes.

"You keep staring at it, little girl, and it's going to notice you," he whispered against my ear, causing me to back up away from him into the dresser.

The dresser slammed forward, sending my body hard against his chest. We landed in a heap of limbs on the bed. I felt something twitch against my cheek, and I lifted, staring down at his cock that I'd been laying on. His throaty laughter sounded from beneath me, and I groaned in horror, wiping the wetness from my face.

"Oh, God, you got pre-cum on my face!" I whined,

much to his amusement as he laughed, watching up at me. I tried to push away from him and stand, groaning as the giant bed shattered the moment I was off, smashing my foot. "Ouch!" He laughed harder. Sitting up, he grabbed my hand. "It's not funny!" I wiped his wetness from my cheek, glaring at him. "You're disgusting."

"You landed with your face against my cock. It is funny."

Pounding started at the door, and he stood, kicking off his boots and socks as I held onto him, allowing him to step the rest of the way out of his pants. The knocking continued, and he acted as if it didn't bother him that someone was pounding on the door while he peered around his disheveled room.

Rhys moved toward the door, and I stammered. "What are you doing?"

"Telling my men that you didn't attack me before they storm the room to investigate," he stated, arching a brow with a silent question. I released my hand on his hip as he watched me. The ceiling above me started to crack, and he shook his head, reaching for my hand. His fingers wrapped around my wrist, yanking me forward. "You are destroying my house, Silversmith."

"You cursed me, so deal with it." I started to cross my arms over my chest, but it was futile with Rhys holding my arm. Abandoning the action, I frowned as he walked us toward the door, pulling me with him.

Rhys cracked it open far enough that it revealed several heavily armed men outside of it. "Everything is fine, gentlemen. Just rough sex happening in here,"

Rhys declared, causing me to sputter in horror at his announcement. Closing the door, he turned and yanked my body against his, brushing his hand against my cheek. "Now strip, woman."

Chapter Eight

Rhys walked me toward an open doorway, and once we were inside the room, I gasped at its elegance. His bathtub was large and sunken, with rose petals floating over the top of the water. Candles covered the ledge, and the scent of sage and roses rushed through me, calming my frayed nerves.

"You used witches' herbs and a soothing mixture in the water, didn't you?" I accused softly, noting that I was relaxing entirely too much to be naked around him.

"Yes," he replied. "You're young, and your body is still something you think should be hidden. I thought it wise to help ease some of your modesty before climbing into the tub with me."

"That was actually thoughtful," I said, deflating. "Can you turn around?"

"You think that's going to make it where I cannot see you?" He peered around at the room full of mirrors.

Exhaling, he smiled tightly, giving me his back, still holding my wrist. "Place your foot against mine, Remi."

I gave him my back, staring at the large bare foot with the heel toward mine. Brushing my foot against his, I swallowed down the thought of the intimacy at seeing his bare foot. For some unknown reason, I'd always found it intimate to see a man's feet without shoes, as if it somehow held a broader meaning, which, of course, it didn't.

His hand released my wrist, and I lifted the borrowed shirt over my head, slowly unbuttoning my pants while leaving the skimpy panties on as some line of defense against him. Silently, I turned toward Rhys, sucking my lip between my teeth as his eyes lowered to my naked breasts that my arms slightly hid.

"You're not naked, little Silversmith," he murmured.

"I'm not getting naked with you near me. This will have to do," I frowned, lifting my eyes to the heated blue depths that smiled, even though his mouth remained in a tight white line. Without warning, he lifted me and stepped into the tub.

"Put your feet into the water, Remi. Make sure it isn't too hot," he said thickly as my body slid down his.

Rhys held me steady as if my weight didn't bother him at all. The water was hot, but not scorching or uncomfortable. I stepped away from him, but his hand remained on mine until I was sitting comfortably in the tub. My eyes closed against the enticing scene of his delicious body on full display, which didn't seem to bother him at all.

Rhys's foot brushed against mine, pressing flesh to flesh as he sat in the tub resembling a large, shallow hot tub rather than an actual bathtub. I sat opposite his large body that spread out in the tub, staring at me, waiting expectantly.

"What?" I asked after another moment of silence sent my nerves rising.

"You're very beautiful," he stated softly, slowly sitting up as he moved closer.

"What are you doing?" I demanded, but he grabbed me, pulling me forward and turning me until my back was against his chest.

"I'm washing your hair, since you can't do that and cover your pretty titties. So, I figured for the sake of your modesty, which I am trying to respect, it's the least I could do."

"Oh, okay—" I was the most awkward person alive, apparently. I stopped my lips from moving. Feeling his body against mine was intoxicating, but being around him naked was worrisome. My body reacted to his touch, much more so than any man before had ever caused me to respond.

Rhys brought a cup up, soaking my hair slowly as if he had done this before. Once it was fully saturated, the scent of lemon zest tingled against my nose. Fingers kneaded my scalp, stealing a moan from my lips as I dropped my head back. Momentarily forgetting where I was and whom I was with, I sat back up. I didn't recall my mother detailing anything about scandalized bathing or hair washing in her tirade of Van Helsing men.

"My mother hates you guys," I said into the silence of the room.

"It's warranted," he shocked me by agreeing to it without argument. "Our families are very much at war, Remington Silversmith. I won't sugarcoat it for you as others would do to win you to their side. I'm sure she told you never to trust a Van Helsing with your back?" His fingers trailed down my spine, and I shivered.

"Yes, among other things they shouldn't be around." I swallowed, internally mentioning me as a whole that shouldn't be around them. "I'm going to guess I shouldn't allow you around my vagina, either."

Deep laughter sounded behind me. I turned, studying the way he watched me. His eyes slid to my hair, and he made the motion to turn back around with his finger. I obeyed as his legs lifted beside me, and something very male touched my spine.

My breathing hitched while I felt it growing, along with the heat filling my cheeks as we both ignored the monster in the room. I shuddered against the feel of him. Slowly turning my head, he rinsed out my hair. I spun around the moment he finished, pushing away from him, only for the candles to crack and wax to shoot toward me.

Rhys moved faster than I could see, blocking my body with his as he grunted. I stared into dark blue eyes that lowered to my hands, which were now wrapped around him as the scent of copper filled the tub. Lowering my eyes to his chest, I grimaced at the glass protruding from it. I'd left his touch, and he'd used his body as a shield to protect mine.

"Sit back," I urged, watching as he complied. His eyes slid to the candles and back to mine as I moved with him, never leaving his touch. I straddled his lap awkwardly, feeling his hands settling on my hips. "Thank you. I don't heal quickly, which is probably something I shouldn't be telling you, I'm sure."

"You're mortal still, Remi. It's a given that you wouldn't heal fast. I do have fixers and healers on the property for those who are yet to rise to immortality, but they can't fix you if you're dead."

I nodded and swallowed, dropping my hands, expecting his stare to lower to my naked breasts. Instead, he held his eyes on my face while I pulled the glass from his chest. His grip tightened on my waist, encircling it with his large hands. My head leaned over, licking his wound with saliva that could heal injuries as his blood's coppery tang danced on my tongue.

He growled, his muscles tensing beneath my tongue as my eyes lifted to lock with his. I smirked at the wide-eyed look he gave me as his cock jerked against my belly. My tongue slid over the smooth cut the glass had left, kissing it softly when it had fully healed.

"Silversmiths cannot heal with their saliva, Remington," he rasped huskily.

"No, they can't. I can, though," I smiled, rising to peer into his heated depths that threatened to swallow me whole. My hands lifted to rest on his broad shoulders, feeling the muscles straining against my touch.

"Interesting." Rhys watched me a moment before

his mouth closed the distance between us, claiming mine hungrily.

I moaned into the kiss, allowing him to devour me as my insides trembled with need. His hands slid up my back, and one held my head. The other lowered, lifting my rear, pulling me closer to him. The room spun around me as I rocked against the hardness of his cock with my soaked panties. By the time the kiss broke, we were both gasping for air. He used my hair, turning my head so his mouth could brush against the rapidly beating pulse in my throat. Rhys's hand lowered, cupping my naked breast as his thumb traced over my pierced nipple, causing a loud moan to escape my lips.

"This is where you tell me to stop, Remi," Rhys growled, resting his head against my shoulder as his fingers pinched my nipple, twisting it until I cried out. His dark head pulled back as glowing blue eyes locked with mine. "Because in a moment, my demon will come out, and he won't care that you're basically an untouched woman who has never been claimed by something like him."

"Oh," I whispered huskily, shocked by the sound of my voice.

"Remi," he warned, noting the war I fought within my mind.

"Stop." I swallowed past the yes that perched on my tongue. Denial at what I'd actually said, instead of what I really wanted, sat like a rock on my tongue. Rhys rose without warning and abruptly released my body, exiting the tub, which shattered into large glass pieces as water gushed all over the floor.

"Don't move," he warned, grabbing me up in his arms, staring down at the mess covering the floor. "How long does the curse normally last?" he asked through gritted teeth, his eyes on my white panties, which were now sheer and doing little to hide my hairless apex from his burning gaze of blue flames dancing within the fiery orbs.

"Eight to ten hours, depending on how much magic I released. We're at like five hours, max, but I am unsure of the time. You relieved me of my watch, and I usually set an alert the moment I use magic to create weapons or bullets."

"Put your hands around my neck and hold on to me," he warned.

The moment I'd grabbed on, the world went off-kilter, and I groaned as my stomach clenched and rebelled from the immortal speed he used. I could use the speed, but it was different when another used it without the mind grasping that took place.

Rhys placed my wet body onto the bed, checking my legs for injury. No emotion shone in his eyes while he touched my thighs, parting my legs to check each one. Once he was confident the glass tub hadn't harmed me, he reached for the sheer gown beside the bed, handing it to me. Quietly, I pulled it on over my head before lifting my derriere to shed the wet panties. I held them awkwardly before his lips curled into a knowing, smug expression.

"I don't have anything else to wear, do I?" I asked in a high tone.

"You don't need panties to sleep. I won't assault

you or push the issue. We're going to sleep so that when you wake, I don't have to hold your hand. How do you manage the curse without a Van Helsing around?"

"I have a cell that I use in my room at E.V.I.E. that's safe for me to be within, but my whole room is pretty much a safe zone. It's reinforced steel, and once the curse becomes active, I retire there until it has run its course. I try not to use more than a tiny amount of magic when crafting weapons. That way I don't have to deal with it for very long."

"How did you end up at E.V.I.E.? I doubt your mother supported your choice to hunt vampires and other creatures before immortality claimed you."

"Elizabeth hates that I joined. She spent my entire childhood running from your bloodline, and I just wanted to stop running for a little while. Every story and every lesson was about how to prevent detection until I couldn't take it anymore. I left at seventeen, and I remained hidden until Winchester found me and made me call my mother, who had gone mad during my disappearance. I guess it was rather selfish to run from the one person who had stuck around to make sure I survived to adulthood. I was a child running from a parent who was a little more than smothering, I guess."

"Who is Winchester?" he asked, reaching for the whiskey beside the bed. He sat beside me, pouring us both glasses.

"She's no one," I swallowed, knowing she'd use to me to test out her newest arsenal if I discussed her with a Van Helsing.

"Judging by her name, I'm guessing another of

Eliza's daughters?"

"How do you know it's a girl?" I demanded.

"You said *she* was no one, meaning female. I guess in this day and age, it could be otherwise. I'm guessing you never entered a public school or got to see much of the outside world. Knowing Eliza, you would have been raised off-grid, kept out of the eye of the world. You never learned how to be human because she never intended to leave you alone until you turned twenty-five and ascended to immortality. She'd have taught you how to survive in the wild, but on her terms. She probably taught you to control silver from childhood and use magic. Your mother was a fierce woman and had the patience of a saint for her children."

"You knew her after you burned her home and family to ashes?" I asked curiously. He flinched, filling my glass before doing the same to his. "You didn't know her after, because you said she died—" I cringed, lifting my eyes to lock with his. "My mother had other children, didn't she? She never spoke of them if that is the case."

"It was war, and both sides struck fast and hard, Remi. Grief makes people act out, and most of the time, it's with the intent to inflict the most amount of pain you can cause. We set their house on fire without warning. We hit your family fast and hard, and we offered no mercy. Your mother lost her mate and children in the fire, or so we assumed. Considering we thought she was dead, it is possible others made it out alive as well."

I swallowed, nodding while biting my tongue. I lifted the glass to my lips, chugging his expensive whiskey without stopping to sniff or swirl it as he was doing. I didn't care if it cost fifty grand. Personally, I thought it was stupid to drop that much on whiskey when people worked their asses off just to make enough to live day-by-day. He and I wouldn't be friends under normal circumstances, I realized.

I had spent hours one day watching people stand in line at a check-cashing place. They were exhausted from long hours of working tirelessly. Yet there they were, standing in line for a payday loan just to be able to afford things for their families.

I'd added money to accounts of strangers, paying off layaways for school or Christmas with the checks that were wasting away in my account from E.V.I.E. since I needed very little to maintain my lifestyle. It was something I could do to give back, and, well, the animal shelters only accepted so many donations before they started to think I was obsessed with them, as most were run by men around Seattle.

"This is where you start to hate me, and it gets tediously awkward," Rhys sighed.

"I don't hate you," I admitted, lifting my eyes to his, which were narrowed on me as if he didn't like my answer. "What happened was because both sides made mistakes. I wasn't there so I can't say who was wrong, but I know our bloodline has a lot of hotheads because I am one of them. Do I think you're faultless? No, because there are always two sides in every war throughout history. And on each side, there are always two varying beliefs on who is right and who is wrong."

"For someone so young, Remi, you think beyond your tender years. Your leg is bruising," he stated, not looking away from me.

I looked at my thigh, and I scrunched up my nose. "Perk of being mortal and fair-skinned. I bruise easily. A perk of being me. I don't feel it, not much anyway. You could kiss it, though, make it better for me?" I laughed only to have it get stuck in my throat as I gazed up, finding him smirking devilishly. "That was a joke."

"That isn't where I want to kiss you, Remi."

"Where do you want to kiss me?"

His lips turned up at the corners, and heat filled his pretty eyes. "I want to push you down on this broken bed, spread your legs apart, and devour your pussy until you come for me."

"You want to kiss my pussy?" I asked in a high-pitched tone as my nipples hardened and my body heated.

His smile turned blinding, and his head tilted slightly to the side, staring at my erect nipples through the white nightgown that hid very little. Butterflies exploded in my belly as he leaned closer, brushing his mouth against the shell of my ear.

"No, I want to fucking devour your pussy until you drip down my chin because you come so fucking hard that you're soaked with arousal. Would you like that, Remi?" he asked, and in the same breath, he asked, "care for another drink, Love?"

"Yes," I mumbled.

"Yes, to me devouring your pussy, or yes to a drink? Or both?"

"Drink me." My eyes rounded in horror as what I

said echoed in my ears. "Pussy my whiskey—oh my God, shut up, Remi!" I groaned, covering my face.

"I'm willing to drink my whiskey from your pussy, if you're game."

"Pour me another drink, Rhys, and stop taunting me. You're flustering me on purpose."

"I enjoy your blushes, Love. Not many women I know still blush or grow flustered when I speak to them. Let me enjoy it."

"Do you often ask women to drink from their vaginas?" I asked, feeling as though he'd dunked my head in a bucket of ice, forgetting to add the water first.

"Actually, no," he said huskily. "That's a new one for me. Surprising, considering my age and the fact that your bloodline cursed me to fuck to feed. Hungry? I'm starving."

"Make that drink a double," I whispered while swallowing down my embarrassment mixed with desire. Rhys's lips tipped up, and his attention dropped to where my body physically clenched under the intensity burning in his eyes. "This is going to be the longest night of my entire life. You should probably know that I've never slept beside anyone before, other than my mother. So I might snore, drool, or even kick in my sleep."

He poured the whiskey before scooting back against the headboard which was attached to the wall for decoration. Following him carefully while trying not to soak the mattress in whiskey, I sat on my knees beside him. I brought the glass up to my nose as my eyes caught him observing me. The liquor smelled woodsy, with a hint of citrus. I sipped it, swirling it around in my mouth before swallowing.

"I don't see the point of doing that," I admitted.

"It enhances the flavor, warming your pallet up to the ingredients."

I frowned, doing it again to end up with the same results. Rhys mimicked what I'd done, drinking it slowly. I snorted, tipping the glass up to down the contents before I reached over him, placing the glass on the nightstand. Gazing down into his lap, I brought my hand back. His cock was hard, ready to do some serious damage considering the sheer size of the appendage. I drew back away from him, shaking my head.

I'd been with men before, but none of them had looked like *that* down there. It was thicker, longer, and I was pretty certain it had *known* I was looking at it. Sucking my bottom lip between my teeth, I smiled nervously. His attention shifted to my mouth as if he wanted to taste me, and at the moment, I wanted him to. I was in so much trouble right now. My hand balled into a fist as the need to learn the silkiness of his flesh entered my mind.

"Goodnight, Rhys," I whispered huskily, turning away from him, pulling the covers up, and slipping beneath them while he helped untuck them, forcing my body to fit against his.

"Goodnight, Remington."

Chapter Nine

I was running over foreign soil. I wasn't sure how I knew it was unfamiliar, but everything around me screamed I wasn't within the United States. Dirt covered my white nightgown, and my palms ached, forcing me to lift them, peering down at the rocks embedded within my flesh. I turned, watching shadows move as I took in my surroundings.

Stars glittered against the velvet sky as the wind kicked up, sending my hair whipping against my face painfully. I pushed it away as the scene around me vanished, and a large mansion replaced the meadows. My heart raced as flames licked over the home, peeling wood with the intensity of the blaze. Windows shattered, and I jumped back, shaking my head as the sounds of people screaming within it echoed through the night.

My feet moved over the ice-cold earth as I closed the distance to the house. An explosion sent my body backward, tumbling through the air to land on the ground. Sitting up, I stared at the face of a woman who peered out of the house, her silver-blonde hair glowing against the fiery backdrop of the inferno now raging through the home.

Turning, I recognized Rhys and Cole, who watched the woman with regret marring their expressions. Rhys had tears running down his face, and his hands balled into tight fists as if he wanted to run to her aid and undo what he'd done. Others stood behind them, watching, unaffected by the scene unfolding before them. Cole turned, staring at Rhys as if he wanted to speak, but whatever he wanted to say remained unsaid. More Van Helsings joined the grisly scene, some gasping as the beauty caught fire, and dropped to the floor.

Rhys moved, but Acyn grabbed his arm, saying something I couldn't hear. Silver shot from the house at the men who erected a wall as the silver pelted their shields, embedding but not piercing them. My eyes slid over the craftsmanship of their shield wall and winced, realizing it was Silversmith silver, which other metal couldn't penetrate. Not even Silversmith silver found a way through it. The sounds of children crying drew my eyes to the second story of the home, where children no older than in their teens, begged for help to no avail.

Cole stared up at them, his eyes flooding with tears. He screamed, turning to the men as he pointed toward the children, and yet the others shook their heads at his words. One man with a cold sneer slapped Cole, shouting back with hatred burning in his vehemently horrid tone. It was malevolence, fueled with poisonous loathing, which knocked the wind out of me from the intensity.

Standing, I stepped back from the chaos of the scene unfolding around me. Rhys still hadn't looked away from where the woman had fallen, as if he could will her out of the inferno with his mind. Men pushed swords into their leather sheaths, continuing to stand silently as the angry man snarled at Cole, who was forcefully dragged away from the scene. Another explosion sounded, and men jumped while Rhys silently watched the spot, still, causing my heart to clench with the pain burning in his eyes.

I closed my eyes and opened them, finding myself back in the meadow, bathed in moonlight. Turning, I watched a half-naked Rhys entering the field with a cocky smile on his lips. His gaze lowered to my bare legs, and I narrowed mine on him. As he got closer, I stepped back, his eyes no longer the turbulent blue of the clear summer day sky, but black. It was as if obsidian had swallowed the whites of his eyes, changing his face's chiseled angles into something sharper, more defined.

I turned away from him, rushing through the meadows. My feet slapped against the earth, followed by those of the predator chasing me. I had no doubt that he was all demon and no man.

Entering the forest, I continued blindly moving through the woods until a house came into view. Moving deftly up the stairs of the entrance, I rushed inside without closing the door. I spun in a wide circle, watching women dance around in old-fashioned dresses, while men wore breeches and long coats.

Rushing toward the grand staircase, I paused as

power erupted into the room. Rhys smiled coldly, watching me from the doorway, cocking his head to the side. The people inside the room continued dancing, unaware of what was happening. He stepped forward, and power slithered over my legs, causing heat to clench in my belly. Spinning, I rushed away from him.

I ran up the stairs urgently, only to discover an entire hallway filled with closed doors. I turned knob after knob, finding nothing but locked doors as Rhys's power slid against my flesh. I swallowed the fear wrapping around my throat, forcing the scream to remain in my chest. One of the doors at the end of the hallway opened, revealing light. I ran blindly toward it, turning to close it, but hands grabbed mine, shoving me into the room. Rhys followed me in, closing the door and locking it without speaking.

"What do you want?" I whispered as my chest rose and fell with fear.

He turned, staring at me through his endless obsidian depths. I continued walking backward until my ass hit something hard. Turning, I stared at the large oak desk in the middle of the room. I started to turn back to Rhys, but his hand grabbed and captured mine, pinning them to the small of my back as he shoved my head against the desk.

Rhys pinned me to the desk, his mouth lowering to nip against my naked shoulder, stealing a yelp of surprise from my lungs. His foot kicked my legs apart, the hand on my head trailing down my spine before pushing against my naked flesh. I whimpered as he pressed his fingers into my body, slowly exploring my core. Moaning loudly, I trembled from the absolute pleasure and heat his touch delivered. When he withdrew, I groaned and rocked my hips with an invitation to explore further. He chuckled darkly, turning me around, lifting and placing me on the large wooden desk.

Rhys's mouth crushed against mine, but unlike the urgency he normally had when kissing me, he slowly devoured me. A growl rose from deep in his chest, causing my body to clench, tightening with a need that excited and terrified me. He gripped my hips, pressing my body against his, showing me his pulsing need. I lowered my hands to his waist, freeing him from his pants, continuing to kiss him as if he were the air that filled my lungs. Power slithered over my flesh, achingly addictive power that fueled the inferno raging within me.

I felt silver against my flesh, felt the coldness of it against my shoulder before the strap of the nightgown severed, revealing my breast as Rhys repeated the action on the other shoulder. Tossing the blade aside, he ripped the nightgown apart down the middle, exposing me to his demon's hungry gaze. He grabbed my breasts, squeezing them until I cried out, and those sinfully dark eyes lifted, holding mine prisoner in their endless pits.

His head lowered, and I watched him slipping his mouth over one pierced tip, suckling against it before his teeth softly nipped. The heat of his mouth caused me to moan louder. He laughed, increasing his delicious assault against the raised peak. I pushed my hands through his hair, holding him there with the need for him to continue. He reached up, silently removing my hands, pushing me down against the desk, and lifting my legs while he smiled coldly.

Rhys didn't speak, didn't look away from me. He lowered his mouth to my core, inhaling my scent, and I fidgeted with shyness. His tongue snaked out, slowly sliding through my arousal. I moaned unabashedly, dropping my knees apart, giving him unobstructed access to my most delicate place.

Rhys grabbed my calves, lifting them against my shoulders, spreading them apart as he sucked on my clit, and I raised my hips as a cry escaped my lungs. He continued lapping greedily against my sex, growling against it, which only caused my body to tighten more. The sounds of pleasure escaping us had the orgasm building within me at a dangerous speed.

I felt something slithering over me as the sensation of dark magic skipped over my flesh. The room was filled with the scent of cologne and aftershave. Cedar, woodsy, and primal male scent tingled in my nose, dancing tantalizingly against it. Something pinched my nipples and slid against my skin as if Rhys was touching me everywhere all at once. My spine arched for him while the orgasm danced just out of reach, teasing me as Rhys continued licking and sucking my core hungrily.

His head lifted, and I stared into sightless eyes that threatened to consume my soul. Rhys leaned closer, kissing me hungrily. His fingers entered my pussy, stretching my body while his thumb rubbed small, perfectly erotic circles over my clit until pained noises in my throat emerged as I whimpered his name.

I kissed Rhys with a crazed need, sucking his tongue while he groaned. All at once, I exploded, crying out his name while light burst behind my eyes and ringing started in my ears. He growled, and his kiss turned frenzied. He continued forcing me to come until it changed from pleasure to pain.

I felt something soft against my opening and wiggled against the velvety flesh that promised more pleasure, but it never pushed into my body. I pried my eyes open, staring into the endless zeniths of his stare, watching the blue warring with the black in his eyes until he broke the kiss, peering down as he pushed against my sweat-covered body.

His hand lowered to his throbbing need, continuing to rub it against the wetness of my arousal covered core. He pushed the thick head into my body, and I trembled, rocking my hips to accommodate him. Lifting his blue eyes to mine, he watched me move my head as my body screamed with the uncomfortable fit of his girth. Rhys was hugely endowed, and it wasn't going to be a comfortable fit.

I lifted my hands to the edge of the desk, grasping onto it for leverage as I whimpered and moaned, uncertain why he wasn't moving yet. His head lowered, clasping onto one nipple as his hand moved between our bodies, rubbing against my clit slowly. His husky laughter at my eagerness was unnerving, but I was strung tighter than a bowstring. His other hand lifted, smoothing its way up to my mouth as he pushed his finger between my lips. I sucked it willingly, maddeningly, as he let loose a pained noise.

Another inch of his cock pushed into my body, and I cried out in pain. He withdrew his finger from my mouth as his head lifted. Striking blue eyes locked with mine as Rhys continued his assault against my clit, removing his cock, letting my nipple pop out of his mouth with a loud noise. Rhys lowered to my apex, never letting my eyes leave his as he flicked his tongue against my greedy core. His fingers pushed into my body, and I lifted against the invasion, rocking with the silent invitation.

He strummed my body to an ageless beat until I cried out, and everything within me collided into the hardest orgasm I'd ever had. I trembled violently, and bright violet light burst into my sight, filling it until I gasped. The room spun around me, whimpering his name like he was a saint, and I was a sinner who needed him to save me.

He groaned, standing up to stare down at me as he held his cock tightly, causing the thick head to turn purple in his hand. I sat up from the desk, dropping to the ground at his feet, peering up at him, silently asking permission as he studied me.

"No, Remi," he whispered huskily.

I smirked wickedly, flicking my tongue over the thick head of his cock. His eyes grew hooded, silently peering around the room. Something in his stare worried me, but I didn't care; I couldn't, with the power I felt on my knees before him.

I wanted him.

I wanted to watch him come undone for me, and he would.

He grunted, moaning while he watched me wrap my lips around his need. His hand released his heavy cock, and I replaced them with my own, unable to close my fingers around his girth, slowly caressing his cock as I learned him.

The salty taste of his cock danced over my lips. I took more of him into my mouth, working it in an unhurried movement with the clumsiness of someone who had never done it before. His hands captured my hair, pushing it away from my face with tenderness. I guided him into my throat, swallowing around him as Nyx's voice sounded in my mind. I remembered her words on how she drove men insane with her mouth, adding her dauntless instructions to my actions.

She'd be so proud of me if she could see me now.

I moaned around him while he ran his thumb over my cheek, and I slowly took more. He groaned, slowly rocking his hips as he watched me through heated eyes. My movements grew hurried. The need to please him consumed me, driving me to be brazen. I worked my hand, hollowing out my cheeks, swallowing him as tears filled my eyes from the need to get air into my lungs. It became an overwhelming need, warring with the need to make this alpha come for me. He grunted, tossing his head back as his body tensed, and hot spurts of arousal filled my throat. I swallowed, staring up at his gaze while he watched me slowly backing away.

"You didn't have to do that."

"No, but I wanted to."

His hands reached for me, pulling me close while he placed a kiss against the top of my head. I kissed his chest, peering up at him as the room faded away, and the scene changed. Frowning, I took in the bedroom and then stared at where we should have been. Swallowing hard, I licked my lips as the startling realization hit me.

"I'm dreaming," I whispered thickly, my throat raw from what I'd done to him. "I was dreaming!"

His dark head shook from side to side. My stomach dropped, plummeting to the floor at my feet. "No. You were merely dream-walking until I caught you. Then it became a reality. I told you that you didn't have to do that. It was the moment I became aware of what was happening. I'm not always in control when my demon pulls someone into a dream walk with him, which is his world to control."

"You didn't think you should warn me that I might wake up sucking you off?" I asked, embarrassment flooding my cheeks.

I'd been brazen because it had been a dream!

I'd sucked his dick!

My heart thundered in my chest as he swallowed hard. The tick in his jaw hammered wildly while he watched the horror unfolding on my face. His emotions slammed shut, and he smiled coldly.

"Get the fuck into bed, Silversmith. I'm exhausted after you drained me. Rather greedily, too, I must add." His smirk was cocky, and I wanted to slap it off his face. "Now. Or you can deal with whatever befalls you from the curse on your own, woman. Your choice," he stated, moving to the bed as the wall cracked behind me, forcing me to move toward the bed, or deal with bringing his house down around me.

"I thought I was dreaming," I said after settling on

the bed beside him.

"You were at first. It was a nice surprise to wake up buried in your throat. Did we do anything else?"

"No," I said quickly, turning away from him. I felt his stare on my back but ignored it as I settled into bed beside him.

"Remi," he chuckled darkly. "If we didn't do more, how come I can taste you on my lips?"

I grabbed the pillow, covering my face as embarrassment washed through me. How hadn't I noticed it wasn't Rhys? I'd seen the eyes, noted the difference within him, but I didn't know he and his demon weren't the same creature. Why, out of everything my mother taught me, wasn't that among the important things?

Hands wrapped around my waist, pulling me flush against his muscular body seconds before he ripped the pillow from my grasp and rolled me beneath him. Heated blue eyes stared down into my mine, and I glared at him with irritation.

"I ate your pussy, didn't I? That's why you were on your knees for me. What else did you allow me to do?" he asked in a raspy tone that caused my nipples to harden. He studied my face, and there was something worrisome in his expression. It was as if he was jealous of his demon and assumed we'd done more.

The really messed up part about the entire ordeal? I was naked, because that had happened too! I could feel every inch of him above me, along with the fact that he was already hard once more. Rhys lowered his gaze, taking in my naked breasts as he shook his head.

"What else happened?"

"Nothing," I whispered huskily.

"Did I fuck you?"

"No, it didn't go that far."

"Good," he grunted, rolling off me, only to collect my body against his once more, placing my head against his chest.

His heart raced, as if he had feared we'd gone all the way. I gazed up to find his long black lashes dusting against his cheeks. His heart calmed, and his breathing grew even. I closed my eyes, hating myself for not realizing I was on my knees in *this* room.

Sitting up, I stared around the room, searching for the desk, not finding it. My nightgown lay upon the floor with both straps cut, and next to it sat a switchblade with the blade still exposed. I peered down, finding Rhys observing me.

"What did he show you?"

"You and your family murdering mine," I muttered.

"And still, you allowed him to have you, knowing what we did to your people?"

"Obviously, I let my guard down, lesson learned. I thought it was a dream, and nothing more." I looked at the white sheets, finding them covered in dirt, along with my feet from running in through the meadow. "I was there, wasn't I?"

"Part of you was there, but your soul was here. You can't be harmed in a dream walking state. Not unless I'm there too. I wasn't the one chasing you. I woke up to those pretty lips wrapped around my cock, and your clumsy fucking hand stroking me. I'm guessing you've never done that before either?"

I groaned, lying back down as his hand lifted, cradling me. "That obvious, huh?"

"You are a rarity, Love. A dangerous one that others will want to taste if they think you're susceptible to dream walking. Very few can come out of a dream walk awake. Most are still slumbering, unaware that they fed a monster in their dreams."

"So why wasn't I asleep?" I pried.

"I don't know, but you also heal with your saliva, which isn't part of what your bloodline can do. Throughout our history, your line hasn't ever been able to breed with another race except your own. Werewolves, vampires, and incubus can heal with saliva. Yet you do. So who the fuck is your daddy, little girl?"

"I don't know," I replied honestly. "My dad left when I was little. My mother said he caught her sacrificing a chicken, packed up, and was gone before she could stop him from leaving us."

"And you bought that lie?" he asked carefully.

"Why wouldn't I?"

"Your mother is a powerful witch. Do you honestly think someone would just walk away from her, and she'd allow it to happen?" Rhys snorted.

I adjusted on his chest, lifting to stare at him. "If a man wants to leave you, what else can you do other than let him?"

He blinked at me, and his lips tugged down into a tight frown. "You're really young if that is how you think our world works, Remington."

"Why do I feel like you're putting me down as being dense when you use my full name?" I countered. "And as I said, if someone wants to leave you, you let them. You don't force them to stay if that's not where they want to be. What the hell kind of relationship would that end up as in the long run?"

"The kind your family expects. Once someone is theirs, that's it," he snorted. "If a man takes another woman when dating a Silversmith, they end up murdered by said Silversmith, and placed in a shallow unconsecrated grave. The men don't ever leave, not alive anyway. That is your family's legacy. Once you agree to be theirs, it is forever. Until death do you part," he muttered crossly.

"None of us have fathers," I pointed out. "You're wrong, Rhys. People can change, and it's been a very long time since you've known my mother."

"I don't care what you think, little girl. Your mother is just like her sister, Roslyn. Even when she had a mate, Elizabeth couldn't keep her legs closed to other males. You're lying to yourself if you think she changed without her mate to hold her sanity together."

"You don't know my mother at all if that's what you think. My mother has never taken a lover throughout my life," I gritted out tightly, anger clenching my jaw.

Rhys snorted, closing his eyes as if he'd just dismissed me outright. I bristled, turning away from him, and then cried out as part of the ceiling landed between us. Rhys reached over, yanking me back toward him as his other hand picked up the drywall, tossing it aside.

"Do try not to die while I sleep from that meal I just gorged on, *Remington*. I'd hate to have to bury your corpse before breakfast."

Chapter Ten

I awoke to someone stroking their hand through my hair. Pushing up from the bed, I took in the disheveled Van Helsing, smiling sleepily at me. Yawning, I sat up, stretching my arms before smiling at him, right up until I noticed his gaze had dropped to my chest. My hands covered my breasts, and I groaned. He sat up, capturing me before I could move away from the bed.

"Good morning," he murmured, running his nose over the shell of my ear in a sleepy tone.

"Morning," I replied, touching his chest as I felt his mouth curving into a smile against my throat. "This is where you let me go so we can figure out if you can stop touching me, Van Helsing."

"Is it?" he chuckled, running his heated lips over my shoulder, softly kissing my hypersensitive skin. "What if I like touching you, Remi?"

"I think it is better that we don't touch each other,"

I whispered thickly, turning my mouth to his as he lifted. I leaned forward, claiming his mouth, and a moan escaped my lips to be swallowed by his lips as he kissed me hungrily.

"I think that's probably for the best," he agreed, leaning closer as he leisurely kissed me. His hands lifted, one capturing my chin to allow him unobstructed access to my mouth, while the other threaded through my hair, turning my head so he could slowly devour me. "Did you enjoy my mouth on you last night?"

"I kind of want to lie here," I groaned while his mouth brushed against mine, smiling as he pulled back to take in my heavy hooded gaze and kiss-swollen lips.

He pushed me down onto the bed, using his body to pin mine against the mattress. Rhys used his knees to spread my legs apart as he studied me. His hand slid down my belly seductively, his finger dipping lower, trailing through my sex, grinning when he found it wet for him.

"I want to devour you in a very sinful way, Silversmith. I hate that I didn't get to watch your pretty eyes light up as you came for me. I bet you make the most delicious noises when you reach your precipice and cry out in pleasure." His finger pushed into my body, and I arched my spine, running my hands over his broad shoulders.

"Rhys," I moaned as his eyes sparkled and danced with amusement.

A knock sounded at the door, and he turned his dark head in that direction, slowly moving to his knees. He turned back, staring down at my body on display, and before I could prevent his descent, he lowered his mouth to my core, licking through it until he reached my clit, sucking hard against it as his teeth scraped the delicate flesh.

"You do taste fucking delicious," he groaned. He slowly eased from the bed, watching my hand cover where his mouth had been. "You start touching it, and I'll fuck you, little girl. You rubbed against me all night, and I have never lain with a woman I didn't end up fucking. Especially not one I craved as much as I am craving you. I'm trying to be a gentleman here. Either invite me to fuck you or stop touching yourself. You have exactly ten seconds to decide what happens next, Remi."

The knock sounded again, and Rhys dragged his heated stare toward the door. I scrambled beneath the covers, hiding my nakedness beneath them. Burning blue eyes turned their attention back to me before he grabbed a pair of shorts from the broken dresser. Shoving his legs through them, he adjusted his hugely endowed cock before answering the door.

Nyx's singsong voice entered the room seconds before she did. I stared at her as she placed her hands on Rhys's chest, leaning over to smile at me, wiggling her brows.

"It smells like sex in here. Did you fuck him? Oh, my word! Remi, tell me you rode his cock like a drunk cowgirl at a rodeo!" She released Rhys, clapping her hands slowly until she took in the silent tension in the room.

"Rhys wouldn't fuck a Silversmith," Acyn answered for us from where he leaned against the doorframe.

"Oh, but this one intrigues him," Cole stated, moving into the room to sit on the bed, taking in my disheveled hair and lack of clothing. "You're naked, and you smell like…" he leaned closer, his mouth entirely too close to mine for comfort. "Did you suck his dick? I didn't see that happening considering your age. I am impressed."

"That's none of your business," I snapped, and Nyx gasped.

"You sucked him off? You finally gave someone a blowjob? Good for you, Remi! I couldn't be more proud if I watched it happening myself!"

"Because that wouldn't have made this more awkward than it already was, right?" I groaned, noting the lack of agreement in the room. "I need my bag so that I can get dressed."

"Indeed," Rhys grunted while his eyes slid over the thin sheet covering me.

"Details, Rhys. How *did* you achieve landing her so quickly?" Cole asked as he leaned closer to me, kissing my shoulder. "And is she interested in sharing?"

"I am!" Nyx announced, uncaring that the men ignored her offer.

"She's rather shy," Rhys chuckled. "I also told you that I didn't intend to share anything with you. Why are you in my house, Cole?"

"I'm a Van Helsing, and, well, this *is* House of Van Helsing. You need me to draw out those dots for you, brother?" Cole asked, slowly running his fingers over my naked arm as he stared at me. "Come on, sweetheart. You know you want us both. Hell, Acyn would probably join us for a night you'd never forget. All three of us lavishing you with pleasure at the same time, making your body come undone for each of us. I could fuck that ass while Rhys destroyed your pussy, and Acyn could bury his cock in your welcoming throat. Come on, little Silversmith, let us fuck you. I promise to finish last because the good guy always finishes after his queen."

"No, thank you. One demon is enough for me," I stated firmly, shivering as Cole continued kissing the curve of my shoulder.

"Rhys can't handle you alone. I would be on my best behavior."

I yanked the sheet from the bed, moving into the bathroom, only to pause at the sight of the shattered bathtub. Slowly releasing my breath, I turned toward the room full of people with only Rhys's sheet offering any resemblance of modesty.

"Everyone out," Rhys growled sharply, noticing my face burning with embarrassment.

"Is she blushing?" Cole asked, rolling from the bed to stand between me and the others. His hand lifted, softly dragging his fingertips against my heated cheek. "Beautiful."

Cole grabbed me, tightening his arms around me before his mouth brushed against mine. Heat enveloped me, swallowing me whole. The room started to spin in my vision until someone else touched me, jarring me back to reality. I peered down at the sheet now pooled at my feet, grabbing for it while stepping closer toward Rhys.

"Get the fuck off of her, Cole. She isn't interested in your dick. Go find a whore to fuck in your club. She's off-limits unless she decides otherwise." Rhys grabbed my hand, pulling me with him toward the connecting door on the far side of the room. We entered the room, and he closed the door behind us. "Sorry. I wasn't expecting an audience, Love. The bathroom is through that door," he pointed to the far side of the room. "Shower, or do whatever you need to do. I'll have your bag brought up shortly."

Rhys walked through the door, closing me into his bedroom alone. The sound of something slamming against the wall filled the room before another smash sounded, the impact shaking the wall. Silently, I moved through his bedroom, noting the huge bed that sat in the middle of the room with midnight blue bedding that was plush and inviting. Around it was a frame that caged it in with silver curtains to close it off from the rest of the room.

I stepped closer to the bed, testing out the mattress's firmness while inhaling Rhys's scent. My fingers moved over the metal before a painting of a woman on the wall in front of the bed caught my attention. Chewing my lip, I slowly moved closer to the image.

The woman had waist-length silver hair, and silver lines of magic moved through her, which the artist had captured beautifully. Her face was hidden, and yet I didn't need to see it to know whose image adorned Rhys's bedroom wall. The woman was leaning against pillows, with her legs bared beneath the exquisite dress she wore. It would have been a risqué pose for that era, considering the style of clothing she wore. I felt a pang of regret that another woman from my family had won the honor to hang on Rhys's wall.

Dismissing the image, and the tightening in my throat, I entered the lavish bathroom that screamed luxury. Reaching into the shower stall, I adjusted the water to a comfortable level and pulled the sheet from my body, folding it before setting it on the white marble countertop.

A bottle of cologne sat beside the single sink, and I grinned. Moving closer, I picked it up, inhaling the rich, sensual scent of Rhys before placing it back on the counter. I found an iPod dock and looked at the wall, noting that it sat on a shelf. Thumbing through the recently played list, I smirked, finding *Simple Man* by Lynyrd Skynyrd, and pushed play.

I stepped into the shower, closing the glass door behind me. Steam billowed from the heated spray. The guitar strumming soothed my soul with the help of the water. I leaned against the stall as water shot from multiple showerheads, massaging my sore body deliciously. My hand lifted, touching my lips, remembering the feel of him against my mouth.

My thoughts slid back to the taste of him, and the way he'd looked finding pleasure in my clumsy attempt to give it to him. He'd felt right against me, his hand on my throat should have terrified me, but it hadn't. He was dominant, or his demon was. His touch stroked my body into a raging inferno that burned hot with a need to match it.

I was the world's biggest idiot, but I hadn't known about dream-walking. I hadn't known it was even a remote possibility, and yet I'd woken on my knees, fully awake from what I'd assumed was a dream. It should have terrified me, but I wasn't afraid. I'd felt embarrassed, sure. Who wouldn't have? Most people would be mortified from feeling brazen in their dreams, only to discover that they hadn't dreamed it at all.

There was a wealth of embarrassment, but I'd liked making him moan with the knowledge that I was creating the storm within him. It was empowering to make a dominant male weak with need. And he was weakened. He'd been powerless to do anything other than accept what I'd done to him with my mouth.

I slid my soapy hands over my body, remembering the look of liquid heat pooling in his eyes as he'd discovered me taking him hungrily between my lips. He was surprised with a hint of worry banked in his eyes, but that heat I'd seen caused my body to clench hungrily for his thick cock. He hadn't feigned shock, and he'd tried to warn me, but I pushed his hands away because I had wanted to taste him. When reality crashed down on my head, it rendered me speechless that I'd done something so brazenly sexual, and was angry at myself for being naïve.

My fingers pushed against the swollen nub, gasping at finding the flesh so sensitive. I worried my lip with my teeth as my eyes fluttered open to find Rhys leaning against the counter with his arms folded over his chest. His narrowed gaze followed my hand, and I stalled my movement, as those fiery-blue eyes lifted to lock with mine, his smile turning wicked as my knees weakened.

Rhys tilted his head toward the music, hiking one brow up in silent question before he vanished from sight. The music changed, and I shifted nervously as he reappeared naked. *I Put A Spell On You* by Nina Simone started as he stepped into the shower without an invitation while jazz filled the room.

"That's a good song," I groaned, stepping back, sliding my eyes over his hard, muscular body with a hunger that I couldn't hide.

"It is, and rather fitting considering what you're thinking about in my shower," he smirked, turning toward the showerhead, letting the spray of the water sluice down his immensely powerful body before he turned, smiling as he moved closer to me.

"What happens now, Rhys?" I asked, grabbing the soap as I started washing my arms.

"Between us or from here?" he countered, turning facing the shower to wash his chest.

"From here," I amended.

"You're going to show me where your mother lived, and why you think something happened to her."

"No, I am not!" I scoffed, staring at the smile curving his generous mouth. "I'm not taking you to my mother's house. She'd murder me."

His eyes darkened with heat pooling in his gaze as they slowly slid over my naked flesh. "I will scan every inch of this place for that cabin with or without you, Remi. I will find the location now that I know it's here. This is my town, and your mother was here the whole time without me knowing. I already have runners searching every alpha house for any news of her whereabouts," he stated, grabbing the soap from my hand. "Turn around."

"Believe it or not, I can wash myself, Rhys."

"I wasn't asking, woman. I like touching you. Unfortunately, you're entirely too delicate to do what I really want to do to you. Not to mention, you still think fucking is something more meaningful than just two people needing release. This is me meeting your sensibilities halfway, trying to give you time to adjust to what is happening between us."

"And what is it that you think is happening between us?" I asked huskily. I swallowed hard as his smile deepened, and he turned me around, running his hand that held the soap over my skin.

"What do you think is happening between us?"

"I think its mutual attraction and chemistry in play."

"You think because our parts fit together that it's some kind of flirtation happening here?" he chuckled darkly, which sent a shiver of unease rushing up my spine.

"I do," I replied in a whispered breath. His fingers found my shoulders and massaged them, causing a moan to escape my lips. "Sometimes it isn't the universe intervening, and it's just mutual attraction. I don't think there's something cataclysmic happening here. You're a man, and I'm a woman. Our parts do fit as you've pointed out. Sometimes it is just as simple as that, Rhys."

I, of course, didn't buy my explanation. I could feel the intensity of Rhys's touch. The pull to throw propriety to the wind, giving in to the overpowering, carnal need demanding I mount him like a steed. I wanted to give in to the baser needs coursing through me. I wasn't some bitch in heat and the universe, or some pre-ordained curse, didn't get to decide who got to dance in my vagina. It was as simple as that. I was the boss of my body, and I wasn't created like Nyx. I needed some sense of something more before I gave in to the needs of my body.

"Maybe you're right, Remington," he growled against my ear, pressing his large erection against my spine. "Maybe five-hundred years of being cursed to become besotted to any Silversmith woman with a working womb has left me jaded. Finish your shower and get dressed. I have other shit to do today besides trailing through the woods to look for your mother."

Rhys placed the soap into my hand and vanished from the shower, leaving me shivering without his warmth. I quickly washed my hair and body before climbing out of the shower, finding my pack on the counter. I withdrew my white camisole, knit shirt, and a pair of tight-fitting jeans. Slipping into a pair of panties, I pulled on the jeans and top before stepping closer to the mirror.

I peered at my tired reflection, braiding my hair into a tight updo. I added mascara and a light coat of clear lip-gloss before dabbing on a tiny amount of perfume behind my ears. Pushing everything back into my bag, I exited the bathroom to find Rhys fixing his slacks, lifting his eyes to pin me where I stood. His gaze dipped to my exposed midriff before leaving me cold as he turned to grab a white long sleeve shirt.

Starting toward the opposite door, he snorted, and I narrowed my stare on the tight smile that was anything but friendly. He looked like sex personified with his dark hair messed up and out of place, as if he'd slid his fingers through it in frustration. He glared at me as his jaw hammered against his cheek, angrily.

"What?" I asked, and he stared at me without looking away. Something had pissed him off between him leaving the shower and now.

"You're wearing jeans and a knit top to go into the mountains?"

"You're wearing a suit." I crossed my arms over my chest, raising one brow in irritation.

He paused, looking down at the expensive Italian suit he wore, and frowned. He started undressing, and my eyes studied every inch of flesh he revealed to my greedy stare. Once he pulled off the white shirt, he vanished into his walk-in closet, dispelling my blunt eye-raping, as Nyx called it.

Rhys returned a moment later wearing relaxed jeans and a dark, tight-fitting button-up, which hugged his muscular form like a second skin. Instead of his Italian loafers, he wore black boots that hardly made a noise as he made his way to where I stood. He grabbed my bag, withdrawing a zip-up sweater, and tossed my things to his bed without a word. Threading his fingers through mine, he pulled me with him from the room.

My stomach churned at the idea of taking him to my mother's cabin, deep in the mountains. If she knew

I was bringing a Van Helsing home, she'd have my flesh taken from me in a heartbeat. I was betraying our family's biggest rule: Don't bring a Van Helsing home under any circumstances. The thing was, Rhys was my best shot at finding my mother alive.

Chapter Eleven

The drive to the cabin was in awkward silence. I wasn't just bringing one Van Helsing home, but rather three brothers, who all glared at me. It was such an uncomfortable ride that even Nyx was surprisingly silent. Chewing my lip, I leaned over Rhys's lap to look out the window as we passed one of the curves in the bend. If he minded, he kept it to himself. I sat back, wondering why the brothers looked as if they were expecting a fight.

We pulled into the driveway of the cabin, and the car rolled to a stop. I paused, silently studying the house. The chair had been righted and sat further back on the wraparound porch. I kept that tidbit to myself, praying my mother didn't come out with bullets flying toward the Van Helsing, who sat next to me. Rhys opened the door, and I grabbed him back, noting his raised eyebrow as he allowed it.

"Problem, Silversmith?" Rhys asked pointedly,

hiking one brow higher than the other before he slid his eyes to the house to scan the area.

I worried my bottom lip with my teeth, considering what to say, if anything. His attention settled back on me, and I exhaled, releasing my lip with a pop.

"My sister may or may not be here. It would be unfortunate for you if Winchester is on the property."

"You think I can't handle a Silversmith hunter?" Rhys studied my face before snorting and exiting the vehicle without fear. "I've hunted your people down for over three-hundred years, Remi. I smell blood."

His abrupt change in subjects caused my brows to shoot toward my hairline. I climbed out, standing beside him. I lifted my nose in the air, confirming what he'd said. Today the blood was more pronounced, and the coppery tang had turned putrid.

"Maybe you should wait in the car, Silversmith."

I snorted, rolling my eyes heavenward, stepping around his hulking frame. "You wait in the car, I don't need to be protected—" Power entered the clearing, halting the words that sat perched on the tip of my tongue.

"Get inside the damn vehicle, Remi—"

A blur of movement caught my eye. Turning, I cried out as something rushed toward me, but a flash of silver intercepted it, and something wet splattered my face. More blurs entered the small, cramped space between the car and the house. I was grabbed and held against a solid chest as Rhys moved with one arm around me, the other holding his sword while he protected me. It felt like we were dancing, my arms wrapped around his body while he deflected blow after blow from an unseen enemy. Rhys moved toward the car, depositing me back into the door while Nyx laughed, her eyes flashing with approval.

"That was one of the hottest things I've seen in my life!" she exclaimed, hooting and hollering as Rhys deftly swung his sword again in a high arch. Spinning around, he struck out in a wide swing, slicing the attacker into three pieces before I'd even noticed he'd swung again, let alone three times.

Watching Rhys Van Helsing fight was like watching dancers who were skilled and elegant. Only Rhys was lethal, and his moves were eerily proficient in the way he dispatched the creatures attacking. Every wide swing of his blade was timed perfectly. The attackers lunged with inhuman speed, and Rhys swung before they reached him. Men in dark tactical clothing moved into the fight, making a complete circle around the car.

My gaze slid to Acyn, who had exited the car with Rhys. He used dual blades, slicing and dancing as he killed the *vampires*. My attention slid to the sun and then back to the vampires who were attacking at noon. They shouldn't be awake yet, but here they were, attacking in broad daylight!

"It's daytime," I yelped, jumping back from a head that slammed against my thigh. Reaching down, I grabbed it and held it up. Gagging on reflex as blood dripped from the severed neck, I tossed the poor vamp back out of the car while fighting the churning in my stomach.

"That is rather peculiar, isn't it?" Nyx said, her eyes still locked on Rhys's ass, covered in tightly fitted jeans. "You landed a hottie, and I think for the first time in my life, I'm jealous of you."

"For once, maybe think with your brain and not your vagina? Why would vampires chance becoming a pile of ash to be out in the daylight?"

"They're wearing sunblock?" I scrubbed my hand down my face as she chuckled. "I'm guessing they've yet to finish their change. Rhys is now taking down three in one blow, and I wish he was fighting in much less clothing. I bet his muscles constrict with every subtle move he makes. Is his cock large? Please tell me he's the full package deal."

I turned away from the fight, peering at Nyx's hopeful gaze. "Very large, and considering he's an incubus, I'm going to guess he is confident enough to know where that spot is. I could get my first real orgasm." I wiggled my brows, turning to stare into azure eyes that narrowed on me as he cocked his head to the side.

"You didn't tell him that the others never got you to the end of the danger zone?" Nyx snorted, but the sound was one of pity. "You're already one up on them, Van Helsing. Since you made her come on the table and she broke it!"

"Indeed," he grunted, turning to take in the sizzling corpses. "Remi, I thought you said your mother had hidden this place? You seem to have a pest problem here."

"Now do you believe me that something

happened?" I asked, slowly climbing out of the vehicle. Staring toward the house, Rhys grabbed my arm and pulled me back as Cole and Acyn stepped in front of us.

"Check the house," Rhys ordered.

"Send a knight in first," Cole snorted, crossing his heavily tattooed arms over his chest. "I don't intend to die by entering a Silversmiths home without an invitation. Their wards are nasty, and I don't intend to writhe in pain because we fell for some bullshit excuse of a missing mother."

"If you would be so kind as to stop this primitive caveman act and release my elbow, I could drop the wards so you wouldn't need to sacrifice a knight. I assure you, the wards are very active." Rhys snorted, but he listened, releasing my elbow with a warning look.

My hands lifted, and the glowing symbols that surrounded the house became visible. The men stepped back, eyeing the cabin as if it were alive and utterly terrifying. I memorized the wards, closing my eyes, and whispered the spell to disarm them, then smiled coldly. The wards shot outward, and I exhaled.

The Van Helsing men, along with the knights, dropped to their knees, howling in pain. Watching them for a moment, I let the small victory slither over me. I peered down at the brothers, smirking as I grabbed Nyx, and started toward the house.

"Hurry," I urged, turning the moment we were inside, and sealing the door closed with another ward. Exhaling, I opened my eyes to find Nyx glaring at me.

"Excellent plan, Remington. Minus the part where we are stuck inside this house with no electricity, no water, and, oh yeah, no food," she grunted, peering around at the disheveled house. "Did I mention that I'm team Van Helsing right now? Rhys is totally into you, and you just dropped them all like hot potatoes, which doesn't bode well for us."

"He's my enemy! They're all my enemies. My mother is missing, vampires are day-walking, and the entire plan I had is now worthless. I sucked him off! Do you have any idea how damaging it is to a woman's sensibility to suck someone off in a dream, only to conclude that I did it, willingly? Not to mention, my family is probably never going to forgive me for doing something as stupid as that, ever."

Something slammed against the door, and I yelped in surprise. I sent magic rushing through the wards and then groaned. I'd yet to perfect magical wards or learn to hold them, and considering I felt the lack of wards, I had probably accidentally disarmed them. The door shook again, and I stepped back, staring at it, looking around the room for the silver, finding the wall empty of the bullets that had peppered it last night.

The door opened abruptly, squealing I backed up until my butt hit the wall. Rhys prowled into the house, entered it with duel blades in his hands while angry eyes locked with mine. The tick in his jaw hammered, and his mouth was an angry, white line.

"Go outside, Nyx," he hissed, barely loud enough for me to hear him.

Nyx hesitated, but Rhys's attention slid to her as his blades hummed with power, as if he was considering removing her head. His rage was so thick that I could taste it in the air. She started to argue, but I cut her off.

"Go, Nyx. I'll be fine," I whispered, chewing my lip as my attention moved back to the angry Van Helsing. "Do not hurt her."

"She didn't try to murder us," he sneered coldly. "You did."

"No, I didn't. The wards would have only hurt for a few moments. Just long enough for us to get into the house to escape you."

He snorted, stalking toward me slowly. "They just tried to eviscerate us. Luckily for us, you're not skilled enough to accomplish that feat yet, Remington. Had you been more skilled, we'd have to regrow and heal organs because of that shit you pulled."

Maybe I should have been paying more attention to my mother's tireless teachings instead of watching reality TV dating shows. I winced as he sheathed his swords before placing one large hand around my throat as he grunted in pain. Azure eyes searched mine, and his hand tightened before he tore them away from mine, looking around the small cabin with an upturned lip.

"This shit-hole isn't Eliza's house. She'd never lower herself to live in such squalor," he snapped. I started to speak, but his hand tightened as a cold smile lifted his lips. "What game are you playing at, Silversmith?"

"This is where my mother raised me, Rhys. Behind this wall is my bedroom, and the one next to it is my mother's room. Below us is an armory, and out in the woods is a shooting range where she taught me to shoot and ensure my guns were precisely tuned to murder anyone stupid enough to think to harm me. I am not playing a game. I may be in over my head, I will openly admit to that, but I also didn't ask you to come here. You brought me. Your mistake was thinking that I wouldn't run the first chance I got."

"No. No games, right? You stepped right into my path by chance. I brought you home with me, where you proceeded to act shy and all modest, right up until you sucked my cock. Was that to make me lower my guard against you, or to make me think you actually liked me? The first moment you got your chance, you tried to murder me, just like the rest of your murderous family, Remington Silversmith. My mistake was assuming you were different." His hand tightened, forcing me to suck in air before he could cut off my airway. The moment he cut the air to my lungs off, he lowered his mouth to brush his against mine, smiling against my lips as a soft moan escaped. "If you try to harm my brothers or me again, I'll slit your pretty neck, and fuck your throat while you bleed out. That is the only warning you are going to get from me, and that's because your lips look good wrapped around my cock."

His hand released my throat, and my hands rubbed where he'd held me. Rhys's dark stare held mine before he snorted, moving toward the kitchen. Cole, Acyn, and Nyx entered the house. Cole's eyes held mine briefly, lowering to the red handprint, surely marring my porcelain skin. Nyx moved toward me silently, grabbing my hand, and her worried eyes noted the tears swimming in mine.

I didn't need to put into words what we were both thinking. We shouldn't have come here, not even if it was my mother missing. We should have assembled a team and come in carefully, but I hadn't thought my mother was missing.

I'd figured she'd just been ignoring my calls or had harmed herself by working a spell that took more than one witch to cast. I'd never assumed there would be a Van Helsing close to where we lived, let alone several of them.

I exhaled, slowly opening my bedroom door as screeching started. My hands lifted, covering my ears to stop the pain that struck so hard my vision swam. I dropped to my knees, along with the others inside the cabin. My head felt as if it was splitting in two. Nyx howled, and I turned, staring at her as blood dripped from her nose. The Van Helsings weren't faring any better, either. I moaned the spell to undo the wards, groaning as the pain intensified.

Bringing my hand up to my teeth, I bit into the palm to draw blood, slamming my hand down on the floor, which stopped the deafening, piercing scream of the safeguard spell. No one moved, not until Nyx screamed and grabbed me, staring down in horror at me.

"What the hell is happening to your face, Remi?" she stammered.

Gazing up at her, I saw the runic symbols written in golden writing over my flesh. My mouth opened, closed, and then repeated the attempt to speak several more times. I watched as she wiped away warm liquid from my eyes, staring as I started to sit up, only to be gently pushed back to the floor by Rhys and Cole, who studied my face.

"That's new," Rhys said carefully, his finger tracing my forehead.

I pushed his hand away, slowly getting back to my feet. The dark room exploded in violet light, changing to an eerie blue as glyphs moved along the walls and ceiling. I stepped back, colliding against Cole, who wrapped his arms around me, ignoring Rhys's warning glare over my shoulder.

The glyphs pulsed, and every single pulse seemed to drain me until I swayed on my feet, and they vanished as quickly as they'd come. Rhys moved to the bedroom doorway I'd tried to enter, and twisted the knob, pushing it open.

I stared into a nursery, frowning as my head tilted to the side. Cole continued holding me until I shoved him away, pathetically weakened by whatever was happening inside the house. Entering the room, I moved to the crib, lifting the blue blankets before bringing it to my nose.

"Okay, this wasn't like this when I left." Sure, I hadn't explored the room last night, but how had I missed a crib, or that my entire room was converted into a nursery?

"How long has it been since you were home?" Cole asked beside my ear, causing a shiver to race down my spine as his heated breath fanned against my flesh.

"Almost five years," I swallowed. "She never mentioned a baby. My mother would have mentioned being pregnant. It would be a huge celebration. When my sisters have babes, it's a full family gathering, and we party for like a week. They have not had any in years, though, nor has my mother been around men, that I am aware. It's also almost Beltane, which is a huge celebration for witches. So she would be here making preparations." My face filled with heat as I turned, eyeing Rhys with the reality of what would happen if I was stuck in his house during Beltane.

"The festival of fucking," Cole chuckled, heat pooling in his eyes as he smiled at me. "That's this week, isn't it?"

I nodded, frowning while turning my attention to Rhys, who studied the pink in my cheeks. Ignoring the heat that pooled in my apex at his narrowed stare, I opened the door to my mother's room, stopping in my tracks as I noticed the blood covering the bed. Daylight had added more sinister sights to the once cozy cabin in the woods.

"That can't be good," Nyx whispered beside me.

The blood left my face, along with the feeling as my pulse thundered in my ears. Nausea rolled through me violently. It took everything I had in me to move to the bed. I walked to the other side, yanking the blankets back to see what was moving beneath the covers, and screamed as snakes slithered off the mattress.

Rhys reacted faster than I could, yanking me away as a snake shot forward. I cried out as he pushed me behind him. His thumb ran over my wildly racing pulse, and I calmed from his silent reassurance as he issued an order. The knights moved into the room, grabbing the reptiles and disposing of them outside. I didn't tell Rhys that snakes terrified me, or that they usually signaled a snake in the ranks. They were a warning to anyone within our bloodline that someone in the family was compromised. Or worse, someone had turned against us. As in me, who had brought home a Van Helsing?

Spinning on my heel, I exited the room, moving toward the kitchen. Opening the fridge, I brought my hand up to my mouth at what I found. Body parts sat in jars, blood coating them as if whoever had been bottling them hadn't cared about cleanliness. The smell was obnoxious and made my stomach heave repeatedly. Rhys reached over my shoulder, closing the grisly scene.

"Fucking witches," he muttered. "Dead vampires, jarred body parts, and a missing Silversmith that may or may not be breeding. A very young, mortal Silversmith, who tried to kill the Van Helsing alpha, along with two other House of Van Helsing males," Rhys pointed out without sugar-coating his words while staring me down. "Anything else you want to add the growing list of *what the fucks*, Remington?"

"No. That pretty much sums it up nicely. I need to go down into the armory, and I don't suggest you come with me. It's highly booby-trapped against anyone else getting in. I don't know if I can disable the wards, and I'd hate for you to fuck my throat, and all that jazz," I hissed, glaring at him as his lips curled into a dark, sinister smirk.

"Your throat was surprisingly welcoming. You sure you don't want to try that one again?"

"No. Once was enough for me. At least for this lifetime, asshole," I muttered, pushing past him to shove the fridge out of the way, exposing the hidden doorway that led downstairs. Pausing, I frowned, finding the door missing from the hinges. "That's not good at all."

"Edger, enter, and tell me what you find down below. Remi, back the hell up in case something comes up the stairs," Rhys ordered as Cole and Acyn stepped in front of me.

Rhys's hand didn't release me, not until I jerked my arm out of his grasp, and refused to look or acknowledge his presence. My fingers lifted to my throat, finding it sore but undamaged. I could feel the heat of his stare, noting that I was touching the injury he'd given me, and yet I refused to meet his pretty eyes. My mind ran wild with scenarios of what was happening and came up blank.

There were snakes in my mother's bed, covered in blood. I was pretty certain it was deadman's blood, something used to inject into a vampire, rendering them paralyzed. Vampires had attacked during daylight hours. The question was, were they sent to protect the house, or to keep us out of it?

Screaming sounded from below, and then the horrifying scent of burning flesh filled the room. We all remained silent, staring at the empty stairway until something started moving toward us. Rhys pushed me further behind him, protectively, as Edger moved up the stairs, crawling his way to us. By the time he'd finally reached the top of the stairs, his flesh was little more than leather covering his skeleton. Smoke rose from his skin, and my stomach rolled, fighting the bile that entered my mouth. My arm lifted, covering my mouth while my horrified stare remained on the corpse.

"What the actual hell?" I whispered, looking down the stairs. Someone stood at the bottom of the staircase, bright glowing red eyes peering through a hood before all hell broke loose.

The cabin began to shudder and shake as Rhys grabbed me without warning, rushing toward the door as he breached the threshold. The entire house heaved, and wood started creaking and splintering. Rhys dove toward the open door of the Humvee, slamming the door shut behind us. He barely had time to shove me to the floorboard before the window shattered as wood shot through it, and the car door.

It sounded like a bomb was going off outside. All I could do was hold on to Rhys, who pressed his forehead against mine, watching me as more shrapnel hit the vehicle. His dark head lifted, and he started to speak as something shot through the car door, and he grunted.

Blood splattered my flesh, and my hands shook as I turned him over. Peering down at his stomach, I cried out, finding a large chunk of wood sticking out from his side. I looked around the car for anything I could use to stop the bleeding, but found nothing. His hand moved to his side, ripping out the wood while I lifted my shirt over my head, holding the knit top to his stomach. Rhys groaned as I pushed the fabric into the wound, lifting my eyes to find him observing the tears sliding down my cheeks.

"Please don't die," I whispered through the emotion wrapping around me. I leaned against Rhys, adding my weight to the wound. His hands slid up my sides, pausing at the sides of my breasts.

"I can't die, Remi. I'm a Van Helsing." His eyes watched mine as I slowly nodded, using my arm to wipe away the tears. "You worried about me, little one?"

"No. I don't even like you right now," I lied, chewing my lip while releasing the breath I'd been holding as relief washed through me.

"Liar," he whispered, cupping his hand against my cheek. I pulled back to look at him. "Look outside and tell me what you see, Remington."

I leaned up, peering through the shattered window of the Humvee. The entire cabin had exploded and turned into little more than firewood. Nyx was on the ground, grunting beside Cole and Acyn. Men had moved around them, preparing what looked like medical stretchers to carry them out on.

Something touched my nipple, and I yelped, staring down at Rhys's lips as he smirked around the puckered flesh that his teeth had captured. I started to lean back, but his hands prevented me from doing so, holding me in place as he opened his mouth and sucked the pebbled flesh between his lips, running his tongue over it leisurely.

My eyes rounded to the size of saucers as pleasure danced through me. His tongue flicked my nipple, slowly sliding over the peak. Moaning, I whimpered as my body shuddered with need. I felt his smile against me and pulled away, staring at him before lifting the shirt from the wound, finding it still seeping blood.

"You don't have time to be sucking nipples, you're bleeding out like the stuck pig you are!" I huffed in an aggravated tone.

"I've survived a lot worse than being hit by

shrapnel. Jerald?" he called in a commanding tone.

"Yes, Sir Van Helsing?" a male voice answered from within the Humvee, causing the blush in my cheek to intensify at not being alone.

"Drive us home, the others will meet us there momentarily," Rhys stated, rolling me beneath his heavy body, uncaring that he was getting me bloody in the process. "Call ahead, and tell them three wounded Van Helsings will need feeders available, and one female nymph as well. Have the feeders accessible and waiting. My knights will require healing and feeders."

"You're going to feed?" I asked through a tightening in my throat that bothered me.

"Unless you're offering to feed me, Remi, I have to, so that I can heal. I'm cursed with immortality, but healing isn't something that happens naturally. Not since I was cursed to become a monster by your family."

I stared at him for a moment and then considered what it was he was asking. "Sex, right? That's how you feed to heal?"

His azure eyes searched mine, finding the wariness burning within them before he snorted. "Indeed, but don't worry. You aren't on my menu tonight, Silversmith. I doubt you're skilled enough to handle my demon in bed."

I bristled before considering my words carefully. "I doubt he could handle a real woman, anyway. You can feed from some basic feeder bitch, because after the shit you did today, you deserve some basic, nameless feeder, asshole. I could handle your demon at his worst.

The thing is, I don't want to. I don't want either of you ever again."

He smiled cruelly, lifting to press his erection against my belly. His eyes dared me to feed him, but I wasn't stupid enough to allow him that part of me. I may not like that he had to feed from someone else, but I wasn't going to give him the satisfaction of knowing it bothered me, either. I turned to stare at the floorboard, dismissing him the best I could manage with him looming over the top of me, watching me closely.

His hands lifted, and he peered over the edge of the seat before lowering back down, grabbing my chin between his fingers while he smiled. Before I could judge his intentions, he claimed my lips in a bone-melting kiss that turned me inside out and left me more confused than I was already. Rhys closed his eyes, resting his forehead against mine.

The Humvee rolled to a stop, and Rhys lifted out of the car, turning to issue orders to the people milling about in front of the mansion. I watched him walking toward the house while a knight moved in beside me. I was silently escorted into the house and escorted up the stairs to the room I'd stayed in last night. I scanned the wreckage and moved toward the bed, pulling the pillow over my head as I screamed in frustration. I almost wished for Winchester to find me, just so I could work out against her, burning the pent-up need and energy that was building every moment I was stuck here with Rhys.

Chapter Twelve

Hours of nonstop grotesque and obnoxious screaming came from the room beside mine. Rhys's feeder screamed his name so loudly that my head actually ached from her cries, and if I never had to hear his name again, I'd be happy. After the fourth hour of listening to flesh meeting flesh, and her screaming she was coming, I abandoned my room.

I hated the idea of him feeding from someone else. It also bothered me that I would even care that he was with someone other than me. He was my sworn enemy, and I wasn't here willingly. So why the hell would I care? I didn't; I told myself. I'd said it a million times in the last couple of hours. I'd said it the moment he opened that door, staring at me with a look questioning if I'd join him or not. I'd verbally told him to get fucked, and he had. So what if he literally had to fuck to heal? It wasn't my problem. That was what I repeated inside my head like a mantra.

"Miss, you can't be in here," a woman called from the doorway of the room where I stared at the portraits of the men in armor. Her eyes held mine before she noted that I peered at the pictures inside the room, smiling. "It's the Van Helsings," she pointed out, using her cane to move closer to me.

I took in her silverish-blue hair and aged form. Laugh lines had added character to her face and made her aging process look more beautiful. Her body, while tired, moved surprisingly fast toward me with a soft look in her eyes while she peered up at the family adorning the walls.

"All of them?" I queried, not wanting to return to my room.

"Yes, miss," she said, pointing to the largest picture with pride burning in her soft grey stare. "That's them together, painted with their parents."

The picture was of thirteen sons that stood around a small, petite woman with red hair and glowing blue azure eyes. Next to her was a man I assumed was her husband and the boys' father, considering the dark hair and skin that spoke of eastern heritage.

They looked happy in the picture, carefree. Rhys's hand was on his mother and father's shoulders, but his mother stared at Cole with visible love. Thirteen Van Helsing sons around her, and she stared at her youngest with the love of a mother, who probably had the patience of a saint to handle that asshole.

"This one is right before they lost her," the woman pointed to another portrait, nodding to one where Rhys stood off in the background, while another of his brothers stood behind their parents. The brother looked cold, merciless, and bitter. His eyes burned with malice as he stared at the artist. "Mikel. He's the one you're looking at. He's a cold-hearted man, but he adores his family."

"How did you know I was looking at him?" I asked carefully, wondering if she was clairvoyant.

"Because you shivered," she chuckled, turning smiling grey eyes toward me.
"Sons of the first House of Van Helsing from front to back are Mikel, Nikolas, who we now call Cole, Acyn, Rhys, Silas, Cadmus, Illeron, Sorin, Xanth, Arryn, Kaden, Dagen, and Xavier. Their mother is pregnant with Lady Nyota in the picture. She died five days after birthing the little princess. They were murdered by that bastard Donte Silversmith for no good reason other than jealousy. Arthur was a good husband to her, and you can tell by their brood of children they adored one another. Handsome bunch, are they not?" she asked, turning to find me grimacing at her assessment.

"Very much so," I agreed honestly. "And this one, she must be the Lady Nyota?"

The picture was of a female with black hair, much like Rhys, but where his eyes were blue, hers were a startling crystalline blue that held an emotion that left me shivering. She was posed in a chair with the brothers standing behind her.

Gone was the carefree Van Helsings, and in their place were cold, hate-filled men that didn't care what the artist captured. Cole was the only one with any emotion other than hate filling his eyes. His eyes held a sadness that caused my stomach to tighten with the pain he exuded.

"We should get you out of here before one of the brothers finishes feeding," she whispered while placing her hand on my shoulder.

"Indeed, since I instructed you to keep my *guest* out of the family room, Isa," Rhys's voice slithered down my spine, noting the coldness in his tone.

"Don't get angry at Isa. I was already in the room when she found me. I couldn't stomach the vile noises coming from the room next to mine," I stated, turning to glare at him.

"Ask me if I care, Silversmith," he grunted, and Isa turned, looking at me coldness burning in her eyes.

"You're one of those bloody bastard Silversmiths that killed our Lord and Lady?" she growled, spitting at my feet before she turned on her heel, leaving the room.

"She's lovely," I muttered, turning to walk past Rhys, only to find a blonde female stroking his arm silently, staring at me through malice-filled eyes.

"Problem, Remington?" Rhys asked softly, his eyes narrowing on me as I took in his meal with jealousy I couldn't understand and didn't care to examine.

She wasn't just pretty; she was beautiful with a smooth, alabaster complexion. She wore a sheer red nightgown, uncaring that it exposed her ample breasts or landing strip between her thighs. Her hair fell in gentle waves to her hips, sexily mussed from hours of endless sex with Rhys. She lowered her hand, stroking over his crotch with ownership burning in her glare.

"Okay then," I whispered, moving past him and his

feeder. I started toward the bedroom, dismissing them both. His hand shot out, grabbing my wrist as my chest rose and fell with an emotion I didn't understand.

"Were you looking for something?" he asked softly.

"An escape hatch or the kitchen," I swallowed, yanking my arm away from his grip. "In all the excitement of you guys getting back, and heading off to eat for hours, I wasn't provided sustenance. Unlike you, I don't eat from my dick. I need actual food, so after hours of listening to Miss *Thang* here scream your name to the bloody rafters, I decided to go looking for the kitchen to see if I could get something to eat. I didn't realize I wasn't allowed to walk around inside your home, my bad. I'll return to my cell," I growled, stomping off toward the staircase.

I entered the room, closing the door behind me, staring up at the newly fixed ceiling. I shed my clothes, heading toward the bathroom to shower. I grabbed my bag off the bed, tossing it onto the counter before moving to the shower to start the water. Seeing the stereo, I messed with the station, finding a soothing song before opening my bag.

Pulling out a pair of lounge pants and a soft white camisole top, I placed them onto the counter with plain white panties. My eyes studied my reflection, frowning. I was gaudy compared to the model-looking woman Rhys had healing him tonight. My hair was a mess, untamable on my best day, and naturally curly. It was a mass of red hues, along with blonde highlights oddly scattered throughout the mess of tresses.

I had porcelain skin but tanned easily enough in

the summer months. But it wasn't spring in the Pacific Northwest. That meant tanning or even sun for that matter was months away. My breasts were perky, but on the smaller side, barely filling a C-cup with the help of hormones. My electric-blue eyes were my saving grace, directing the eye away from the freckles that covered my nose and cheeks, adding to the redhead stereotype in which I fit perfectly.

Shucking my clothes, I moved into the shower, sliding beneath the blissful heat spray. I washed my hair, lathering it, and repeating the process. Once it was clean from the craptastic day I'd had, I smothered my hair in conditioner. Rinsing it out, my fingers ran down my body and paused over the swollen nipple Rhys had sucked on, nipping it with his teeth. He'd taken my piercings, the backup silver that never left my body in the event that I needed it.

Asshole.

I exited out of the shower, drying off before I slipped into my clothes. Quickly braiding my hair into two parted sections, I stared at my pale reflection, rubbing my eyes. Rolling my dirty clothes up, I put them into the second pocket of my backpack, and then pulled the knit shirt back out, moving toward the garbage to toss it in before exiting the bathroom.

Rhys was seated on my bed, shirtless. He lifted his head, letting his eyes slide down my frame before they moved back up slowly. He didn't speak for a moment, swallowing past the heat burning in his gaze. I rolled my eyes, staring anywhere but at him and his magnificent body.

"What are you doing in here? Shouldn't you be off

feeding or something?" I snapped dismissively, moving to the other side of the bed, setting my bag down before the smell of cinnamon hit my nose.

Turning toward the small table, I took in the food covering it. My stomach growled, and I padded on bare feet toward it, pausing to take in the assortment of food. Fresh fruits, stuffed French toast, cinnamon rolls, and an array of meats and cheeses with fancy crackers covered the entire tabletop, with a single bottle of whiskey sat in the middle.

I grabbed a cinnamon roll, bringing it to my nose, inhaling the delicious scent of freshly baked bread. It wasn't store-bought. Someone had actually made it from scratch! I bit into it, moaning around the mouthful before closing my eyes at the orgasm happening to my taste buds. Polishing it off without care that I had an audience, I reached over the food, grabbing the whiskey, pouring a glassful, and holding it to my nose before scrunching it up at the aroma.

I still failed to see why people did that, or what purpose it had. It would still taste the same whether I sniffed the crap before or after I downed the cup's contents. I took a long drink, turning to gaze at the male watching me through narrowed eyes.

"They made this stuff from scratch?" I asked, uncertain how they had accomplished it since I'd been in the shower. The cinnamon rolls were hot, as if they'd just come out of the oven moments ago.

"I keep several cooks on staff, and this one was cooking for the staff's children. They enjoy waking up to freshly made biscuits and bread in the morning. Eat another cinnamon roll, woman. You're too skinny.

Didn't they feed you at E.V.I.E.?"

"I'm not skin and bones. Just because I don't have curves like your feeder, it doesn't mean I'm skinny. I'm average, which, by the way, works for me. I don't need your damn approval," I seethed, turning back to the ruined meal as a strange feeling settled in the pit of my stomach. "You can go."

"Dismissing me?" he asked coldly.

"I am exhausted. You tried to strangle me today, and then I got to listen to you have sex for hours while I sat here starving. For the record, Van Helsing, I am mortal, as you should know since you keep throwing in my face. I need sustenance to maintain my mediocre figure, as you so delicately pointed out. I want my piercings back too. I weaken without silver, and your house seems to be lacking it."

"Your figure is perfect. If I had tried to strangle you today, you'd be dead. I reacted badly, but I am a bit jaded where your bloodline and mine are concerned. I am sorry for overlooking the fact that you require food in my need to heal from my wounds. You aren't getting your piercings back because I know exactly why you have them, and what they can do. As for the screaming, I was pretending the feeder was you, and I may have lost control a little bit. I wish I had fed from you, but being you're not immortal yet, I didn't wish to stress that I wanted to fuck you. Unfortunately, I didn't have much choice in the matter without seeming like a complete asshole."

"Oh," I said breathlessly. "Look, I get that I'm not very knowledgeable about what is happening here. I'm not an idiot, though. I'm not as weak as you think I am.

I could handle you, just for the record." He smiled a lopsided grin, standing up as he tilted his head. "I didn't mean right now. I'm not interested in sloppy seconds."

"I wouldn't take you after soiling myself on a feeder, Remington. You're a woman. You deserve respect in that aspect. Considering the conversation with Nyx, you've never reached a climax with anyone but me?"

"We're not having this conversation," I blushed, turning toward the table, refilling my glass. "Whiskey? You should drink too because then your lips are busy and Lord knows those lips need to be busy… On drinking! They need to be busy drinking. Let's get drunk. No," I said, shaking my head. "No, we probably shouldn't get drunk. I'm a pretty easy drunk, so we shouldn't do that together. Shut up, Remington!" I shouted, turning horrified eyes on him. I watched his lips twitching as he fought laughter. "Drink?" I growled, holding out the bottle because fuck it, I wasn't doing well around him.

"Are you always like this when you're nervous?"

"I am not nervous," I lied, turning away from his heated stare, embarrassment filling my cheeks. His hand grabbed my braid, pulling on it.

"You're nervous, and it's cute, Remi. You are so innocent that it's intriguing. Now sit down and eat, because I have it on good authority that you require food. I enjoy listening to you eat, as well."

He grabbed a cup as I downed the second glass of whiskey, holding my glass out for more. His brow lifted as his eyes slid to my lips. I sucked my bottom lip between my teeth, watching him pour a double shot into my glass.

"I'm sorry my family killed yours," I stated softly, holding his surprised stare.

"I'm not sorry mine killed yours," he returned, and I winced.

"Ouch."

"Tell me about your mother. The Elizabeth I knew wouldn't live in a hovel for even mere moments. She'd have found it beneath her. And those glyphs, what were they?" I swallowed, staring at him before I reached for a cinnamon roll, shoving the entire thing into my mouth as his eyes narrowed, and a smile tugged at his lips. "No moaning this time? What a shame. You make the most delicious noises, little one. Go to sleep. Tomorrow we will finish this conversation, and you'll make me a sword to prove you are a Silversmith. Sweat dreams, and if you find me within them, do try not to suck my cock. I won't let you finish me off the same way again. Next time I wake up with you sexually participating, I'm going to consider it an invitation to do more."

Chapter Thirteen

I stared at the glass room in the enormous basement of the mansion. There was a large assembly of knights moving in and out of what appeared to be some kind of control room. Outside of that room was a long table with chairs around it, and big TVs covering several news outlets. Rhys had an entire surveillance room in his basement where he watched the outside world in high definition.

He had an amazing setup which was something I hadn't expected. I'd known he'd be articulate with his men, but he was eerily efficient. Rhys wasn't an alpha by mistake. The way he controlled the room and dominated it with his presence was proof of his status.

Today he'd forgone his suit and wore a faded shirt with dark, loose-fitting jeans. His boots were expensive Italian leather, designed with his family crest. He'd pulled his hair back away from his face, revealing his sharp, angular features. He'd also skipped shaving today, which made my fingers itch to trace the 5 o'clock shadow to see if it was as soft as it looked.

"How does this work?" he asked, and I smiled tightly.

"I normally create bullets, but you've asked for a sword which will take magic since silver is a soft metal. I'll need copper, bronze, and silver. The room needs to have extreme temperature settings. It will take several hours at least to make a sword strong enough to wield against bone. It's not a simple process by any means. I'll have to melt the metal, cool it, form it, and then reheat it. At that point, it becomes tricky. I'll use magic to enhance the blade with the Silversmith silver in the actual design, adding potency to the blade's magic. I'll then repeat the process until the final heating steps. After that, I'll have to cool it slowly to reinforce the metal and ensure it doesn't weaken in the process."

"How many hours are we talking?" he asked, canting his head to the side, studying me.

"I've made two swords in my lifetime. One was a mistake that I melted down once I'd finished. The other is still being used today by Nyx. Unlike others in my line, any blade I create becomes infused with magic that adheres to the one who will wield it."

"How does that work?"

"I'm different from others in our line. When they craft, it is merely Silversmith silver that is the end result. However, when I do it, something else is added to the weapon. Nyx's sword molds into what she needs, and occasionally, it's more penis-shaped than an actual blade she wields."

His eyes narrowed, and a smirk replaced the frown on his mouth. Rhys turned my words over in his mind, and I saw his eyes burning with more questions, as if he found me a wealth of information. I now saw why Winchester was always telling me to shut my craw, as she called it.

"I can't say how long because that depends on the metal, magic, and the room you provide. It looks pretty state-of-the-art and probably has everything I need. However, it isn't my armory, and that will slow me down. If I was in my armory using my tools, probably four hours, max. However, I'm not, so I'd double that time."

"Trust the process," Nyx interjected, sliding up against him as she smirked at me. "Reporting for duty, hooker. I'll be your captain today, buckle up, bitches. It's about to get hot in here, so take them clothes off, and let's work it, woman!"

I scrunched up my nose, pulling my shirt over my head to hand it to Nyx. She tossed it over her shoulder and wiggled her brows while holding out her hand. I looked down at my shirt, watching Nyx deflate as she huffed, moving to pick it back up, making a show out of folding it. I hooked my thumbs through the warm-up pants and pushed them down to reveal the tight spandex shorts I wore when I forged.

"And you're wearing next to nothing. Why?" Rhys asked, turning to toss an irritated look at the knights and his brothers. There was a crowd gathering, slowly moving to sit around the table.

"Because the room is too hot for clothes," I admitted, shrugging. "I can't wear a bra because the wire would cause damage, and I prefer underwire bras or nothing else. Does my lack of clothing bother you?" I asked, lifting a brow with the question, crossing my arms over my chest, studying the tick in his jaw.

"You're wearing a tank top that is showing off those perky nipples that I want to suck on. Your shorts, if you can even call them that, expose every curve of that tight little body, leaving very little to the imagination. It's making me want to bend you over the nearest hard surface, spread those tight thighs apart, and fuck you hard. So, yes, Remington, your lack of dress *is* bothering me." His gaze scorched a trail over my exposed flesh, leaving me in a smoldering pile of ashes at his feet.

"Yeah, so that happened, and it was hot!" Nyx announced, licking her lips as she hiked a thumb toward Rhys. "You need to say yes."

"He wasn't asking," I argued, still holding Rhys's heated stare.

"My word, Remi," she chuckled, patting my cheek. "You're so clueless it both hurts and endears you to me immensely. When a man says your lack of clothing makes him want to bend you over, that's an invitation because he wants to do it, telling you about it in explicit detail. If he's saying that, he's literally imagined it in his mind a few times. So the word you're looking for is *oh, hell, yes*."

"That's three words."

"Point in case, I just drew you a map with crayons, and you're worried about how many words I used!"

"I have to make a sword, and my brain is trying to

focus on that at the moment!" I gritted out. I was trying to concentrate on the steps to make Rhys a sword that would knock his ego down a few pegs.

"He is offering you *his* sword!" Nyx argued, staring at me with a pointed look dancing in her eyes.

My attention turned, narrowing on Rhys, who was watching us argue about his so-called offer. His gaze dipped to my mouth where my teeth worried the plump bottom lip, and I imagined him moving to the table, bending me over it, and doing what he'd stated he would. A soft moan slipped past my lips, and I rolled my eyes for falling for Nyx's overactive imagination.

"You just imagined him naked, fucking you! Oh," she said, bouncing from foot to foot. "You're growing up! My little girl is growing up! I couldn't be more proud if you started making porn!"

My jaw dropped, and I shook my head, snapping myself back to reality. "That escalated quickly."

"I went too far with the porn, didn't I? I mean, it's not like I think you should videotape it. At least not until you're sure he won't put it online. I have so many videos, but I mean, people know who I am, and that's not bragging. Yeah, a few need to see certain parts before they believe it is me, but hey, a girl has to eat, after all. Right?" She took in my horrified expression and snorted. "Yeah, I lost you again, didn't I?"

I rubbed my temples before counting to ten. "Let's just begin, shall we?" I asked, not sure I ever wanted to look online again in my lifetime. There were just certain parts of your best friend you didn't want to see, ever. "I will try not to take too long, but I do take pride in my work. Swords are a lot more work than arrows, arrowheads, or bullets. I don't half-ass anything, Van Helsing. Also, no one should try to enter the room until I've hit the last cooling phase."

I stepped into the room, closing it behind me, moving to the thermostat, and cranking it up to five-hundred degrees. Nyx started the timer, knocking her knuckles against the glass before I nodded, tying my hair up, preparing to work.

I grabbed the bars of metal, weighing each one before tossing them into the cauldron on the glowing coals. Sweat beaded on my neck, running down my temples as I peered up at the thermostat. My gaze swung to Nyx, who was watching me, her eyes slightly widening at the sight of sweat.

"Adjust it by forty minutes," I said before grabbing the body patch that kept track of my temperature to slap it over my shoulder.

Rhys had a top-notch metalsmith room that was about to kick my ass. I placed the mold on the table before me, grabbing the cauldron without gloves or protection, and dumped the contents of the melted metals into the blade mold. Once I finished pouring, I set the cauldron down, pushing my bare hands into the ice-cold water set beside the table. I turned to gauge Rhys's response outside the room. His eyes were locked on my hands as if expecting them to be charred.

After a few moments had passed, I poured cold water over the mold to solidify the metal. The hiss of steam comforted my mind, soothing over me as a soft smile played on my mouth. I loved creating weapons, but Winchester had warned me several times not to make anything other than ammo. Though, she had never told me why or what was so dangerous about the process.

Next, I pulled the glowing red blade from the fire and carefully placed it into the water, looking over the shape. I pulled it out quickly, and set it back onto the coals to keep the metal at the heated temperature I needed, placing it on a long table, grabbing the hammer beside me. I started shaping the sword slowly, pounding the hammer against it as sweat dripped down my face, sizzling against the glowing metal. I beat it slowly, forcing it into the correct shape, solidifying the metal together.

Once the metal became too hard, I placed it back into the forge and hummed with magic, slowly holding my hands over the blade to enhance its strength. Silently, I added detailed runes, slowly etching them into the dragons I engraved over the blade. As an extra touch, I added the Van Helsing crest on the chest of the dragons. Rhys's name sat on the other side of the sword, written in old lettering that enhanced the weapon's overall look.

I repeated the steps until I was satisfied with my creation. Moving to the thermostat, I turned the temperature down, spinning on my heel to stand near the glass wall where Nyx waited. Her lips turned up as she and I began to do jumping jacks, her eyes never leaving mine, laser-focused as the room started dropping in temperature at a dangerous speed.

My forge had been built by me, allowing the temperature to drop over time. Rhys didn't have that option, which meant I'd have to keep moving or chance hurting myself. I'd known that coming into it, since most didn't plan for a person to be within the room as the weapon finished curing.

My eyes fluttered closed, and Nyx slammed her hands on the glass, jolting them back open. "Look at me! You keep moving, Remington Aliana Silversmith. You don't close your eyes. Understood?" she snapped, her eyes wild with worry.

"Got it," I stammered, and immediately started moving again.

I followed her lead, dropping to the ground to do pushups, lunges, and then back up to do more jumping jacks. She kept her eyes bouncing between my armband that told her my temperature, and my eyes that grew heavy. My body fought the urge to go into shock at the extreme temperatures with the sluggish movements we made.

"What is happening?" Rhys demanded.

"It's normal. At least when Remi makes swords," Nyx snapped, dismissing him to focus on me. "She isn't a bladesmith. She's a damn silversmith. Swords are harder because they need more metal. High temperature is needed and frigid temperatures too. It just went from being 500 degrees in there to 100 below freezing."

"That's impossible. She's mortal."

"Have you never watched a Silversmith work before?" Nyx asked, and my eyes narrowed as ice dusted my lashes.

"No one has," he growled.

My head turned, staring at the room packed full of

men, all watching me do jumping jacks. I scowled and would have rolled my eyes had they not been trying to freeze in the position they were currently in, forcing me to blink repeatedly. I paused, moving to the thermostat to bring it back up, then withdrew the blade from the fire to grind it down.

My family was going to crucify me. No wonder they never let me outside. I hadn't known that no one had never before watched a Silversmith forge a blade before, let alone how we created our pieces in extreme temperatures. Winchester was going to skewer me, and I was going to deserve it.

I held the sword to the machine, watching as sparks flew from it before lowering it to eye-level. Turning off the grinder, I gazed at the sides, then running my hand over it, bringing up a bloodied palm. I held the blood over the blade, watching as it dripped on the design, turning the metal golden in color as my blood magic fueled the protection runes.

I whispered the magic enhancement spell, lifting the sword to place into the cooling water, and then lifted it out to test the metal's temperature, making sure it was safe to touch. I stepped on a button on the floor, as a wood statue emerged from the ground, covered in gouges where other blades had left marks, and I smirked.

Holding Rhys's stare, I lifted the blade as I spun, sending the sword in a spinning move before releasing one hand and slammed the blade through the wooden frame. I never broke Rhys's gaze as the statue severed into two pieces, proving that I was worth my weight in gold—or silver. The door buzzed open, and I walked out of the room covered in sweat, still holding the blade in my hands.

"For you, Rhys Van Helsing," I stated over the excited chatter in the room. My words stopped all talk. Rhys narrowed his eyes on mine, lowering them to the artwork of the blade.

"Are you sure you want to do that?"

"It was made for you. I'm pretty sure no one else will want it with your name engraved on it." I frowned, noticing the expressions on the men's faces. It was just a damn sword. So why did they look worried?

"Remington Silversmith, are you sure you want to give me your silver?" Rhys repeated carefully, holding his hands out.

"If you don't want it, brother, I'll take it," Cole chuckled, but his eyes held wonder as he looked between Rhys and me, and then turned to Acyn, who looked frozen in place.

"I made it for you, Rhys. Why is everyone acting weird?" I asked. I stepped back from him, but he grabbed the blade before I could step back any further or change my mind.

"I accept, Remington Silversmith. I accept your silver and your blade."

"This is weird, even by my standards," Nyx stated awkwardly.

"I may need that sword back," I frowned, watching his eyes smiling like a cat who just tasted cream for the first time.

"Once a Silversmith offers a Van Helsing her silver,

it's unbreakable," Rhys said, holding the blade so his brothers could take in the details.

He didn't seem impressed by the sword and had barely looked at the fine details. Instead, he watched me like he'd captured me or just found something so unique that he wasn't sure how to handle it at all.

"Why do I feel like I just did something foolish?" I asked, swaying on my feet as Nyx steadied me with her hand.

Rhys smiled and turned to see his brothers and his men salivating over the sword I'd made. They pointed to the dragons and their family crest before noting the runes etched within the dragon's scales.

It was the finest weapon I'd ever crafted, and I had taken some precautions. You know, because I wasn't a total idiot. Rhys couldn't use the blade to draw Silversmith blood or it would shatter.

Nyx caught me as I swayed on my feet. Rhys sheathed the blade, stepping to me and lifting my sweat-covered body into his arms. The grin was still smugly on his face as he walked us out of the room and started up the winding staircase that led to a secret passageway into his bedroom.

"My room is fine," I grumbled.

"That is the finest blade I have ever seen in my entire life, Remington. Thank you for the gift of your silver. You'll stay in my room tonight, as Cole is staying as well. I'd rather you be near me when he is in residence. I am uncertain of his newest plan to pay me back for the Silversmith he lost, and I'd rather he not use you against me, all things considered."

"All that animosity is over a Silversmith who played you both?"

"Roslyn was supposed to become my wife until I found out she had lured my mother to her father and betrayed me."

"Ouch." Rhys laid me down the softest mattress I'd ever been on in my life. I sank into it as it formed around me, cradling me. "Our families really went at one another, didn't they?"

"They did, but none of yours had ever offered their silver to us, until you, Remi."

"Shit, I did do something dumb."

He smirked as he stripped and undressed, staring into my eyes. "That depends on how you look at it."

"I can't look at it, Rhys. I have no idea what the hell it even means."

"You offered me a part of your soul, Remington. Our curse is a blood bond created by powerful magic. You and I are already bonded by that, since we sort of shared body fluids." I grimaced, and he chuckled at my response. "Now, the deepest bond a Silversmith and a Van Helsing can ever share is when he vows to protect her against her enemies, and she gives him her silver. I vow to protect you against your enemies, for they are now mine. You are a part of me, and I am now a part of you, Remington Silversmith. From this day forward, you are my silver, and I am your strength and protection."

"What did you do?" I gasped, fighting to sit up past the spinning in my head as light blinded me. He held my hand, smiling wickedly while watching my panic unfold.

Pain filled my chest, as if something within me clicked, and settled into place. I shook my head, anxiety rushing through me, while blinding pain throbbed in my head. Rhys gritted his teeth, holding his chest as if he felt the same pain. Still holding my hand, Rhys lowered his mouth, claiming my lips in a pain-filled kiss that sent lightning rods rushing through me as tears slipped from my eyes.

"It hurts, Rhys. Stop it!" I pleaded, but he couldn't, and I knew it without him having to tell me. I heard his teeth gritting together, grinding over enamel as he groaned against my mouth.

"Remi," he whispered, lifting his eyes to study the tears swimming in mine. "Breathe, beautiful girl. Stop fighting me. Just let it happen."

"It hurts!" I screamed, feeling like my insides were filling with lava instead of the blood that had once run through my veins.

"That's because you're fighting the part of me that is combining with you."

"What the hell? Why would you do this?" I whispered thickly, swallowing past the pain.

"I did it so that you can never harm me with your silver, and in return, I can never raise arms against you. I outplayed you, and your mother. The glyphs that glowed on your pretty face inside your home? They're the sign of a newly born alpha to the House of Silversmith. I wasn't certain at first, since it's been hundreds of years since anyone has seen the glyphs of a newborn alpha heir. You are the strongest Silversmith I have encountered, which means your mother strategically chose your father to breed a new alpha."

"I'm more of an omega." I shivered as his eyes dipped to my mouth, slowly lifting to hold mine before he continued speaking, ignoring my outburst.

"The Silversmiths have always had a female alpha. Your house will not rise again, because you're now my silver, and I will never allow it."

So that happened.

I was going to end up helping my sister crucify me at this rate. I should have known there was a reason he wanted a sword. Why would my family ever think waiting to tell me this shit was a good idea?

He'd just outsmarted me, and I thought I was the one being smart! My mother hadn't taught me anything. And our lore? It wasn't in books. The stories were rumors, because we had people who went around erasing any trace that we'd ever existed from records. There was no correct history about us in the libraries, only fictional shit that people romanticized. So how was I supposed to know what not to do, or to do, if no one told me?

"Rhys, I think we should break up. It's not you, it's me. I'm a dumb ass. I am so stupid! They're going to hang me up, and I am going to hand them the bat to use me as a human piñata!"

"First, they'd have to get to you. Second, you're mine to protect now, so that scenario isn't happening. Get some sleep. Beltane comes this week, and I can't have my silver worn out before the witches' celebration.

I am throwing a ball that is open to every Alpha House and their family members. I can't wait to show you off."

"I'm going to be sick that day, sorry."

"Go to sleep, woman. You worked for fourteen hours straight on a blade today. You were sexy in that room, dripping sweat as you held burning metal in your pretty, bare hands. How did you hold the metal straight from the fire? Better question, Silversmith, how did you live through being in a room that was 590 degrees as a mortal?" I swallowed as his eyes narrowed on the pulse beating wildly on my neck. "That's what I thought. They didn't die in that fire, did they? It's why they never allowed anyone to see them work. It wasn't to keep the magic a secret. It was to keep other aspects of their nature a secret."

Yup, I was a dead woman walking. I hadn't even considered that when I'd felt the urge to make his blade. I'd wanted to impress Rhys, and by doing so, I'd exposed my family's secrets. I'd watched that fire burning, and while the children had more than likely perished, their parents had snuck out through the secret panel in the library and lived, and I'd known it. That hadn't clicked, though, not until just now as he'd asked the questions on the edge of my brain, the ones I'd shoved into a box to look at later, once I was free.

I hated *ah-ha* moments, but worse; I now understood why no one had ever told me the important things. I was an open book, a source of information without even realizing I was spewing it until I'd fucked up so badly that I couldn't take it back.

"Don't beat yourself up too bad, Remi. I've had a

couple of lifetimes to learn how to get the things I want without torturing my prey. You're young. Give it time, and you'll learn how to keep those secrets better."

Chapter Fourteen

The next morning, women came to my room to take measurements, fitting me for a dress. This situation was made more uncomfortable by Rhys sitting in the room, pretending to work while the women measured me in my panties and tank top. I'd bathed for over an hour to alleviate the aches and pains from standing in front of the forge the day before. I hadn't even realized I'd been in that room for fourteen hours straight until Rhys had told me.

The forge was my safe haven. The place I escaped to when things weighed down on me. I wasn't shocked to learn I'd been within it for hours without realizing exactly how long. I was surprised to hear people speaking about the sword I'd given to Rhys today. They acted like I'd gotten down on one knee and proposed. Which, I guessed, was what I had involuntarily done in the way our world worked? It was insane archaic type of shit, for sure.

"Stand up straight, ma'am," someone whispered. I bristled, standing up to square my shoulders while Rhys's eyes lifted from the laptop in front of him, locking with mine.

His mouth tipped up at the corners, watching me fidget beneath his intense stare. I felt like I was on display. Lifting my arms, multiple sets of hands measured every inch of me. I wanted to hide from them, sneak back into the forge, and create more weapons, but mostly to use on the obtuse jerk who had outwitted me.

I was so out of my league here. I wasn't sure why my mother had ever thought it wise to wait to educate me about our enemies. Had I known anything about the Van Helsings, I may have armed myself better to deal with Rhys. Instead, I was in his mansion, being fitted for a dress for Beltane.

"Finish. Remi needs to eat," Rhys said, lowering his stare back to his laptop as he began typing quickly. The sound of the keys was almost soothing compared to the silence of the room when he stopped. "Have the ingredients for her bath ordered as well. Roses and daisies are preferred. See that she has them available to her. I want her dress to be silver, but to keep to tradition, have ribbons that match her pretty eyes added to the corset, along with the necklace I had made for her. I also want what lies beneath her dress to match as well. Make sure there is a pouch sewn into her dress. It needs to contain rosebuds, primrose, mint, and the rowan tree's bark within the pouch. Come, Remington. Let's get you something to eat and drink before we head to the sanctuary to meet with the other alphas who wish to verify your existence."

"I don't wish to be displayed like something you own. You don't own me, Rhys," I stated, crossing my arms to glare at him while he slowly moved toward me.

"Everyone out," he ordered.

I watched the women scuttling out of the room. I swallowed as Rhys settled in front of me, smiling with heat pooling in his eyes. Before I could guess his move, he reached up and ripped the shirt from my body. Stepping back, he watched as I lifted my hands to cover my breasts. My breathing grew labored beneath the smoldering intensity of his stare.

"You're beautiful, woman."

"You needed to rip my shirt off to say that?" I asked, lifting a brow.

He vanished from sight, and I stood there silently, looking around the room. I started to move away from the spot I was in, but hands grabbed me from behind. One snaked up around my throat, while the other settled on my belly, slowly moving down to push beneath my panties. I whimpered as his fingertips pushed through my sex, feeling the pull of his magic as he walked me toward the couch he'd been sitting on.

Rhys pushed me down, staring at my body, lowering himself between my thighs. I started to sit up, but he grabbed my legs beneath my knees, pushing them up until my back was leaned into the couch. Rhys lowered his mouth, slowly dragging his heated breath over the inside of my thighs. He smiled at the moan that escaped my lips, watching my chest rise and fall with the storm he created.

"I want to spread you apart and devour your pretty

pussy. Do you want me to do that? You let my demon savor you, and I only got to lick your sweet taste from my lips, little one. Can I make you come for me, Remi? Can I drink you, and hear your sweet noises?" he asked in a hoarse voice that ran up my spine, creating heat that pulsed in my core dangerously.

His hands lifted to my hips, hooking through my panties, removing them smoothly. His passionate gaze feasted on my flesh, and before I could voice any denial, his mouth lowered to my pussy, lavishing it like his favorite flavor of ice cream melting on the cone. I cried out as pleasure rushed through me, my hips rocking for him as he chuckled darkly.

Releasing my legs, Rhys allowed them to drop onto his shoulders. He pushed two fingers into my body; slowly groaning as I moaned at the fullness they created. My entire body pulsed with pleasure, red-hot desire that fueled ecstasy burning through my core enveloped me.

Rhys moaned against my clit, as if my pleasure turned him on. I pushed my hands through his hair, holding him to me as my body started to unravel. I cried out as light burst behind my eyes, trembling violently as his fingers moved faster. He sucked my clit harder until I was held in the thralls of the release, needing more from him.

He sat up, working the buttons of his suit pants with the urgency to give me what I needed. I hurried him, rocking my need before his greedy stare. His thickness pressed against my opening, and I arched, working the thick tip into my body's tightness. He smirked at the sight of his cock, which wasn't going to be an easy fit.

Someone pounded on the door, and he growled an inhuman noise, turning as his head cocked to the side, listening. I shivered, watching him as he turned back, gazing at my core that he still stroked. He leaned over, clamping his mouth around a nipple, and I moaned as he laughed against the heated peak. He worked his cock, rubbing it against my core.

I closed my eyes against the multitude of sensations he was creating. He started to move forward, stretching my body as I whimpered, but the pounding at the door intensified until he pulled back, grinding his teeth as he watched my body trying to accommodate his.

"Do not move, woman," he ordered, standing without warning.

I grabbed the throw blanket from the back of the couch, staring at him as he adjusted his cock in his suit pants. He smiled down at me as I realized what I'd been about to do. Blinking, I watched him silently moving to the door, opening it to reveal Cole, who entered without invitation.

"Are you intending to keep the alphas waiting? That's just bad manners, and so unlike you, brother," Cole stated, sitting on the couch beside me, placing his hand on my naked thigh.

He smiled, lowering his pretty eyes to the panties that sat by my feet, and then slowly slid them to the blanket I held against my body like armor.

"I have an hour before I'm expected at the bar, asshole. Did you actually need something?" Rhys asked, licking his lips slowly, which caused my cheeks to heat.

"There was an attack today, which you would know if you weren't trying to get balls-deep into Remi. The factory was broken into, and five workers were injured severely. Don't worry, *bro*. I sent a team to handle it. Care to share her?" Cole asked, lifting me onto his lap. Staring at Rhys, I grasped on to the blanket. "Stop squirming, Remi. I'd hate to hurt you," he growled, pulling my legs apart as he removed the blanket.

Cole's fingers held the inside of my thighs, forcing my legs apart. I watched Rhys's eyes dip to my core, heating with need as they slid over the arousal he'd created. He didn't move, didn't show any emotion as I was held open for him. Cole's lips brushed against my throat, holding Rhys's stare before he released his hold, letting my legs rest on his before his fingers brushed against my sex.

"Can I destroy you, Remington? Let me fuck your tight cunt while Rhys watches me wrecking you. I want to see him fight that monster within him, knowing you are coming for me. I bet he'd uncage the demon for you." Cole's hands moved, slowly parting my sex as tears filled my eyes. My heart pounded against my ribs while Rhys just stared, and worse, he was turned on by watching Cole play with me.

"Let me go, now," I growled, standing up the moment he released me.

I didn't wait for either one to speak or apologize. I threw open the door and started out of it, only to hear crashing sounds behind me. I came face to face with two knights wearing actual armor. One pulled his cloak off, rushing forward to offer it.

"Ma'am," he whispered, taking in the tears rolling from my eyes. "Please take it before you incite a riot with your beauty."

I accepted the cloak, covering my body as the sound of glass shattering filled the hallway. Grunts and groans followed it, and then the entire wall shook as something slammed against it. I didn't wait to figure out what was happening or if they were fighting. I just wanted the floor to open up and swallow me whole.

Rushing up the stairs, I entered my bedroom, rushing into the shower. Turning on the water, I slid beneath the spray, dropping the cloak onto the shower floor. Angry tears burned my eyes as I reached for the soap, washing my body until it was red and sore. I fought to remove both men's touches.

The door opened, and I spun around, staring at Rhys, who peered down at the soaked cloak in the shower. His eyes held worry, and yet he didn't look apologetic. He looked pissed off at me.

"I can't stop him from touching you. You can, though. If I do it, he'll only want to hurt you more to get to me."

"Get out," I whispered, turning around to dismiss him.

"I'll have food ordered at the bar for you. Get dressed and be downstairs in twenty minutes. If you're not ready, I'll take you to the bar naked, Remi. Don't make me into the bad guy. If I had reacted, he'd only worsen in his need for revenge. Cole has never forgiven me for what he saw as a trespass against him, even though the woman he loved was nothing but a murderous Silversmith whore. He couldn't see her for the monster she was, and he was too young at the time to see the bigger picture unfolding. I do not intend to share you, but I also won't give him what he wants, which is to make him think you're a weakness for me. You're not, and to pretend otherwise would only paint a target on your back. You have sixteen minutes now. I suggest you climb out of there and get over whatever it is that is bothering you."

"I was just spread apart and violated, and you did nothing!"

"I couldn't react."

"I don't belong here," I groaned, exiting the shower to grab a towel, shouldering past him.

I walked to my backpack, pulling out a skirt and blouse. I dressed quickly, feeling his burning stare on my spine. I ran a brush through my hair, slipping a band around it, creating a messy bun, then slid my feet into sandals.

"Ready, asshole."

I left him standing in the room as I walked down the stairs to where Cole stood with a smug smile on his lips. He watched me approaching him silently, opening his mouth to speak, but my hand cracked across his cheek, forcing his head to snap to the side with a comforting noise. Slowly, his eyes settled back on me with heat burning within them.

"Don't you ever fucking do that to me again," I hissed. Cole looked at Rhys before he turned back toward me, smiling as if he found me intriguing. "If I want to fuck you, I'll let you know. Otherwise, don't touch me, Cole Van Helsing. I'm not yours or Rhys's fucking plaything. Don't use me to get revenge for something that happened before I was even born. That isn't fair to me, and I sure as shit have never wronged you. Don't wrong me."

I took in the pain that entered his eyes and watched it vanish before I could investigate it further. His cocky grin slipped back into place, and he stepped closer, running his finger over my cheek.

"Careful, Silversmith," Cole said huskily, as if hurting him had turned him on. "I consider that foreplay, and after smelling your arousal, I'm officially fucking interested in you. You smell fucking addictive, and I like addictive things. Especially when they come in such a pretty package," he chuckled. Pulling me against him, he lowered his forehead to rest against mine. "I'm going to have you one way or another, Sunshine. Do hurry up and let Rhys down gently, yeah?"

"Go to hell," I whispered, pushing Cole away from me, even though he didn't budge.

"Enough! We'll be late," Rhys said from beside me. I followed the knights out of the front door, listening as Rhys grabbed Cole's arm. "Take the hint, asshole. She isn't interested. After your little fucking stunt, we'll have to pick another brother to seduce her, so that we can finish this. Stop working against me and start working with me if you want revenge against the Silversmiths."

I didn't hear what else was said as I crawled into the limo, finding Nyx waiting for me. She smiled, holding out strawberries and a flute of champagne.

"It's the good stuff, taste it!" she smiled, dropping it in the bucket as she took in the anger burning in my eyes.

"We have to get out of here, Nyx," I whispered, barely loud enough that it was audible to my own ears.

"Fucking try it, Silversmith," Acyn chuckled, peering around Nyx, where she sat on his lap, gulping down champagne. "You gave Rhys your silver. He owns you now. Welcome to the world of immortals, where every good deed gets you fucked harder than the last one." His nose lifted, and his pierced eyebrow brushed against his hairline. "You already get fucked hard, sweetheart?" he asked, narrowing his eyes on Cole, who climbed into the car, sporting a black eye, his lip freshly cut open. Rhys sat beside me, peering over at Acyn, who grimaced at the black eye Rhys now wore too. "Bloody hell," he growled. "Choose a cock, sweetheart, and ride it already. I can't endure another pussy war like the last one."

"I choose neither," I snorted as the door shut, and we started down the driveway.

Chapter Fifteen

The bar was empty, other than the few men who sat around a large table set in the center of what I assumed was the dancefloor, considering the lights around the area. Rhys walked me to a chair, pulling it out as he waited for me to sit, pushing me closer to the table before sitting beside me at the head of it.

Men, and I use that term loosely, turned to take in my features. Their stares burned my flesh with the intensity of the way they studied me. Only a few females had joined, and they looked me over with ridicule and boredom, as if I belonged on the bottom of their stiletto heels instead of at the table with them.

"Ladies and gentlemen, welcome to House Van Helsing sanctuary." Rhys placed a card on the table, and one by one, the creatures around it reached for it to sign. They passed the card around, silently handing it back to Rhys with everyone's signature.

"Really, Van Helsing? What game are you playing?

This... child is not a Silversmith. Her coloring is all wrong, and she is rather... mundane. I've seen prettier creatures in the back of a whorehouse." I turned, studying the cold persona of the woman that spoke. Violet eyes narrowed on me as she smiled, tilting her head. "You couldn't even pass her off to newborns as a Silversmith."

"I agree. She lacks, well, everything that would mark her house," another woman stated, her eyes smiling as they took in the frown playing on my face.

"If you wanted me here to fuck me, Rhys, I assure you, you didn't need the others. I rather enjoy your cock enough to come willingly," a woman stated, heels clicking over the floor as she reached the table. Placing her blood-red nails on his shoulder, she leaned over, kissing his cheek. "I have missed you while I've been away, Love."

"Sit down, Eloisa. I didn't call you here to fuck," Rhys stated, his eyes turning to lock with mine. "I assure you, Remington is indeed a Silversmith, and full-blooded at that."

"That's impossible, darling. She doesn't even have the telltale markings of a Silversmith. Her hair, while gaudy, is naturally red. Her eyes are also not hidden beneath contacts. Witch, maybe. Silversmith, not a chance in Hades' whorehouse. And I should know, I've visited it often enough over the centuries." Eloisa grabbed my face, turning my cheek, and I yanked back, glaring up at her as she narrowed her eyes. "She looks like Roslyn, or at least her eyes do," she said breathlessly, gripping my chin until it ached.

"Indeed, she does," Rhys agreed. "She is her niece,

after all."

"That's impossible, and you know it. We helped you murder the Silversmiths, Van Helsing. All of us jeopardized everything to help you find justice for your mother and your brothers' wives and children. There are no full-blooded Silversmiths left alive."

My stomach clenched as Cole snorted, and Acyn joined him, turning cold eyes on me. Acyn lifted his hands and folded them on the table, staring at me as he spoke. "I'm aware of what you all sacrificed and placed on the line after the Silversmiths murdered my mother, and hunted down my children like animals, butchering my wife and leaving her womb outside her body with my dead, unborn son rotting inside. This girl is a full-blooded Silversmith, and that's a fucking problem for everyone. She's mortal. That means there's a full-blooded mother who birthed her into this world running around out there somewhere," Acyn hissed, holding my gaze.

Rhys placed the blade I'd made onto the table, and everyone stood, looking at the craftsmanship. "Lucky for us, Remington wasn't taught much about the war between our bloodlines before she ran away from Elizabeth," Rhys stated, and everyone turned to look at him before examining me once more. "She made this sword and gifted me her silver."

"You accepted it? Was she forced? If she was, it's invalid. Do you intend to offer her your protection? Elizabeth was the best Silversmith they ever produced, born of a pure lineage. Her children were always stronger than the others, and you think to claim this girl in the ancient ways of their line? You've gone mad, Van

Helsing."

"How so, Griselda? I claimed the strongest Silversmith I have ever encountered. By claiming Remington, I have ensured that she can never raise silver against me or my house. Look at her work and tell me that it isn't better than anything Elizabeth or Roslyn ever created in their lifetime. But even better than that, I was shown exactly how a Silversmith creates their silver. In fact, my brothers and my knights also watched her crafting the blade before you."

"And what did you learn?" Griselda asked, her eyes lowering to hold mine.

"That the Silversmiths probably sacrificed their staff and their own children to escape the fire, which I assure you, they could have lived through easily. Remington worked for fourteen hours in a room where the heat was five hundred degrees, and yet the room burned hotter due to the forge where she worked. It reached five hundred and ninety degrees, and her body temperature during that time reached a full seven hundred degrees."

Everyone slid their gaze from the blade to me, and I glared at Rhys, who continued. I watched the way every immortal in the room hung on his every word. He was respected by more than just the women who had eye-raped him harder than I had, and that was saying something.

"Things have started to go awry for houses out of nowhere, and nothing has added up. Not until this little Silversmith walked into a fight between Cole and me, murdering a half-blooded Silversmith, shattering her into slivers of silver. Newborn vampires are being created without a sire. We all know a witch can make day-walkers that appear to be vampires, and the wolves have been attacked during the new moon when they're at their weakest points.

"We thought it to be hunters because the bullets weren't fully silver, just laced, but enough so to still kill them. Half-breeds have been turning up dissected, yet still alive with no memory of who took them, or how they were wounded. Only a few creatures can erase memories so deeply that others cannot pull them from their mind." Rhys tapped the blade, smirking. "Then I went to her mother's house, who Remington claimed was missing."

My eyes narrowed on Rhys as the tick in his jaw slowly pulsed. "What I found was the glyphs to control an alpha in their younger years pulsing on the wall when Remington, herself, touched the door to her bedroom. The same glyphs appeared on her flesh. Being that we were very young that last time we'd seen the symbols, it took us a while to add it all together," he explained, and the eyes narrowed on me intently, causing me to fidget beneath their stares.

"What are you saying, Van Helsing?" Griselda asked carefully.

"The house held all the signs of a rising son, but in this case, a daughter since we all know the only alphas in the Silversmith lineage are females. Snakes in the bed of the reigning alpha, a mark that means their time is short as another comes to take it by force, and blood beneath them to signify a sacrifice made. We didn't make it down to the armory, but then none ever do when they try to reach one owned by a Silversmith, as the unknown being protects it. The armory exploded, almost ending Remington's life in the process, but I protected her. I have given her my vow of protection, and she has given me her silver. In the eyes of the old world, she is my wife."

"Excuse me?" I glared, staring at him through narrowed eyes.

"You did it, you claimed her fully. No Van Helsing has ever claimed a Silversmith in the way of the old world, because it was forbidden to protect their house from ever falling. Why would they leave something so precious unguarded in her most vulnerable time?" One of the alphas asked, his lime-green eyes searching mine as if he could find the answer within me.

"Remington ran away from Elizabeth at seventeen. She joined E.V.I.E., and I think Elizabeth thought she was safely hidden within their organization. Had Remi remained in their hold, none of us would have looked for her there. She was their weapons master. She used metals along with her silver, which none of us would have noted unless a solid silver weapon was wielded against us. We'd have had to survive to realize what silver had been used. Remington's silver is powerful, and I'm willing to guess that few have survived it or lived to tell anyone they'd felt the Silversmith silver again."

"I'm not your wife, asshole," I interjected, watching as the tick in his jaw started, but he continued ignoring me. "Is the bar open?" I asked, watching his azure eyes turn toward me for the first time in the last several moments.

"Remington, I'd advise you to hold your tongue."

"I'd advise you to hold your fucking breath, but I don't think you'd die from suffocation, which would make the entire point moot. Now, is the bar open? Because I am reserving the right to get rip-roaring drunk tonight, and, hopefully by doing so, I'll forget what you and your brother did to me. Obviously, you don't need me for your little party. I was just here so you could stroke your male ego at what you found unguarded. I'll go get drunk, and you get your back patted on such a good job for catching a little mortal Silversmith, and using her naïveté to fuck her over."

"You're not moving from your chair. If you'd like to drink, I can order you something. Do you understand me?" Rhys asked, narrowing his eyes as I smirked.

"Yes, Daddy, I understand," I smiled darkly, leaning back while I surveyed the others who watched us with curiosity.

"Now, where were we?"

"At the part where I was hiding in E.V.I.E. where I signed a ten-year contract that is only breakable through death," I stated pointedly, noting he didn't seem to fear them coming. "That means they're coming. My family will also come to get me. They're never going to allow you to keep me. I apparently have a super big mouth, and giveaway shit that I wasn't even aware was a secret. I also tried to be nice and make you a badass blade, which now you assume makes you my husband. Which, by the way, that's some medieval bullshit mentality. I mean, I thought handfasting was outdated. But blade trading? Whew, that one outdates the books, I guess. I've read hundreds of books, and none included the bitch giving him the blade, but lots of them had the rhetorical cock, aka, sword, entering her vagina and bam!" I slapped the table, causing the immortals to jump in their seats, which was a little soothing to my bruised ego. "Bitch is married to Sir Dicks-A-Lot. But hey, you want my sword? I'll peg you so fucking hard you feel me fucking your throat, Van Helsing. I'm down to be dirty with you."

"Are you finished yet?"

"No. Not even close. I did mention my *super* big mouth, right?" I asked, watching his eyes sparkling with anger. "I'm not here willingly, Rhys. You expecting me to sit beside you like a good little bitch, well, that's just unrealistic expectations on your part. I didn't murder your people. I sure as hell wasn't around when our families went to war. I wasn't a part of your twisted as shit backstory, and I don't want to be either. I'm just a girl who likes to make pretty weapons that kill nasty monsters. Is that too much to ask?"

"Actually, it is, Sweetling. You are responsible for the deaths of my creations," a scathing voice slithered down my spine. I turned, watching a blonde move toward me with pale-skinned men beside her.

Vampire.

"Laura, I'm surprised you would lower yourself to come tonight, darling," Cole muttered, glaring at the vampire.

"And miss finding the little bitch that is helping E.V.I.E. hunt down my children? As if. Nikolas, you, of all people, know how attached I am to my children," she sneered, her fangs extending as he smirked, licking his lips as the queen evil bitch gave him a lusty stare.

Her cold ice-blue eyes slid to me, and she slowly moved closer. "You're the weapon master for the Seattle branch, are you not?"

"I am," I said carefully, showing no fear as I faked it until I made it, which was out of this encounter alive, or so I hoped. "They do scream so beautifully when the silver shreds their non-beating hearts. If you want your children to live, all they have to do is follow the rules agreed upon by both you and E.V.I.E. If you can't manage to control your own child, Laura, how the fuck do you manage an entire branch of your house?"

"You're what, twenty, twenty-one at most? You're an infant in this world, and I could end you before you blink, little bitch."

"It would be a fatal flaw to underestimate me right now, Laura. You see, I am very young, but I am highly trained in the call of silver," I stated, standing to come nose to nose with her as my finger lifted, trailing down her cheek. I felt Rhys rising behind me, standing ready to protect me, unaware that I wouldn't need it. "At the moment, I can sense the Ben Wa Balls shoved up that pussy of yours that you're clenching so hard to hold in. There's also a hint of silver sitting in your ass. I'm willing to bet it has enough within it that when I call, it will come. You won't, because well, I'm not trying to get you off here, after all. You have piercings in your nipples, your naval, and your clit. I dig it. Did it hurt? I've actually been considering getting mine done, but I was iffy about it since vaginas are very sensitive areas. Also, the clit has about eighteen thousand nerves in it, and one fuck-up and bye-bye orgasms. Oh, I'm off subject, aren't I? *Anyway.* Before you strike me, those

Ben Wa Balls will come out your eye sockets, ripping their way free through them via every major organ in your body. That bullet in your ass? I'll call it too, and instead of your eyes, it will come out your mouth, which would probably be a shitty deal for you, pun intended.

"Those nipple rings will go into your body, shredding that worthless organ in your chest. And while it doesn't beat, it is needed to run everyone else's blood through your ice-filled veins. That clit ring? Well, I'll just let it rip that vital part of your anatomy apart, because I'm a total bitch like that. I'll be a darling and leave your naval alone, since by then, you'll already be dead enough for me to grab that sword and take that pretty head of yours off your neck. So, I mean, you could try, but in the time I've wagged my tongue, I've called your silver, and I'm willing to watch it work for me, because honestly, I want to see how big those balls are that you're clenching so hard, trying to hold onto." I crossed my arms, watching the anger burning in her eyes as I gave a little yank on the silver, and she shivered. "I can't believe you'd be so stupid to get a text message sent to you about a Silversmith and run right over with all that silver, just begging me to play with it inside your body, Laura. Considering I have been hunting you down with my silver for the last five years after you murdered a ten-year-old child because you wanted her fucking ice cream, that's rather sloppy."

"I will fucking destroy you."

"No, you won't."

She lunged, and I ignited with power, watching as she dropped to her knees. The silver rushing through her as it ripped her apart. My eyes swirled as my veins glowed, filling with power. My hair floated, igniting as the power surged through me. I grabbed the blade, swinging it in a wide arch as the other vampires moved forward, following their maker to their grave as their heads bounced across the floor.

I smiled coldly, bending with the blade in my hand to wipe it clean on Laura's gaudy dress. I placed the sword back on the table and sat down with a bored expression as Rhys slid his hand to my thigh silently.

"I didn't know Laura would come intending to harm her, Rhys, you have to believe me," Eloisa said through trembling lips, slowly moving to stand beside him as she slipped into his lap.

Her arms wrapped around Rhys's neck, and she tried to kiss him. But Cole pulled Eloisa over to him, his eyes slowly noting Rhys's hand on my thigh. I relaxed, grateful that I wouldn't be exposing my weakness to a room full of immortal alphas who would seek to use it against me.

"Now, Eloisa, why the fuck would we believe you? Haven't you murdered the last nineteen women that Rhys showed interest in seeing for more than just feeding?" Cole asked, chuckling coldly as he stared at me. His smile turned dark as Eloisa gagged. My eyes lowered to her chest, where Cole's hand protruded through the center, holding her heart out in front of her on display. "Hear me very clearly, everyone. Remington Silversmith is under Van Helsing protection, and an attempt on her life is an attempt on ours. You all know who wins in this fight if we go to war. Remington may have promised Rhys her silver, but her heart," Cole stated, popping Eloisa's like a mushy, oozing balloon of slime, "isn't claimed yet, and at the end of the day, I couldn't give two fucks about who owns her silver, as long as I get her heart." His eyes held mine, forcing me to stare at the blood dripping from his hand.

Rhys snorted, gripping my thigh tightly. He turned, studying me before his eyes dipped to the corpse beside us, who unfortunately wasn't dead yet. Not unless I picked up that sword and removed Laura's head, or Rhys did it. That would start a war, though, and we both knew it. I was willing to do it, considering how evil the cold-hearted bitch was. Killing children was a hard limit for me, and anyone who enjoyed their deaths deserved to die.

"As Remington Silversmith has given me her silver, I stand beside my brother's claim. Other than him claiming her heart, as I have claimed her for myself for now," Rhys stated, watching me carefully to see if I would argue with him. "If anyone has an issue with that, I will hear it now and challenge them and their house to honor my promise of protection. As you all know, a Van Helsing can only give one woman his protection in a lifetime, and I chose Remington Silversmith. I am duty-bound to protect my silver, and I mean to keep that promise." Did that mean he'd married me too? I was so confused about how this shit worked.

"If you're serious about her being the strongest Silversmith you've ever met, then Lord have mercy on you, Rhys Van Helsing, because I don't think she intends to," Griselda said, smiling as she took in the disgruntled look my face. "However, my house will stand with yours, as we have since the beginning. I do, however, think I will remain close by, in the event that something larger is brewing, and you need me at your side, and yours, Silversmith. You may not have the correct coloring, but you hold the fire of a forge within you, which Laura's unfortunate ire exposed."

"Thank you, Griselda," Rhys acknowledged, bowing his head.

One by one, the houses gave Rhys a vow to honor the bond between us, whatever that meant. I hadn't quite figured that part out yet. Nyx's eyes held mine from where she sat on top of the bar, tapping her finger on the glass she held. There was worry in her eyes, and it sent a tightening to the pit of my stomach as she looked away.

If I were a better friend, I'd send Nyx away from the mess I had ended up in, but I was certain after I'd just harmed the alpha vampire's second-in-command, he would be seeking revenge against me in any shape or form he could get it.

Chapter Sixteen

I sat at the bar, gulping down my third margarita as Nyx danced seductively to a heady beat. Acyn watched her with heat banked in his eyes, while Rhys argued with someone over the phone at the bar's far end. Cole sat beside me, our legs touching to maintain contact, to counter the effects of my curse. He studied me as if he stared long enough, I'd cave and fall into his lap. Every few minutes, Rhys would go silent and turn to stare at Cole with a murderous expression. I just wished the alcohol would work quickly, and I could forget the sight of the Ben-Wa balls coming out of Laura's eye sockets.

No matter how hard I lied to myself, I hated inflicting pain on people, even murderous monsters such as Laura. I much preferred to remain in the armory with the forge, creating weapons to wage the silent war against them. It might make me seem weak to these beings, but at least I didn't suffer nightmares for days afterward.

"You keep looking like that, and I'm going to assume you need me to kiss those dark emotions away, Sunshine," Cole said smoothly, pulling my attention toward where he sat.

His long fingers ran over the dew that dripped down the side of the glass from the condensation of ice and alcohol. The smile on his mouth twisted in my peripheral vision as he noted where my attention had gone. His finger slid through the wetness, moving toward his mouth, where his tongue flicked it erotically.

"Penny for your thoughts?" he asked, turning to face me as his eyes slid down my outfit. "I do miss women wearing dresses instead of pants. So much easier to lift them and taste their pretty petals. I bet you make the most delicious sounds when being devoured, Sunshine."

"Does that work on women?" I asked carefully, somehow managing to keep my body from reacting to his seduction. Cole grabbed my hand before I could pull back, and the room faded away from us.

I was seated on the couch from earlier in the day, my legs spread over his thighs, but Rhys wasn't there. Instead, Cole held me, slowly rubbing his thumb in a clumsy circle over my clit. His mouth kissed against my shoulder as he groaned hungrily.

"You were so wet for Rhys, where's my cream, kitty? I want to lavish your pussy until you drip from my tongue. This pussy clenches for me, doesn't it?" Cole asked huskily, pushing his fingertip against my opening. "Can I play with you too? I promise to share you with Rhys. You're a greedy little bitch, and you'd enjoy all of us fucking you. I can sense your desires, your needs, Remington. You're a hungry girl who needs feeding, and Rhys alone couldn't sate you. Not without unleashing his demon, and he's too afraid that he won't be able to shove that gluttonous bastard back into the box once it comes out. I enjoy letting mine play, and he wants to fill this pretty flower full until you're stretched around me, screaming my name as you come. Can I make you come, naughty girl?"

"Stop this," I uttered huskily, closing my eyes and pushing away from Cole as the sound of glass shattering filled the bar. My hands released the shards of glass, and I stared at the blood coating my fingers.

"Fucking idiot," Rhys snapped, grabbing my hands as he peered down at the damage. "Give me a clean towel, Payne."

The bartender handed him a fresh white towel, which Rhys placed on the counter and set my hands on it. His fingers slowly ran over the sliced flesh, finding and pulling out the shards in silence. I winced as Rhys extracted the glass and then watched in trepidation as he nodded to the bartender, who smirked, sidling up to me as he leaned over the bar and licked my wounded flesh. The flash of his elongated fangs had me fighting Rhys's hold on my wrist as the vampire healed the cuts to my fingers with his saliva.

"Stay the fuck out of her head unless she invites you in, brother," Rhys warned Cole, his fingers slowly tracing over my wrist.

"She did invite me in, Rhys. If she hadn't been interested in me, I couldn't access her mind, now could I?" Cole taunted, the tick in his jaw matching Rhys's as I sat between them.

"I'm starting to feel like a bone you dogs are fighting over," I grumbled, lifting the new apple margarita to my lips and downing it in a single drink. I regretted it instantly as the brain freeze hit. I rubbed my forehead, turning to Rhys as his phone chimed again, and his eyes lifted over my shoulder to hold Cole's.

"Take her home, and try not to molest her, at least until Beltane, Nikolas. I have matters that need my immediate attention, Remi. I'll see you later at home," he said absently. "You sleep in my room now. Your things were moved earlier today."

"No, thank you." I snorted, nodding toward the bartender for another drink.

"You've had enough alcohol. If you drink any more, you won't be able to walk. Since Nikolas has left a mess of creatures mucking up my streets for me to handle, you'll more than likely need your wits until I return to you."

"Did you get the part where I said, no thank you? Or are you choosing to ignore me?" I answered pointedly, watching his eyes lift from his phone to hold mine.

"The bed in the room you slept in is broken and tossed into the trash until a new one is ordered. Unless you'd prefer to sleep with Cole in the guest chambers, my bed will have to suffice. I am not willing to compromise your propriety or force you to do anything you don't wish to do, Remington. Cole, on the other hand, would use his magic to create an illusion where you'd be unable to tell fiction from fact, and you'd wake up in a compromised position."

"Like when I woke up sucking your cock?" I asked, enjoying Cole's choking as his drink went down the wrong pipe.

"Indeed. Exactly like that."

"So the difference would be what, exactly?"

"I warned you that you didn't have to do that for me. He'd enjoy it, and you'd end up waking to Cole doing much more than I would have allowed to happen without your consent." Rhys pushed his phone into his pocket, lowering his eyes briefly to my mouth, then lifted them once more to hold mine in silent challenge, daring me to argue with him.

"So you didn't enjoy it?" I asked, narrowing my eyes to the heat burning in his pretty azure gaze. He swallowed, smiling wickedly as he gave me a pointed look.

"I came for you, didn't I?"

"Indeed, you did. That isn't the point. Any bitch can make a man come; men are easy like that. The question wasn't whether you came; it was whether you enjoyed it?"

His eyes moved up and down my face before he chose his words. "I've thought of little else than the feel of your pretty pink lips wrapped around my cock since you smiled with my erection between them. Is that what you wanted to know? If you're asking me if I crave those soft lips around my cock again, Remi, I assure you that the answer is yes."

I swallowed as heat pooled in my core, which clenched as his lips curved into a sexy smirk. He stepped closer, wrapping his fingers through the hair on my nape, and brought his mouth flush against my ear.

"I intend to finish what we started earlier when I get home tonight. I hope to find you naked and waiting for my return. If you're asleep, I'll take that as your denial, and wait for you to be ready to accept this thing between us, woman," he whispered huskily, the gravel embedded in his tone running against my flesh. "Please be naked and waiting, so that I can give you what you crave, and what we both need."

He dragged his soft lips over my cheek, slowly releasing me. Rhys gave me a pointed stare before turning and walking away. I watched him as the knights at the bar entrance turned and walked out behind him, disappearing into the night. My eyes slid from where he'd vanished to Nyx, bent over a table with Acyn behind her.

"That escalated quickly," Cole muttered as he chuckled. "Looks like it's gonna be just you and me tonight, Sunshine. Unlike Rhys, I don't think you've had nearly enough to drink yet."

I exhaled a shuddered breath, grabbing my cup to turn away from the couple going at it, uncaring that everyone here could see them. Of course, it was just me, Cole, and the bartender now, but still. Talk about a hussy. Freaking nymphs, they had one goal, and that was to get off, however, wherever they could. If only life could be so simple. I was almost jealous of her, considering the current need and state of my body. I'd been messed with more in the last few days than in my entire life put together.

"Once Acyn comes, we'll head to the house," Cole

muttered. The groaning and unsexy noises grew louder. "Finish your drink, she's about to use her power to drain his balls."

Cole pulled out his phone, smiling at whatever flashed across his screen before he pushed it back into his pocket. He pulled out a fat cigar, cutting off the end before he lit it. The sickly sweet scent of tobacco filled the bar. I turned my attention to the embers at the end of it. Exhaling, he puffed a cloud of smoke into the air, forcing my eyes to his lips as he licked them slowly. My eyes moved to his reflection in the mirror behind the bar, watching galaxies move in his eyes as he grinned.

"Or we can find a room here, and you can show me how those pouty lips of yours look around my cock, Remington."

I lifted my drink, downing it as I felt the alcohol catching up to me. Cole smiled before taking another puff of the thick cigar. "Chicken. I bet you shocked the shit out of Rhys when he woke up with your pretty lips wrapped around him. Rhys seems whole, Remington. But he isn't. He doesn't allow anyone to get past the shields he erected over his heart after what Roslyn did to us. She fucked us harder than anyone else ever had. The moment he fucks you, his interest will wane, and you'll be another broken-hearted female he'll add to his long list. Of all of us that Roslyn toyed with, she fucked Rhys the hardest. He was the loyal knight who jumped when she called, doing what she asked without question. Rhys loved her. He thought she wanted to marry him and make a life and give him children."

"But not you?" I asked softly, watching the

darkness pooling in his gaze.

"I knew she was a monster. I was okay with that. I was okay with her fucking my brothers and her obsession to conquer the entire Van Helsing male population with her loose cunt. Rhys, though, he loved that evil bitch even though I don't think he realized it until after she'd died. When she helped her father murder our mother, Rhys was the one she used to lure Mother to them, and then she made it known to the world that our mom died because Rhys Van Helsing was weak and unable to deny her anything. I hated him for it, but not because of Roslyn." Cole swallowed, lifting his drink before he took another drag from the cigar.

"Our mother was gentle and everything beautiful. Rhys thinks I hate him because he was her knight, but I never wanted to be a knight. I wanted to be a monster, and in that aspect, I got my wish. I hated him because he couldn't see who that evil whore was, not even after I proved it by fucking her in front of him and bringing women and men for her to use while she made him watch without joining. Don't get me wrong, Sunshine. We're all fucked up, and we enjoy what we've become. Rhys took it as a punishment and has refused to allow his other half out to play. He was always the better man, the knight who needed to save the world. Roslyn just exploited it and him until he faced the truth. Rhys will fuck you, and when he's finished, he'll walk away because he's Rhys Van Helsing, and to punish himself, he won't let anyone love him again. I, on the other hand, will be waiting to catch you after you fall, Silversmith. I'm always the second choice, and I've learned to live with it."

"You should never be anyone's second choice, Cole. Nobody should ever settle for second place, because you are someone's first choice. You just have to find her." I studied the way his eyes tightened, and he shook his head.

"Just don't fall in love with him. He isn't interested in more than a one-night stand. I don't want to see you fall and end up hurt, little one. And those who fall for Rhys, they always fall the hardest."

Chapter Seventeen

We piled into the stretch limo, and I leaned my head against Nyx's as the car lurched forward in the direction of the estate. Cole spoke to Acyn in a hushed tone, and I ignored them. What Cole said earlier ran through my head and worried me.

I didn't assume I'd end up falling for Rhys. But then, people didn't ever plan to do anything so stupid. If I were being honest, I wouldn't admit to wanting him if asked. The thing was, I only wanted him for a one-night stand, and if Cole had been trying to sway me from that course, he hadn't.

My eyes closed as the car moved down the highway toward a housing development still in the midst of being built. I'd actually considered buying one of the condos for when I came to visit my mother, but quickly squashed the idea when I saw the hefty price tag that came with the yearly maintenance fees.

A light caught my eye as a whistling noise filled

the night. I sat up, watching as it sailed toward us. My eyes rounded, and my mouth opened to scream out a warning, but it was too late. The car was struck, and began flipping non-stop until it finally came to a rest, upside-down.

My ears rang as screaming sounded. The muffled noises reached my brain as I watched Cole and Acyn, righting their large frames in the car. Cole withdrew his phone, punching in a code before shoving it back into his pocket. Hands grabbed me and pulled me out of the bent, twisted metal. The scent of fire singed my nose, and I gasped as everything went silent. Acyn set a dazed Nyx beside me, reaching into the car, ripping the seats apart as he produced blades.

"Remington, are you alright?" Cole asked, studying my face between his large hands. "Answer me, woman! Dammit!" he snapped. Peering down at his glowing pocket, Cole withdrew the phone, staring up at Acyn, who watched the direction from where the missile had come. "She's alive, asshole. Hurt, but alive. Yeah, I fucking know it isn't good. Send a fucking team and get us the fuck out of here now." Cole hung up the phone and touched the side of my head, causing me to wince.

Shouting started from nearby, and Cole growled, leaning into the burning car, withdrawing a pair of wicked looking blades. What the hell? We'd been sitting on an arsenal of weapons without knowing it!

"Do not move, do you understand me?" Cole warned, his eyes sliding to the side of my head, where I could feel a throb and wetness. "Bloody hell, that looks bad."

"They're not going anywhere, but we're about to

be fucking surrounded, Nikolas. Let's release some steam, brother," Acyn chuckled. The sound of the wickedness in his tone sent a shiver racing up my spine.

The moment the brothers were out of sight, I turned, finding Nyx glaring at me. Her tawny head shook as she looked in the direction the men had gone. She frowned, moving her attention from my eyes to the side of my head that dripped blood.

"You're going to make me run, aren't you?" she asked, and I nodded, wincing at the pain. "He has a really nice cock, Remi. It's a shame to abandon it. It's tough to find a decent looking guy, who actually knows how to use his nice cock."

"We have to go now," I grunted, crawling to my knees to watch as the men engaged the creatures swarming them. "They're outnumbered. If they fall, we're toast."

"Can you feel any silver?" she asked, frowning as I shook my head. "Fine, let's go."

She moved to me, helping me to my feet as we turned, staring at the vacant condos that were little more than wood structures. Nyx didn't let go of me, moving into the shadows of the night, slipping behind one of the large buildings to take a breath. Her eyes zeroed in on my head, and her hand lifted, touching the wound.

"We probably should have stayed and let you heal before we made a daring escape from captivity, Remi. Your head looks bad."

"I've had worse before. We need to keep moving."

She nodded, even though she didn't look

convinced. I swayed on my feet as we ducked inside a building. Cutting through it, we made a run for the woods. Once inside the foliage, Nyx stalled, turning to look over her shoulder.

"Someone is following us, and it's not a Van Helsing." She grabbed me, holding up my weight easily, rushing us toward the sound of gurgling water.

At the large body of fast-running water, she twisted and peered through the darkness as we entered the creek and began floating. I didn't need a play-by-play to figure out it was immortals tracking us, and that more than likely, they were doing so by the scent of my wound. I dunked my head beneath the water, using my fingers to scrub the blood away from my scalp. Nyx pulled me with her, moving us toward an overhanging rock that jutted out over the bank.

We slipped beneath it, and I lowered the wounded side of my head into the water to keep the scent moving with the flow of the rushing creek away from our location. Thankfully, we were in Washington, where creeks were the size of rivers in most other states.

"I smell them. One is definitely bleeding."

"No shit, idiot. The others won't be able to keep the Van Helsings busy for long. They're fodder for their blades. We need to find the little bitch now and get the fuck out of here before their alpha shows up. He knows we set the traps to lure him away by now, and I don't plan on dying over some bitch that may or may not be worth her weight in silver."

"This way," the other grunted. "You saw him looking at her. He's fucked her, or he intends to. You know she won't allow the little bitch to live long. I say we take her to the cabin and have some fun with her before we hand her over."

"Are you fucking stupid? You don't think she'll notice we fucked her? She's an alpha. She'd know, and I don't intend to die over some worthless pussy when the women she gives us to hurt will suffice and fulfill those itches you want to scratch."

Nyx's hand tightened on me, her inhuman senses much stronger than mine. She pushed me down the moment I had sucked in air, cutting off whatever they were saying. I watched feet entering the water close to where we hid. Nyx's body blocked mine, but when the feet turned in our direction, they moved back and appeared to be struggling to stay upright. The bodies slid beneath the water, stirring up unsettled algae from the creek's bottom, marring the ability to see anything.

More feet moved through the water, pausing to turn in our direction before turning back the opposite direction. My heart echoed in my ears, and my lungs began to burn from holding my breath. I lifted from the water, silently inhaling before slowly dropping back beneath the surface, watching the feet pause before moving toward us again.

We didn't move, not even when they were inches away. Wet jeans brushed against my shoulder before the male exited from the other side of the creek bank. I pushed from the water silently, ensuring I didn't disturb it, sucking air into my starving lungs.

My teeth threatened to give us away from the ice-cold water sinking into my bones. My fingers and legs were going numb, but we didn't dare leave the water.

Instead, we let our survival training kick in, huddling together, waiting within the chilled creek for time to pass. Eventually, we became numb to the cold, and it no longer bothered us as hypothermia became a real fear.

When dawn started to rise, Nyx dragged me to the far side of the bank, pulling me out of the water. I shivered, staring at up her as she dropped to her knees, crying out as she landed.

"I'm a fucking prune," she groaned. "My vagina probably looks like a ninety-year vag right now!"

"We have to find somewhere to hide and change out of these wet clothes."

"I smell men, which means there's more than likely a cabin someplace close to the creek. They smell like fish, so I'm guessing they're here on a fishing trip instead of hunting. Come on, let's move. You do know I could be riding some good dick right now. Instead, I have a wrinkly pussy, and we're in the middle of Nowhere, USA, in the woods."

"It won't be wrinkly as soon as it dries, hooker."

"Slut, I saw you, eye-humping Rhys, more than a few times. I know you want to ride him. I can smell you when you're turned on, woman. Remember, nymph here. I know all about sex. I'm like a sex addict, with a master's degree in human needs. You even look at a man with lust, my high beams go hard, and my instinct is to get to your prey before you reach that goal. So, I know things before you even know that you're considering slipping down that cock. You, Remi, want that Van Helsing dick with a fever burning through you."

"Can we move before I end up with an actual fever—mortal, remember?" I muttered, hating that her words spoke true, hitting home so hard that I couldn't argue with them. I wouldn't lie to her, not to Nyx. She was my person when I needed to vent or when my emotions conflicted with my priorities.

"Tell me I'm wrong, Remington. Tell me you don't want Rhys," she continued, holding my arm, starting us in the direction of where she'd smelled men.

"You know the truth, so why ask? You know me better than anyone else. The thing is, he is my enemy. Not to mention, I don't trust him. Every time I start to let my guard down, he pegs me so hard in the ass that I feel him in my lungs. He called every alpha to his bar and announced to them all that I existed. He's just placed a huge target on my bloodline, and my mother is still missing. I had enough shit to worry about before I met Rhys Van Helsing, and now he's just another thing that I have to deal with."

Male voices sounded from somewhere in front of us, and Nyx fixed her wet hair, smiling as we entered what looked like some semblance of a yard. Two men turned, staring at us as we made our way closer to where they watched us.

"Are you guys okay?" one asked, slowly stepping closer.

"Great, wrinkly vaginas and all," Nyx snorted. "Can one of you be a sweetheart and suck the other off for a few?" she asked sweetly. My eyes dropped to their skinny jeans; her biggest pet peeve. One of the men wearing loafers with matching jeans and a tight tank top blushed and grinned to himself, turning away from his friend as he considered Nyx's suggestion.

"We're not together. Not like that," the other snorted, although the thought didn't seem to put him off as he puffed out his chest, magnifying the embroidered trout on his very non-salmon-colored pink shirt.

"Oh, well, you can stand guard then, and make sure no one gets past you into the cabin until morning." She smirked as their eyes studied her with lust.

"I'm going inside," I muttered, moving into the house to peel off the wet clothing.

In the bathroom, I turned my head, staring at the large gash above my ear. I fumbled around the bathroom until I found a first aid kit and used gauze to clean the wound with rubbing alcohol. Once I'd tended to it and several smaller abrasions, I entered the cabin's main room and pulled a shirt out of the dresser, slipping it over my head. I searched for sweats, finding some in the last drawer, pulling them on and tying the waist as tight as it would go.

Lying in bed, I stared at the ceiling. The sound of moaning men filtered in from outside, and I sighed. When Nyx entered the cabin, I frowned, peering between her and the window where the moaning continued.

"It is wrinkly! Oh my God, it looks so wrong."

"Nyx, stop playing with your grandma vag and get in bed."

"You did not just call it a grandma vag! Take it back! I'll never forget you said that. It's mean, seriously mean. I thought we were friends?"

"It will only be a grandma vag until it dries. Stop overreacting. You know, even if it were wrinkly, men would still want it."

"That is true," she agreed, and the sound of her searching the room replaced her complaints as my eyes grew heavy, and sleep settled over me.

Chapter Eighteen

Something touched my head, and I groaned. Opening my eyes, I stared up at Rhys and Cole, who both watched me before taking in the crumpled male clothing. My eyes slid to the window, revealing it was light outside, and yet Nyx continued to slumber, oblivious to the men in the room, which told me I was dreaming. She was one of the people you couldn't sneak up on because people had too much sex running through their minds nonstop, which gave them away.

"Go look around the other room, Cole. Find an address," Rhys ordered softly, his hand still examining the wound. "You're hurt, Remi. Why the hell would you run?"

"Because you're the enemy, Van Helsing," I groaned, sitting up as he backed away, lowering to his haunches in front of me, silently staring.

I reached up, yanking the gauze from the wound on my head, pulling off dried blood. I gasped and grimaced as I brought the bandage in front of me, staring at the hair stuck to it. Sliding my legs off the side of the bed, I tossed it aside.

"If I'm dreaming, why did that hurt?" I asked, and his smile turned darker, which caused my body to tighten.

"Cole is controlling the dream-walk, which means if I hurt you here, you wake up wounded." Cole entered the room, scratching his head. "Figure out where our little minx ran off to?" Rhys asked.

"Yeah, and men outside fucking screaming about them being here, and, well, they've been at each other for long enough that they're rather hoarse. So, our pretty bird flew, but she didn't fly far. She's a mile from where our bodies are."

"I didn't think she'd get too far from us, not wounded. Not smart, Remington, to run from a Van Helsing hunter, tracker, and assassin. You may be good under E.V.I.E. standards, but I assure you, we're much better."

"If we wake up now, we can reach them before people start milling about. Considering it's Monday, and humans are about to start waking up and heading to their day jobs." Cole leaned over Rhys, checking my wound with a wince. "Bloody hell, woman," he muttered.

"Let's go, Cole. The sooner we get to Remington, the sooner a healer can tend to her wounds."

The dream faded, and I turned, shaking Nyx awake. "Get up now. They're coming."

"I was almost coming too! Acyn was just about to do that thing with his tongue where he flicks my clit. You're a horrible person to wake me up before he made me come!" she whined, tossing the pillow over her head, bellowing into it.

"It probably wasn't a dream. Cole and Rhys were just both in mine, and they figured out where we are hiding. Let's go," I said, slipping my feet into the sandals before grabbing the keys off the nightstand.

"You're a slow driver, give me the damn keys," she groaned, slipping on her shoes before she moved toward the bathroom. "If you need to use the bathroom, do it. I don't intend to stop until we're at least over the mountain pass."

We piled into the Land Rover and started down the small dirt road, hitting the highway. I had just leaned back and exhaled when Nyx slammed on the breaks, bringing the SUV to a stop. I peered through the windshield, staring at Rhys, leaning against the dark Jeep with his arms crossed over his chest, dressed in tactical gear. His eyes held mine as he uncrossed his feet, standing up. Their SUVs blocked the entire road. I groaned, turning to look at Nyx.

I wanted to slap the smug look on his face, violently. Car tires screeched behind us as a motor revved, causing my body to swivel in the seat. Trucks blocked our retreat, and then the car lurched, and I turned, noting the side road.

"It's gravel," I pointed out, and she shrugged.

"It's the road less traveled, and those shows always talk about taking them."

"I think it's supposed to be a metaphor, not literally. Especially not when being chased," I pointed out, gasping as we hit a bump.

"Van Helsings surround us. Would you rather we attempt to drive through them?"

I sat back, frowning as the car hit a dip, and my head slammed against the top of the interior. Reaching over, I grabbed the seat belt, pulling it across my lap as Nyx turned on the music. Queen's *Another One Bites the Dust* started playing loudly, and she smiled brilliantly, nodding.

"So, let the prey become the hunted," she mused.

"Hey, I'm not the prey. It's just that Rhys is so…" We hit a bump, and I yelped, "mean! Jesus, stay on the damn road, woman. Remember, I am mortal!"

"I can't help it. The road is filled with craters the size of Texas!" She rounded a corner, and I groaned, staring at the end of the road. "Okay, I'm going to get out and run one way, and you're going to go the other. Every movie has the blonde captured first, and the redhead is smarter, so she makes it further into the movie."

"That's in the movies, Nyx."

"Yeah, and when she gets caught, she gets fucked. Sounds great to me," she snorted, shrugging her delicate shoulders.

"Murdered, she gets murdered," I groaned, climbing out of the Land Rover.

"Stop ruining my fun! I like my version better."

The sound of cars moving toward us forced our

attention back the direction we'd come. Nyx wiggled her fingers, using her inhuman speed to zip into the woods. I groaned, moving toward the heavily wooded forest beside the dead-end road. It was almost as if they'd wanted us to take it. My eyes rolled, and I started moving as if the hounds of hell were chasing me.

If I'd known they would find us via my dreams, I'd have taken caffeine pills to stay awake, and we could have been miles away from them before they'd figured it out. But no, I was mortal and young, and my brain worked with logical facts.

Facts like men didn't really walk into your dreams and figure out where you were hiding from them. Or, you know, wake up with their dick buried in your throat, because hey, hussy, I was trying to impress dream Rhys with my unskilled throat.

Tripping over a low-hanging branch, I caught myself before planting my face into the forest floor. I could hear the sound of my heartbeat thundering in my ears loudly, which made it harder to discern anything else. I started at a decent pace, wishing I'd done all those suicide lunges in training instead of pretending I had.

I spun around as my lungs burned, noting the forest floor grew more thickly covered in debris as I started up a rock cliff, digging my fingers into the jagged rocks to pull my weight up until I reached the top.

Staring out over the barrage of trees, I deflated with the lack of anything or anywhere to hide. I moved forward, reaching the trees as the wind kicked up, and something brushed against my arm. I turned toward it, finding nothing there. Stepping backward, I shivered as the oversized clothing allowed the wind to send chilled air against my skin.

I moved through the woods until I hit a meadow, stopping on the edge. I wanted to stomp my feet at the nothingness in this place as I peered into the empty field. Slowly, I moved away from the cover of the trees and entered the clearing. Flowers bloomed everywhere I stepped, and a deep growl caused me to pause, turning back to look toward the direction I came. A shadowy figure stood on the edge of the meadow with the morning sun to his back, blocking out his features.

I stepped back, slowly moving as he started forward. My heartbeat hitched, beating relentlessly against my ribs until it filled my ears. He slowly moved toward me at an unhurried pace. I spun around, rushing toward the woods, but slammed against something hard and unmoving. Rhys peered down at me, watching as I fell to the ground ungracefully.

The moment my back touched against the ground, he dropped and easily captured my arms, pinning them above my head as his gaze searched mine. His knee parted my legs, and he smiled coldly. My chest rose and fell as he remained unnervingly silent.

"You ran from me, woman," he growled, pushing his knee against my apex, studying my reaction.

"You're the bad guy," I whispered breathlessly.

His smile widened, and he lowered his mouth to kiss my racing pulse. I moaned from the heat, my frozen body still yet to thaw fully from the ice-cold water we'd hidden within for hours. My knees lifted, cradling his body to retain his heat.

Rhys didn't release my hands, not even as his mouth claimed mine hungrily. His tongue pushed past my lips, dominating and controlling the kiss, nipping my lip before he pressed his tongue against mine.

I rocked against his muscular frame, unable to stop my body's reaction as need coursed through me. It was like his mouth held all the answers to the world, and when it brushed against mine, all my worries and troubles melted away. The only thing that mattered was getting him deeper into my soul.

Rhys pulled back, searching my face before he spoke thickly. "If I'm the bad guy, Remington, why do you kiss me like I'm your fucking savior?"

"I didn't say it made any damn sense. I was just pointing out facts," I replied softly, peering into eyes that studied me.

"If you run from me again, I'll ensure it will be the last time. I won't give you another warning," Rhys growled, lowering his mouth to crush against mine as my legs lifted, cradling him against my body.

Moaning, I allowed him to continue distracting me, holding my hands above my head as he showed me who was in control. Rhys didn't just kiss. He dominated, devoured, destroying you for every other male on the planet. His lips were sin, wrapped in seduction, and the moment they touched you, you were lost to him before you even realized his game.

He pulled back, releasing my hands, chuckling darkly at how weak I was to resist him. I hated him a little for knowing that he held that control over my senses. Rhys pulled me up from the ground, and

I moved my knee, hitting him in his balls. I started forward as he dropped to the ground hard.

I ran toward the forest without peering back, knowing I'd merely bought myself a few moments before he'd catch me again. I wasn't entirely sure why I thought that kneeing him in the nuts was wise. I had enjoyed the shock on his face as I'd landed my knee against his groin. A moment before I would have pushed through the forest line, a large grey wolf exploded from the brush, and I skidded backward, trembling with fear.

"Bad doggie! Please don't eat me. I'm not old enough to be tender yet and haven't had enough time even to marinate to taste good!" I cried, only to have a firm, large, very angry Van Helsing shove me behind him.

"Stand down, mutt. She's mine," Rhys growled, and I peered around his shoulder to see if the wolf listened.

My eyes widened as power rushed through the clearing, and the wolf trembled, growing hands before the rest of him started mirroring human parts. He lifted from the ground, baring teeth that had yet to finish turning blunt, and Rhys snorted.

My attention lowered to the enormous appendage between his legs, and my mouth dropped open. "Holy dick," I whispered in amazement as Rhys turned his head, glowering at me with annoyance. "What? It's huge and very hard to miss!"

"Stop looking at the mutt's cock, Remington," he hissed, moving his attention back to the man, who had just shifted into a human.

"Why's your bitch on my land, Helsing? My pack is hunting tonight to feed, and this isn't the time to be having some honeypot out in *my* fucking woods. Not to mention, judging by the scent of her trailing from the road, she's fucking mortal."

"Conrad MacGregor, meet Remington Silversmith. If you'd have answered the fucking summons, you'd know who she was. She's also under my protection. Make sure the other mutts and savages get that memo because I won't give it again."

I slowly lifted my gaze from the man's very thick, large appendage to meet his heated stare. He had sharp features, and he didn't look friendly in the least bit. Dark hair was disheveled, which looked pretty damn hot on him. His arms were covered in black and grey tattoos, while his chest held scars and a full moon over his heart. My stare dipped down again, and his cock jerked, forcing my gaze to lift to the wolfish grin marring his sensual mouth.

"Silversmith, and under your protection? Are you planning to fuck her then, Van Helsing?"

"That isn't your problem. Is it? She's untouchable unless I say otherwise, MacGregor. You have yet to respond to my invitation to Beltane. I suggest you respond to it soon. The heads of the houses will all be in attendance." Rhys stepped in front of me when Conrad continued staring at me as if he wanted to say something else.

"Funny, last I remembered, my pack wasn't worth your fucking time. Now, all of a sudden, a Silversmith shows up, and you want us at your party?" he asked, lifting a brow in challenge.

"I was being generous asking for your attendance, asshole. It wasn't a request. Vampires have turned up in daylight, and they're unresponsive to the normal shit that should be killing them. That's a problem, and with Laura currently recovering from wounds inflicted during a conflict with my little *honeypot*, as you referred to her, all heads of houses have been called here for Beltane."

"You took down the evil bitch?" Conrad asked, moving around Rhys, inspecting my borrowed clothing and disheveled appearance. "Did she do that to your head?" he questioned, stepping closer to sniff me. "If she's yours, Rhys, why the fuck does she smell of other men? Losing your touch at seducing women in your old age?"

"The caravan she was in was attacked last night. I am currently retrieving her from her own stupidity."

Conrad whistled, lowering his mouth to lick over the cut on my head as Rhys snorted, holding me still as the wolf tended to my wound. It was awkward and disgusting, but the moment he'd started licking my head, the dull throb had relieved. When Conrad finished, he stepped back, uncaring that he was naked in front of us.

More wolves escaped the woods, mid-shift to human as bones cracking and reforming sounded in the meadow. A woman silently made her way to where I stood, lifting a dainty nose in the air before glaring at me. Her hand moved toward the alpha with a territorial look as she began stroking his hard erection in front of us. His head fell back and rolled on his shoulders before his eyes turned to hold mine. I swallowed, uncomfortable with the blatant erotic scene unfolding.

She dropped to her knees, intending to do more, but he growled, and she bared her teeth at him, growling back. Other women slinked out of the woods, joining her to caress him, and he smiled at the blush filling my cheeks.

"She's young, Van Helsing."

"Very young," Rhys agreed, pulling me against him as one of the women moved toward me. "She's mine, Caroline. Remington is off-limits."

"She's beautiful and smells unsatisfied. I can help her," Caroline offered, her hand moving to her large breasts.

"She isn't interested in being an omega to your pack," Rhys snorted and lifted his eyes to the last female who entered the clearing, moving directly toward Rhys with purpose. She lifted on tiptoes when she reached him, kissing Rhys with wild abandonment, causing my brows to rise and a growl to build in my throat. Rhys didn't kiss her back, but he didn't stop her either. "Abigail," he grunted as she tried to push her hand into his pants.

"I've missed you coming to find me when I am in heat, hunter," she purred, turning her stare to me as it dripped with indifference. "I want to fuck."

"I'm busy," Rhys said, pulling me against him. "See that you come to Beltane, and bring your bitches. I'm sure everyone will eagerly welcome them, MacGregor."

"You know I don't like sharing my bitches."

"You can't fuck them all on Beltane, asshole. Let's go, Remington," Rhys stated, grabbing my wrist painfully, which told me he was a little hot over me kneeing him. "You ever do that again, and I'll pull your pants down and spank your ass until I'm confident that you've learned your lesson, or maybe I'll leave you to the wolves."

"I'm not a child," I muttered. "Honestly, you should have seen it coming. And I can handle wolves on my own. I don't need saving. I could have talked it down, or done something."

"You would have ended up pinned to the ground, fucked into submission, and then eaten for trespassing on their land. Those bitches would have picked their teeth clean with your bones," he growled. When I snorted, he turned, moving in a direction as if he had changed his mind.

"No!" I cried out, pulling his arm as he stopped, turning angry azure eyes on me. "I don't even know if I like doggie style." What the fuck? Did Nyx just really come out of my mouth? I had to stop listening to her talk when it was about sex.

His lips twitched as his eyes narrowed on me. "You'll figure that one out soon enough. I've imagined your pretty thighs parted, and me holding you apart as I fuck you from behind. You'll come for me like a bitch in heat when I fuck you like that."

"You imagine me being fucked… by you?" I stammered as he walked me backward until my back touched against a tree.

"Indeed, Love. I have dreamed of little else since meeting you. I'd show you, but you seem to have left my balls in my stomach and killed my erection. Now fucking walk, because the others are starting to assume I have beaten you into submission, and are giving us privacy so that I can fuck you."

"Oh," I frowned, turning on my heel to stare into the woods. "My sense of direction in the forest isn't great," I groaned. He smiled, threading his fingers through mine as he directed me out of the meadow, where the cars waited. "I didn't make it very far, did I?" I muttered.

"No, but it was cute that you thought you could outrun me."

Chapter Nineteen

I drove back to the estate with Rhys in silence, sulking at my inability to give him a decent chase. Of course, my job at E.V.I.E. had been to create weapons and make ammo ready for the operatives that actually hunted down vampires. My fingers tapped on the side panel and seemed to annoy Rhys, who continually swerved until I stopped.

Turning, I silently took in his angry profile. His bone structure was perfectly asymmetrical, with the five o'clock shadow that normally wasn't there. "Where's Nyx?" I asked curiously.

"Being taught a lesson as to why you don't run from Van Helsings," he said without looking away from the road.

"Excuse me?" I demanded, turning to face him.

"She's being punished. Do you need me to spell it out for you? She hasn't complained about it, and Acyn seemed rather inclined to show her that she couldn't escape him." He snorted as I huffed, crossing my arms to stare at him as we drove through the estate gates.

"Take me to her now," I hissed.

"You sure?" he asked, and when I just continued glaring at him, he shook his dark head and exited the car, moving around it to open my door. "I'm not sure you want to know what Acyn's punishments include, Remington."

"Now!" I demanded, following his stare toward the house.

He shrugged as if it didn't bother him one way or the other and started forward. We entered the silent house, and I followed him until he leaned against the wall, nodding at a door. I opened it just as a scream ripped from Nyx's throat, stopping dead in my tracks as my eyes rounded.

Cole was holding her up as Acyn moved behind her, both of them buried in her body. Cole turned dark eyes on me, slowly letting them drift down my body with open hunger. Cole's body rippled with power as he spread her body further, showing me his thick cock in the process. My teeth worried my lip, and my heated stare slid up the heavily tattooed muscular build of his body. Nyx screamed, her noises mixed with pleasure and pain as Acyn slammed into her, turning his blue depths to stare at me.

"Either strip and join us or get the fuck out, Silversmith," Acyn growled.

I slammed my hand over my eyes, realizing I was watching the threesome happening with open curiosity.

"So much dick," I groaned, moving to the wall beside Rhys, who reached around me, peering into the room before closing the door.

"Curious little thing, aren't you, Remi?" he asked, turning to stare at me with glowing blue eyes. "Would you like to be punished?"

My eyebrows hiked to my hairline as my mouth opened and closed. I was stuck in a house of sex! He stepped closer, cupping my cheek as he inhaled my scent. His hand released my face to push against the wall as he pinned me between his arms.

"Can I spread you apart and fill you, wrapping you around my cock until you're in pain? I bet those other boys you let play with you never made you ache as they fucked you, did they?" he asked, lowering his mouth to kiss the side of my neck as he captured my hands, pinning them above my head.

Rhys's mouth brushed over mine, and I chased it even though he held it out of reach. Pushing my legs apart with his knees, he used his other hand to lift me, urging me to wrap my legs around him. His groan echoed through me as he walked us down the hallway, and I continued chasing his mouth, which he never allowed me to have. It wasn't until my teeth caught his lip, nipping it and pulling against it that he smiled, opening the bedroom door and entering it.

Rhys closed the door, pressing me against it hard. He lifted the oversized shirt above my head, cupping my breasts as he claimed my mouth hungrily. He spun me around, still held against him with my legs wrapped around his waist, slowly lowering me to the bed. My hands slid down his body, untucking his shirt as I worked to get him bared to my touch.

He pulled away, breaking the kiss long enough to peel the shirt off, tossing it aside as he captured my hands, holding them in his much larger one above my head. He sucked on my neck, laughing darkly while I rocked against him, eagerly needing him to hurry it along before some other asshole knocked on the door.

Rhys rose, staring down at me, pulling the sweatpants down and noticing the lack of panties. He smirked, lowering his mouth to kiss my stomach. His eyes lifted, holding mine as his fingers pushed into my body, and I cried out at the fullness they created. I rocked against him, needing him to strip and give me what I really desired and wanted from him.

Dark laughter brushed against my flesh, sending his heated breath fanning against my core. He sat back, and I leaned forward, working his pants to free him, and when he was, I kissed the thick top of his cock, lifting my eyes to hold his as he brushed the hair away from my face. My hand cradled him, wrapping around his length. I took him into my mouth as he groaned, pulling my mouth away from his cock.

"Not this time, little giver. I plan to give," he instructed. "You get to take."

"Hurry," I groaned, laying back to spread my legs to show him my need.

His hand smothered over his mouth, and he pushed his pants down, stepping out of them. Rhys pushed my legs apart and, pinned my hands against my belly as he settled between my thighs. Leaning over, he clamped his heated mouth over one nipple and sucked hard.

I moaned loudly, rocking my hips with a need that threatened to burn me to nothing more than ashes.

His fingers slid over my opening, and I shivered, claiming his mouth as it brushed against mine. He groaned, turning his head as footsteps sounded in the hallway. Sitting up, he shook his head, lining our bodies up as someone pounded against the door.

"No, no fucking way!" I groaned. "If that is Cole, I will skewer him myself!" Rhys laughed wickedly, slowly rubbing his cock against my opening while his heated eyes noted my body's need glistened against his cock.

"Van Helsing, your family is here!"

"Fuck!" Rhys growled, standing up. "Bloody hell."

I sat up. "Get your dick back here!"

He turned, looking at the plea burning in my stare before he grabbed his pants, pulling out his phone. The sound of Nyx screaming out her pleasure filled the phone as he snorted.

"Tell the nymph to shut the fuck up for a goddamn bloody minute. They're here, get the fuck out of her pussy, and meet me in the hall," Rhys hissed, ending the call to move back toward me. "We're not finished, Remi."

"You could finish it now," I replied, but the look in his eyes told me he wouldn't. I exhaled, moving out of the bedroom, wrapped in his blanket. "The universe hates me," I groaned, resting my head against the counter as he moved into the bathroom, starting the water.

"My family is here, Remington. They won't be kind to you. It would be best to stay close to me, Acyn, or Cole from now until they leave. Understand me, Love?" He turned, staring at me with a frown. When I nodded, he smirked, coming to a stop before me as he pushed the blanket away from my body and lifted me onto the counter. "You are so beautiful, woman," he growled, cupping my cheeks as he held my mouth in place to claim it.

"You don't need flattery for a *yes*, Rhys," I whispered against his mouth, nipping his bottom lip while he pushed my thighs apart, slowly delving his fingers into my body as I moaned against his mouth.

"I don't want a quick fuck from you," he whispered, pulling his mouth away from mine. "I want you in every way possible. I want to show you what it is like to be with a man. I want to taste you come on the tip of my tongue and feel your body tightening as you come around me. I don't want to just bend you over and fuck you like some dirty little feeder. I want you to know what it is like to be with me as I watch those pretty blue eyes grow wide with wonder as you come undone for me and me alone. Five minutes isn't long enough to make you feel owned or wanted. I want that for you, and while I could easily spread you apart and fuck you hard enough that we both come in moments, you would feel used, and that isn't something I ever want you to feel from me."

"I hate you right now," I groaned, leaning my head against his shoulder as the bedroom door opened, and Cole moved into the bathroom doorway, watching as Rhys and I both turned to stare at him. Rhys added a finger, and I gasped, burying my face in his shoulder.

"Pretty, so bloody pretty," Cole muttered before he vanished, and Rhys lowered my feet to the floor, turning me around with one hand while slamming the door closed with the other.

His knees parted my legs, and before I guessed what he intended to do, his body leaned against mine. The counter bit into my hips as his finger found my core, pushing into my body. His other held my hair, pulling it back to his mouth as he sucked against the pulse hammering in my neck. Rhys's fingers curled, dancing over the spot that hit every nerve ending perfectly.

My eyes held his in the mirror. He stroked the fire, slowly moving his fingers inside my body until everything began to unravel within me. I whimpered, opening my mouth as a cry escaped, and the world spun around me. He didn't stop, didn't slow his thrusts, sending me toppling over the edge again. Rhys kept me dangling there until I was slamming my body against his fingers, crying his name as everything became too much to bear, and my body grew hypersensitive.

"You're going to love being mounted from behind, pretty girl," he groaned, lowering his mouth to my shoulder, kissing his way down my body. He kissed along my spine and over the rounded portion of my ass, dipping lower to kiss against my opening. He licked once through my arousal with a loud moan before he stood, turning me around and kissing me hard, forcing me to taste my pleasure on his lips. "Shower, and the knights will escort you to me when you're ready. Tonight, we eat dinner with my family. It should be interesting for them to meet the Silversmith that gifted me her silver."

"Is it possible to just forget that happened?" I asked, holding his stare as he smiled.

"Not a fucking chance. I'm the only Van Helsing ever to receive such a gift from your line, Remington. There's no way I'm not screaming that to the entire world."

"Damn. Cocky much?" Cole snapped from outside the door. "Are you done making her come half-assed? Let me in, and I'll finish her off for you, brother."

"Fuck off, Cole. She's my girl," Rhys growled, kissing me hard before he moved me toward the shower, slapping my behind and enjoying the yelp that escaped my lips. "I might like you running from me. You're a hot little thing afterward, Remi."

"Great," I muttered, stepping into the shower. "And Cole, I don't accept sloppy seconds, man-whore!"

"I can get into that shower with you, woman. Just say the words, and I'm all yours, Sunshine."

"I'll see you downstairs," Rhys said to me, moving to the door before exiting. "Get the fuck out of my room, assholes. I said to meet me in the hallway."

"Just seeing that you tap that ass soon, brother," Acyn grunted and then snorted. "Do it, Rhys, or someone else will, and they won't care what she thinks. Hell, she's almost succumbed to Cole on a few occasions. You know the rules. Finish it before you lose the only leverage you have against them."

"Not here, asshole," Rhys growled.

I swallowed against the door, frowning as I listened to the brothers. When the room went silent, I slipped back into the shower, resting my head against the stall. I had to stop kissing Rhys because I lost my ever-loving mind and did stupid shit when I did.

Chapter Twenty

I sat on the bed, staring at Nyx, who frowned, studying me quietly. I told her what I'd heard, and she'd come up blank on what it could have meant. Something was happening, and neither of us had any idea what it could be. It left us unsettled, but the fact she was walking funny added some amusement to the evening.

"Are you okay?" I asked, watching her move around as I winced for her.

"Van Helsings don't play around, Remington. I mean, I'm good at orgies. This wasn't an orgy. Normally, I'm the one feeding. They fed, and damn did they feed. I came so many damn times that I was begging for mercy. Me, a freaking nymph," she groaned. "I don't beg for mercy, ever."

"Until now," I pointed out, finding her bruised ego a little humorous.

"You watched, pervert," she smirked. "I don't

think their Beltane and ours are on the same level. Fair warning."

"Why do you say that?" I asked, remembering Rhys asking the alpha wolf to bring his *bitches*. How demeaning was that?

"Oh, I don't know. The fact that Acyn and Cole mentioned sharing me with the crowd that hadn't known the pleasures a nymph brought to the bedroom. Plus, they're also bringing in a bunch of feeders since it's the one night Rhys can't fully control his monster. Everyone loses their shit on Beltane, and it turns into one big orgy. I have a feeling this one is going to be lit."

"He's bringing in feeders?" I asked, needing her to clarify.

"I don't know, but it sounds like he may need them. He is the alpha to the incubi and the Van Helsings. He's the only alpha who has a combined house, of which I know you're aware, since technically it's your family's fault."

"He's called in all the alphas to deal with the vampires. We need to get out of here and get home."

"About that, Remi," she said, sitting beside me, patting my hand. "You know how E.V.I.E. has always had a silent benefactor? One who actually runs the Seattle division, even though he never comes to check on things?" Nyx asked, and my stomach did a somersault.

"Yes?"

"It's Rhys. He's the head of Seattle's E.V.I.E., and we can't go back. If we leave, we can't go there anymore." She grabbed my hand, holding it as I stared at her with my mouth wide open.

"You're sure?" I asked through a tightening in my throat.

"I called to check-in, and they told me to stay with you. I asked if they had heard anything else about your mother, and they told me the benefactor had it under control. That unless Rhys Van Helsing said otherwise, we weren't allowed to go back to the center," she whispered, peering carefully at the door. "On Rhys Van Helsing's command, we are officially jobless and homeless. I have money saved up, though, and we can find a house to rent. We're going to be okay, Remi. You and me, we always make it through things together. This is just one more thing we'll have to survive."

"My armory," I moaned, rubbing my hand down my face.

"Rhys's armory is ten times better than yours. Acyn said he was already moving people to allow you full access to it. It isn't like you can't make guns anymore, or ammo. You just have to make them for him."

"So that he can use them against other alphas and play God, Nyx. If I make his weapons and they're all created of Silversmith silver, he could rule the entire alpha community. He'd be their judge, jury, and executioner, and I'd be handing it to him."

"The thing is, Remington, he already is. You're just handing him silver to reinforce his hold on them. Rhys Van Helsing is the one creature no one is willing to challenge. He is lethal and sinister when he dishes out his punishments. You've already been working for him without either of you knowing it, so it's not like it will be any different."

"It's different because my mother is still missing, and Rhys is sneaky. He's using my stupidity against me, and I don't know what I can or can't say because he took my phone. He cut off all my outside communication. No one within my bloodline knows he has me, and no one is coming to save us, Nyx."

"You're not a damsel who needs saving, Remi. You're fucking bulletproof, and you literally can have the world at your feet. If you and Rhys end up together, you will be the '*it*' couple in the immortal world. You're already his silver, whatever the hell that means. That one has me stumped, and nothing anywhere says shit about it or what it means. I know it isn't good for you, not where your family will be concerned."

"I'm aware of that. I'm afraid that the snakes in the bed were for me. A warning to others that I'd become a traitor. It can actually mean a few things, but considering where I am and who has me, I'm almost certain it was Winchester, sending up smoke signals to anyone coming here."

I moved from the bed, peering into the bathroom at the dress I wore in the full-length mirror, remembering the feel of Rhys against me as he'd watch me unraveling for him. How was it he touched me and I disappeared? All the survival training I could use to flee him fades to black, and I became lost within him. Unless he was using his incubus magic against me, and I was succumbing to it?

I pulled my hair up into a ponytail and walked out of the bathroom, finding Cole sitting beside Nyx, running his hand over her thigh. His eyes slipped over the black dress I wore, resting on the wrap-around heels. Exhaling, I slowly moved toward him, wondering if he'd tell me what I wanted to know.

"What does it mean to offer a Van Helsing your silver?" I whispered, tilting my head as he frowned, studying me.

"It means you are Rhys's, and everything you fear it means, Remi. It's like offering him your soul, and once accepted, it cannot be undone. You sold your soul to the devil, and I let you do it. Can't say I blame him, or you for choosing him. Rhys is honorable to a point, so don't push him. He's never given his protection, nor have I added mine to back his. You're special."

"Because I'm untrained and don't know what I should hide from you and your brothers?" I pointed out, rubbing my arms as he stood, moving closer to me.

"No, because you're innocent," he whispered softly. "You know we're monsters, and you don't care that we are. You know we murdered your family, and yet you say it is in the past. You don't condemn us for what happened yet, and you're right, maybe you being naïve helps that. Remi, you had yet to choose a side. But by giving Rhys your silver, you chose ours. An accident led by being naïve, but it is done. You're wed to him, and that's deeper than any Silversmith has ever allowed to happen. In our family's history, no Silversmith has ever awarded us a weapon to use against our enemies; bullets and arrows, but never weapons. Weapons give us power, even the power to take down other Silversmiths."

I swallowed, shaking my head. "Not my silver, it is

cursed."

"What?" he asked carefully.

"My silver cannot be used against Silversmiths. I will never allow it. Rhys's sword, while lethal, isn't lethal against my bloodline. I may be naïve and foolish and led by an overactive libido where he is concerned, but I will always protect my family, even from myself."

"Sneaky, but we expected that already. You do know we read runes, right? We've had centuries of boredom to endure, Sunshine. Now, I'm here to escort you to dinner, since you are keeping everyone waiting, which Rhys considers a personal slight since he instructed you to be down shortly… three hours ago."

"I had to get blood out of my hair, Cole," I stated icily, moving past him to the door as Nyx followed us down.

"Indeed," he stated, passing me down the stairs at an inhuman speed as if he needed distance between us.

"That wasn't weird at all," Nyx groaned.

We slowly walked down the stairs as the real-life version of the people in the paintings turned, glaring murderously at me. My heart kicked up, thundering against my chest, and I paused as anger and malice slithered over my flesh in warning. My feet wouldn't move, and everything within me said to run, to get away from them as silent tears pricked my eyes.

"Fuck this!" someone shouted, and I was thrown backward, up the stairs, slamming against the wall to slide down, hitting the ground hard. The male rushed toward me, but Rhys appeared before me as if he'd materialized from thin air. He slammed his fist into the man's face, sending him toppling down the stairs.

Rhys was slammed against the wall by a small, petite woman, who he lifted, slamming against his knee before he tossed her toward the stairs as well. His eyes turned, holding mine as I remained on the floor, shocked and uncertain what to do.

I started to sit up, but the air moved around us, and Cole slammed into a body before it could reach me. Acyn joined, and together the three formed a wall around me while I fought the urge to crawl into a ball and hide.

Feet became visible past Rhys, and he shouted, the voice coming out in layers. "Enough! I am the alpha. Unless someone wishes to challenge me here and now for my claim, back the fuck off and stand down," he snarled.

"She's a Silversmith!" a male voice shouted.

"She is, and she's mine!"

"She deserves to die for what they did to us. You are the alpha. It falls to you to handle her, and yet you protect her? Why, brother?" another sneered.

"Because she gave me her silver," Rhys growled, and everyone went silent.

"Are you out of your fucking mind?" the woman asked, groaning. "Now it makes sense. You do realize that others will come to take her, even by force. Have you bred her yet?"

I blinked, shaking my head.

Cole snorted. "Of course, he's started the process,

sister. Luckily, they're not breeding yet, or we'd be having a much more damaging conversation due to your willingness to throw her around. Now wouldn't we? See that you don't do it again, as she is mortal."

"A mortal Silversmith walks into your lap, hands you her silver, and you question nothing about it?" the woman demanded icily. "Did she ride your cock first before sucking your brains out through its tip? Or did you see her name and believe her words? There are no mortal Silversmiths because we left none alive to breed the little bitch."

"And yet she carries the curse and controls silver. She stands inside a forge and touches the silver with her pretty delicate fingers, Nyota. In a room that had a temperature of five hundred and ninety degrees. We watched her work for fourteen hours to create a sword, unlike anything I have ever seen. When she gifted it to me, I accepted it for what it was, even though she had no fucking clue what she was doing. She is young, very young, and alone. So, yes, while I question everything about her, I also have ensured that she cannot wield her silver against me."

"But that means there's another Silversmith who survived the fires," she swallowed, her hand pushing Rhys aside to peer down at me. "Eliza?"

"Indeed. Remington is her daughter."

"The coloring is wrong. Is it dyed?" a man asked. I remained on the floor, staring at Rhys's feet as they talked about me like I was some rare creature he'd found in the pet store.

"Natural. A rare occurrence maybe, or designed to

hide in plain sight. I don't know yet. Remington took down Laura like she was child's play, and you and I both know she isn't. She is powerful and very deadly. And she's mine now," Rhys stated, and I lifted my eyes, glaring at him.

I was so not sleeping with him tonight.

"Can we eat now? It's been a very long time since we've had everyone here," Nyota whined, and Rhys bent down as if to help me up.

I forwent his offered hand, getting to my feet as pain moved up my spine. I reached behind my arm, feeling stickiness as I dropped my hand, kneeling to remove the broken heels while everyone watched.

"Remi," Rhys groaned, touching my shoulder.

"Get the fuck off of me," I snapped, glaring at him. "I can manage to get my shoes off, believe it or not, Van Helsing. I did manage to live without you for twenty-one years, and I could have made it to my ascending without you too." I removed the heels, stepping through the crowd of Van Helsings to walk down the stairs, feeling his angry glare on my spine as I ignored him.

And to think, I'd almost had sex with him! I was nothing more than leverage to wield against his enemies and sit his ass upon some legendary throne of immortals. I was an idiot to come here. In hindsight, I'd had good intentions, but my execution left a lot to be desired. I had just turned twenty-one the week before coming home, and with how things were going, I would be lucky if it weren't my last.

Chapter Twenty-One

I pushed the food around my plate as the Van Helsings studied me like I was some freak they couldn't stop gawking over. I kept glancing toward Nyx to make sure I hadn't grown another head, but she was the only one not looking at me. Rhys snorted, and I slid my stare toward him for a moment before dismissing him.

"Do you know what burning human flesh smells like?" one of the brothers asked, and I lifted my eyes, finding the question directed at me.

"Intimately, yes," I replied, setting down my fork to reach for the whiskey, downing it as a server raced to refill the glass. "Why? Would you like to set me on fire? It might not end as you'd hope. I'm willing to allow you to try if you'd like. It matters little to me which option you choose."

"You think I wouldn't set you on fire?" he countered, studying my face.

"That isn't what I said," I stated dismissively. Picking up my fork, I continued pushing around the food that was now little more than mush.

They'd served plates of steaming hot food that, at any other time, I'd have devoured. I didn't enjoy being the focus of the table, or that they were all exuding vibes that stated how badly they wanted me dead. It was causing my stomach to turn, and an uneasy feeling was rolling through me. I'd also been drinking on an empty stomach, which made me tired and bitchy.

"Let's go outside and try it, shall we?" he offered, and I stood, only for Rhys to grab my arm, pulling me back into my chair.

"Let's not set her on fire, okay?" he grunted, never pulling his eyes from me.

"She's passingly pretty. However, she lacks the silver coloring of the Silversmiths that made them beautiful," another brother stated, but which one I didn't know because I'd given up caring or paying attention to names. "Remington. What a boyish name. Maybe they named her such because of her rust coloring?" he continued.

"I don't know. I find it fitting for a mythical gunsmith to name her daughters after those with less ability than she has," Nyota said, and *almost* complimented my mother.

"You haven't touched your food," Rhys pointed out, and I turned to look at him blankly.

"Between being thrown against a wall and having your family try to murder me repeatedly, I seem to have lost my appetite. One of your brothers wants to set me on fire. Another thinks I'm passingly pretty and have a horrid name. The others are wondering how to fuck me before you get to me and breed my womb because you all think it holds some kind of mythical tether to my silver talent. You're parading me around like I'm some fucking trophy, and you think I'd still have an appetite. Why?" I asked pointedly, glaring at him. "Oh, let's not forget that I almost let you into my vagina tonight, too. Not that it will be happening now. I'd rather fuck the sword I made you than let you touch me again tonight. So, there's that."

Cole choked on his liquor as the others watched Rhys to see what he would do. My fingers tapped the table, something I knew bothered him. I waited for Rhys to do something, anything other than stare at me with his pretty stupid eyes.

"Eat," he demanded coldly.

I reached for my whiskey, downing it as the server moved closer. Rhys shook his head at the server who veered away from the glass he'd been about to refill. He pushed my plate closer, and I shoved it away. He continued until I lifted it, tossing it over my head to smirk as it shattered against the wall.

"You're acting childish, Remington," he pointed out.

"And you're a dick who enjoys treating me like some fucking pet he trapped," I muttered.

"Go to the bedroom, Remington," he growled, and I stood without warning, pushing the chair out before he could. For all his faults, he was well-mannered.

I felt his eyes following me as I silently made my

way up the stairs. I didn't understand why they forced me to endure their company when it was clear they wanted me owned or dead. I entered the room I'd first been in, staring at the new bed, replacing the one I'd broken. Glaring, I peered up at the ceiling and walls they'd repaired in the last few hours.

Climbing onto the bed, I shed the dress, wincing at the wound on my shoulder, and sat up. I walked into Rhys's bedroom, grabbing the curling iron out of my bag. Slipping into the bathroom in my room to plug it in, I tapped my fingers on the counter, leaning against it while I waited for it to heat up. After a few minutes, I turned to look at the wound on my shoulder in the mirror, holding the curling iron against the cut flesh until it sizzled.

I turned, staring at Rhys, who watched me silently through narrowing eyes. Ignoring him, I pulled the iron away from my shoulder, peering into the mirror at the healed flesh. Reaching over the sink, I unplugged the iron and placed it where it wouldn't melt or burn anything.

Grabbing my toothbrush, I applied the paste and set to scrubbing his taste out of my mouth while he watched. His stare slid over my naked frame, slowly lifting back up to my shoulder with curiosity.

"Heat heals you," he pointed out, and I rolled my eyes at his brilliant deduction. "You're fireproof, aren't you?" he asked, and when I didn't answer him, he slipped in behind me, watching me in the mirror. "That's what you meant when you said he could try, but it wouldn't end up as he wanted. Isn't it?"

"Mmm," I said around my toothbrush. Bending

over, I spit out the toothpaste before grabbing the mouthwash. My eyes caught his in the mirror, reminding me of earlier when he'd done devilish things to me. He moved quickly, planting his hands to box me in against the counter. I continued staring at him as those memories flashed in my mind. "Stop it."

"Stop what, Remi? Stop touching you? Stop learning you?" He studied me; his smile curving his mouth while his eyes sparkled with dark amusement burning within them. "You're going to need to elaborate on what you want me to stop doing."

"Stop using your magic on me, Rhys Van Helsing."

"I can't make you want me. If that is what you think I am doing, you're mistaken. I can only enhance your pleasure. I can't make you want those dirty thoughts playing out in that pretty head of yours. That's all you," he uttered huskily.

"Do you have bleach?" I asked softly, turning to run my hands up his chest slowly, watching the smile deepening on his lips, wrapping his arms around my waist. He pressed his erection against my stomach, proving I wasn't the only one remembering earlier.

"Now, why would you need bleach?" he asked, lowering his mouth against mine.

"To erase every image of you from my head," I smirked against his mouth, patting his chest. "Good night, Rhys," I snorted, ducking out from beneath his arms. I walked toward the bed, only to be picked up and carried into his room. "I am not sleeping with you!"

"You're sleeping in my bed, woman. It isn't up for negotiation at this time. When my bastard brothers leave, you can ask again. I have no intention of sleeping in this room just to keep you safe from them, not when you can sleep in my bed."

"You've done a smashing job of keeping me safe so far, asshole," I grumbled, and then cried out as he dumped me onto the bed.

"My job is to protect your life, Remington. You're alive, aren't you?" he muttered, pulling off the suit coat, and then slowly unbuttoning his shirt. I watched him silently, hating that his body made my eyes need to take inventory of each contoured line in detail. "How did you figure out that you were fireproof?"

"How long have you run E.V.I.E.?"

"I don't run it. I only run a portion of the Seattle division. I hand out assignments that won't need my assistance. It prevents me from spreading my knights out too thin, leaving them available for more pressing issues. How much does it piss you off knowing that you can't go home, Remington?" he smirked wolfishly, victory shining in his azure stare.

"It wasn't my home. It was just somewhere to pass the time," I lied, rolling my eyes at his snort. "Of course, a Van Helsing would run the hunting guild. It actually makes perfect sense as to why we weren't allowed to slaughter the blood bags. You had a Silversmith right beneath your nose and didn't notice me, which must burn your alpha ass."

"Admittedly, a little, but then I was coming to investigate the little spitfire that had climbed the ranks so rapidly. You see, I was aware of you, just not of what you were. I would have found you, Remington, even if you hadn't returned home. There are not many who could do what you did, and certainly not in the time you did it. Most weapon masters take decades to learn their craft and adapt to what their role demands."

I bristled under the compliment. I felt uncomfortable with the praise and was uncertain how to take it, so I ignored it. Rhys slid his thumbs through the waist of his slacks, pushing them down before standing back up to step out of them. My attention lowered to his thick cock before I turned away from him. I moved up the bed, slipping beneath the covers to lie down, facing the opposite direction.

"You're upset that I am showing you off?" he asked into the room's silence.

"I am. I feel like a pet that's made you proud. I am not a pet, Rhys. I am young, and everything it entails. I have emotions, and while they may seem stupid to you, they're not to me. You think it is fun to show me off to immortals that want to use me, abuse me, and murder me. Before you, the only immortals I was around were my family, and then at the center at E.V.I.E., where I knew I was safe. Here, I don't feel safe. I feel like at any moment, everything is going to go crazy, and my life will become forfeited. Either by accident or because my family slighted another's before I was even born or created. You expect me to sit and be a good pet, but I will run, and I will keep running until I am free. I don't want to be caged.

"I agreed to work with you, and the first chance you got, you made it permanent because I am naïve, and you used that against me. Cole held me open for you to look at and play with because I'm easy to manipulate, and because every time you get close to me, all my inhibitions leave me. When your mouth touches mine, my worries slip away, and the world feels right. That alone terrifies me because, at the end of the day, you don't actually want me. You want the magic I wield."

The sound of clothing rustled in the room, and I silently fought the tears that threatened to fall. My throat tightened while I waited for his reply.

The door opened and closed, and I sat up, staring at the empty room. I frowned, pulling my legs up against my chest to drop my head to my knees. I'd just poured my heart out to Rhys, and he got bored and left. I was marking this one up as one of the biggest mistakes of my life, right next to running in to save him, and waking up on my knees with him between my lips.

Chapter Twenty-Two

Days went by where Nyx and I spent hours in the armory, charged to rearrange it, much to the horror of one knight. He would sigh, frown dramatically, or snort when I moved something. My babysitter, Acyn, would watch every single move I made. Either Cole or Acyn supervised me since the night I'd bared my soul to Rhys, only to have him slip out of the room like it hadn't mattered to him. For the last three days, other than sleeping beside him, I hadn't seen much of Rhys.

"You cannot possibly think this is right. There's a system in place. How will we find anything in a hurry?" the knight groaned. Acyn's lips twitched, and his stare landed on Nyx, who purposely bent over, showing him that she'd forgone to wear panties today. "I want to speak to the alpha about this before she destroys everything!"

"You have copper bullets mixed in with silver ones. If you were to shoot a wolf with copper, you'd end up with a dead knight assuming he'd made a kill shot, when in reality, all he'd manage to do is piss off that werewolf. You have bronze arrow tips in with the brass, and there are shavings everywhere, clinging to those tips. One single shaving on an arrow can mean the difference between life and death if it affects the arrow's trajectory when released. A sharpshooter expects his ammo to be in firing shape. Yet your bullets are scuffed, tossed into freaking drawers, unboxed and unprotected. In short, you're a shit weapons master who hasn't mastered how to catalog, let alone store his ammunition properly to assist those in the field.

"You literally had one responsibility here. And in case you are unaware of what it is, it is to ensure everything is in top firing order and prepared for the men counting on you to ensure it is so. You have an assistant who orders for you when supplies are short, yet you've failed to utilize him since half the supplies are low or gone. There's another knight who ensures weapons are stored properly, and he catalogs them in every night. They're cleaned, reloaded, and restocked into the safe, stored in zero moisture because he goes above and beyond to ensure the rice and vapor barriers within the room are changed out every three days. You, on the other hand, are a mess. If they're doing their jobs, and you're doing a shit job, their jobs don't matter. Weapons need ammo, and you are the one responsible for storing that ammo correctly. So either sit your pompous ass down and shut your whining mouth, or get in here and help me to fix your mess, sir!" I snapped crossly.

Acyn lifted a brow to the knight glaring at me, and yet the others didn't stand behind him. Neither did they argue over what I had said.

"You are what? *Twelve?* You don't know shit about what it takes to do my job!" he stammered with a red face.

"I've been the weapons master at E.V.I.E. since before my tits reached their full potential. I have used guns and bows since the time I could stand up. I am a Silversmith, and my entire life has revolved around manufacturing weapons, unlike anything this world has ever used or fired before. I could pour silver into bullets and perfected the process before I was old enough to discover my love button or that it had an actual function. I am a marksmanship champion against an entire line of hunters. While I may look young and inexperienced, I assure you that I am not. If you or your alpha intends to add my silver to this shit-hole of a mess, you have inside this armory, then I expect you to do your fucking job, or find another one you can handle."

"And you thought she might need your help?" Cole's voice filled the room, forcing my eyes to his before they slid to Rhys, who stood beside him with his arms crossed over his broad chest, staring at me.

"Indeed," Rhys said, shaking his head as his eyes slid to the knight beside me. "You're being reassigned to a new post. Acyn, find someone who knows their cock from their hand and send them to Remington to see if they fit her expectations. When I learned that we had a new weapons master in Seattle who was a spitfire, I should have known it was a fucking Silversmith," he admitted, rubbing his hand down his face. "Acyn, see to the completion of the other preparations as well, and report to me when you're done," Rhys announced, his eyes never leaving mine.

Rhys wore a white button-down shirt that molded his muscular frame. The collar was left unbuttoned, and the sleeves rolled up, exposing the colorful tattoos that moved as he unfolded his arms over his chest, watching me as the knight opened his mouth to argue.

"I am being generous, Carson, and considering your laziness has been mentioned repeatedly over the last few months, you're lucky I didn't reassign you to Antarctica. Leave now. If I have to ask you again, you won't like me." Rhys's eyes never left my face, studying me through heated blue depths. "I'll be in my office. When you're finished here, I'd like a few words with you."

I stared at him, narrowing my eyes before I went back to arranging his arsenal as his knights helped me. It took more than four hours before I'd finished and stepped back, scanning over every box of ammo and every arrow that now was precisely where it belonged. Turning on my heel, I asked one of the knights where I could find Rhys's office, and then was escorted there, which had become a new normal.

I knocked on the door, stepping inside when he called out for me to enter. His eyes slipped over my shoulder, and the guard exited, closing the door behind him. Rhys's office was huge and masculine. He had large filing drawers, with weird writing on the front next to a large wooden hutch that had dragons and the Van Helsing insignia carved into the front. On the other wall was an extensive display of books. Placed in the middle of the largest, widest shelf was the sword I'd crafted for him, prominently on display.

"Sit, Remington," Rhys exhaled tiredly. I moved forward in the jeans and corset top I wore, sitting in the chair, crossing my legs while I lifted my glare on him. "Tomorrow is the celebration of Beltane, and with it, we observe certain traditions."

"I understand," I said dismissively.

I hadn't spoken more than a few curt words to him since he'd left me in bed. Last night, he'd finally agreed to let me move into the other room on the condition that the knights stood guard. They stood there all night long, and to top it all off, Rhys demanded the door connecting mine to his remain open. No amount of arguing had changed Rhys having an open door into my room.

"Is that it then?" I asked, standing up.

"Sit down," he said, studying me as I looked anywhere but at him. "It's going to be rather stimulating and sexual compared to what you are used to."

"I'm a witch. It will be fine."

"Everyone will expect you to pick a partner for the night," he announced, and I paused, turning to look at him.

"Okay," I said, holding his stare without blinking. "I'll find someone."

The pen he held snapped into several pieces. His eyes narrowed as the sound of his back teeth grinding together almost brought a smile to my lips, but I hadn't found anything to smile about lately. I had felt somewhat normal after being able to be inside an armory again. It wasn't mine, though, and I wasn't the weapon's master of his armory. I dropped my eyes as he cleaned the ink off his hand, continuing to watch me silently.

"A partner to sleep with, Remington."

"I didn't assume you meant a dance partner, Van Helsing." I swallowed past the tightening in my throat, turning to gaze at the sword that had sealed my fate.

He had it on display like a trophy. Go figure. He probably wanted everyone who entered to see and notice it. Rhys cleared his throat, drawing my attention back to him. I studied his face, noting the tight corners of his mouth and eyes as he decided on what to say.

"It's not a trophy. It's a display of honor, Remi. Before I placed your blade there, my father's prized sword occupied that space. It, too, was a work of craftsmanship and held a special place in my heart. I replaced it with yours to remind me that changes are happening, and we're evolving. The changes in how we will deal with one another are going to be a process, and sometimes we need a reminder close at hand to make them happen. I'm not used to dealing with young people. Cole normally has that responsibility. As alpha, I make the hard choices that protect my people at all costs. Having a full-blooded Silversmith appear from thin air, well, it isn't easy for any of us. Your family wasn't loved, mostly because they came from nothing and then ruled everything without a care who they hurt in the process."

"Is this where you tell me how low we were? How unworthy of being in your prestige graces I am?" I asked, hoping to skip over the holier-than-thou speech.

"No, this is a tale from rags to riches, and how power corrupted what was once a decent family of strong women. Your family enjoyed coming into power, but that wasn't enough for some. Some wanted to sit on the throne and to control every alpha house. That is how the Silversmith started to become hated by every alpha. The code is simple: take care of those who count on you and remain in the shadows. Roslyn wanted more power, and so she simply took it, and I helped her accomplish that goal, blinded by her beauty. When I was with her, everything seemed right. All my troubles faded away, and I could be me, the knight who swooped in to protect her and keep her safe. It wasn't enough for her, nor was I. She reached for entire houses, which forced me to step back. I began to see her lust-filled stares at anyone she wanted because no one was ever enough," he said, swallowing hard against the words.

"When Roslyn asked to speak to my mother, I was blind to what she truly wanted. I allowed it to happen, Remington. I walked my sweet mother into that viper's house, where Roslyn handed her off to her father to rape and murder with Silversmith silver. My mother was the first alpha to be murdered by your family, but she wasn't the last. I spent my time serving Roslyn, pretending to be her knight, which made my family hate me more than they hated her. I did anything she asked, and then I took her down. You think I want the immortal throne, but I don't need it. I have it already. You think I need your silver, and again, I don't, not really. I need a Silversmith to show the others that when your family returns, they cannot slaughter us. Your presence guarantees peace among a race that is lethal, and I will do whatever it takes to win against your bloodline."

"If you're trying to turn me against my family, save your breath," I snorted, holding his intense stare. "Over three hundred years have passed, and you don't know if they intend even to return. Here's the thing, you all made horrible mistakes. I didn't. I'm just a girl who wanted to make weapons and hunt down the bad guys. I didn't want to spend my life hiding, so I ran away. I came back because something was wrong, and ended up as your silver, and I don't even fully understand what it means. It must be something huge if none of my family has ever gifted it before. I get that I'm basically your medieval wife, or whatever, but that's where my knowledge ends. You're no better than my mother. She kept so many secrets, and by the time I was old enough to be told the truth, it was too late."

"Had I taken your silver, and not given my vow, our arrangement would have been one-sided, Remington."

"That means nothing to me, even though I know it means something to you."

"Your soul belongs to me and mine to you. Whether we're going to end up lovers, friends, or enemies, well, that will depend on us. What we choose to be to one another will determine our path when we're reborn." Rhys stood to grab the whiskey from the hutch, setting a glass in front of me. I fought the panic threatening to consume me. "Our arrangement isn't just for this lifetime. It's something souls do when they're given. In this case, between our bloodlines, it is silver weapons, or a promise of a knightly duty that, once given, cannot be taken back. If I hadn't taken your silver, Cole would have, even with my name on it. You're innocent. Cole would have asked, and you'd have handed it to him. I accepted your offer, so that you wouldn't become his because the thought of you belonging to anyone, well, I couldn't allow it to happen."

"You could have told me what it meant and allowed me the choice to melt it back down. You could have told me that I was sealing not only the rest of my life but every lifetime after this one too, Rhys. You don't even like me, so why would you do this?"

"To ensure peace remains, and that your family doesn't rise up to start World War III, slaughtering humans in the process, as they did last time. It wasn't just my family who stood outside your family's house, watching them burn, Remi. We all did. Every alpha in every branch helped us trap the Silversmiths into that mansion and set it ablaze. Do you think your sweet mother is going to forgive us? Or do you think she will want to avenge the children we slaughtered? Her children and her mate were within that home, and I assure you, they weren't immortal. I know, because I buried them.

"My family returned the next day and gave yours eternal rest because we did owe them that much because not all of them were evil. It was more than they had done for my mother. Knowing what I do now, that some survived, I'm willing to guess it wasn't any of the good ones because they'd never have left those children behind to die by fire. Fire isn't a good death, not when the flames moved faster than the smoke, offering them no relief from the pain. So no, Remington," he stated, handing me the glass of whiskey, "I couldn't let you walk away because you are going to mean the difference between winning this war and losing it." His eyes held mine, and I lowered them, peering anywhere but into the cunning stare that was smug as shit.

"You are not evil. Not yet, anyway. I could have done this differently and told you the truth, but had I done that, you'd never have believed me, let alone trusted me. At the end of the day, I'm a Van Helsing, and you're Remington Silversmith. You were born my enemy, and I chose to become yours. Don't choose an alpha tomorrow, because then I'll have to kill them to claim their child should you produce one during the festival of fertility. I respect most of the alphas because we've worked very hard to bring order to our world since it crumbled at the hands of your family. As an alpha, I can take the child of a beta as my own and raise it. I'd never wish to remove a child from its father, but in this case, because of the nature of the blood you carry, I would. You can go." Rhys stared at me as I sat there, numb from what he'd dropped in my lap.

As I processed his words, my heart thundered against my chest, and I wanted to slap him, scream at him, or do something to release the pain his words had caused. I was stuck with him for eternity, and any child I had, he would take. Was I supposed to just accept that? Fuck that and him.

"That dark look of absolute rejection burning within your stare, Remi," he mumbled softly. "The pain you're feeling? That's why I didn't tell you. I'm a sadistic bastard who enjoys my role, but your pain doesn't bring me joy. I sort of hate you for it because it tells me you're a weakness I cannot afford."

I downed the drink, holding the glass back out for more, watching him hesitate. "You just told me that I'm stuck with you one way or another until the world blows up, and even then, I can't escape you in our next life. I don't see it happening soon enough for it to be relevant, so pour me a damn drink, Van Helsing. Tell me about the festival. Or tell me something not horrible about this world in which I was born."

"Your dress is finished. I allowed it to be silver to symbolize your house. You'll wear the only silver ribbon as well. When you choose a partner, you tie it around his wrist, and at the end of the night, if he chooses you, you will be his for twenty-four hours to procreate. Most can't create life anymore or have lost the ability because of what they've become. As you know, Beltane is the only time of the year that immortals are fertile. Therefore, any children born to immortals are off-limits in feuds, since breeding is such a rare occasion."

"Unless they're Silversmith children? In which case, you'd take them from me," I countered harshly, watching his throat bob at my reply. "That was an asshole thing to say."

"But true," he admitted without removing his heated stare from mine. "They're off-limits again, though. That shouldn't have happened. Rage, grief, and fear create monsters. They don't think before they act, and when they do, it's done harshly and without care to those they harm. We didn't start out as monsters, Remi. We became the monsters to prevent a war, unlike anything the mortals would have ever seen. Us giving into our demons allowed us to prevent the humans from perishing to a greedy bitch who wanted too much. Had Roslyn gotten her way, she'd be the immortal queen of all the houses. But her greed wouldn't have ended there. She'd want the entire world. Roslyn was tired of hiding who and what she was. She wanted it all. She'd do something so horrid and then cry for forgiveness afterward, and everyone always forgave her."

"Almost everyone," I whispered, sipping the cup. "Someone needed to stop her," I admitted, sipping the whiskey while lifting my eyes to hold his stare. "Evil is evil, and sometimes it is blood. Roslyn sounds like a psychotic, murderous bitch. I'll pick a beta, because if I have a child, no one is taking it from me, Rhys. Not even you. As I said, I take pride in the things I create, and if I create life, I will assure it is perfect, and I will raise my children myself because that's important to me."

"I figured you would want your child, Remington. You're the kind of woman that men look for as a mate. You're smart, beautiful, and there's a loyalty within you that not many people can even begin to understand. I went through your files from E.V.I.E. last night. You entered under an alias, Remi Cordova, and earned the entire division's highest marksmanship scores. You marked higher than pure born witches in magic skills, and yet you chose to make weapons. You could have done anything you wanted within E.V.I.E. and gone straight to the highest-ranking level of hunter, but you chose not to do so. Why?"

"Because your bloodline cursed mine, and that limits me. I'd have put others in danger, and that wasn't something I could allow. Sometimes we have to accept our faults, see our limitations, and understand what they mean for others and ourselves. I know mine, and I know what they mean for others. I can't expect others to save me all the time. So, I stayed where I could help E.V.I.E. the most. I am a good shot, powerfully blessed with magic, and I can hunt down my enemies. The thing is, to do so, I'd have had to lie about being cursed, and I am many things, Rhys, but a liar isn't one of them. Sleep well, Van Helsing," I whispered, setting the glass on the table and leaving him to ponder my words.

Chapter Twenty-Three

I stared into the mirror, amazed and blown away by what the women working for Rhys had been able to do with my appearance. The dress he had commissioned for me was a work of art. Silver beadwork covered the corset, with a flowing bell skirt creating layers of fine silk that flowed to the floor beautifully. The only jewelry I wore was a simple silver necklace containing an infinity symbol dangling from a thin chain. It was delicate, simple, and beautiful. Rhys had dropped the necklace off earlier, and I wasn't sure if it was for my protection or a gift. Either way, I was thankful to feel some resemblance of defense tonight.

My hair was curled and placed into an updo with a few strands left down to frame my face. Makeup was applied, but only to enhance my eyes and lips with light color since tonight wasn't about transforming into something we weren't. It was about freeing yourself from the constraint of the modern world.

Beltane was all about new life. It was the celebration of a man and woman coming together to create life. It was also the celebration announcing summer to the world. They lit fires to fill the world with new light while heating it with renewed warmth.

"I look like a goddess!" Nyx bounced from foot to foot in her red dress that had a deep V-line neck exposing the curves of her ample breasts. "I cannot wait for them to undress us, because I'm literally wearing nothing but panties beneath this dress!"

I swallowed, lifting my narrowing eyes to glare at her, shock filtering through my expression. "Excuse me?"

"Oh, he didn't tell you, did he?" she winced overdramatically, even though her smile was firmly still in place.

"What didn't he tell me?" I asked, assuming she was referring to Rhys. When she cocked her head to the side, slowly frowning, her mouth puckered into a tight line, and I groaned. "Spill it, Nyx!"

"Halfway through the night, they bare the maidens to the men. They strip us down to our undies before parading us through the courtyard. They do it so men who haven't chosen a consort for the night can make their final choice on who to take into the forest until dawn."

"Do they actually go into the forest?" I questioned, turning as a knock sounded at the door to my room.

"Well, no. Everyone has a room to sleep in, of course. Some will choose to go into the forest as is tradition, but pinecones in the vagina is a hard limit for some of us. Pine needles hurt in certain places, and they poke your ass as well." She dabbed her finger against her ruby-red lips, fixing her lipstick before moving to the door, peering out into the hallway. "Your jailers are ready to escort us down," Nyx called over her shoulder, and I exhaled a soft sigh.

I had knights escorting me everywhere since Rhys had started allowing me to move freely throughout his home. I was unable to escape them, even during mealtime. It was unnerving, but it made me feel safer while his family was here.

Moving to the door, I paused. Nyx grabbed me, turning me to face her as if she had something important to say. "You're wearing something sexy beneath the dress, right? Like something that will knock Rhys's dick right up to punch him in the nose?"

"It wasn't that big of a dick, Nyx." Swallowing, I listened as the knights choked or smothered their laughter with coughs. "Besides, he isn't interested in me. He told me to choose a beta for tonight. That way, if I created a child tonight, he could take it. He isn't choosing me tonight."

"He named you the May Queen, and himself the Forest King. He basically wrote his name on your vagina, woman." Coughing exploded outside of the room, and I stepped into the hall as my knight, Luis, smothered a laugh as he reached behind us to close the door.

"You look beautiful tonight, My Lady," Luis said, bowing his head, which made me smile at the chivalry he was displaying.

"Thank you," I replied, moving further down the hall. The knights surrounded us as other guests filtered from their rooms and into the hallway, making their way to the courtyard.

"Rhys wants you, Remi. It's as simple and complicated as that. The issue is, he's *the* alpha."

"He doesn't want me like that anymore. If he did, he'd have finished one of the times he started, but he'd rather answer the door or whatever, and leave me needlessly hanging."

"He's alpha, Remi. It's his job to be available to people who need him. He must continue being the alpha because his brothers are all cold bastards and would let a war begin. Rhys wants to stop it from happening. I understand what he is doing, even if he did go about it horribly wrong. As your best friend, I know you understand it too. You've seen what creatures like us do to humans, and if we go to war, they will suffer needlessly."

"It doesn't make it easier for me that I was thrown into this shit hazardously. I have no choice in anything I do, and Rhys uses my age against me to trap me into positions that I shouldn't be."

We paused as we entered the courtyard, silently taking in the multitude of people talking and drinking already. I swallowed down the urge to tuck tail and go back to my room and hide. The knights closed in behind, preventing my retreat and anyone else from moving onto the stairs as I began to descend.

The steward announced my name, and the entire assembly went silent. I exhaled a shaky breath, taking in the eyes that examined me. I moved my feet carefully down the stairs, and locked eyes with Rhys, who stared at me as if I was the only woman in the room. I focused on getting to him without falling and breaking my neck.

"How uncomfortable is it to know that everyone here wants to murder you?" Nyx asked, and I almost missed a step, turning my wide eyes toward her.

"It wasn't until you mentioned it," I groaned, turning to look at Rhys, who was now glaring at Nyx. "Let's try not to say it too loudly. I am sure some people in the back didn't hear you."

"Well, I mean, not everyone wants you dead. I don't," Nyx chuckled as we stopped in front of Rhys and Acyn, both bowing at their waist, lifting to offer their elbows to escort us into the courtyard.

"You are stunning tonight, Remington," Rhys whispered against my ear.

"You clean up pretty good too, Van Helsing."

"Were you ever taught to dance?"

"I can dance," I swallowed, noting he was heading straight toward the dance floor, and all around us, couples were following our lead.

"Good, because everyone is watching you." Rhys stopped in the middle of the floor, turning toward me as he smirked devilishly.

I paused to look around, noting that everyone *was* watching us. He held his hands up, and I placed mine against them, waiting for the music to begin. The moment it did, he closed the distance between our bodies, sliding one arm behind my back. He slowly turned us toward the others on the dance floor, moving forward before turning me yet again.

"What dance is this?" I asked, panic slowly sinking in.

Rhys didn't answer. Instead, he turned toward me, encircling my waist as my arms wrapped around his neck. His eyes watched me, lowering to my throat to see my wildly racing pulse. There was a wicked smile playing on his mouth, but his eyes slid to something over my shoulder.

The music changed, as if whoever controlled the tempo noted that we'd changed dances. It was a slow song, one that allowed Rhys to move us fluidly across the dance floor. His hand reached up to mine, claiming it before he spun me around and yanked me back until I was flush against his warmth.

"You're safe, woman. No one here will touch you tonight. Not unless you wish it to be so, Love," he whispered into my ear, and then lifted me into the air while holding my waist.

Rhys stared up at me through heated eyes, my hands held on to his shoulders, and slowly, so very slowly, he lowered me to the floor. Smiling boyishly, he grabbed my hand, spinning me around the moment my feet touched the floor. He danced like it was a battle, one he raged against me as we spun around, coming body to body repeatedly. His mouth would lower precariously close to mine, but he'd move away every time I lifted on my toes to claim his lips. On the last few notes of the song, he dipped me back, his hands holding me as I slowly lifted my eyes to his, finding them filled with naked heat pooling in their endless depths. He slowly pulled me up, holding me close until his forehead pressed against mine.

"Cole is off-limits tonight, Remington. I suggest you choose someone wisely," he swallowed, stepping back to watch me. I struggled to control the emotion that dancing with him had created within me.

I opened my mouth to tell him that I wanted him, but a blonde woman stepped in front of me, tying her ribbon to his wrist while he held my stare. My throat bobbed, and I smiled tightly, turning to flee the dance floor. I stopped in front of the bar, slowly calming the burning inferno of jealousy and need rushing through me.

"You do realize that if you don't tie your ribbon to his wrist, he can't agree to be yours, right?" Nyx muttered from beside me, leaning over the bar to gain the attention of the bartender. "Also, you ran away before lighting the fire, so you're going to have to go back and finish the job with him," she said, turning to look pointedly at me. "I suggest you tie your ribbon to him then."

I peered over my shoulder, watching Rhys, who stared at me through the crowd as women continued tying their ribbons onto his arms. Snorting, I rolled my eyes before turning back to tell the bartender what I wanted, asking if it was possible to get the entire bottle now. He chuckled like I was cute, and I stared at him without cracking a smile.

"Yeah, she's serious," Nyx chuckled and turned, exhaling. "Hey, Rhys, nice turnout tonight, don't ya think?"

"Indeed, very nice turnout, but then they're here to see Remington," he said, grabbing my hand, turning me to look at him. "I need you."

I swallowed against the warmth his words filled me with and then groaned out loud as I realized he meant to light the fire of Beltane. I nodded, allowing Rhys to pull me toward the large fire pit as people watched us. We stopped in front of a torch, and he handed me a candle, and together we touched the wicks against the flickering flame before turning to drop the candles into the large pit.

I turned to speak to Rhys, but he was already moving away from me to stand beside an ethereal brunette who smiled coyly when he reached her. Scanning the room, I noted several people were openly pointing and speaking about me and my odd complexion that they were strangely fascinated over.

Worrying my lip, I walked away from the fire, heading back to the bar. I accepted my glass that Nyx held out, downing it in one swig before placing it on the bar and nodding to the bartender for another. Nyx moved away when someone asked her to dance, and I spun around, watching her, noticing others were staring at me.

Illeron, one of Rhys's brothers, stopped in front of me, placing his hands on the bar behind me, caging me against it. His dark blue eyes swept over my face, studying me as I stared back silently. His dark head leaned closer, forcing me to lean back, watching a cruel smile play over his mouth. He dragged his nose against my throat, slowly moving it to press against my ear.

"Is your pussy really that good? You have both

my brothers drooling over your cunt, so it must be magical to have ensnared them so deeply. I wonder if you'd let me fuck you too, so that I could make an educated opinion about it as well? Can I fuck you too, Silversmith whore?" he asked as I shook, closing my eyes. His hand slid to my side and closed around my breast until I yelped in pain.

"I have not fucked either of them, so no. You may not fuck me either, Van Helsing. You can, however, get the fuck off of me. I am not a whore, nor do I intend to be shared among brothers for yours or their enjoyment. Excuse me," I said, and yet he didn't budge from where he pressed me against the bar.

People had stopped what they'd been doing to watch us together. My heart thundered against my chest, and panic was sinking in while his knee lifted, pressing against my apex as he nipped my ear, growling against it.

"Illeron, have you still not figured out how to tell when a lady isn't interested in your cock, brother?" Cole asked, sliding in beside me. The moment Illeron started to back up, Cole pulled me in front of him, wrapping his arms around, resting his chin on my shoulder, daring his brother to argue with him for me.

"She's already fucking both of you. Why not share her with the rest of us?" Illeron asked, lifting a drink to his lips, glaring coldly at me.

"Oh, my. Do you feel left out again? I mean, you did always go after our discarded pussy when we'd finished with it. Here's the thing, brother. Remington hasn't slept with any of us yet. Therefore, we're not finished with her. It's Beltane, and there's pussy everywhere. Go find one that will gift you her ribbon willingly. This isn't the medieval times where you can order a woman to hand you their ribbon. Now go, before I forget you're my brother and that you're one of the few I actually like."

I watched Illeron until he disappeared into the crowd of people, finding Rhys watching me as a woman brushed her fingers against his chest. I turned my attention to Cole, crawling off his lap and grabbing the drink in front of him, downing its contents as I ignored the crowd's curious stares.

"Are you okay, Remi?" Cole asked, slipping his hand around me. He pulled me into the heat of his body, cupping my cheek before his eyes searched my face.

"I'm fine," I muttered, closing my eyes before peering up at the sky filled with stars. The night sky was always soothing to me, even as a child.

"Dance with me, Sunshine," he said, grabbing the whiskey glass from my hand and placing it on the bar. Cole pulled me behind him out onto the dance floor, smiling at the worried expression on my face. Once there, he slipped his arms around my back, slowly moving us to the beat of the music. My hands lifted to rest against his chest, and he smiled when I leaned my head there too, resting it for a moment and closing my eyes. "You're the most beautiful woman here tonight, and yet you look the most miserable, Remington. Tonight is a celebration of life. Stop caring what everyone else is thinking or doing. Just be you, and you'll be perfect," he whispered against my hair, inhaling deeply.

I opened my eyes, looking over Cole's shoulder,

locking eyes with Rhys, who glared at me from the opposite side of the room. The tick in his jaw hammered against his cheek, and his arms crossed over his muscular chest, displaying a multitude of ribbons on each wrist.

He wasn't happy that I was dancing with Cole, but he'd left me on my own tonight. So far, the only people who had approached me were his brothers. I looked away from Rhys, staring up at Cole, who also watched Rhys. I parted my lips to speak, and he lowered his mouth, claiming mine in a sinfully wicked kiss that stunned me speechless.

Cole didn't simply kiss. He fucked you with his tongue, leaving you dazed and struck stupid as you tried to figure out what the hell had just happened. I moaned against his lips, sliding my hands up his back, feeling his muscles tensing beneath my touch. Tilting my head for better access, Cole slid his hand to the back of my neck, deepening the kiss while barring any retreat.

He devoured me until I was trembling against his lips while he deepened the kiss further. Something brushed against my back, and then arms wrapped around me, pulling me back from Cole's mouth as a soft cry of regret escaped my throat.

I was pulled from the dance floor while Cole remained on it, canting his head to the side, watching Rhys yank me toward the shadows. Rhys slammed me against the wall and slapped his hands against it, on either side of my head. He caged me in as I peered up into his angry azure gaze. My hand lifted, touching my swollen lips from Cole's dominating kiss.

"What are you doing, Remington?" he demanded

icily, glaring as I continued touching my lips. He grabbed my hands, pushing them above my head, leaning closer. He kissed me hard and fast until I was moaning against him, easily erasing Cole from my mind. "Kiss him again, and you'll learn what voyeurism is when I rip your dress off and show all my guests how prettily you cry out as you come for me, little girl. I warned you that Cole was off-limits to you, and I fucking meant it. Don't push me tonight. Not tonight, please."

"Rhys... I...," he turned, leaving me dumbfounded. I watched him moving back to the crowd, "want *you* tonight," I whispered to myself.

Leaning my head back against the wall, I watched him move to a male who turned, eyeing me before they vanished together through the crowd, moving up the stairs silently.

"You and I have some unfinished business, Silversmith," Laura snapped, strolling toward me, even though she'd sounded like she was directly in front of me. I swallowed, and she smiled coldly, but a petite woman stepped in front of me before Laura could reach me.

"Not tonight, you don't, Mon Chéri." The newcomer was barely over five-feet-tall, and yet the power she exuded was immense. She waited for Laura to snarl, baring her fangs before she turned, followed by a male vampire that slipped silently out of the shadows.

I took in Laura's shadow as he turned violet eyes on me, his silver-colored hair, making him look more fae than vampire. He smirked, and I swallowed hard as he turned to look at Laura with a dark smile playing on his seductive mouth.

"If you cause a scene tonight, Laura, I assure you that it will be your last one upon this earth for the next thousand years." Laura stepped back, turning on her heel as vampires I hadn't even noticed standing around her, slithered from their spot, taking her away with them.

The vampire turned his violet gaze on me, smiling, hitting me with the watts of a thousand lights. The tiny female turned, lifting her hand to my temple, sending pain ripping through my head as she whispered softly.

"You feel no pain, my pretty girl. You're safe, and you feel nothing," she cooed reassuringly.

"Sure, except for the part where you're trying to rip through my memories," I groaned, holding my hand against hers to push it away, immediately pulling from the bloodbath of her memories. "Just ask me what you want to know. I will answer you honestly."

"People are never honest, sweet, naïve girl," she chuckled unkindly.

"People are assholes."

"Your mother, who is she?" the male asked.

"Who are you?" I countered.

"I can try again," she offered, staring at me.

"Ian Macleod, King of the Vampires."

"Elizabeth Silversmith."

"Impossible, as she's dead."

"No, she is not. She's very much alive, or at least

she was when I last spoke to her. She escaped through a library within the mansion and lived."

"Do you intend to start a war?" Ian asked, canting his head to the side, moving to stand in front of me, blocking me from the other partygoers. I leaned over, staring toward my protection detail. I caught sight of the knights behind him, and the vampire turned, smiling as if their presence amused him.

"I do not intend to start a war. I simply want to live without having to hide. I have never wronged anyone. Okay," I stated, holding up my finger. "I did make weapons to murder vampires, but I only did it so that we could keep them from breaking the laws, which you maintain. I have never actually murdered one, but I also firmly believe that keeping our presence unknown to humans is *very* important. There's nothing worse than a horde of humans on a high horse, holding pitchforks, fueled on by panic."

Ian's lips twitched while his eyes sparkled with amusement. "Why are you here?"

"Because I am young and foolish," I swallowed while doing my best to answer honestly. "I witnessed what I thought was going to end with people murdered and stepped in to break up a fight. It turns out that my stupid ass tried to save Rhys Van Helsing from Cole Van Helsing, and now I'm rather stuck here."

He threw his head back, laughing, which caused me to jerk back in surprise. Ian narrowed his eyes as he extended his elbow toward me.

"Dance with me, Silversmith. I won't take no for an answer."

I slipped my arm into his, knowing he probably *wouldn't* take no for an answer. For the vampire alpha, Ian was everything that they said he wasn't. I'd heard the lore about him, listened to horror stories of what he'd done to hunters who had murdered one of his enforcers, or those who held his houses. However, Ian seemed down to earth. But he was still one of the alphas that had stood outside my family's mansion, watching them burn.

Chapter Twenty-Four

Ian moved me gracefully around the floor as he talked about the changes in the world and what he enjoyed about them. He was a wealth of information and never tired of speaking. When the fifth dance ended, he paused as someone caught his attention. I followed his stare to where Rhys waited on the edge of the dance floor, watching me with the vampire alpha. Ian leaned down, kissing my cheek before reaching into his pocket and tying his ribbon on my wrist.

"You're a pleasure, Remington Silversmith. Save a dance for me when you shed this dress, please," Ian said smoothly, running his lips over my artery, causing my heart to kick into overdrive at the brief brush of fangs against my flesh. "I promise not to bite you unless you beg me to do so. Most do," he stated, grabbing my hand to place a gentle kiss onto my palm.

"That was pretty smooth," I whispered.

Ian smiled, throwing back his head to give me

a belly laugh, which caused everyone in the room to pause and stare at him. "You're refreshing, and either lack fear, or have the protection of the Van Helsing. Which one is it, Remington?"

"She has my vow of protection, and I have her silver, Ian. I'm glad to see you crawled out of that pile of rubble you call a castle to come tonight, old friend," Rhys stated, peering at my wrist with a narrowed look burning in his stare.

"No!" Ian whispered, turning to look at me to see if I'd argue Rhys's claim. "You sneaky devil, how did you manage that?"

"Surprisingly, it was rather easy. Remington is rather naïve in her young age." Rhys lifted his eyes from my wrist to hold my stare with anger burning in his. "If you'll excuse us, Love. I do believe Nyx has been looking for you for the last hour that you've kept Ian busy."

"Actually," a deep voice said from behind me. "I'd like this dance if Ian has finished monopolizing the May Queen. I didn't get a chance to introduce myself formally."

Rhys ground his back teeth together before he turned, staring at Conrad. "Indeed, at least this time your is dick covered, mutt," he growled.

"If I remember correctly, she liked looking at my cock, old friend."

My cheeks heated, and Ian smiled, lifting his hand to brush his fingers over my cheek. "She blushes beautifully."

"What the hell is up with you guys and blushing?" I asked without realizing I'd asked aloud.

"When you're as old as we are, nothing amuses us. Finding a pretty maiden on the cusp of her immortality that still has some sense of morals, is something we don't often see," Ian answered, dropping his fingers. "How is it she doesn't have the normal silver hair and ice-blue eyes of a Silversmith?"

"That's the mystery of the hour, isn't it, Remington?" Rhys asked, watching as Conrad lifted my arm, securing his ribbon onto my wrist while Rhys glared at us. "Shall we, Ian? Excuse us, Conrad, Silversmith." Rhys nodded to Conrad before leveling me with a chilling look of warning.

I watched Rhys turn away from me, moving toward the stairs again. Conrad waved a hand in front of my face, studying me when I turned my attention to him.

"He'll never allow himself to love you. He's charged himself to the eternal agony of never knowing real love. Rhys is a glutton for punishment. When Rhys hands out a punishment, he doesn't go back on it, ever. You look like the type of woman who would need more from a man than a quick fuck, Remington. Something tells me that you're more mate material than a girl who would allow herself to be used and then set aside."

"Don't confuse curiosity with being stupid, Conrad. He's claimed me in a way that doesn't allow me to escape him; even in death, I won't be free of him. Rhys is willing to take advantage of me, so why shouldn't I figure out a way to repay him tenfold?" I asked, lifting a brow. He slipped his arms around me, peering down at me with serious amber eyes that held keen intelligence.

"Don't do that," he warned softly. "I have met only a few men I wouldn't cross in my lifetime, and Rhys Van Helsing is one of them. Don't make him your enemy, Silversmith. Right now, you have the advantage because you confuse his duty with his need. The moment you cross that line from friend to enemy, you won't ever come back from it."

"I don't intend to use or harm him or screw him over as he'd done to me. I just want him to know that I am not a weak female," I grunted, turning as someone slipped in behind me, their hands smoothing over my dress to cup my breasts.

"So pretty," one of the female shifters whispered. "We're claiming, alpha?"

"I have placed my ribbon for her tonight," Conrad answered. Leaning closer to me, he inhaled deeply. "You've seen what I can offer you. I would be gentle, and my pack would give you pleasure as well." Someone grabbed my arm, and multiple hands started placing ribbons around my wrist as Conrad smiled. "Have you ever been cherished, pleasured by an entire pack, Silversmith? I assure you, those who have never leave because it is most pleasurable to be with us," he assured me.

"The song ended five minutes ago," Cole stated, narrowing his eyes on the females that continued placing their ribbons on my wrist. "Kinky, even by my standards, Sunshine," Cole smiled, slowly pulling me back against him. "Do you want to see what Conrad has to offer you? I can show you what it would be like, but I'll be honest, I intend to enjoy it too."

"I'd like this dance, gentlemen," a silky voice injected, and both men stiffened. "Aw, it's a tradition for every alpha to dance with the May Queen. Rhys should have realized that when he named her such. Remington Silversmith, I am Hunter, alpha to the otherworld creatures," he said in a voice layered in thick lust.

I turned, staring straight into turquoise eyes that reminded me of the blue seas in the Caribbean. His hair was midnight black, pulled back to show off the angular planes of his chiseled jawline. His lips tipped into a smile, and he tilted his head to the side, searching my face as he held out his hand, waiting for me to accept.

"I promise to be on my best behavior, considering you're mortal, and I am not. May I have this dance, Silversmith? No other woman here seems capable of matching your beauty."

I remained in place, peering into the galaxies of his eyes. They swallowed me into the abyss of waves, washing over me soothingly. His smile turned wicked as he stepped closer, placing his fingers beneath my chin to close my mouth. I lifted my hand, checking for drool. A loud snort sounded from beside me, and I turned to find Rhys watching me with something akin to resentment banked in his gaze.

Hunter grabbed my hand, sweeping me out onto the dance floor without waiting to see if I had agreed to dance. I couldn't remember if I'd spoken or not. He was ethereal and way too pretty. He lowered his mouth to my ear, whispering against it in a layered voice, and the dance floor vanished, and we were in some type of room. I swallowed, pulling my hand away from him while he watched me.

"You have tongues wagging everywhere, Silversmith. Drink?" he asked, and I shook my head. "You've heard of us, have you?"

"I'm going to pass on food and beverages from the King of the Fae, Hunter. You're the legendary hunter who murdered the High King of the fae and took his throne by force. You're the creature the immortals warn their misbehaving children about at night."

"You have heard of me," he chuckled, and we were once again on the dance floor. I turned, finding Cole and Rhys both glaring at Hunter. "Your wrist, my darling," he chuckled, unperturbed by the men who looked like they wanted to use his head for target practice.

I lifted my wrist for him, watching while he turned it over, kissing my racing pulse before his ribbon appeared without him moving his hands. He pulled me against his body, whispering into my ear. He turned my head at the last moment, claiming my lips softly, which created a throbbing need between my thighs.

"I was created for pleasure, and to please a gluttonous queen. Choose me tonight, and I will make you my queen for eternity, Remington," he stated, dropping my hand, turning to nod at the men who both stared at my wrist before lifting their gaze to mine.

I swallowed, moving away from the dance floor to reach the bar, swallowing hard past the heaviness of my tongue. Nyx lifted my wrist, snorting as her eyes went owl-like in shape.

"Are you promising some major head to men, or telling them you're some blushing virgin? I need to know because I only have five ribbons, and I'm the nymph! I am made for fucking! The shame!" She placed her hand over her eyes dramatically, and I groaned.

"I need a drink," I stated as someone tapped my shoulder.

"I'm not fucking you!" I snapped, coming face to face with Nyota, who lifted a dark eyebrow, crossing her arms over her chest.

"I would hope not, I don't swing that way," she snorted, sliding in beside me. "Rhys will never allow you to get close to him. You're only hurting yourself with your delusion that he'll ever care for you." She looked over at Nyx, who tried to hide that she was listening, but failing miserably. "Go find something to fuck, nymph."

"No," I stated icily, glaring at Nyota, watching as her eyes slid back to mine. "She's having a drink with me, and if you're here, to tell me how Rhys will never allow himself to have me for more than a quick fuck, I've heard it already tonight, several times."

"Rhys wants you, Silversmith. Of that, you can be certain." Her eyes slid over my face before she sat at the bar and nodded for me to join her. "Sit and listen, because whatever it is you've done to Rhys, it's given him a spark. That isn't something I've seen since your murderous whore of an aunt fucked him over." I slid onto the stool, nodding at the bartender who peered at Nyota and then bowed before pouring our drinks. "He will allow himself to have you once, and then he will be stoic, distant, and cold. Cole will sweep in to pick up your broken pieces. After a while, he will grow bored with you. When Rhys doesn't rise to the occasion to argue for you, Illeron will then try for you, and then they will pass you down the line of my brothers, and that is the ugly truth. It's been that way since that bitch burned inside that mansion, if she actually did. Cole only wants you because he's made it his mission to force Rhys to forgive himself. Illeron, well, he's an asshole. The rest, well, they just like to be sure that they've tasted whatever flavor Rhys tasted first.

"I want my family healed, of that, you can be sure, too. You're not the one who can do that, Silversmith. You're the enemy. So fuck Rhys, let him get you out of his system, and then fuck off. If you don't, know this: I am the one person Rhys will never hurt. I can murder you, and he'd forgive me. Maybe not right away, but he's always forgiven me of my crimes. Don't make me murder you, because you seem innocent in this. But then so did Roslyn, until she revealed her true colors. Rhys is trying to stop a war with you, but you're going to be the one who starts it. If you fuck Cole tonight, you can end this before it begins."

"You're intervening where you're not warranted," Cole growled, his tone sending a shiver up my spine. "Rhys might forgive you, sweet sister, but I don't. Now fuck off and leave her alone. Remington, it's time for the real party to start. Finish your drink. You're going to need it."

I started to place my hand into his, but a giant hand gripped mine. It yanked me from the chair violently, pulling me forward. Cole swore beneath his breath, and the entire assembly seemed to go silent around us.

"Dance. You dance... me, please," the giant said.

I lifted my eyes to his, barely schooling my

response in time. He had a scar that ran across his face from one ear to the other, giving his face a caved-in appearance. My pulse kicked up while Cole stepped back, and Nyota swore beneath her breath. The surrounding silence was deafening, and I fought to control my response to the giant's sheer size.

"You… dance… me," he stammered, his words hitching.

"I will dance with you," I stated, smiling softly.

He smiled, and the entire room released a breath. His head tilted as he watched me. His disfigured smile was unnerving, but there was an innocence to him that dispelled the fear I'd felt. He easily stood over seven-feet-tall, with dark, cropped hair that hung to his shoulders.

He smiled again, leaning closer to me to whisper, which came out in a scream that tickled my ear. "I… Thurston!"

"I am Remi," I grinned, watching as he nodded joyously.

He pulled me behind him, forcing me to step quickly, so as not to be dragged behind him. Thurston stopped on the wooden dance floor, and others scooted away from him. He nodded vigorously to a woman who stared at me with a warning in her eyes.

I didn't have time to wonder about it as American Authors' *Best Day of My Life* started, and the giant began jumping up and down. I smiled wide, shaking my head at his dance moves. I started dancing with him, and he paused, cocking his head to the side. He laughed and mirrored my movements, which was like a carefree idiot that wasn't watched by an entire assembly of immortals who wouldn't forget it anytime soon.

I threw my hands in the air, and Thurston followed my lead, shaking and twisting. I danced with him until the end of the song. The moment the song ended, he grabbed me by the waist, lifting me over his shoulder as he patted my ass. My eyes widened as Rhys chuckled, chasing after us until the woman stepped into Thurston's path.

Rhys slowed the moment Thurston paused, his demeanor changing. "I fuck... her!"

My eyes grew large until they mirrored saucers, and Rhys shook his head at Thurston. "She's mortal, Thurston. You'd kill her. She's delicate like a flower." Okay, that was taking it a little far. I wasn't *that* delicate.

"I want... her. She's... pretty... laughs from... deep. I... go deep... in... pussy." I frowned, peering over my shoulder at Rhys, who snickered.

He better save my ass!

Thurston's hand patted my ass, and I jerked as he slammed his beefy hand against my rump a third time. The woman reached up, slipping her ribbon over his wrist. He turned, staring at her with interest.

"Remi is very beautiful and very delicate," Rhys stated, his voice calm and without the panic I felt. "Carla wants you tonight, isn't she pretty? You won't break her."

Thurston slammed me into Rhys's arms, and he barely stopped us from both going to the floor in a pile of limbs. Rhys turned me into his chest, smiling at Thurston. We didn't move until he and the woman were on the stairs. Rhys pulled me toward the bar, sitting me down. I took my first breath of air, slowly exhaling. The bartender handed me a whiskey, and I turned, staring at Rhys, who observed me carefully as if he thought I would break down or something.

"Thank God for Carla," I muttered, shaking my head as his lips twitched. "I'm glad she accepted him."

"She's the first love of his life," he announced. I felt the other men settling around us, asking if I was okay.

"That's sweet. Before he was wounded?"

"Indeed," he agreed.

"Well, glad she wanted to have him tonight. Saved me from having to turn him down for sex," I stated, taking a pull of whiskey.

"She's his mother," Rhys stated, and I spewed whiskey all over the bar, choking.

My eyes turned to his, and I opened my mouth and closed it. "She's going to have sex with him? She's his mother!" I gasped as the bartender laughed, handing me a towel to wipe my face off while the men around me laughed.

"No, his father will be waiting in the hallway to inject him with a tonic that will allow them to lead Thurston to his room. He was wounded in battle before he was immortal, and they became sterile soon after Thurston was born. We all made a pact, allowing them to keep their child, and not put him down as was done in those days. We agreed that no one would treat him as anything less than a giant deserving of respect."

I swallowed as tears pricked my eyes. "That is sweet."

"So were you for not turning a scarred man down. You knew he was dangerous and damaged, and yet you made his year, Remi. He will never forget the beautiful May Queen who danced with him and laughed like you didn't have a care in the world. No one else would have done that."

"Well, then they suck. Or maybe they realized Thurston was going to caveman a bitch and carry her off to fuck her hard," I chuckled, drinking as Rhys watched me with a smile on his lips. I reached for my ribbon, and a knight approached him, whispering in his ear as his eyes slid to mine, narrowing.

"Excuse me," he stated, strolling away with the guard while I picked at my ribbon.

"Come on, let's get you out of that dress," Cole whispered, pressing against my ear. "Stop hesitating, Sunshine. You're the May Queen, and no one can get fucked until you choose a partner. You know that you'll choose Rhys, it's a given." I turned to face Cole, staring into his pretty blue eyes as he grabbed my wrist. My eyes found Rhys standing across the room, watching us. "But in case you're not certain, a Van Helsing has to claim you as well. Can't have all the alphas holding a claim and none of us, right?"

He smirked boyishly, his teeth worrying his bottom lip. When he'd finished tying on his ribbon, he held out his elbow, and I slipped my hand around it, holding him tightly. The undressing was precisely that. We were stripped down to our panties and paraded around the room with me, leading all the women.

Rhys stared openly, slipping his gaze down to the tiny panties that luckily covered my ass, which I was sure was his doing. Once we'd finished walking in a circle around the dance floor, we moved from it, and I swallowed, walking to him as he smirked, turning his head to peer up at the stairs before moving toward them.

Closing my eyes, I nodded to the women who held my dress, slipping back into it before heading to the stairs as everyone watched me. My heart sat in my throat, and yet it was probably for the best that he hadn't allowed me to tie my ribbon to him. He obviously had chosen someone else, and avoiding me seemed to be his way out of dealing with me tonight.

"What the hell is happening?" Conrad asked, turning to look at Ian.

"I'm guessing she gifted herself the ribbon and intends to fuck herself tonight?" Ian snorted loudly.

"Can she do that?" Hunter asked.

"She's a Silversmith. She can do whatever the hell she wants with Rhys's protection. Good for her," Cole muttered, but there was a catch in his tone that tugged at me.

The knights walked me back to the room, where I silently removed my heels and rubbed my neck. Stretching it out, I reached behind me, unclasping the necklace. I started for the dress's zipper, but hands stopped mine. I lifted my eyes to the azure gaze in the mirror.

"Tell me to leave, Remi," Rhys whispered huskily.

"Stay," I swallowed, holding his heated depths while he reached for my arm, turning me to face him.

Rhys flicked a blade open, slicing through the other ribbons on each of our arms, freeing them as he set the knife down. Carefully, he secured his ribbon to my wrist while his eyes held mine prisoner. Once he'd finished, I tied mine to his, and he smirked wickedly, turning me around as he unzipped my dress to watch it pooling on the ground at our feet.

"You have no idea what I intend to do to you tonight, Remington. I intend to use every single second of the next twenty-four hours with you until you're screaming and begging me for mercy. You should know, I don't have any," he growled, turning me toward him as he began walking me slowly backward. "Tonight, you're mine, woman."

"About time, Van Helsing," I whispered breathlessly, crushing my mouth against his in a kiss that showed him I meant business. He groaned, lifting me, pushing my back against the wall, and capturing my hands above my head in one of his vise-like grips. His other hand grasped my chin, taking control as he devoured me hungrily, growling until I was moaning against his hard body with need.

Rhys pulled back, and I studied the blue of his eyes fighting the darkness of the incubus for control. It mattered little which side of him won tonight, as long as it ended with me getting relief from the need pulsing through me.

Chapter Twenty-Five

Rhys didn't just kiss me. He slowly seduced me, holding me helplessly pinned against the wall with his body. His tongue caressed mine, deliberately moving in and out of my mouth. It was as if he was showing me exactly what he intended to do to my body tonight. My stomach tightened with need, my core clenching greedily to be filled by him. Moans escaped my mouth, only to be swallowed and captured by his hungry kiss.

He pulled away from my mouth, kissing my neck as his fingers threaded through my hair, forcefully turning me around until my forehead pressed against the wall. His mouth brushed over my shoulder, nipping the skin with his teeth. Rhys's fingers worked the sides of my corset, becoming impatient and ripping it away from my body instead.

He slipped his hands around my front, grabbing and squeezing my breasts as he continued kissing the back of my neck. One of his large hands slid down my stomach, where his fingers glided against my opening. He growled wickedly, finding my body ready for his, pushing his fingertips in and out of my body while he continued kissing my shoulder.

"I need you now," I pleaded, but he didn't answer.

He was slowly kissing my spine, his hands gripping my breasts while his thumb played with the hardening tips. He chuckled when my hands reached behind me, searching for his body to free his thick cock. Releasing my breasts, he captured them with one hand, gripping my wrists and pinning them against my lower back.

"You'll get what you want soon enough, Love. Right now, I need to taste every inch of you and learn every curve. I have craved the taste of you dancing on my tongue. I plan to make you come so hard that you fight me to escape the pleasure that consumes you. You're not in control right now. I am. Now spread your legs so I can see how drenched you are with the need to be fucked by me," Rhys ordered huskily against my ear. I parted my legs, arching my ass, even though he continued holding my arms against my lower back. "Good girl, Remington. Are you wet for me?"

"Very," I admitted, blushing. His hand pushed my panties aside and skimmed over my naked heat again, enjoying the gasp of need that escaped my throat. "Rhys, please fuck me."

"I plan to, woman. You're not leaving here for twenty-four hours. When you do, you'll know what it means to be fucked stupid. When you leave this room, you'll want for nothing because nothing will compare or come close to what I'm about to do to you. Now shut up and fuck my fingers so I can feel this wet pussy clenching against me, begging me to fuck it hard and deep," he growled, pushing two fingers into my body, and I cried out as he laughed darkly.

His fingers moved slowly, torturing my core, which tightened with the need to hold him in place. I felt Rhys staring at my opening, and then my hands were lifted and pressed against the wall as he slowly pushed my panties down, revealing my naked need to his heated gaze.

"Such a messy girl," he whispered, bending down to blow against my heat. His fingers entered me again, and his tongue slid around them. I balled my hands into fists, closing my eyes as my body tightened, and he lapped hungrily at the arousal he created.

He was wearing entirely too many clothes for him to do what I needed. Pressure built in my core, and butterflies fluttered against my stomach as the sounds of pleasure escaped my throat. Rhys pulled his fingers away from my pussy, and I whimpered at the loss of them. I turned as he stood, lifting me by my hips, forcing me to wrap my legs around his waist. Rhys walked us toward the desk. His arm swept over it, sending his files and laptop clattering to the floor.

Setting me down, he lowered himself between my legs, pushing them apart to gently kiss my apex as I watched. I slid my hands through his hair, and he lifted, kissing me hungrily until I almost came from the intensity of it alone. I grabbed his suit jacket, undressing him hurriedly. He growled against my mouth, capturing my hands to place them onto the desk behind me.

Rhys stepped back, silently taking in my naked body. I blushed from the power burning in his eyes. His fingers worked the buttons on his dress shirt, slowing revealing the rippling muscles and beautifully etched curves of his body. Swallowing past the dryness in my mouth, I lowered my stare to the V-line that led beneath his slacks. Much to my disappointment, he didn't shed them before stepping closer.

I lifted my hands and lowered my mouth, kissing his chest in the middle before raining soft kisses over the edges of his six-pack. Rhys was built for war. The perfect design of sleek muscles and hard edges that drove women crazed to be conquered. My teeth found his pierced nipple and pulled against it playfully. His hands slipped through my hair, removing the pins as it fell freely down my back.

"I'm not going to last very long if you keep teasing me with that hungry mouth, Love," he warned, cupping my cheeks to lift my mouth to his.

"I'm okay with that," I whispered against his lips, hearing his moan that empowered me to act brazenly. Rhys slowly pushed me down onto his desk, parting my legs and pushing my knees up, spreading me fully before him. He held me there, staring at the arousal coating my sex with the need he created.

Rhys leisurely kissed his way down my body, slowing when he reached the middle of my breasts, turning his attention to one with renewed hunger. His teeth worried the rose-colored tip, his tongue brushing against it slowly. He stared at me as I writhed on his desk, my hands lowering to the edge, holding it tightly while he learned my body intimately. He moved to the other breast, showering it with the same heated kiss before he once again started toward the one place I needed him most.

The moment he reached my wanted destination, he turned his attention to my thighs, slowly kissing his way to my ankle. His fingers brushed over the back of my knee, sending my pulse racing to my core. He laughed huskily, standing to lavish the other leg with the same attention, moving his way back toward my center. His heated mouth claimed my clit without warning, sucking it hard between his lips, causing me arch off the desk, coming without warning in a violent orgasm.

He moaned against my core, staring at me while I blinked, trying to figure out what the hell had just happened as moans left my throat, and the room spun around me. Rhys didn't release my clit. He didn't even pretend to care that I'd come harder than I had ever come before in my entire life. My whole body vibrated with a shudder that continually escaped past my lips as a whimpered cry.

Rhys picked me up, kissing me hard while walking us toward the bed, dropping me. He watched my still trembling body bounce on the mattress. I smoothed my hands over my belly, but he stopped them, capturing them to pin above my head. He settled between my thighs, peering down at me with heat glowing in his azure gaze.

"That belongs to me tonight, woman. Do not touch it unless I tell you that you can. Spread your legs and drop your knees apart. Show me what belongs to me, Remington," Rhys ordered, lowering his mouth to mine, sucking my bottom lip between his teeth. He bit into it softly, pulling back with a growl that reverberated through his chest, sending a shiver rushing through me. My legs dropped open, and he smiled, releasing my lip as he sat back, staring at the mess between my thighs that he'd created. "Good girl."

He stood slowly, backing up a step, working the buttons on his suit pants. He paused to make sure he had my undivided attention as he grinned, freeing his huge, thick cock that jutted up proudly against his stomach. He allowed the pants to slide down his legs, easily stepping out of them as he gripped his pulsing shaft, watching me hungrily licking my lip as the tip glistened with cum.

"Sit up," he ordered, and I did. I sat up and leaned forward, pushing his hand away from the silken flesh as I kissed it, gazing up into his eyes. I let my tongue glide over the rounded top.

The tick in his jaw hammered, and his neck muscles constricted. The moment I took him into my throat to his base without warning, he gasped loudly. His fingers pushed through my hair, moving it away from my face. I pulled back, smiling around him, lavishing the sensitive edges while he studied me through hooded eyes. He allowed me to bring him to the edge, his chest tightening as his breathing grew labored. The muscles of his stomach clenched, and then he pushed my body back, trapping me beneath his. Darkly hooded eyes searched my face, and then he grabbed my hands, holding them above my head, parting my legs with his knee.

Rhys lowered his mouth, kissing me softly while

I squirmed with need beneath him. I felt his hardness against my core, felt his thick cock pushing against my opening before he pulled back, and thrust his hips forward, watching me cry out while he stretched me painfully full. He buried himself within me to his base, and my body reacted violently, coming undone with the abrupt, painful entrance.

I whimpered his name, and he stared at me as my eyes blinked to dispel the blotches of light that filled them. My ears rang, and sweat covered my body. He released my hands, sitting back to stare down at where we were connected.

"Bloody hell, Love," he grunted painfully while my body clenched against his throbbing cock. "You're certain you have been fucked before?" His eyes held mine before they lowered, his fingers slowly parting my pussy to show him how tightly my body gripped against him. My core clamped down around him, trying to dispel his oversized cock.

"I ache," I moaned, the burning stretch he created making my body pulse with the need for him to move. He was largely endowed, filling every inch of me full with his throbbing cock.

"You're so gorgeous." His eyes lifted, watching me trembling through the storm that refused to abate. His lips tugged up in the corners, watching yet another orgasm explode through me the moment his fingers grazed over my clit. "You're so tight around me, sucking me off while you come for me."

Rhys slowly moved within me, and I cried out his name. My hands wound through the blankets, twisting in them as he rocked against my apex. He groaned loudly while my body gripped him tightly, milking him while he slowly danced me back to the edge. The moment before I would have danced over the edge again, he stopped, lifting my body against his. He rose to sit back on his knees, kissing me breathless, moving us until I was straddling him as he lay back on the bed, peering up at me through burning eyes that searched my face.

"Ride me, woman. I want to watch your pretty eyes glow with wonder while I am buried within your tight cunt. You're so fucking responsive to my touch," he murmured, smiling at me with mischief dancing in his pretty gaze.

Rhys reached up, squeezing my breasts before dragging his heated stare down my body ravenously. He placed his hands on my hips, directing me to move slowly. He watched everything. The motion of my body. The speed I moved my hips in. When I started to unravel, he held me in place, denying me. I moaned, rocking my body with the need to come again. He smirked, leaning up to suck one nipple into his mouth, moving his tongue in a circle around the hard, pink tip. He lay back, directing my hips again as he slowly moved within me.

He continued denying me until I grew frustrated, which I knew he was aware of his effect on me. Lowering his eyes, he watched his fingers stroke my clit, growling from deep in his chest at my hooded stare, burning with need for him.

"You're so fucking tight and perfect around my cock, Remington."

"I'd be more perfect if you let me come," I

murmured huskily, shocked at the silkiness and need buried in my tone.

"You light up when you come for me," he hissed, lifting my hips, slamming me down hard on his thick erection. "Do you want to come for me?"

"Yes," I murmured, leaning down to claim his lips.

He slowly controlled the speed of our bodies, slamming me down every few moments until it hit on every nerve ending, firing them all up at once while he watched me pulling back to assist in my undoing.

"Look at me and don't close your pretty blue eyes. I want to see them light up with wonder when you come on my cock," Rhys ordered, slowly rocking my hips until I was assisting him. The coil in my stomach tightened, and I started to sweat as he slowly brought me to the edge of another orgasm.

He didn't release my hips, guiding my body and the angle in which he entered me. I lowered my head, holding his eyes while everything with me began to unfurl. Rainbow prisms filled my vision, and butterflies took flight within me.

My skin broke into goosebumps, and he lifted me, slamming me down onto his cock repeatedly. The scream ripped from my throat. His name escaped my lips like he was my savior, and I'd worship him until my dying days. Rhys continued thrusting into my body, extending the length of the orgasm until tears escaped my eyes. The beauty of the pleasure rocked my foundation and forced my walls to break apart and crumble, and he watched it happen.

"Goddamn, Remington. You're the hottest fucking

thing I've ever seen." Rhys rolled us until I was beneath him, then he withdrew from my body, kissing my back while adjusting me on the bed.

He placed me on my belly, lifting my hips, before spreading my knees apart with his. Rhys slid his hands over my hips and pushed into my body, going further than any man had ever gone. I whimpered, jolting from the fullness and pain it created. His dark laughter sent a chill racing up my spine seconds before his fingers followed the trail of it to my neck. Fingers twisted through my hair, and he pulled me up, forcing me flush against his body as he slowly worked his hips, grinding his cock into my flesh.

"Remember when I told you that you'd like this position?" he asked huskily.

"Yes," I replied through whimpers while he worked my body slowly to a boiling point once more.

"Let me know what you think of it when I'm finished wrecking your cervix," he growled, pushing me down as he let loose.

His fingers bit into my hips while he moved behind me, chuckling when I exploded around him. I cried his name while he slammed against my hips. I grabbed the blankets, biting them to muffle my screams, while he took me to the cliff, forcing me to dance upon it as the sounds of our bodies slapping against one another filled the bedroom. Rhys tensed behind me, and I felt his cock jerking within me. Then, he leaned over, kissing my spine, moaning as he released into my clenching need.

"Remington," he growled while I bucked against him, gluttonously needing more.

"I don't like it, Rhys," I whispered, smiling into the blanket. Rhys tensed behind me, his hands still holding my hips. "I love it, and I need more. I need all of you. I hope that wasn't everything you've got to give me. I'm a greedy bitch, so I need you to destroy me more," I moaned, rocking my ass against him, feeling his smile curving against my shoulder.

"I'm so glad you said that because we've got twenty-three hours left, Love. Round two starts now." His hand slapped against my ass, and my head fell back screaming his name while I impaled myself hard on his thick, pulsing cock. "You're a naughty little bitch. You're about to get wrecked, and I promise to leave you a sated, whimpering mess."

Rhys hadn't been lying. He used every moment of the time we had together, stopping only to feed me or supply whiskey to keep us hydrated. He'd even poured it over my pussy, lapping against it hungrily while he cracked jokes about me offering it to him the night we'd met.

In the morning, I woke cradled in his arms with my head against his heart. Instead of feeling sore or preventing him from another round, I let him have me outside of the time allotment, and slumbered more, only to repeat it until my body cried out with the need to rest. Even then, we didn't stop touching one another. It was as if some invisible tether was tied securely around us.

Chapter Twenty-Six

I awoke to someone playing with my hair, and my lips curled into a sleepy smile. Lifting my head, I peered into sleepy azure eyes before Rhys pounced on me. He pushed me down onto the bed, running his nose over my cheek. I moaned as he spread my legs apart, entering me hard and fast. It forced a soft cry to escape at the delicious soreness he'd created, lifting my mouth to his, which he pulled back, grabbing my hands to hold me down.

Opening my mouth, I gasped, shattering as he sent me over the edge quickly. He joined me as his body thrust a few more times before it stiffened, and he smiled, pressing his forehead against mine.

"You were made for me, weren't you, Remington?" he asked huskily. His eyes widened, and he slowly pulled out of my body, rolling from the bed to grab a pair of sweats from the floor.

I sat up, pulling the wrinkled sheet up against my

body, smiling at him. He sat on the couch, studying me. I could feel him closing down as if he'd not meant to say what he had. Swallowing, I stood and plastered a fake smile on my face.

"Thanks for last night, and this morning, Rhys," I whispered awkwardly. I started backing up while his stare followed me as if he weren't sure what was happening. "See you later." I waved clumsily, never having done the walk of shame before, even though our rooms were connected.

"What are you doing, Love?"

I hiked my thumb over my shoulder in the direction of the door. "I'm going to go, because I've never had to deal with the whole morning after, and you're looking at me like you're about to let me down. I get that you do this whole punish yourself shit, but this was just a man and woman fucking, so don't beat yourself up over it. It was fun, right?" I said awkwardly, chewing my lip, and he tilted his head, narrowing his eyes to angry slits.

"Come here," he growled, sitting back in the chair.

I slowly moved toward him, apprehension fueling my nerves. When I reached him, he pulled me down to him, forcing me to straddle his legs, causing the sheet to drop away from my body. He held my waist, watching me chewing my bottom lip nervously.

"It was fun? You think what we did was *fun*," he laughed soundlessly. Lifting his fingers through my hair, he twisted my head, pulling my mouth down close to his. His lips brushed against mine, and he lifted his hips to show me he was ready for more. "You don't get to dismiss me, Remington," he warned.

Standing up without warning, he walked me backward with his hand directing me until I was flat against the wall. His mouth lowered, claiming mine in a toe-curling kiss that stole a soft moan from my lungs. He released my hair, lifting me by my hips as he opened the connecting door, slowly walking us toward the bed in the other room.

He laid me down, lifting his head. Rhys's mouth brushed against mine. His eyes searched mine, and he smiled wolfishly. His erection pushed against my apex, and he snorted, feeling me rocking against him, eagerly ready for more.

"Your pussy is delicious. I enjoyed sucking the arousal from it as you begged me to fuck you. I enjoyed wrecking your tight cunt and listening as you screamed my name for hours. It was *fun* fucking you, Remington. Watching your pretty eyes grow hooded as I hit that spot within you that no other man had found before, also *fun*. It's been *fun* seducing you and learning how innocent you really are. You should have told me to leave last night. I warned you," he chuckled, lowering his mouth to devour me slowly as my stomach clenched. His hands braced his weight on either side of my head while he pushed up, tensing his chest muscles. "It's too bad that you weren't more than a pussy I intended to claim. You really are beautiful, and rather amazing in bed, even with your clumsy moves. But Remington, that is all you are, and will ever be." He watched the tears filling my eyes. He swallowed, turning on his heel to stop at the door. "That's how you let someone down the morning after, Silversmith. They are serving breakfast downstairs. See that you're in attendance. My staff isn't going to wait on you hand

and foot. I'll see you down there, oh, and stay the fuck out of my room now that I got what I wanted from you."

He closed the door, and I laid there, staring at where he'd slipped into the other room and locked the door. Something crashed against the wall, and I jumped, sitting up to stare at the door. I slid from the bed, silently moving into the bathroom to wash him off of me.

I dressed, slipping into a soft blue dress before adding lip gloss and mascara. I silently tied my hair up, moving from the room. The knights fell into step behind me, none of them speaking. I moved purposely to the dining room, sliding into a chair as everyone watched me. Rhys came in after me, sitting in the chair beside me at the head of the table.

Cole scooted his chair closer to me, staring at me while I remained mute and unnerved by Rhys's cold dismissal. Servers moved around us, and Cole leaned over, kissing my cheek. I ignored him. Illeron watched me, his eyes smiling as he leaned his arms against the table and spoke.

"This is where you fuck Cole, and I get you after he gets bored of your snatch," he snorted, licking his lips. Nyota elbowed him and turned angry eyes to Rhys, who silently watched it unfolding.

"You ready to be mine, Sunshine?" Cole asked softly, reaching for my hand.

I stood slowly, moving my eyes to Illeron, Cole, before finally settling them on Rhys. "You're a bastard, and you need to forgive yourself. You fell for some stupid whore's game and thought her innocent, and people got hurt. It isn't your fault you fell for a tight pussy that was attached to the villain. Many men before you and after you will also slip and fall into cunts just like that one. It's like the idiot guide to adulthood. You," I said to Cole, holding his stare.

"You deserve more than to pick up the broken pieces of those that Rhys discards like trash. You're better than that, Cole. You may want everyone to think you're a prick, but your heart is huge, and it deserves to be someone's first choice. You, Illeron, you're a fucking idiot. Nobody sticks around for sloppy thirds. It isn't even a real thing! You are all seriously fucked up. I wasn't alive when this shit happened, nor am I a part of it. I get that our families have history, but if you want to live in the past, do it without me. I prefer the future and learning from mistakes we've made so that we don't repeat them. Nyota, I am not some evil bitch here to hurt your family. I am not here willingly, and as of this moment, I'm a freaking hostage." My eyes slid to Rhys. "Do not expect me to take your shit with a smile on my face anymore. If you'll excuse me, I need to wash you out of my vagina again, as you disgust me, and I can still feel you there."

"What the fuck just happened?" Cole asked.

"I think you finally met someone with enough self-esteem to tell you assholes right where to shove your little game of *pass the snatch around*," Nyota muttered, her eyes meeting mine briefly with regret.

I pushed away from the table, and everyone watched me walking away with my shoulders back, and my head held high. I hit the stairs, skipping one, moving up them quickly before I burst into tears where they could hear me.

The knights rushed up the stairs, finding it difficult to keep up with my angry strides. I entered my room, slamming the door closed before moving to the connecting door, pushing the large dresser against it. Next, I angled the bed in front of the other door and moved into the bathroom, running the water as hot as it would go. Shedding the dress, I slid into the scathing hot water, slipping beneath it to scream. I watched the bubbles rising as the sound of something hitting the door caused me to lift from the bath, glaring.

Rhys stormed into the room with Cole and Illeron on his heels while Nyota shouted at them. I watched them all filing into the bathroom, stopping in their tracks to take in my mottled flesh and the steam rising from the tub. I stood, glaring at them.

"Get out," I hissed, pointing my finger at the door they'd just rushed through, and noted their eyes sliding down my body with shock.

"Get out of the bath now," Cole snarled, grabbing a towel and pulling me out. "You're burning yourself!"

"I won't burn," I growled, shoving him away from me. "You're all unwanted in this room. Get out, or I *will*," I warned, and when no one moved, I shoved through them, marching toward the bedroom door, and continued through the house until I reached the glass room with the forgery, slamming the door and locking it behind me.

"Open the door, Remington," Rhys snarled, and I turned, flipping him off as the towel dropped.

"Remi?" Nyx screamed, entering the room. I stepped back, and her eyes took in my red flesh. "No, you don't get to do this again. The last time sucked!"

"So did this morning," I snorted, turning to hit high on the thermostat, listening to her hands slapping against the glass.

"Don't do this. He isn't worth it," Nyx pleaded.

I turned, smiling brokenly at Nyx. She placed her head against the glass and then backed away to set the timer on her watch, and I shook my head. I needed a total reset this time, and there was the only way I knew how to do it. Sure, the Van Helsings would figure out more secrets about me, but I was sure Rhys had no intention of ever letting me leave. So what did it matter? He'd made it abundantly clear that he planned to use me, and that was how I felt now—used and discarded.

"Remi, open the damn door," Cole growled, his eyes lifting to the thermostat maxed out at three thousand degrees.

Nyota worried her lip, picking at her sleeve while Illeron stared at me in shock, his brows nearly disappearing into his hairline. I stood there stark-ass naked as more alphas were entering the room to figure out what was causing all the commotion. Hunter, Conrad, Ian, and others filled the room, and I shut them all out, turning as the heat filled the armory, causing my skin to sweat.

I fired up the forge, sliding the silver into the mold, and watched it glowing red before I pushed my hand into it, dripping the liquid metal over my fingers. I could hear them gasping behind me, knowing they were freaking out at the show. I lifted myself into the fire and laid down on the coals. My eyes slid closed, and I exhaled.

The flames kissed my flesh, heating my soul while I exhaled the pain of hearing Rhys's words. Even though I knew he rejected me because of his self-punishment, it didn't make the words any easier to swallow. I could hear people screaming as the fire hid my body within the flames.

Some women were created from flames, and I was one of them. I'd discovered it in an accident that should have ended my life. The car had rolled down a hill, and after bouncing several times, it burst into flames. I'd screamed, begging for someone to help me until I felt the pleasure the flames brought. I'd sat in the car on fire, listening to the crackling of metal as it burned so intensely hot that it had melted and twisted the frame. When the fire began to simmer down, I crawled out of the car and walked home naked through the woods.

I'd told my mother everything, and she'd hosed me down as if she'd been expecting it. We hadn't spoken about it afterward, other than to promise to keep it a secret. Speaking of my mother, I highly doubt Rhys had even looked for her. Where was my family? Where were Winchester, Sig, Weston, Smith, and Sauer? I mean, I understood them not rushing in to save me, but no one here had even mentioned them. If my family were here, people would notice.

I sat up, sliding my legs over the forge, and walking toward the water. Slipping into the bath, I watched the water bubble as steam hissed loudly. I turned, smiling coldly at Rhys, who watched me with a dark look in his eyes. Yes, asshole. I wasn't just a Silversmith. Whoever my mother had chosen to sire me was also a part of who I was.

She'd chosen each father for her children based on what they were. That much I knew. Each of us had a unique skill set, but I burned things to the ground where others created beautiful works of art. Where my siblings were driven by the need to reach for things they desired, I never reached for or expected anything. I accepted that I was different and that even my mother feared me. Alpha? No. I wasn't created to be the alpha to the House of Silversmith. I was crafted as a weapon to hold the house up, once erected.

I slipped from the water, noticing that Nyx held up a robe outside the door. I shook my head, turning the heat to freezing, and waited for it to cool down enough that it wouldn't harm those outside the glass room. Ice settled on my flesh, and I ignored the ache that filled my bones. Frost dusted my lashes, but I didn't blink to dispel it from forming around my eyes or covering my body in an icy layer from my sweat. When the timer on the thermostat dinged, I opened the door and stepped out, forcing the ice to crack with my movements.

"That was stupid," Nyx whispered as if the entire room of immortals wouldn't hear her.

"I needed to feel the flames before I ended up doing something stupid. I have clarity now," I admitted, tying the strap of the robe around my waist. Nyx stepped back, and everyone continued staring at me with worry in their eyes.

"Phoenix?" Cole asked, and my eyes moved to his.

"Do I look like I have fucking feathers?" I countered, pulling my hair out of the robe.

Dismissing them, I moved toward the long hallway that led back up to the main floor entry. I didn't stop, even though all the immortals followed us. Once I reached my room, Nyx slipped inside, and I closed the door as Rhys held my cold, dead glare.

They could guess what I was, since I didn't even know for certain. I was the only child my mother hadn't planned, as my father had chosen her. A love affair that had ended when he'd caught her cutting the head off a chick in the woods. That was her explanation for his departure from our lives. I didn't buy it, not for a moment.

I'd always known my father had found her, intending to breed, but the why of it escaped me. Not that it mattered. No one cared what I was beyond a Silversmith witch with the ability to create weapons that could kill immortals, sending them to their long overdue graves.

"What do we do now?" Nyx asked, chewing her thumbnail nervously.

"Now we rent a house and figure out how to live as mundane mortals. My savings account has a little over ten thousand in it, which should be enough to find somewhere to live, and tide us over until we can find jobs."

"I don't think that our skillsets are in high demand. What are we supposed to put on our applications? Will hunt down the undead for you? Good with sharp objects and killing people you want to send to an earlier grave?"

"I'm a gunsmith and you're a nymph. We'll be fine," I stated, sitting on the bed, exhaling slowly.

"What happened, Remington? You never lose your shit like this."

"He was amazing, Nyx. He cherished me and my body, seducing my mind and soul, and then I tried to leave the room before it got awkward. I said I'd had fun, but that I'd never had to deal with a morning after, and tried to go back to my room. So he took me to my room, where he told me I was less than nothing to him. I could have told him to leave or just gone to sleep. I wasn't even upset about having to deal with his self-induced punishment. It was the coldness in the way he told me I was nothing to him. At breakfast, Cole started flirting, and I was rather blunt on where I stood with them. I went to bathe in hot water, since it helps me soothe my emotions. They all decided to crash my bath. My emotions started to unravel, and I panicked. I knew I could make it to the forge, so I did. I'm sorry that it scares you so much, but I told you that I am fireproof."

"Your silver fails you, though. What happens if one day you're not fireproof? Being immortal doesn't mean you're invincible. You're still mortal, for Aphrodite's sake! I can't lose you, Remi. You're all I have."

"I love you too, even if you occasionally get so horny that you try to hump my leg."

"Dogs do it on occasion, and people never point it out to them," she pouted.

"Actually, they do. They just don't bring it up often since the dog doesn't understand them," I explained, leaning my head against her shoulder as she hugged me. "Who did you end up with last night?"

"Acyn," she smirked. "I think he likes me or my vagina. It's either one or the other. He covers my mouth a lot when we're going to pound town, so I'm leaning toward my vagina."

"Nobody calls sex pound town, Nyx."

She snorted, patting my head. "I just did."

"Yeah, but you also call your vagina a man-eater or cake."

"People call it cake all the time. There are literally music lyrics that call lady bits, cake. I think it's because they eat it."

"Is that why?" I laughed, smiling. I stared at our reflection in the mirror. "We're going to be okay. We have to be. We're together, and at the end of the day, that's all that matters."

"Except we're both prisoners in the hands of your family's mortal enemies," she pointed out, smiling at me in the mirror. "Your mother is still missing, and you're falling for your enemy."

"I'm not falling for Rhys."

"Honey, I'm your person. I am the one person who knows you and doesn't judge, no matter what you do. I know your faults and your strength, and I know when you fall hard for someone. I know the look that fills your eyes when you're in pain, and right now, you're in pain. I hate him for it. I hate that I cheered you on and that he made you feel like less than nothing."

"More fool am I because I knew what would

happen. I still agreed to be his. The saddest part is, I wouldn't change who I chose last night. I'm glad I allowed it for one night, but I won't be his punching bag. I won't fall into Cole's arms and then have him hand me off to Illeron. I won't be their toy or play their game. I'm Remington Silversmith, and while I may be naïve and young, I'm not weak."

"That is why we're friends. You fall, but you never stay down for long. I'll see about finding us a house to rent, or one to buy. I do have money, you know."

"Do not buy a house here. We won't be staying long enough for that. Just long enough to find my family and then move somewhere far away, where men like Rhys aren't hovering, and we're not at the bottom of the food chain."

"I am not moving to Antarctica. I'd starve to death!" Nyx blurted, and the door that connected the rooms opened.

"Get out, Nyx," Rhys growled, crossing his arms, glaring at me over the bed. "You and I need to talk, Remington."

"I have nothing to say to you, Van Helsing."

"Now it's Van Helsing? Pretty sure last night, my name was your fucking savior as you came for me."

"That was last night. A lot changed between then and now, and I still have nothing to say to you."

"I'm going to go," Nyx said, leaning over to kiss my cheek. "Not because he said to, but because I'm having hormone issues with the full moon, and I don't want to hump your leg like last time."

"It's okay. I'll be fine," I whispered, watching her exit the bedroom. "You have five minutes before I pass out."

"You don't get to decide how long I have to speak to you."

"No, I'm sure I don't. The thing is, once the fire is gone, my body needs rest. You have four minutes now before slumber claims me, and I am helpless to stay awake."

His eyes searched my face. My eyes grew heavy with the need to succumb to the siren's call of sleep. I swayed on the bed, watching as he rounded it to stand in front of me, cupping my cheek before my body jerked, and my eyes closed. He pushed me back, and I hissed.

"Stop the shit, Remi. I'm helping you to bed before you end up hurt," he growled, righting my body before adjusting the sheets. Shedding his shirt, he climbed in beside me.

"What are you doing?" I demanded.

"Just because you're asleep doesn't mean you get to escape me. I'm a male incubus demon. Once you enter sleep, you're in my world, little girl."

Chapter Twenty-Seven

I stared at the side of the hill, watching for the car to roll over it in a spinout. One, two, three, four, five... My black Chevy Camaro rolled down the steep incline on cue. It never changed; the dream of when I learned I was something more, something else.

Rhys stood silently beside me, watching the car flip repeatedly until it came to a stop, and my cries for help went unanswered. One, two, three... It burst into flames. A spark hit the gas leaking from the twisted frame, and it erupted into an inferno. The screams stopped and became groans and whimpers of fear. I turned my eyes to the dark shadow standing on the cliff; her face hidden within the shadows of the bright sun shining behind her.

"This is the moment you learned you were fireproof," Rhys whispered, and I moved away from him as the next scene came into play.

My mother stood with her back to us. The hose she

held sprayed my body down, while steam rose from my flesh. It made a sizzling noise as ice-cold water touched the blistering heat of my skin. She hadn't cried and didn't even seemed fazed by the fact that my skin was flaming red due to the blaze of the wreckage. My mother had been so calm it had terrified me, which only pulled a snort from her lips. My mom was never warm and fuzzy by any means, but I'd expected some reaction from her. What I got was cold disdain instead.

The scene changed again, turning to the day Winchester and Sig returned home for a visit, but it wasn't the one I normally had. The new memory was blurred and unfocused, replaced by a new scene that I didn't recall. Winchester and Sig were still there, but instead of a happy homecoming, we all stood outside in the firing range, staring at living targets tied to the trees behind our house. A man and his son screamed as Winchester fired her gun, missing one while hitting another who pleaded for mercy. I was barely seventeen years old, and the memory of the event suddenly assaulted me, and I stumbled backward as more memories began to flood my mind; terrible, horrifying memories.

Another shot rang out, the sound echoing through the woods, and my attention focused back to Sig, who smiled, having shot the target dead-on without even looking. Tears pricked my eyes, my throat closed, and my chest tightened. How could I have forgotten that this had happened? How could I have blocked this from my memories? Stunned, I watched the execution unfold as silver filled the target's eyes and dripped down his face.

"Your turn, Remington," Winchester announced sternly. "Relax your shoulders, stand straight, and don't hold back. He's a Van Helsing."

I swallowed bile, suddenly transported as a passenger into my seventeen-year-old body to relive the memory as if it were happening for the first time, unable to do anything but watch the events unfold. I lifted my bow with intent, yet I'd purposely missed my target, something I had never done. Sig chuckled, turning his sapphire eyes to Winchester, who exhaled, sliding her attention from the target to me.

"You have to learn to kill, Remington," she stated, sliding closer to me. Her hand lifted, cradling my cheek. "Mother will punish you if you cannot learn to murder her enemies. We all have a part to play in her revenge. You are the greatest piece on her board. We will try again tomorrow, and you will kill the Van Helsing. Do you understand the importance of this lesson?"

"I don't want to kill people," I whispered softly, turning my stare to the teenage boy who was barely older than I was. "I just want to make weapons."

Winchester sighed, her hand dropping away from my face while she sucked her lip between her teeth and shook her head. "It's what we do. It isn't easy, but you'll understand the importance of it one day soon."

Silently, I watched my brother and sister undo the body of the dead male. He'd slighted my mother somehow, and in return, she'd ordered us to kill him and his son. Winchester turned, studying me carefully. The boy continued to sob with fear, and my heart clenched for him.

"Do not speak to him, Remington. Once you know them, it is much harder to murder them," she warned, and together Winchester and Sig left the clearing, leaving me alone with the boy.

"Please," he begged, his arm bleeding profusely from where the silver arrows had pinned him to the tree. "I just want to leave."

I chewed my lip and silently turned my attention back to picking up the arrows. Placing my bow into the pack, I listened as the boy continually pleaded and begged for mercy. Finishing up, I turned to look at him as he watched me with azure blue eyes.

"You don't want to kill me, do you?" he asked softly.

"No," I whispered in a small voice. The boy smiled, and I sucked my lip between my teeth. "You want to kill us, though. So why shouldn't I kill you first?" I crossed my skinny arms over my chest, watching him furrowing his brow.

"It is a legend they tell us from the cradle. It says one Silversmith left alive can kill every alpha and erase immortals from the world."

"Why would we do that? That would be a horrid thing to do," I stated, dropping my arms, looking around the woods guiltily.

"You could prove that you're not evil."

"How?" I asked, stepping closer.

"Release me. Let me go."

I shook my head, turning to look around again while I spun in a circle. My heart hammered against my ribcage, while I moved a little closer to him. He smiled reassuringly, his eyes studying my face. He was one of the first boys I'd seen up this close, other than my brothers. It had made me feel weird at first, and then warmth spread through me, which had made Sig laugh. He'd constantly teased about my red cheeks and gaudy hair, making me ugly. *Dick.*

"You're very pretty, Remington. Is that your name?" he asked. His pretty azure eyes smiled while he watched me moving closer. At my nod, he beamed wider, revealing handsome dimples. "Have you ever been kissed?"

I shook my head, scrunching up my nose. As if Mother would let me leave the woods to know what it was like to be kissed. My experience with romance was from chapter books and bad reality TV. I tilted my head, touching his naked chest, feeling him tense beneath my fingers. My eyes slid to his, and he smiled, swallowing hard.

"Let me kiss you," he stated firmly. "If I am to die, I would die happily, having tasted your lips, Remington."

I blushed deeply, pushing my hair away from my face, considering my path. I didn't want him to be here tomorrow. I didn't want to murder him or anyone else, and if he remained here, they would force me to end his life. I stepped on my tiptoes and reached for the arrow. He whispered encouragements, leaning his forehead against my shoulder, which had caused heat to pool in my stomach.

The moment he was free, he slammed me against the ground, stomping on my face. I cried out in shock, sobbing at the red-hot pain that ripped through me while he assaulted me. I turned, curling into a ball as he attacked.

"You actually think I'd kiss your poisonous lips? Ugly little bitch. You are nothing. You're less than nothing. Your kind deserves to die, and when I bring your head back to my alpha, he will praise me for my bravery, facing off against a monster like you." He reached down, yanking my head up by my hair. He ripped my shirt open, squeezing my breast while laughing cruelly. "I may take you back whole, and use you for sport," he chuckled.

I couldn't see past the blood in my eyes. I didn't see what hit him, or who landed a kill shot to his forehead. Only that he released me and hit the ground with a bullet through his head, and pink brain matter sprinkled on the forest floor. Blood from both of us covered my face, and I shoved him away from me, righting my torn shirt.

"You are such a disappointment, daughter," my mother's distorted voice filled the forest, and yet I couldn't see her or pinpoint her position. "Get up, Remington." I didn't move. I couldn't.

Sauer grabbed my hair, yanking me to my feet. I sobbed in pain as my bones cracked and a rib pushed through my chest as he snorted. He held me in front of him, and our mother stepped out of the shadows, covered in dark robes.

She shook her head before she slapped me. "You are nothing if you cannot do what I created you to do! If you cannot become what is needed, I will remove your heart from your chest and try again. Do you understand me, Remington?" she asked. I continued to cry and scream. "Stop acting like a child!"

"She is a child, mother," Winchester whispered, her eyes pleading for me not to say something stupid.

"She's a waste of resources if we cannot train her to kill, Winchester. Her age doesn't matter. None of you held back when required to handle an enemy. Remington has failed me and will be punished. Place her in the armory. She will spend six months there, and when she gets out, we will hunt another young Van Helsing for her to murder. The younger, the better, so that she knows no emotional influence can prevent her from our course. Do not heal her, do you understand me?"

"She's your daughter, mother. Not some criminal in need of a lesson," Winchester hissed, and Sauer slapped her, causing her head to slam against the tree. She whipped it back, baring her teeth at him.

"Do not speak to our mother that way, Winchester."

"Meet me in the meadow, Sauer. Any time, any day, asshole," Winnie snapped, her eyes flashing silver as she glared at him in challenge. He stepped back, the only sign of fear he'd ever shown before our mom. "Come on, Remington."

Winchester helped me toward the shed that led down into the armory. Once inside, she turned, peering down at my exposed ribs. I looked over her shoulder as Rhys watched us, his jaw hammering wildly, anger pouring from him at the dark memory. It was one of the few times my mother had harmed me, but I'd let a Van Helsing go, one who had intended to rape me, according to my mom. She was trying to protect me. She'd been trying to teach me how vile and evil his kind would be to me if I failed to kill them before they discovered what blood ran through my veins.

"The door will be unlocked tonight. I suggest you run, and don't stop running until you're free, Remington," Winchester whispered, pushing money into my pocket with the E.V.I.E. flyer. "You're not made for war, no matter what our mother thinks you are. You're kind, gentle, and I'm pretty damn certain you couldn't murder a bee, even if it stung you. E.V.I.E. is in Seattle, and you will be untouchable there. Everyone is going to sleep soon, and you're going to run." Her hand pushed the rib back into my chest, and I shivered. She slammed her hand against my mouth to hide my screams of pain. "Shh, my sweet sister. You're okay. Do you understand what I am saying?" she asked, and I nodded. "Good. Call me when you get to Seattle. Once you are settled and accepted into E.V.I.E., you're going to need to call mother to let her know you're safe, but you won't do it right away. Now, look at me," Winnie whispered. My eyes lifted, and her hand touched my cheek. "You won't remember what happened tonight. You will block all the bad memories from this place, only remembering the need to run because our mother smothered you. Remington, you're an amazing girl who has an amazing future creating weapons, but you won't hunt beings. You know your limits, and that it would hinder others. I want you to make weapons within the protection the compound will provide you. Don't come back home. You will not leave the base until such a time in which you're strong enough to fight back, okay?"

"What about us?" I asked, tears slipping from my eyes.

"I'll find you when the time is right. I'm leaving Washington tonight to return to Paris. I can't be here when she finds out you're gone. I love you, Remi. Live, and don't let her turn you into the monster she wants you to become."

The scene changed, and I turned, gazing at the child version of me on the porch who wept as a man packed his belongings into a dark-colored truck.

"Why am I experiencing some of these memories as a passenger in my own mind, and others I can watch from a distance, like a movie?" I asked, knowing Rhys was beside me.

"Some memories scar too deep, and only return as nightmares you are forced to watch play out. Others are so deeply embedded into what you have become that you will always relive them as a passenger, through your younger self's eyes."

"I'm seeing memories previously lost to me. The fire must have cleansed more than my body when I reset. I've never allowed myself to lie amongst the flames for that long."

Rhys was quiet for a moment, before he shook his head. "You saved a Van Helsing who returned your kindness with betrayal, and yet you still stepped between Cole and me."

"In my defense, I thought Cole was the Van Helsing and totally planned to fuck him up," I muttered, turning as my mother entered the scene playing out before us.

Winchester rushed toward my three-year-old self, lifting me into her arms. She whisked me away from my mother to the shadows of the porch. My sister's eyes held hatred, but who she directed it at, I couldn't tell. The hate burning within my mother's eyes aimed at the man loading up his car, oblivious to the child on the porch who was begging him to stay. I inhaled sharply when he turned, and I realized the man was my father.

"Why is your mother's image blurred, and her voice distorted in your dreams?" Rhys asked, taking in the silver hair and blurring face blocked from his sight.

"It's a defense spell, so that if someone captured us, mind readers or other beings couldn't learn that she had survived. She did it to protect herself and us from being discovered by your family and the other alphas."

Silver shot through the air and slammed into my father as he tried to scramble to the car door. He went down hard, screaming in pain. Winchester tried to cover my eyes, but I cried for my dad. I hated this memory. I loathed it so much, but I forced my eyes to stay focused through my tears, needing to see what happened. I silently watched as my father lifted from the ground, laughing while my mother screamed in frustration. The memory froze. All except for my dad, who took in the scene on the porch before turning glowing red eyes in our direction. He silently studied me, eyeing Rhys briefly before returning his attention to me, determination burning in his gaze.

"Daughter, it is time. You know what you have to do now. Save them all, or we will all fall beneath your mother's need for revenge. Remember me when you wake this time. I am proud of whom you have become, and I am coming to find you." He burst into flames, slowly moving toward the porch to stare at the child version of me, smiling while I held my arms out, weeping for him to take me with him. Everywhere he stepped, flowing red flames covered the ground.

"That isn't possible," Rhys whispered, turning to look at me carefully before he spun, finding my father inches from us.

"Van Helsing, be kind to my child. I created her to save us all, so your services are no longer needed. You've played your role, so tread very carefully where my daughter is concerned. You have no idea what she is capable of doing, but the entire world will know soon enough."

"What are you, Remi?" Rhys asked as the scene changed into a bedroom. "Was that the last time you saw your father?" he demanded.

"I don't even remember seeing him *that* time. I know it happened, just not why or when. Why am I telling you this? I don't even like you anymore."

"Because I'm a demon, remember? Plus, I took control of your dream the moment you fell asleep. You are currently grinding your body against mine, and that is giving me more power and control of you in your dream state."

"Peachy, I'm a leg humper when asleep. Nyx will be so relieved that she isn't alone in that division."

"What?" he asked, and I rolled my eyes dismissively.

The lights turned off, and I peered down at my

suddenly naked body. "Put my clothes back on! This isn't a memory. I have never in my life worn anything this ridiculous!" I wore a sheer pair of panties with tassels on my nipples. Reaching up, I pulled them off, groaning as they left my nipples sensitive.

"Oh, this isn't a memory. It's your naughtiest fantasy playing out for me. Let's see how dirty you really are, Remi," Rhys chuckled. The scene changed into a dark room with candles lit in sconces on the wall. "A dungeon? I have to admit, I didn't see that coming."

"That makes two of us. Are you sure it isn't your fantasy?" I asked, feeling his hands as they slipped around me from behind. His mouth kissed my neck, and I frowned, noting that another version of Rhys stood in the corner, watching himself fondling me. "Because this isn't weird or anything, right?"

Rhys captured my hair, turning me around, and lifted me from beneath my thighs to claim my mouth hungrily, walking us toward the bed. He chuckled from where he now stood beside us, watching as his fantasy double devoured my lips, grinding his erection against me.

"Your fantasy is me?" he questioned in disbelief.

I moaned, unable to answer him because my tongue was busy. Fantasy Rhys was way less drama than actual Rhys. He lifted my body, slamming me down on his cock as my head pulled away from his, a scream bubbling up to erupt from my lips.

"Really? You tell us to stay the fuck out of her head, and here you are, pulling the cheat card by learning her darkest desire. Why is she fucking *you* in her darkest desire?" Cole asked, and I turned, staring at him from where he stood next to Rhys, who watched his body-double thrust into my body, pulling out, before spreading my legs to gaze down upon me. "Jesus, isn't that a pretty pussy?"

"You assholes," Acyn growled, his eyes narrowing while he moved toward the bed. Kneeling beside it, he reached out, touching my clit. "Pretty little flower, Sweet thing." I moaned, hating them all for being in my head.

"Bend her over so I can fill that tight ass," Illeron growled, exiting from the shadows.

I shivered with rage as Rhys shoved into my body, and I exploded around his cock. I slammed the mental walls around me, blocking out the Van Helsings. My body jerked, and I jolted upright, screaming. I turned on Rhys as he slowly lifted from the bed, his eyes scanning my face, studying the way I trembled.

"Stay out of my head!" I yelled and turned at the echoing sound of men rushing through the hallway toward my room.

"How the fuck did you do that?" Rhys questioned.

"What the hell just happened?" Cole demanded, entering my room with the others on his heels.

"Good question because it couldn't be what I think just happened. No one has ever thrown me out of their head," Illeron snorted.

"It's impossible to eject an incubus demon from your dream once he has access. She just ejected four of us," Acyn stated, folding his arms over his chest to stare pointedly at me.

"Five," Nyota groaned. "Sick bastards. Some shit I don't ever want to see you doing. Trying to make Remington want you when her entire fantasy revolved around Rhys... Well, that is one of them."

"I don't think she came out okay," Cole stated, watching me trembling.

"Get out," Nyx screamed from the doorway. "All of you, now. Rhys, if you intend to stay, strip naked and cuddle her. The fire is gone, and she's freezing eternally."

"Who the fuck made you the boss, nymph?" Rhys growled warningly.

"I am her person! I am the one who knows what to do when something goes wrong. I know Remi's secrets, her dreams, and I know when she is in trouble. She's in trouble! Are you willing to measure dicks over this and lose her in the process? I'll save you the trouble. I don't have a dick, which most of your brothers can verify! Her core temperature is dropping, Rhys Van Helsing. You will lose your advantage if she dies, and if her temperature gets too low, she will die! It has to be gradual. Her body has to reach its natural temperature on its own. You woke her up too early, so get her comfortable, now. Heat her body, so that her body can slowly regulate its temperature."

Silently, I watched Rhys stand, pushing down his sweatpants, while he stripped naked. Nyx made a strangled noise of need in her throat, purring as he glared at her. "Get the fuck out, all of you. Now," Rhys snapped. He slid the robe off of my body, pulling me close against his heat. My hand lifted, curling around his hand to bring his palm against mine. "You're okay, Remi."

"Worst day ever," I muttered, burying my face against his chest, inhaling his enticing scent. Heat enveloped me, and the feel of his body against mine comforted my mind while I allowed sleep to consume me, to heal.

Chapter Twenty-Eight

I awoke alone, stretching out on the bed, before lifting my head to find Rhys studying me. I could see the questions dancing in his gaze, but I didn't know their answers. My mother hadn't been forthcoming with anything. I'd barely remembered the ordeal before I'd left as a teenager, which I now knew had been altered by Winchester.

"Winchester protected you from a woman who told you that you were nothing," he snapped, surprising me with the anger in his tone.

"Maybe you and my mother would get along, after all," I offered. Shrugging when he didn't reply, I pulled the sheet around my naked body.

"Your mother allowed the male, who I assumed was your brother, to hurt you. You're still mortal, which means she was willing to let you die. Yet you race back here to save her? You're either blindly devoted or incredibly stupid, Remington." Rhys leaned forward, steepling his fingers in front of his mouth.

"As you saw, Winchester took the memories, and I think she's done it more than once. That's her gift. She has the ability to mess with people's memories, replacing them with blank spots inside your mind. I am not blindly devoted to my mother, but I do love her, Rhys. She gave me life, and that is something I appreciate. You loved your mother, and just because you assume mine is a villain, well, it doesn't mean I don't love her."

"You kicked five incubus demons out of your dream like we were weak. I assure you, that is not the case here. I am the strongest incubus demon within the world, so you need to explain to me how you, a fucking mortal female, kicked me out of your head."

"Your brother was being obscene with his language, and what he wanted to do to my backside." He smiled wickedly while heat smoldered in his gaze. "I was worried you would let him, or dream you would allow him to hurt me. My fantasy wasn't him, or them, Rhys Van Helsing. It was you and only you that I wanted. Once it changed, I felt the pull to expel you all to prevent harm to my body. I also found it very unromantic that you would steal my fantasy, which is something, very private and personal to me."

"I liked knowing it was me in your darkest desire, and that you want me. I don't like that you had the power to kick me out of your mind, though. No one has ever kicked me out before you, and I need to know how you managed to achieve it."

"I don't know, Rhys. I knew I didn't want your brothers touching me. Acyn had no right to touch me where he did, and Cole was removing his clothes. Illeron planned to force himself into my body, where no one has ever been. That was wrong, considering if I had to choose someone to do that, it would be you. I didn't want to be shared by them. I had thought I made that fact very clear during breakfast. I am not the kind of girl who gets passed around simply because it amuses you. It did not amuse me that my fantasy was turned into a family spectating event. So, we both had something happen that we didn't want, and you're about to tell me to deal with it. So, Rhys, deal with it."

"I didn't know they would enter your mind when I searched for your deepest, darkest desires. I also didn't expect for me to be a part of it, Remi. I don't like that your mother knew you and her other children could end up in her enemies' hands and spelled your mind to shield her identity. Why would she let you go? Why not find you and bring you home?"

"Because by the time I called home, I was deeply vetted and protected within E.V.I.E., which Winchester ensured by hiding my memories and giving me new ones. I thought I left a loving mother behind, and since waking up, I can see several times that she was less than loving to me. Honestly, I don't know what to think about the memories we saw or the new ones that I now recall. You took away my phone, so I can't call my sister to ask her either."

"You'd tell them where you are, and that would be a mistake."

Rhys stood, slowly moving to sit on the bed, brushing his fingers over my shoulder. I watched his eyes follow his hand, sending a shiver of need rushing through me. After a moment, I scooted away from his touch, staring toward the doorway pointedly dismissing him. He exhaled, dropping his hand before he pushed me down, slowly pinning me to the bed.

"You're gorgeous. Perfectly imperfect and naïve in a world where people aren't what you need them to be. To you, sex is personal. It's intimate and special. To everyone else, it's just fucking sex. It is two bodies finding mutual release and pleasure together. You're young, and even though I hate to think of it, your views will change, and you'll become as cold and indifferent to the world as we are. Life's a bitch, Remington. Your family threw you into the fire, and while you burn beautifully, every fire eventually burns out."

"Not if you fuel the flames," I argued, watching his mouth lowering toward mine. I turned away before he could reach my lips, brushing him off. "You don't get to dismiss me and then kiss me like you want me. I am not that naïve to realize that I mean nothing to you. I got the message, clearly."

His hands released mine, turning my head before his mouth crushed against my lips. I moaned, wrapping my legs around him as he devoured me whole. By the time we broke apart, I was panting as he watched me.

"Wear my necklace." Rhys reached into his pocket and pulled out a delicate silver medallion engraved with the Van Helsing insignia. "It's a mark of protection. It's also the mark you were born to carry, Silversmith. Flipping the medallion over, Rhys pointed out two beautiful diamond-etched snakes forming an infinity symbol, signifying the joining of a Van Helsing and Silversmith. Right now, this mark is forming beneath your ribcage. In a month or so, we'll both have it, indicating we're a mated couple." Dropping the necklace in my hand, he lifted from the bed, sitting beside me to study my face. "I'm leaving for a few days. Cole will be your protection during my absence. Keep Nyx close, as well. She's not much of a fighter, but she's another body to throw at anyone stupid enough to move against you during my absence. Ian, Hunter, Conrad, and Acyn will be with me, so I want you at Cole's side at all times. He will be between here and the sanctuary. Don't run from me. Not while I'm gone. My family wouldn't be gentle with you in my absence if they had to come out and catch you, Remi. Sit up and kiss me, and mean it."

"I'm not kissing you," I complained.

His lips had some invisible magnet to mine, and the moment they touched, we ended up sucking face. It wasn't healthy. I had a battered ego, and I wasn't happy about the invasion of privacy he felt compelled to break. He acted like he had a right to invade my memories, push past barriers I hadn't even known were there, taking control of my mind while I was defenseless against him. I'd felt naked and vulnerable.

"I shouldn't have done it," he grunted, scrubbing his hand down his face. "I needed to know if you wanted Cole."

"You could have asked, and I would have answered you truthfully. I find Cole very attractive, but he's a wild card. He needs someone wild like him to match his needs, and that isn't me. Cole is into sharing his things, and I'm not one for being shared, Rhys. I'm a one-man type of woman. So your answer is no. I wouldn't do that, or try to be with him because there's no longevity there."

"Yet you chose to be with me knowing I would push you away. Why put yourself through that?" he demanded as if I were the asshole in this situation.

"Because you're a forever type of man," I admitted, rubbing my hands over my face. "You have teased me, taunted me, and pushed me until I have thought of nothing but you. You wanted me as much as I wanted you, which makes this *our* fault. Not mine, and not yours, but ours together. It was enjoyable. You were great and treated me with respect, which is more than either of my flopped attempts had done. You knew I wouldn't blow your world away when you came to my room. You knew I lacked the experience, and yet you came anyway. It worked, and we both got what we wanted. That's it in a nutshell."

"You're wrong, Remington Silversmith. You didn't blow my world; you rocked it. That's more than any woman has done for me in three hundred years. You were innocent and inexperienced, but you matched me in need and fire, and no woman has ever accomplished that before you. Sex wasn't feeding with you. I have not fucked a woman in three hundred years for anything more than to feed." I blinked, holding his stare, watching him stand after he'd dropped that information into my lap. "Don't tell Cole that, he enjoys the game of bedding feeders he thinks I come to enjoy."

"Why?" I asked softly.

"It gives him some sick sense of enjoyment."

"Not that," I snorted.

"Because I hadn't found anything worth relishing, or allowing myself to enjoy until you," he admitted, watching my face. "If I were a better man, I'd have left you alone last night. I'm not a better man, my Silver. I have built a reputation around being a monster, and it works for me. I have no weakness other than my family. I have given no one anything to use against me, and I'm not about to start now."

"You also won't forgive yourself," I frowned, watching all emotion slip from his face. "Sooner or later, you have to forgive yourself because everyone else has, Rhys. You punish yourself so much that it holds you back. Guilt is a heavy burden to carry, and you've carried it for so long."

"Do not pretend to understand what or who I am, little girl. It makes you look weak and stupid," he growled, slipping through the door to slam it behind him, causing me to wince.

The door to Rhys's room opened and closed, and I turned as mine opened from the hallway, staring at Nyota, who slowly walked toward me. Her azure eyes were framed in thick, dark lashes as she studied my face closely.

"You're not here to hurt us. But someone created the perfect mate out of you for Rhys, to either help him or destroy him, Remington. He's a damn good man and the proudest knight in the entire Van Helsing line."

"He seemed to have lost the chivalry part."

"Chivalry is dead, child." I started to argue her calling me a child, but she lifted her hand for silence. "I am four hundred years old, Remington. To most of us, you're a newborn babe in a world of ancient beings. I do not think you want to destroy Rhys. If you think you can reach him, I will help you achieve it. My family is everything to me, and I have watched them tear each other apart over women or things they desired for centuries. No woman before you has turned Cole down. They don't see the heart behind the malice and pain, yet you saw through his facade. You know he isn't for you, and you called him out on his bullshit. You know Rhys would hurt you, yet you willingly took that chance to see if you could reach his deadened heart, and I think you did. He was out of his mind when you crawled into that forge. Others may not have noticed, but I did. Prove me wrong. Show me who you really are, and I'll help you in any way I can."

Chapter Twenty-Nine

Rhys had been gone days when Cole told me to get into the metallic blue Lamborghini Aventador, which had probably cost him more than a house. Apparently, it was one of Rhys's favorite cars, and Cole had been itching for an excuse to drive it. I eased into the plush, black-leather interior just as Cole stepped on the gas and the engine purred to life, and I smirked as Cole made a purring noise along with it. Silently, I checked the phone that only allowed me to call Rhys, even though I'd refused to use it once since he'd left.

"Rhys does love exquisitely beautiful things, Sunshine." Cole stared at my mouth, grinning when he saw the smile playing over my lips. "And they're so fucking beautiful."

"Are we speaking of the car?" I asked as heat filled my cheeks.

"Among other things he claimed entirely," he grumbled. The smirk dropped, and a tick pulsed in his cheek.

"He didn't claim me, Cole. You're just a heartache waiting to happen, and one Van Helsing is enough for any girl."

"Ask Nyx how she feels about that when we reach her at the sanctuary's bar. She rather enjoyed double Van Helsings, even triple at one point."

"Nyx is a nymph, and I'm not. I'd want you to be mine and commit to only me, Cole. Could you honestly do that? I'm not talking for a little while. I'm asking if you could commit to me forever," I probed softly, chewing my lip while watching his brow crease to push together in the center of his forehead.

"Like one pussy for the rest of my life?"

"Exactly that," I laughed at the horrified expression marring his perfect features. "See, you're a wild card, Cole. You need someone who will want to share you with others. You enjoy a woman who lets your brothers play with her too, and that isn't me. Maybe it is because I'm young. But for now, that is how I am."

"You could be forever," he stated, surprising me. "When I'm ready to give up my sinfully wicked ways." I opened my mouth to reply as his phone chirped, signaling an incoming. I turned, staring out of the window at the sprawling countryside as he connected the phone to the Bluetooth.

"Rhys," Cole muttered, smirking at me.

"Daily Remington report, asshole. Is she moping about missing me?" My eyes shot to Cole in surprise. The hopeful tone in which Rhys had spoken made butterflies erupt within me.

"I didn't notice between her bouncing on my cock last night and this morning. You were right. She does make the most delicious noises when she's being fucked from behind. It's almost a strangled scream and moan of deliciously wicked pleasure that comes out together at once." My eyes widened as Cole grinned, holding a finger to his lips.

"She wouldn't fuck you. She's much too innocent to slip and trip onto your dick, brother. Really, though, how is she?"

"Why? Do you miss her?" he countered.

"I miss the way she rolls her eyes when you say something obtuse. The heat that fills her cheeks when she thinks of my cock in a naughty position, and when she's angry. It's so cute when her tiny hands ball into fists at her sides while she's trying not to strike one of us," he admitted, causing me to suck my lip in as a smile flitted on my face.

"You don't miss her pussy at all?" Cole asked curiously.

"Believe it or not, brother, women have more uses than just spreading their thighs for us," Rhys snorted. "Like when her head is against your chest, and her fingers curl into yours without thought. I personally like it when Remington whispers my name in her sleep as she reaches for me. It's…" Rhys paused, searching for the word. "I can hear someone else breathing and the purr of my prized car, asshole."

"Just me and Remington out for a leisurely drive to the sanctuary for the weekly check-in. Don't worry, she only heard everything, and now knows you enjoy cuddling with her. You might not want to admit that shit to anyone else. It sounds like you watch her sleep, which is honestly rather disturbing." The dial tone sounded, and I glared at Cole.

"You want him happy, don't you?" I asked, watching Cole's eyes turning back to the road as we entered town.

"Is it that obvious?" he asked, and I smiled, patting his leg.

"You're a good brother."

"I honestly don't care about his happiness, Remi. I care that he is holding the guilt of the past for all of us. He wasn't alone in his wanting to please Roslyn. There were several of us that fell into her trap. He was just the one who thought he could save her."

"But you didn't think so?"

"Roslyn was a selfish, sadistic bitch who enjoyed hurting Rhys. She fucked us all over the same way, except for Rhys. He was a gentleman. He adored her, and even loved her, which none of us assumed she was capable of, but he thought he could change her. You can't change someone who likes who they are, and she did. She loved the power that being a Silversmith allowed her, and she wasn't afraid to hurt anyone who stood in her way. Roslyn couldn't change her colors or her greed. No matter how much Rhys loved and adored her, she couldn't love him back."

"That's horrible," I muttered, watching Cole's mouth tighten before he spoke again.

"He'll never forgive himself enough to love you, Sunshine. He can barely forgive himself enough to be around us, and he merely tolerates us because we refuse to let him hide in the shadows. I know Nyota is helping you, but she wasn't around for the worst of what happened."

"Why were you fighting him that day outside the sanctuary's bar?" I asked, noting the curve of his lips.

"It was a test for the Silversmith halfling witch. To see if she'd move to kill him; even after I explicitly forbid it," he chuckled as I rolled my eyes. "The ammo she had wouldn't have killed him, but it would have hurt like hell. I had to know if she was trainable, if she would listen to orders, or was merely tolerating me to get to the Van Helsing alpha. Imagine our surprise when an actual Silversmith stopped the ammo easily. I've never seen a Silversmith use one arrow to stop a barrage of bullets, Remi. *Ever.* Nor can they absorb them, and yet you did both."

"I discovered it by accident. The absorption part, anyway. Nyx entered the firing range inside E.V.I.E., and the student firing their AR-15 hadn't turned on the live firing sign, and was firing entirely too fast for me to stop the iron bullets from hitting her. So I used magic to pull them toward me, and then realized the mistake I'd made too late. Miscalculations don't happen to me with ammo, but the thought of losing my best friend made me act rashly. I felt each one hitting my flesh. I expected pain or death, but instead, I was fine. The arrows, on the other hand, are specially crafted and spelled to eliminate fired ammunition. So it wouldn't have missed her bullets, not even if it had to turn around to stop them before they hit flesh. Once spelled and released from the bow, it calculates which bullet will hit first, and if it can't get the bullets, it takes out the intended victim's Achilles tendon."

"That's brilliant. You mixed magic with weaponry, but you'd have to pay a higher cost to use it, correct?" Cole asked, frowning, and then smiled. "Hence why the curse was worse for you when you used it to save us, even though we didn't really saving," he stated matter-of-factly.

"More fool was I for trying to save Rhys because I assumed *you* were the Van Helsing alpha."

"You thought I was the Van Helsing alpha? Please tell Rhys that," he laughed, pulling into the reserved parking spot next to the front of the building.

Cole's phone rang again, and he smirked, staring at the screen. Answering it, he held up his finger, exiting the car, and came around to open my door. I slipped out of the seat, standing against him. He dropped his mouth against my ear, sucking the lobe between his teeth while I listened to Rhys bitching him out for blindsiding him. Cole pulled the phone away, studying my face before lifting his head, and turning to look behind him.

"I need to call you back, brother. Something is…"

A gunshot echoed in the parking lot. Blood painted my face as I peered through Cole's chest. I screamed, moving to help him. Something slammed against the side of my head, sending me to the ground as pain rang out through my head. Sobs filled my chest. My body was hit repeatedly by something hard, and solid.

Cole dropped to the ground, lifeless. I curled into

the fetal position, groaning as Rhys's voice echoed through the phone beside me. Another blow caused a scream of pain to escape my lips. Covering the phone with my body, grabbing it, I slipped it into my pocket. I was grabbed and dragged over concrete painfully.

My eyes refused to regain focus, pulsing light into my vision. My head dripped a steady stream of blood from a deep laceration in my forehead. Someone lifted me and tossed me into the trunk of a car. Cole was dropped on top of me, smashing me into the jack that stabbed into my neck. The trunk was slammed closed, and I felt the engine's vibration as the vehicle peeled out of the parking lot.

It took everything I had to pull the phone from my pocket, lifting it to my still ringing ear. I could barely make out Rhys screaming orders as I whispered.

"Help us," I pleaded.

"Remington? Are you okay?" he asked with worry etching his words.

"No," I sobbed. "Help us, Rhys. They shot Cole, and he's dead," I cried, covering my mouth with my hand to smother the sobs.

"Tell me what you see around you?"

"The phone is on," I swallowed. "Find us, Rhys."

"You're slurring your words, Remington. How badly are you hurt?"

"Bad… mmm…" I exhaled, losing consciousness as the phone dropped from my hand.

Chapter Thirty

I woke in a barn, chained to two posts with my arms spread, stripped to my panties, soaked in mine, and Cole's blood. Squinting through my swollen eyes, I found Cole's body, dumped on a pile of hay beside the corpses of a man and a woman, drained of blood and discarded like rubbish. I could hear the sounds of feeding and rough sex, raping women, and using them for food while they wept and cried out for help.

Turning to face forward, I saw Laura studying me, sitting patiently while waiting for me to regain consciousness. I lifted my head, only for the vampire beside her to punch me in the face again, causing me to cry out as my head jerked to the side. Spitting out the blood in my mouth, I looked down to see blood pouring from knife wounds that covered my body. They had carved me up, sliced me open, and left me to hang in a pool of blood.

"Do you think I'd forgive you? Stupid little whore.

No one hurts me and lives," Laura ground out, her head moving closer. She sank her painful incisors deep into my thigh, causing me to scream. Her bite sent fire burning through my leg as her nails sliced through the flesh she held. Laura pulled away with my blood coating her lips and smiled, "How does it feel to know you're about to die for what you did to me?" she asked, her eyes glittering with excitement.

I searched for any silver to wield against Laura, but a fist slammed into my jaw, making me focus on the pain. For hours I'd been knocked around, my focus remaining on the pain her companions forced on me. My head dropped forward as consciousness slipped from my grasp. Darkness swelled around me, and then Rhys was there.

"I need you to hang on for me, Love. Can you do that?"

I sobbed, and he lifted his hands, cradling my face as he closed his eyes. In my subconscious thoughts, I was undamaged. I shook my head, not wanting to feel what they were doing to my body.

"Remington, we are close. I will not leave you, but I need to see what you see. Show me who took you. Let me look through your eyes. Open them," he encouraged, and I did.

I turned to where Cole lay staring at the top of the barn, sightlessly. Next, I showed him the dead couple and the women they tortured as the vampires raped their bodies while shredding through their necks. Peering out the wide barn doors, I looked at the quaint little farmhouse that sat glowing beneath the blazing bonfire outside the barn where the drained bodies burned. Horses bayed, snorting, and kicking in their stalls as they shied away from the vampires.

I focused on Laura, feeling the pain of my body, slowly letting my gaze slide down to it. They had removed my panties and bitten my thighs several more times. I silently looked at the pool of blood at my feet and turned to focus on what else I could show Rhys. The vampire's fist connected to my face several more times. Something slammed against my side, and I vomited blood into the puddle.

A vampire settled in the blood pool, staring up with an evil smile shining in his eyes, moving closer toward my unprotected sex. Rhys snarled in my head as the vampire's fang elongated and pushed through the delicate flesh, causing me to let loose a bloodcurdling scream. Pain registered in my mind and sobs filled my chest, hurting my damaged ribs. He pulled away, pushing a sharp nail over my apex's flesh, slicing through it while laughing at my cries of pain.

"Enough, we don't want her dead yet. She must die from Cole's hand when he wakes and feeds so that the feud begins anew. I couldn't find the others, but I know they're here. It must look the same as it did in the past." Laura dragged her nail over her wrist, pushing it against my mouth. I gagged against the coppery taint of blood.

"Drink, you stupid little bitch! I have vowed to renew your family's feud, and you don't get to die unless the Van Helsing murders you. When he wakes, his hunger will be insatiable, and he will need to feed to heal. Cole will not be able to resist the feast we have provided and will feed from you until you're dead. If you're smart, you'll use the silver to murder him before he can rape you. Place him next to her and start clearing the corpses. Rhys Van Helsing won't take long to find this place. He's a hunter and a damn good one at that. It's really too bad he thinks this pathetic bitch is his mate, as it's a waste of his magnificent cock." Laura leaned down, licking my stomach as her fingers slid through my core. "You can save yourself, but to do it, you'll have to use the silver I leave behind," she laughed, reaching for something from the tray beside us, lifting her fingers to her mouth, sucking on something silver.

Laura held three large, shiny balls up in her palms, smirking wickedly before pushing them into my body. I cried out at the size of the Ben Wa Balls, feeling my body clenching to dispel them, but they were too large to come out on their own. I didn't have the energy left to push them out.

"I do hope you find a better exit than your eyeballs, since I need you to murder Cole, ensuring that everything else will fall into place, Silversmith. Your family has worked hard to remain hidden, but hearing that you were raped and brutalized by a Van Helsing... well, Silversmiths will want Van Helsing blood. Van Helsings will once more hunt down the Silversmiths for sending their dirty little murderous whore in to murder one of their own. History repeating itself at the cost of Cole's and your life, well, it's a price I am willing to pay. Van Helsings always go harder when one of their own is needlessly murdered. Roslyn may have moved against them in her greed, but they were not the only ones planning to move against their family. Some of us are tired of the Van Helsings holding us to the same rules. Humans are weak and nothing but food. Yet we are forced to starve, feeding in the shadows. We will rule this world."

They placed Cole on the ground at my feet. His eyes filled with blackness that stared up at me. His body was healing, which sent relief flowing through me. The vampire slammed his fist into the side of my head again, lowering his body to kiss my thigh as he watched my sex clenching.

"I want to fuck her, My Queen," he growled, tracing a pattern into my thigh.

"This Silversmith is about to be fucked hard and mercilessly by a demon blinded by his need to feed, to heal. When he feeds, he will push those balls deeper into her cunt, forcing her to pull them out through her body. Just like she did to me, which is a pity to miss since I can't be here when it happens," Laura purred. Cole grabbed my leg, his eyes lifting to mine. A deep growl escaped his chest while his focus zeroed in on me with hunger burning in them.

My head dropped as the sound of people moving into the barn echoed until someone screamed. Laura turned, screeching as power erupted around us. A sword cut through the air, and I lifted my eyes to see Rhys. He locked eyes with me and exhaled in relief as he turned, slicing through a vampire that shot toward him. Rhys turned sideways, cutting through another male so quickly that my eyes couldn't even process the motion.

Ian was tearing vampires apart, using their legs and arms to trip others. Hunter stood in front of the barn doors, holding a small group of vampires on the ground with an invisible grip while they howled and cried tears of blood. Conrad was chewing through vampires as quickly as Acyn could toss them his way, slicing their heads off in midair.

All around me, alphas fought the horde of vampires that seemed to be flooding into the barn. Something grabbed my leg, lifting itself from my thighs to stand before me. Cole's dark eyes held mine. He leaned forward, pushing against my opening. I screamed, and Nyx appeared, her hand touching Cole.

"I am here, lover. Come feed from me," she offered, but he didn't turn toward her. Instead, he continued trying to push into my body until I sobbed, but Rhys was there, pulling him away as Cole spun on him, hissing and growling.

"You'll kill her, Cole!" Rhys warned, turning to Nyx. "Make that pussy wet, nymph. Get his attention, so I don't have to murder my baby brother to protect Remington."

Rhys walked around Cole, his blade held at the ready. Acyn slipped in beside Nyx, pushing his fingers into her pants as my head bobbed. Cole's head turned, and Rhys slipped his arms around me while someone worked on the chains, releasing my wrists, shredded to the bone, causing me to scream out in pain.

Hunter grunted, reaching around Rhys to place his hand on my shoulder. I was no longer in the barn. The pain subsided to nothing more than a twinge of irritation. I was on a boat in the ocean, and it was peaceful. I peered around at the waves that swept over the ship's deck. Hunter smiled softly, not speaking while he held my hand, staring into my eyes.

"Ian! I need blood now!" Rhys demanded, though

it came from far away. "Her pulse is weakening to a dangerously slow beat. We're losing her."

I tasted the coppery tang of blood and Hunter cleared his throat. The taste of copper changed to something sweet and enticing. A glass appeared in my hand, and I held it against my mouth.

"She's not drinking, Hunter," Ian uttered. "Drink, woman," he ordered as if he could demand I drink it even though I wasn't there.

"It comes with no hidden cost, Silversmith. Just drink it," Hunter pleaded.

I tipped the cup back, peering down when I felt someone licking my stomach, but I only found Hunter's fingers tracing where I felt the tongue sliding against my flesh.

"There are too many fucking cuts. Conrad, get the hell over here and help me heal her wounds. She's losing too much blood, and Ian cannot replace it at the volume she's losing."

"Look at me, Remington. They're helping you heal, and there's nothing to be afraid of," Hunter said thickly, staring down my naked body. "Jesus, there's something inside of her."

Everyone stopped moving. Hunter removed his hand, and I was back in the barn. Rhys shook his head angrily releasing an exhale as his head leaned against my shoulder. "I'm sorry, Remington. I'm going to need to retrieve whatever they stuck inside you."

"It's Ben Wa Balls. They're too big," I warned, watching Hunter's cheek twinge.

"They're rather large, Van Helsing. You might want to wait until she is in a healing sleep, before forcing her to endure more pain. That area of her body is rather—wounded. I'm afraid to ask what that murderous bitch did to her or allowed to be done before we arrived." Hunter's eyes studied mine as tears slipped free to roll down my cheeks.

"She's good enough to travel," Rhys announced, lifting me into his arms. I wrapped my arms around his throat tightly. "I have you, Love. Laura will never harm you again."

"Cole?" I whispered, feeling a sliver of fear.

"Already on his way to the estate with Acyn and Nyx, healing. Acyn will keep Cole from harming Nyx while she feeds him," he whispered against my ear.

I looked over Rhys's shoulder, where Ian, Conrad, and Hunter followed closely behind us, and saw the barn explode. It was a sight to see, the head of the alphas walking behind us, guarding us as we escaped a fiery hell. Men were loading the horses into waiting trailers, and Van Helsing knights watched Rhys carry me out, his cloak covering my naked body.

We slid into a waiting car, and the others climbed into the vehicles behind us. Rhys held me tightly against him, and I noted the tremble in his body.

"You knew that if the phone were on, I'd be able to trace it."

"Yes," I admitted. "It's one of the things taught at E.V.I.E."

"I'm aware. It's something I slipped into the

lessons in case I had to save one of them during capture. I'm glad it helped me find you, Remington. You frightened me, and I don't intend to allow you out of my sight for a while."

"The Ben Wa Balls that Laura placed inside of me are silver. She wanted to force me into ripping them from my body to use on Cole to save myself. She did this to start a war between our bloodlines again."

"Don't worry about those. You have broken ribs, and tendons torn apart in both of your arms. Your stomach is swollen and you are bleeding internally from the blows you sustained by a wooden bat that was discarded and left beside my favorite car. We healed many of your cuts, stopping most of the bleeding, but some still need attention. You have damage to your face from the repeated strikes to your cheeks and eyes, and you're slurring your words. You're going to need to sleep for a while in order to heal the damage. I'll take care of you, Remington. I'll remove the balls when you enter your healing sleep. I should have been here."

"You saved me, and that is all that matters." My eyes grew heavy. His grunt sounded within my ear as he kissed my shoulder. It was probably the only part of me that wasn't cut or broken. "Don't leave me alone when I fall asleep, Rhys. I don't want to relive this in my nightmares. Stay with me, please?"

"I'll be right here beside you, Love. Rest, we're still an hour out from the estate. I won't let you relive this experience again, even if it means never leaving your side."

Chapter Thirty-One

I woke to someone washing my skin, and I jerked away from the hands touching me. Rhys held me tightly while Nyx stared at me uneasily. I was in a bathtub, being bathed by my best friend while the man I'd had scrupulously, delicious sex with, held me tightly against his hard body. I shivered, taking in the unmarred skin on my body. Frowning, I watched as Nyx knelt in front of me, exhaling a shuddering breath.

"I told you she would come back if you put her in hot water," Nyx snorted while rolling her eyes dramatically. "You asshole," Nyx said, glaring at me, "have had us all terrified that Laura broke that brilliant brain of yours."

I tried to speak, but my mouth was parched. Nyx jumped, moving to the pitcher of water she'd had waiting beside the tub. I accepted the glass, downing the contents, before asking for more. Turning my head, I peered up at the IV pole attached to a bag of saline that sat beside the bathtub. I followed the tube to where it connected to my arm and groaned.

"How long have I been out?" I asked, and she dropped her eyes, pursing her lips together tightly until a white line formed over her mouth. "How long, Nyx?"

"A little over a month," she admitted softly. "You had some pretty extensive damage to your body, vital organs, and brain. To put it in a nutshell, Rhys murdered three doctors who said to take you to the farm and put you out of your misery."

"You murdered doctors?" I asked, resting my head against him, hearing his deep exhale while he brushed his lips over my shoulder, kissing it gently.

"Only the ones who wouldn't save you," he admitted softly. "Nyx, tell the physician who lived, that Remington is awake and speaking. Have him standing by outside the room to examine her. I'll finish her bath," Rhys ordered.

Nyx hesitated, watching me. "You promised not to leave me alone. Do you have any idea how terrifying it was to walk outside and smell your blood mixed with Cole's? There was blood splattered all over the car and ground beside it, but we couldn't find a trail anywhere. It just vanished, and I was alone and terrified!"

"I was in a trunk," I whispered, coughing. Nyx rushed forward with more water, staring over my shoulder.

"Stuff it, Van Helsing. She's my person, and I almost lost her. That shit messes with a girl's head, and I haven't reached an orgasm since. Cole ate me for an entire week, and still no orgasm! Although, that was the hottest thing I have ever been through in my entire life."

"Nyx, she needs to be examined by more than you and me right now," Rhys stated calmly, exhaling against my shoulder. It sounded like he was struggling to remain calm in the face of a hyperactive, overemotional nymph.

"I'm okay, Nyx. I probably should see the doctor, though," I laughed at her pouting lips. After a moment, she nodded in agreement. She slapped her forehead, lunging forward without warning to hug me tightly. "Nyx, I'm totally naked, and you can't un-see that, ever."

"I've been self-appointed vagina washer for over a month. You and I are way past first base; we're like…"

My hand landed over her lips, stopping her from speaking. "Oh my God, don't finish that," I chuckled, turning to bury my head against Rhys. "This is so bad," I laughed harder.

His fingers played in my hair while he silently kissed my neck as the door closed with Nyx's departure. Rhys turned me around to face him, and I fell toward him. His eyes slid down my body, and he sat up, placing me onto the opposite side of the tub where Nyx had been leaning.

"How do you feel?" he asked, grabbing for the sponge she'd sat on the tub's edge.

"Weak. I feel very weak," I admitted, watching Rhys slowly wash me like some delicate doll. "Not so weak that you would rub my flesh off if you actually touched my skin with the sponge." His lips twitched, and his attention lifted to the soft smile I offered him. "I won't break."

"You did break, Remi. You almost died nineteen times while I fought to hold you to this world. You flatlined nineteen fucking times, and I anchored you to me with your mind. Ian has been feeding you his blood. Conrad bit you three times to see if we could force a change. Hunter, he wanted to take you to his realm and force you to become one of the spirits that reside there."

"And you?" I asked, slowly taking in the sinewy muscles of his chest, tensing from his movements.

"I held you tight and told you that I didn't accept you leaving me, Love. I want you alive, do you hear me?"

I didn't lift my eyes to his, unable to look into them for fear of seeing something deeper developing there. He closed the distance between us, lifting me onto his lap as something very hard and noticeable sat between us. Rhys's lips brushed against mine seeking permission, and my arms wrapped around his neck, kissing him hungrily. He stood from the bathtub, walking us into the bedroom, where he laid me carefully onto the bed.

A knock sounded at the door, and he laughed, peering up at me, smiling. "I'm going to build a bunker just to have a place for us to fuck so that we're not constantly disturbed."

"That's a little much just to get laid, isn't it?" I asked, and he lifted as to leave. "No, not even," I growled, pulling him down, lifting my hips in invitation.

I shivered as he stretched my body out on the bed, lifting his head as he groaned. His eyes heated while staring down at me, watching me tremble with need. His hips moved slowly, testing me until I attempted to roll him, but failed miserably. His smirk infuriated me with his cocky brows that lifted. Rhys claimed my lips, growling as he devoured me.

He pushed into my core, stretching me full before lifting back, rocking his hips while I gasped at the multitude of sensations he created. He was slow, calculated with each gentle thrust, which I eagerly met as he smiled down at me.

The knock sounded at the door again, and Rhys pulled his lips from mine. "Unless you want to die a slow, painful death, go the fuck away!"

He lowered his mouth to mine, nipping my lip, and I laughed against them at his random outburst that wasn't like him to indulge in. His body moved gently, purposely building the orgasm up until it ripped through me. He pushed his forehead against mine, carefully rolling us until I was seated on him. Lowering his hands, he moved my hips slowly. I placed my hands onto his chest, uncertain I could stay upright.

"You do know she's not healed, right, asshole?" Nyota snapped from the other side of the door.

"She's on top," Rhys snarled, and Nyota chuckled, and maybe I was hallucinating because it sounded as if she'd just said that I was her girl. "You're beautiful, but you're exhausted still," Rhys groaned, rolling us quickly. He moved forward with purpose, edging me toward the cliff again until he groaned, moaning loudly. He placed his hand over my mouth, smothering the cry as lights ignited behind my eyes, and bells rang in my ears. "You should wake up now so that we can do this for real, instead of half-assed inside your head, woman."

"What?" I asked, staring up at him while he smirked beside me on the bed. "This is a dream?"

"Yes, this is an improvement. There weren't monsters chasing us, or crazy shit unfolding this time. You've been asleep for over a month now. I kept you here so that you would let your body heal. I have to admit, some of the shit inside this pretty head of yours is honestly creepy as hell, woman."

The knock sounded at the door, and I lifted my head, peering at it. Rhys moved on the bed, and I blinked, struggling to sit up.

"Slowly, Love. Bloody hell," he groaned, peering down at where he'd tented the blankets. "You're sure you're not part succubus, right?"

"Do not blame your erection on me. I was in a coma, so who's the pervert here?" I whispered weakly, turning onto my side while his fingers pushed the hair away from my face. He leaned over, kissing my forehead, then got up from the bed. Rhys slipped into sweatpants before silently moving back to my side.

"Sit up." Rhys watched me struggling to move and held up his hand. "Hold on," he ordered, pulling out a black silk nightgown from the dresser before returning.

He lifted me gently, careful of the IV taped to my arm. Rhys untied the nightgown I wore, slowly removing it to replace it with the clean black one he'd retrieved. His fingers worked quickly, tying it up before placing me back into bed, pulling the other nightgown out of the blankets, before walking it to the hamper. I silently watched him pour a glass of ice water before returning, handing it to me, before fixing the covers.

"You've been doing this every night since you saved me?" I whispered, narrowing my eyes on him as he nodded.

"You asked me to stay with you. I have not left this room since we brought you back from Laura's hive. Ian, Conrad, and Hunter tracked down and beheaded every vampire she sired in the last fifty years. She and her people won't harm you again. The other alphas saw to it. But I couldn't break that promise to you and go hunt them down."

"Thank you," I whispered, feeling the pull to sleep as he opened the door.

Everyone moved into the room, staring at me. Even the alphas were here, and Thurston, god's love him, burst into the room, screaming his presence.

"Thurston is here!" he shouted.

"Hello, Thurston," I smiled weakly, trying to sit up. Cole moved toward me, fixing the pillows behind me before he leaned down, kissing my ear.

"You, sleeping beauty, scared me to death."

"Are you okay?" I asked, and he nodded.

Stepping back, he sucked his bottom lip between his teeth. "Now that you're awake, I am okay. I'm so sorry that I didn't see the danger that night."

"We lived," I smirked, scrunching up my nose. "Laura's dead and we're not. That's a win for team *good guys.*"

"It's cute that she thinks we're the good guys, right?" Cole asked, turning to look at Rhys.

"It's endearing, if not a little irrational. We're the monsters, but let's wait to tell her that."

"You guys know she can hear you, right?" Nyx asked, sliding to the bed beside me. "What I said in your dream walk? That happened. It really happened. So, should I not tell you out here?" I stared at her while her mouth opened, and her eyes widened. "Got it. Can we redo this and wake her back up later, so she doesn't know that I washed her vagina? She's prudish."

"Stop talking, nymph," Nyota stated, smiling at me. "It's about time you woke up. You asked the alpha to remain at your side while you slept. That makes you an asshole. Just so we're clear. Also, welcome back to the world of the living. I'm… glad…," she paused as her brothers watched her. "I'm glad I didn't have to watch these assholes mope around because you died."

"Thanks, Nyota."

"I'm Thurston!"

"So you are, Thurston," I laughed, turning to stare at Rhys. "I think I need a bath."

"You just had one… Oooo," Nyx stated, inhaling the air before she tilted her head. "You just woke up! And you call me horny? Jesus."

"Someone get the doctor up here to check her out so we can get her that bath she's itching to take," Rhys stated, his lips twitching. I stared hungrily at him, watching his eyes smolder with the hunger to match mine. "Now," he growled, moving to the bed as everyone watched us. Thurston jumped, and we turned as he sailed through the air toward the bed. Rhys lifted me quickly to prevent injury. He moved so fast that I hadn't even known he had until I was in his arms, staring up at him with wide eyes. "Thurston, Remington needs rest. There's a giant pool out back, why don't you go swimming for a bit?"

"Thurston, swim!"

We laughed while watching Thurston excitedly leaving the room. Rhys placed me back onto the bed and sat beside me. He reached for my hand, and Nyota studied it, smiling before she hid it. Rhys adjusted the covers, fussing over me while the entire room watched in silence. He didn't seem bothered by it, not even when the doctor entered and shooed everyone out but Rhys.

Chapter Thirty-Two

The doctor gave me a clean bill of health, and I'd tried to corner Cole for days without luck. I was pretty certain he was avoiding me, but Rhys denied it. Rhys, on the other hand, couldn't get enough of me in his bed. He had demanded I remain with him, close by at night so he could guard me. Not that there was a threat against me anymore.

If I were honest, I'd admit to myself that I enjoyed the feel of Rhys beside me. I would admit that his scent drove me to the edge of sanity and hung me on a cliff of bliss. I'd also say that being with him when he laughed or seduced me was mind-blowingly beautiful. I'd admit that I was falling for my enemy, but I wasn't admitting that shit out loud. That was a double-sided blade that once you fell on, couldn't be withdrawn from your heart.

I watched Thurston dancing, clapping his hands while I followed his lead with his mother and father, both watching us. Thurston was simple. He wanted to dance without a care of who judged him. He didn't mind that the world wasn't black and white, or that we belonged in the edges of those colors in the grey area. What I wouldn't give to feel his carefreeness with him. But I could feel that something was coming. Every day a grey cloud hung above us, threatening to let loose without mercy. We all felt it closing in around us.

Tapping Thurston's hand, I bowed and thanked him for the dance before heading toward Rhys, who had just entered the hall. The moment I got close to him, Van Helsing knights rushed into the hall, striding urgently toward him. My heart dropped as their words echoed in my ears the moment they reached him.

"There's a large force of Silversmiths outside the gates. They're demanding you release Remington Silversmith, or they intend to ensure no one leaves this estate alive," Luis said, turning worried eyes in my direction.

"How many Silversmiths?" Rhys asked, turning to narrow his eyes on me as I slowly approached him.

"If I had to guess? I'd say at least fifty or more," Luis informed, standing back as Rhys watched me.

"Henderson, close the armory so that they cannot access the silver within it. Alert those within the estate grounds to go inside their homes until I say otherwise. Once our people are all inside, let the Silversmiths through the gates. They won't take Remington. She's going to tell them she is staying here of her own accord."

"Why would I do that? I'd be cut off and

disowned."

"Because if not, I will give the kill order and murder them all while you watch it happen. They're unable to cast within the iron gates. The only silver here that they'd be able to wield is in my armory through reinforced iron and steel. The moment they enter my estate, they're defenseless. Unless you wish to watch your family bleed on my grass, you'll do what I say."

"You're a bastard," I swallowed, feeling my stomach tightening while flipping repeatedly.

"I warned you that I wasn't a good guy, Love. You assumed I was, and that is your mistake," he growled, grabbing my arm while pulling me close against him. "Don't do anything stupid, do you understand me?"

"Clearly," I hissed, struggling to get out of his hold.

"Be a good girl, and I will let you ride my cock tonight."

"I don't think that's going to happen ever again, asshole," I snapped, falling back the moment he released my arm without warning, watching as Luis moved to break my fall.

"With me, Van Helsings, and Head of Houses. Let's go welcome the House of the Fallen back from their graves, shall we?" Rhys snorted, holding his hand out for me to accept.

I glared at it with hot tears burning my eyes. Rhys had no idea what he'd just done. For the last two months, everything had been smooth, and we'd lived happily, or as happily as enemies could. I'd allowed him to use me, to comfort me, and the first chance he got, he betrayed me.

I guess it wasn't an actual betrayal. He'd never pretended to be anything other than my sworn enemy. I'd just let my guard down and assumed something had changed between us. I thought that I could become more to him, and I'd been wrong.

Rhys pulled me with him, marching toward the doorway which we exited together. He didn't stop moving until we were on the gravel driveway. I could see my family through the gates, yet I couldn't make out who was who at our current distance. I was surrounded by Van Helsings and the alphas. Doors closed, and runes glowed above the houses that lined the long winding road leading through the compound.

The gates to the estate opened, and my heart clenched as cars slowly started to pull through. One by one, they moved up the long, hedge-covered driveway that led to the mansion. Hooded figures stepped out of the car and slowly moved toward us while managing to keep a safe distance.

When enough of them were out of their cars, the first one spoke. "You will release my daughter, Rhys." My mother shoved back her hood, and I smiled.

"Mother," I whispered.

"Hello, Roslyn," Rhys growled, and my eyes snapped to him, before settling back on my mom.

"It's been a long time, my knight. I've missed you. Have you missed me?"

Nausea swirled through me, burning the back of

my throat. "No," I whispered through the tightening in my throat.

My mother's sapphire eyes moved to mine, glaring at me. "You should have stayed where you were, child. You're such a disappointment."

My eyes slid to Winchester, who was looking between us in confusion. "You're Elizabeth."

"I was never as weak as my sister. I hear my whore daughter is fucking my knight," she stated coldly, noting the tears slipping from my eyes. "Stop being so weak, Remington."

I felt like the world was spinning around me. Everything was off-kilter, and the malice dripping from my mother's lips made me want to retch. Rhys shut down his emotions as everyone else around us whispered in low voices. Shock rushed through the crowd, and then fear entered it, which caused my mother to smile.

"How could you?" I asked thickly.

"How could I do what? Stop being weak like your father? And wipe away the tears, you stupid little bitch. Get in the car, Remington," she hissed vehemently, turning to Rhys. "Did you enjoy fucking my daughter? Was she as good as I was for you, my love?"

"She means nothing to me; less than nothing." Rhys didn't speak more than a few words, as if he were frozen and unable to understand what was happening. His eyes slid to mine, and in them I saw a deeply seated hatred.

He looked at me like I was a stranger. Like I'd

known my mother was Roslyn all along. I started to step closer to him to tell him he was wrong, but her hand shot out, landing against my cheek, jerking my head to the side as pain ripped through me.

"You're nothing to everyone who knows you, daughter. You're less than nothing to me and *my* lover, Remington. You are my greatest failure. Imagine my surprise when I returned home to find you *fucking* my enemies like the little whore you are. I should have murdered you long ago. Just as I did the others who couldn't prove useful," she snarled.

Winchester stepped closer, like she planned to intervene on my behalf. "Enough, Mother," she hissed.

"Stand back, Winchester, or you may join her!"

"In what? In becoming alpha to your house?" I snapped, glaring at her.

"You were never to become alpha to House of Silversmith, you stupid little bitch; that's not your purpose. Did you honestly think I created you to become an alpha?" my mother laughed coldly, and when I moved, she slapped me again.

I remained there with my head bowed, glaring at the ground. A loud pounding started in my ears, growing until it became deafening. She lifted her hand to slap me again, and I sent a right hook sailing toward her face. Magic rushed through me, forcing my hair to rise as if a strong wind had caught it. I hit her again and again, sending her backward with each hit.

Winchester shouted for everyone to back away, her eyes filling with worry as she watched me. My skin turned bright red and continued until my entire body was glowing and pulsing with power. I slammed my mother down, stepping back, using magic to lift her, crushing her body onto a car which flattened beneath her with the force I'd used. Someone moved behind me, and I turned, grabbing Sauer by his throat.

"Enough, you stupid little bitch! She's my *wife*!" Sauer shouted, and I laughed coldly. He sent silver rushing toward me from the palm of his hand. One by one, his bullets hit me. My body absorbed them, melting them as he watched in horrified silence.

Sauer not being my brother, but instead, my mother's husband, was probably the only thing that made sense right now. He'd always been beside her, the only male from her line allowed into the armory with her. Sauer raised his fist to hit me, and my heated hand pushed through his chest. I wrapped my fingers around his heart, and a sickening sound filled the air when I pulled it from his chest. I watched without emotion as his eyes widened, and he began to turn to ash.

"My mommy seems to be missing one, so I have taken yours for her. I do hope you don't mind, *brother*," I whispered barely above the howl of the wind. "I'm also part Silversmith, which means that I am immune to your silver." I grinned at the other Silversmiths, who quickly removed their hands from their pockets, holding them in the air.

Turning, I shot into the air, landing on the car above my mother, watching her cry as the wind picked up her lover's ashes. Her mouth opened to scream, and I thrust his heart into her mouth, pushing my entire fist into it, forcing it deep into her throat. I laughed hysterically, watching her choke on her lover's heart while trying to gain air past my fist. Withdrawing my arm, I peered into her horrified eyes.

"Stop being so weak, Mother! What's the matter, Mommy? You don't like my monster? It's okay; it doesn't like you, either," I chuckled, slamming my fist into her face until her head smashed into bloody bits, and her body turned to ash, just like her lover's.

I dropped my head back, smiling while the powdery remains of her body filtered into the air. I could hear the Silversmiths, the alphas, and their people gasping while trying to figure out what had just happened.

I'd finally let my monster out to play, and she was not going into the box anytime soon. Done were the days of being abused or held hostage. I wasn't some weakling that could be held down by my mother—or Rhys Van Helsing.

Chapter Thirty-Three

I turned slowly, staring at the Silversmiths who watched me wordlessly. Standing, I dropped from the car as it started to compact under the heat of the fire burning through it. Smiling, I walked toward the crowd that had come to save me.

"The House of Silversmith will rise," I stated, turning glowing eyes on the alphas. "Under a few conditions, of course," I corrected, bowing my head to hide the smile.

"Remington," Winchester whispered, and when I leveled a cold, unemotional gaze in her direction, she closed her eyes. "We kneel," she agreed, dropping to her knees before me.

I watched the Silversmith bloodline dropping before me. I didn't want submission. I wanted to live without being told I was nothing. My father did not create me to become an alpha, of that I was certain. I was the enforcer, designed to protect the bloodline from the alphas. What my mother hadn't realized, was that my father wasn't a shifter, or a shape changer. He was the phoenix. An undiscovered breed that had remained in the shadows forged in the fires and grew stronger from them. I'd never known they existed, and yet all signs had pointed to it. It wasn't until Rhys had forced me to remember my father leaving, and Cole's words outside the forgery had played in my head.

My father had called me his little bird, and he'd taken me to play within the fires without the others knowing. Winchester had removed him from my memories, locking away my childhood to protect me from the pain of my mother and her endless hatred toward me. Rhys had opened the doors to those memories, as I had rested in the forge last week, I'd remembered them all.

I couldn't be an alpha, not with the other issue I'd discovered today. I wasn't going to rise because it wasn't my house anymore. I was House of Phoenix, which, as far as I knew, was just me. Soon, there would be another, though.

"Who here challenges me for alpha?" I asked, turning to stare at the men who hadn't fully bowed. One rose, stepping forward. "Do you plan to raise the house without prejudice or malice of the past?"

"I will crush them all for what they did to us," he smiled coldly.

Slowly, I stepped toward him, striking before he could say more, watching his head bounce across the ground until it came to a rest at Rhys's feet.

"Anyone else?" I asked softly. "No? Rise,

Winchester, Head of Silversmith House."

"Remington?" she whispered.

"I cannot be an alpha. I am not a full-blooded Silversmith. My father created me to ensure that history never repeated itself. My father is the last phoenix. Therefore, I will become his heir. His house needs me, and yours has you, sister. You have always done the right thing. I expect that to continue. If any Silversmith wishes to fight my sister, they will fight me as her second before reaching her. That goes for you as well." I turned, staring at Cole and Rhys, who watched me with narrowed stares of condemnation. "Now go, because you're not welcome here."

I stepped back, watching my family pile into the cars, leaving as quickly as they'd shown up. I started toward Rhys, but he stepped back, glaring at me with loathing in his eyes. I stalled before him, frowning.

"Don't be mad. You're the one who opened the gate to those memories," I stated, watching the tick hammering in his jaw. "I'm leaving. Nyx secured a house for us in town. I thought I'd give you the courtesy of the truth." I watched as he turned, and Ian dropped his gaze to my stomach before his eyes rounded.

Rhys swung back, his eyes filled with hatred that was deeply embedded from years of guilt. "The truth? Roslyn was your mother, and you expect me to believe that you had no idea? You came here out of the blue, fell into my fucking lap, and yeah, I questioned it. I never for one second thought you'd be the daughter to the murderous whore who ruined the lives of everyone she touched. So, what the fuck do you have to say to me that could fucking matter now?"

"I'm pregnant," I swallowed, watching his eyes narrowing on me as he laughed coldly.

"Fuck you, Remington. I'm not buying that you're pregnant. I want nothing to do with you, do you understand me?" he snarled.

"She's very much pregnant, Rhys. She has two heartbeats," Ian announced, and Cole exhaled, staring at me.

"Fuck you too, Ian," Rhys growled, gazing at me with cold malice that soaked into my bones.

"You think I knew who she was? I thought my mother was Elizabeth Silversmith. That's who I knew her to be since as long as I can remember. Honestly, I probably would have kept it from you had I known. You questioned me being here, but I never wanted to be here, Rhys. You forced me to stay with you. You took my silver, and while I didn't understand the gravity of it, I know you did. My father found my mother and pretended to be something he wasn't so that I could be born to police the Silversmiths. I don't know why, or what his actual intentions were for creating me with Roslyn. I didn't come here to hurt you. I came because my mother wasn't answering her phone, and all of my memories said she was a gentle, loving mother who cared if I lived or died. Winchester shouldn't have changed or altered my memories. I assume she never thought I would wind up in the hands of the one creature strong enough to destroy the wall inside my head that held the horrible truth locked away."

"I don't care what fucked up shit your mommy

did to you. I don't care about you or your whore of a mother. I get it now. My deep attraction to you wasn't for you at all. I just needed it spelled out for me. You're the daughter of the one woman I ever loved, and she's a part of you. I wanted her so I could save her. I ended up with her lying, conniving daughter instead. No wonder it was so easy to let my guard down around you. I'm sure that was why I wanted your tight pussy so bad as well."

I laughed silently, fighting against the tears his words created within me. I sucked my lip between my teeth, slowly balling my hands into tight fists at my sides. He hated me, and I was very much pregnant with his child. I'd discovered it right before heading into the hall where I'd gotten distracted by Thurston. I nodded, wiping my eyes, inhaling a fortified breath. He watched me expectantly, like he assumed I'd argue with him pushing me away. Instead, I turned toward the Audi, where Nyx sat, having sensed my need to escape.

"You're going to let her walk away with the heir to the Van Helsing House in her womb?" Nyota snapped, her eyes sliding to me and back to Rhys.

"It's not my heir, at least not one I will claim openly."

"Rhys, she didn't even know! She killed the evil bitch! Remington isn't Roslyn. She's danced with dimwits and charmed the entire alpha population without fucking them. Who has ever been able to do that before?" Nyota hissed.

"Roslyn, her mother," he answered, turning to walk into the house while I slid into the car silently.

"Drive," I whispered, closing the door before the car started down the cobblestone driveway.

"He is wrong to do this to you."

"He feels betrayed, Nyx. I don't blame him. I don't even know what to think right now. My mother was the horrid monster, one who enjoyed hurting him. I feel dirty. I slept with a man who loved my mother."

"Yeah, that one is a bit awkward, no matter how you argue it, or I would."

"I mean, it was like three hundred years ago, so that shouldn't make it *as* weird, right?" I asked, and she turned to look at me laughing, slowly shaking her head.

"What are we going to do now, Remington?"

"I'm a Silversmith and a silversmith by trade. You're a nymph, one who has guys eating out of your vagina if you ask them to. We'll be okay. We're going to be okay."

"You're going to have a baby which means you need to be careful. It's going to need a name."

My hand touched my flat stomach, and I smiled through the tears blinding me. "Bullet," I laughed, hating the sick feeling that ruined the moment. Tears slipped free as a sob exploded from my lips. Nyx pulled the car off to the side of the road, sliding out of her seat to come around, opening my door to hold my hand; she knelt, staring up at me.

"It's going to be okay. We're not alone."

"Literally," I said, watching a speeding car swerve to the side Nyx had pulled off on, stopping in front of ours.

We watched in silence as Nyota opened the door with Cole exiting the other side of the car. Both slowly walked up to the open car door while I wiped away the tears.

"I'm coming with you," Nyota announced.

"Excuse me?" I asked, staring up at her.

"I'm moving in with you," she said awkwardly, rubbing the back of her neck. "If it is okay with you, I'd like to move in. You're going to need protection. You're also going to need money since Rhys just froze both of your bank accounts. I won't allow him to make rash decisions that leave you and his child on the streets until he screws his head back on correctly."

"Like our own private ninja?" Nyx asked, and I closed my eyes.

"Thank you for offering, Nyota. You don't even like me, though. Bullet will be fine; we've never used the bank account set up by E.V.I.E. Everyone needs a backup plan, and ours was to escape and build a Silversmith company, with a strip club above it."

"Who the hell is Bullet?" she asked with a frown marring her face.

"The baby," I answered, and her eyes rounded with shock.

"You cannot name it Bullet. You know that, right? Bullet Van Helsing? It's actually not as bad once you add the last name."

"Bullet Silversmith," I frowned, and she frowned too. "And no, that's what I'm naming the baby for now because that's currently its size."

"Scoot up," she said, climbing in the backseat. "Get my shit out of the car, Cole," Nyota ordered as I sat up closer to the dash, allowing her into the backseat.

The moment she slid in, the seat slammed forward, and I groaned, rubbing my forehead. The seat made a cracking noise, and her hand touched against my side, slowly moving toward my belly as if she would feel the baby move. I groaned louder and glared back at Nyota before righting myself in the seat.

"I didn't say yes," I muttered, staring at Cole's stiff spine as he moved to do what Nyota had asked of him.

"You're pregnant, and you just used magic. You don't have a Van Helsing handy to protect you from the curse," she stated, tapping her hand on my shoulder. "Now, you do."

My gaze slid to Cole's, finding him studying me carefully. He had avoided me for days, and he didn't look happy to be here right now. I exhaled and swallowed.

"I didn't know she was my mother, Cole. I murdered her today for things she said, but also for things she did in the past to you and your family. She wasn't kind to me, not as I thought she was. My sister protected me from the truth, which Rhys unlocked when he entered my dreams and took control of them. The same one I pushed you out of." Cole snorted, searching my face briefly. Dismissing me, he stared up the road silently. "Everyone hates me now, and I can't change my parentage."

"It's a big bomb that got dropped today, Remi. Think about it; Rhys let his guard down, and you and he were happy. He had never slept with the same woman twice since Roslyn, yet he did with you. He grew attached to you, allowing himself to be happy finally, and then, he comes face-to-face with the woman who destroyed him. Then, he finds out that the one woman he's allowed himself to be happy with, well, she's her daughter. You also made a fallen house rise, and you technically don't have the power to do that. It has to be voted on in the sanctuary with the other alphas all present."

"How do I go about doing it legally?" I asked, and Nyota's hand tightened on my shoulder.

"You don't because you have me. I'll set it up and make Rhys give you sanctuary for it, or I'll drive him insane until he agrees. See, you'll like having me around. You have no idea of the gravity of what a child will do for us."

"No, I don't. Here's the thing, though, I'm done with everyone keeping secrets from me, Nyota. People have lied to me and taken advantage of me because I was naïve. That's not something I can change, but I can take control of my life from this point on. I can no longer think of only me anymore. Bullet is going to need me to make decisions that will shape the future he or she inherits. I have to do better. The only way I can do that is by surrounding myself with people who care about me, and those who will also love my child. Nyx has my back without question, but where do your loyalties land?"

"With my family," she stated honestly, her hand tightening on my shoulder. "And my family is in your womb, growing. That means you're my family now, too. You're Rhys's silver, whether he wants it or not. He chose to accept you, and he offered you his protection. I vow to you that I will always tell you the truth unless it endangers my brothers. If it becomes an issue, I will live in a tent outside your house."

"Like a stalker?" Nyx asked, popping the button for the trunk. Cole dropped the bag in, and I watched him walk off without a backward glance.

"Exactly like a stalker. Rhys has many enemies, and they'll see his child as a weakness. They don't know that he has disowned it, and they will not stop to ask questions. The entire Beltane guest list was outside for the announcement of his child's existence." Cole peeled out, heading in the opposite direction of the Van Helsing Estate. "My family just broke again, Remi. That pain just became fresh for them, and even though you killed Roslyn for good, it's going to take a few minutes for them to see you had no part of this mess. I can see it because I watched you instead of that murderous bitch during the fight. You had no idea your mother was Roslyn, and actually thought she was Elizabeth. It's both sad and pathetic."

"Uh, thanks," I snorted, chewing over what she said while my chest tightened with pain from the betrayal and Rhys's outright rejection of our child.

"I did just say I wouldn't lie to you. I thought you wanted honesty?"

"Some white lies aren't bad," I admitted while counting to ten inside my head, holding on for dear life as Nyx sped us down the road. "I feel like the most unwanted, blind fool in the world."

"You pretty much are," Nyota stated.

"White lies, Nyota!" I snapped.

"You're brilliant," she corrected.

"Asshole," I muttered.

"Bitch," she huffed.

"I need dick," Nyx announced, and I rolled my eyes while Nyota made a crude noise from where she sat pressed against my seat.

"This is going to be insane. A nymph, a Van Helsing, and a pregnant Silversmith," I frowned. "What could possibly go wrong?"

"Is that the house?" Nyota asked as Nyx pulled into a driveway.

The house looked abandoned with windows covered in plywood, as if preparing for a hurricane to hit, or worse. The grass was yellow and dead, and the porch ceiling was hanging down, as if something had sat on it, crushing it beneath the weight.

"Please tell me this is a joke?" I asked, turning worried eyes on Nyx, who smirked, tapping her fingers on the steering wheel.

"It just needs some elbow grease, right? I mean, you said anything would work."

"I didn't agree to protect you from a fucking house, Remington. It's one strong wind away from blowing over."

Our heads turned back as the porch creaked loudly, and the ceiling crashed to the ground, destroying the steps that led into the front door. I sat back in the seat, exhaling as I rubbed my eyes. I was exhausted, and my emotions were on edge. I'd discovered my mother was a murderous, power-hungry villain who literally hated me.

Rhys told me I had meant nothing to him and that my child meant about the same. I'd become homeless, and the shack that Nyx had purchased wasn't even a safe place to sleep. We couldn't even get into the door to go inside.

Headlights appeared behind our car, and I watched as Ian unfolded his lengthy frame from the driver's seat. Conrad climbed out of the car, staring at the house before sliding his attention to me and back to the house as another board crashed onto the ground. Both paused to look at the house, and Nyota pushed the seat up to grab the door.

"They may be here to hurt you and Bullet," she whispered, pushing the door open as she pulled out a blade. "Halt!"

"Who the hell says halt?" I asked, turning to look at Nyx.

"Scotland Yard police do," Nyx said, shrugging when I looked in her direction. "What? They do! I watched it on Sherlock Holmes while riding Acyn reverse cowgirl."

"I could have lived my entire life without having known that," I said, and jumped as Nyota tapped the window.

"You know, for the person who is supposed to police the Silversmiths, you're pretty jumpy. Rather pathetic, really," Nyota snorted.

"White lies," I whispered, rubbing the bridge of my nose before climbing out of the car to awkwardly hold her hand to prevent the curse from striking.

"You're sure you wish to stay in this place, Silversmith?" Ian asked, narrowing his eyes on me with a look of pity.

"Pretty sure it's condemned, sweetheart," Conrad snorted, grunting as Nyota elbowed him in the ribs. He whistled, and the female shifters slipped from the shadows, clapping as they found me and gathered around me with excitement. "They're rather smitten with you. They wouldn't shut up about being mothers since you dropped the baby bomb on Rhys. So, until he pulls his head out of his asshole, you have us."

"All of us. Stop hogging the poor girl, mutt. She is going to need all of us to get through this shit," Hunter snorted. I turned, staring at him where he was leaning against the side of the house. "This place is a shithole. I could see hiding a dead body in it, but not a beauty like you."

"Yeah? Well, it may be one now, but it's ours. We will fix it up, and Bullet will have a home here."

"Who is Bullet?" Ian asked.

Nyota snorted, elbowing him again. "It's the baby, vampire. Keep up," she stated.

"You're naming the Van Helsing heir *Bullet* Van Helsing?" Ian snorted and then caught the irritation on my face. "I mean, it's a strong name! One he will be very proud of."

"I am calling the baby, Bullet, because it is the size

of one."

"Oh, thank fuck," he laughed and then righted at the look of ire I gave him. "It's cute and catchy."

"He knocked you up on Beltane, that bastard. One child is created a year for immortals, and he got the lucky draw." Conrad grunted, closing his eyes, dropping his head back while rolling his neck.

"And he threw it away," Hunter finished, smiling as I swallowed hard. "Don't you fret, pretty girl. You have us, and Rhys's devoted sister at your side. Rhys will come around eventually, and if the prick doesn't, one of us will gladly become your mate."

"And what, Hunter? Love the daughter of the monster who destroyed him and murdered his delicate, sweet mother? He may come around for his child, but he cannot forgive himself, let alone forgive me. He will never see past that evil bitch that gave birth to me or love me. I don't want that for my child or me."

"So what you're saying is, you're going to need a baby daddy?" Conrad asked, smirking devilishly while he rubbed his hands together, and the women shifters smiled, nodding happily.

"No, that is not what she's saying," Nyota snapped.

"Shh, it's getting to the sex part," Nyx said.

"Rhys and I were never in a relationship. He made it very clear that I am nothing to him and that I will never mean anything to him. I'm his silver, but that doesn't make him my soulmate. He said we could be enemies, friends, or lovers. I'm pretty sure he just forced me into the enemy category by default because of who created me. I'm not looking for some medieval love, dating shit right now, either. All I want is a bed, and to cry my eyes out so that I can wake up from this nightmare. Can one of you make that happen?" I asked, turning to look at them.

"My cabin is free, and it's about a mile from here up in the woods. You can sleep in it tonight, and we can come back and see what needs doing here tomorrow." Conrad scratched his chin, frowning. "I'd send the women, but they're shit for security."

"I'll take tonight's watch," Hunter announced, holding out his hands for the keys.

"You'll be outside, though?" Ian asked, hiking a brow into his hairline.

"Of course," he grunted, crossing his arms over his broad chest. "Remington is exhausted and has been rejected by enough assholes tonight. No one deserves what she went through. Out of all of us, I know rejection the most. It's how I became the king, after all."

Twenty minutes later, I found myself tucked into a bed with enough testosterone around the house that it made it difficult to sleep. The moment I closed my eyes, Rhys was there. His eyes narrowed, and his mouth slanted into an unfriendly grin.

"Are you ready to play, Love? I've been waiting to show you the real me."

The End For Now

About the author

Amelia lives in the great Pacific Northwest with her family. When not writing, she can be found on her author page, hanging out with fans, or dreaming up new twisting plots. She's an avid reader of everything paranormal romance.

Stalker links

Facebook: https://www.facebook.com/authorameliahutchins

Website: http://amelia-hutchins.com/

Goodreads: https://www.goodreads.com/author/show/7092218.Amelia_Hutchins

Twitter: https://twitter.com/ameliaauthor

Pinterest: http://www.pinterest.com/ameliahutchins

Instagram: https://www.instagram.com/author.amelia.hutchins/

Facebook Author Group: https://goo.gl/BqpCVK

Printed in Great Britain
by Amazon